the Only Choice

THE CHOICES TRILOGY, BOOK THREE

DEE PALMER

The Only Choice (The Choices Trilogy Book # 3)
Copyright © 2015 Dee Palmer
Published by Dee Palmer

All rights reserved. No part of this book may be reproduced or transmitted in an form, including but not limited to electronic or mechanical, without written permission from the publisher, except in the case of brief quotations embodied in critical articles or reviews.

This is a work of fiction. Names, characters, businesses, places, events, and incidents are either products of the authors imagination or used in a fictitious manner. Any resemblance to actual persons, living or dead, or actual events is purely coincidental.

This book is licensed for your personal enjoyment only. This book may not be re-sold or given away to other people. If you would like to share this book with another person, please purchase an additional copy for each person you share it with. If you are reading this book and did not purchase to, or it was not purchased for your use only, then you should return it to the seller and purchase your own copy. Thank you for respecting the author's work.

ISBN-13 -978–1512126402
ISBN -10 -1512126403

Warning: This story is on the filthy side of smut and isn't suitable for those who don't enjoy graphic descriptions that are erotic in nature, but for those that do, enjoy ;)
For free stories sign up to my Newsletter on the contact page at http://deepalmerwriter.com/ (Promise No Spam)
or go see
http://eepurl.com/biZ6g1
To receive this freebie

Dedication

For My Husband—All My Love, Always

Chapter One

GOD I MUST have really been out if it for the last six weeks to not have said something, anything abtout this monstrosity I'm wearing. I know she's my best friend and it's her day, but honestly every time I look down or catch a sneaky glimpse in the many reflective surfaces around this lavishly decorated room I feel nauseous. She promised I was going to be Pippa to her Kate and I distinctly remember having my satin ivory court dress with the halter neck and scooped back fitted to perfection. But no, as I stand guard to the gift table in a taffeta lime green tartan puff ball of a gown I am a shoe-in for Mrs Shrek. Still it must have happened because here I am. Although I can't remember much of the ceremony and the faces are a little blurry. Funny I don't remember drinking at all not even to toast the happy couple. It feels all wrong. I have dutifully and carefully placed each gift and thanked the guests as they filter passed. I sway a little, I just feel so sick and it can't just be the dress, although. . . . My wayward thoughts are frozen as I stare into the deepest dark blue eyes, piercing me and searing a fearful panic in my chest. The line of people directly in front of Daniel drift apart and he steps forward, his long arm tenderly draped over the shoulder of . . . No! It's only then I notice Angel is his plus one.

I swallow so loudly I'm surprised I don't interrupt the music of the band playing in the corner of the large ballroom. I grit my teeth and can feel the tension pinch its way to my temples. I steel myself, I am going to be calm. This is Sofia's big day, but seriously, what the fuck! They stand in front of me, his chest to her back, pressed together. His fingers curled protectively on her bony shoulders holding her to him. They are a little too close to me but with the table directly at my back I can't step away, the distance is oppressive. I don't know how, maybe some inherent hospitality training but I actually manage to speak, politely.

"It's lovely to see you, both?" I can't help if I sound disingenuous. Daniel doesn't smile, his face is ever impassive but his eyes are fixed with a familiar heat. Angel is wearing a long velvet evening gown with one shoulder strap. It is simple, elegant and looks like it has been cut to her body perfectly but its black, she looks like she's at a funeral.

Angel's voice is saccharin sweet and is not helping my nausea. "I simply love weddings and when I saw Daniel's invite had a plus one, well, I knew you wouldn't mind. You have been so generous already." Her lips smear into a knowing smile.

I flinch at her words and unsuccessfully try again to recoil and gain some space. I hadn't been generous at all. Daniel chose her. He didn't want me enough but I definitely didn't give him away and here she is rubbing it in my face. She stole my fucking life and he broke my heart and I have to welcome them to the party, well fuck that. I stiffen and straighten my back but before I can react, everything slows down and like watching a painfully slow exaggerated frame by frame sequence of a movie my eyes drift to follow the line of her gaze. She reaches into her ruche silk clutch purse and pulls something long, shiny and sharp. Light flashes and the bright sun reflects on the mirrored surface, momentarily blinding me. I scream at the first plunge and incredible splitting, slicing pain. My hands grasp my belly, holding back the flow of pain, catching the pooling blood that drips through my fingers. I know I'm screaming now and my eyes snap toward Daniel but he hasn't moved. *I don't understand why hasn't he moved? Why is no-one helping me? It hurts so fucking much.* A blinding light makes me squeeze my eyelids tight as my legs give way, my hands leave my belly to protect my eyes from the intensity of the light. My head throbs, my chest feels like it is going to explode, every nerve in my body violently trembles. *I just hurt.*

"What the Fuck!" The gruff, angry voice startles me awake. My eyes blink as wildly as my heartbeat, adjusting to being open. A loud crash as Ethan drop's whatever he was holding on the hardwood floor and kneels beside me. I have gathered my knees up to my chin and wrapped my arms around my legs, holding tight and trying to regain my sanity. "You scared the crap out of me Bets. What are you doing here? I thought you left already? Have you been here to whole time?" His quick fired questions are just a blur. I couldn't answer them if I tried. I just can't get the nightmare out of my head and I can feel my whole body continue to shake, my skin is slick, dripping with shock. "Ok, Ok, you're all right now shhh." Ethan grabs the fur throw from my bed and despite the room temperature probably being in the mid-twenties I am grateful for the instant warmth and can feel my shivers start to subside. Now I just feel awkward and hugely embarrassed, not the least of which because I can now see that Ethan is completely naked.

"Ethan baby, shall I call the police?" A small voice calls from the other side of the bedroom door and I hear Ethan curse under his breath.

"No Sky, it's fine, just go back to bed I'll be there in five." He sighs and although I have regained a normal breathing pattern I still can't bring myself to look at his face.

"Sorry." My voice is croaky and it's then I realise that I must have been screaming blue murder for it to feel so rough.

"No need to be sorry, just a little surprised that's all . . . well more than a little. Look, do you mind if I go and put some clothes on and then come straight back?" He coughs to hide his embarrassment and I instantly feel a little less embarrassed myself. I nod but keep my eyes averted. I am still tucked up beside the bed wrapped in the throw when he returns with a glass of water. I smile weakly, take the glass and sip. "You Ok?" He voices is soft like maybe he is tending a wounded animal and I chance a look at his face for the first time since I woke. His soft brown eyes are filled with concern and he is trying for a comforting smile but I can see he is struggling. I so didn't want this to happen. Why can't I just keep all my crazy shit to myself? I hadn't meant to fall asleep but after Daniel walked out I just collapsed. I must've crawled to the side of the bed and lay on the deep sheepskin rug and fallen into an exhausted coma because looking at the clock on the wall I have been asleep for nearly twelve hours.

"If I said yes would you believe me?" I sigh and give the faintest of smiles.

He lets out a loud short laugh and with it some of the tangible tension. "Um no I don't think I would." He places his hand gently on my knee and gives a sort of mix between a pat and a comforting squeeze. He waits for me to say something.

I take a deep breath. I've woken him and his date up, the least he deserves is an explanation. I just know I will have to keep it brief or I will break all over again. "I had a nightmare, I get them sometimes." He raises a brow as if stating the bloody obvious wasn't quite what he meant so I continue. "Daniel left me. I'm no longer engaged." I rush the words like pulling a band aid but it really doesn't stop the pain it just makes it sharp and instant. "But I can't . . ." I draw in a breath that's already starting to break and Ethan quickly sits beside me and wraps his long arm across my shoulders. I shake my head to try and physically stop the thoughts from entering my brain.

"It's Ok sweetheart . . . you don't have to . . . It's all right . . . you're going to be all right." He pulls me into his chest and kisses my head and that just about breaks the very finest thread I was hanging on by and I fall, crash and burn. Long uncomfortable minutes pass with me barely drawing enough breath to maintain the out pouring of gut wrenching sobs. My eyes are raw and I just want to disappear right about now it hurts so fucking much. "Ah Shit Bethany, what can I do? Please tell me something I can do? You're breaking my heart like this, please sweetheart, stop crying, shhh, come on sweetheart. I know it's clichéd but he is not fucking worth this." His fingers are stroking circles on my arms and he gives comforting squeezes intermittently. After a while, sensing my breathing slowly returning to normal he whispers. "You know Dad's in construction right? Pretty sure we could hide the body, large holes in the ground, concrete, that sort of thing, just say the word Bets. Hell, you might not even have to say the word the way I'm feeling at this moment." He grumbles.

This makes me chuckle and I wipe my sore eyes, my cheeks sting from all the tears but his words have made me sit up. I look into his eyes for the first time in many heart wrenching minutes. "I think I mentioned my abhorrence to violence and like you said he's not worth it." I feel a painful bite in my chest at these false words but I need to practice my own mask if I am to function like a normal human any time soon. I might as well start now. He flashes a brighter smile at this sentiment. "Tired, emotional and a little unstable at the moment but no need to call in the big guns." I let out a calming sigh. "I will be fine. I promise. I know I must look like shit but I feel better." I wriggle and start to stand. "I'm going to freshen up, get some more sleep and I will see you at breakfast." He frowns and looks suspicious but I return my most convincing smile yet and add. "Thank you by the way. I really appreciate everything and I promise, tomorrow will be a fresh start." He stands and walks with me to just outside the en-suite and I hold my breath hoping he is buying my Oscar winning act. He bear hugs me and holds longer than is comfortable and my restricted breathing is starting to make me panic but he releases his grip just before I ruin the moment with a frantic cry and gasp for oxygen.

"All right Bets, if you're sure but if you need anything, call me Ok? You really don't have to resort to screaming the place down to get me in your room naked." He winks and with a cheeky smile goes to leave.

I offer my best attempt at a smile. I know its a weak effort but I am happy that Ethan seems to have reverted to his more normal treatment toward me. I relax a little because flirty is so much better than pity. He closes my door and I start to peel my clothes off, walking into the bathroom I turn the shower on full. I feel like a functioning shell but I am determined to function and practice acting skills, if need be. This tragic life turn will not define me, it will not break me and despite every fibre in my body screaming your wrong, I will survive Daniel Stone because he made his choice and it wasn't me.

I didn't dare fall back to sleep after my shower. I wouldn't risk another dream, another nightmare, besides it was only a few hours until dawn. After I had completely packed and tidied my bedroom and bathroom it was nearly light. I had decided to cook breakfast for Ethan and his guest before I take the train back to London. I prepared most of the food but needed bodies before I could cook the eggs because they really don't fare well in the warming oven. I poured myself a coffee and added lots of milk in lieu of preparing a latte with Ethan's fancy machine because it makes enough noise to raise the dead. With the sun just peaking over the horizon I can selfishly enjoy the spectacle on my own. I lean on the railing of the balcony, steaming cup in hand and suddenly feel very small. The absolute stunning beauty of the breaking dome of brilliant light where the sun kisses the sea and the sparks of reflective light dance on the rippling waves is spellbinding. The early morning chill vanishes as the creeping morning light races across the land and hits me full in the face. I close my eyes and bask in the gentle warmth, so distracted I don't hear the door open and only become aware of company when Ethan nudges his arm against mine.

"Hey." His voice is soft and I look up into his eyes, his brow is furrowed but he thankfully doesn't look too tired.

"Hey." I smile but bite my lips together in an attempt to swallow back all my rising embarrassment from last night. "Look I'm so sorry about last night." I don't want to rehash everything, new day, new start, so I quickly move the conversation on. "I've made breakfast for you and your guest, Full English . . . the works. My smile is brighter than it deserves to be. I lead him back into the kitchen before he can comment although his brows just seem to knit tighter together. "So scramble or fried?" I wave the spatula enthusiastically and turn the gas on.

"Bethany I think we need to—" He snaps his mouth at the same time I hear the light voice from last night cry.

"Oooo something smells good, I do love your. . Oh!" She stumbles to a halt as if she's hit a glass wall and flashes a scowl at me, narrow eyes and tight lips. She is tiny, masses of tight blonde curls. She is wearing one of Ethan's t-shirts that is hanging off one shoulder and reaches her knees. Her skin is sporting a permanent tan which I would think has little to do with a spray can and more to do with endless hours on the beach.

The tension I could cut with my spatula and after a few never ending awkward moments I step forward with my hand. "Hi I'm Bethany, Ethan's sister." The loud scraping of the kitchen chair across the wooden floor causes us both to stare at Ethan as he growls.

"Not my fucking sister!" He is radiating anger and as I've never seen him like this I instantly go into placate and diffuse mode.

"Okaay, you're right of course . . . not his sister but well, anyway I'm cooking breakfast before I head back to London would you like some, there is plenty?" I have laid the table and its clear there is enough but Ethan grumbles.

"Sky's just leaving." Exactly the same time Sky says. "That would be great"

"Okaay," I sort of wish the ground would swallow me now and judging by the look on Sky's face she's wishing that too. I wonder if I look like that when I look at Angel. I silently mock myself, even if I did, it doesn't bloody work. The scowl is still effective, however, in making me retreat. I turn to face the gas and quietly crack some eggs into a pan; without a preference being expressed, fried eggs it is. Stubbornly refusing to turn round despite the hushed heated exchange on the far side of the lounge I only let out my breath when I finally hear the front door close. I have dished up Ethan's plate and a little for me, although I can't face anything on mine right now. Even my normal coffee I've ditched in favour of a peppermint tea. Ethan sits beside me as I chase my food around my plate, stacking and hiding in an attempt to make the portion look eaten. He roughly picks up his fork and stabs at his breakfast like it's going to pay, whatever it's done it's definitely going to pay. God he looks pissed and he always looks so chilled I can't help but feel truly awful that I'm the cause.

I push back from my chair. "I should go." He grabs my hand before I can leave the table and his eyes are wide with shock.

"No don't!" His voice is sharp but he quickly shakes his head and adds in a much softer voice. "Please Bethany, don't go."

I squeeze his hand. "Ethan, you've been so kind and I've had the best time, really but I have made you angry and ruined your date and I do have to get back so I think its best—" I smile because I hate this new awkwardness.

He interrupts but turns his hand to hold mine. "I'm not angry with you Bets. I'm angry with me, I'm angry with Daniel, no I'm fucking furious with Daniel. I can't believe he did this to you, he's such an arsehole!" His gruff voice is fired through gritted teeth but then he relaxes, "but mostly I'm pissed with myself." The confusion on my face must be clear because he quietly continues to elaborate. "Look yesterday you were getting married to that guy." He holds my hand a little tighter as I crumple at the waist and fold like I can again feel that stabbing in my belly. "Sorry, but, well it's true and now you're telling me that you're not. Fuck, I wouldn't have . . . you were engaged for fuck sake! How could I have known? Fuck! This isn't me. No, it is me, but . . ." He drags his other hand through his hair and is clearly irritated, angry, frustrated; whichever or maybe all three and again I feel like shit because it's my fault.

"Ethan, I'm not sure where you are going with this but I don't judge, I really don't. You've been the best but I can't see past my own shitty mess right now and that's going to take everything I've got. He was my life Ethan. It was his choice to leave and no, I don't understand it and yes, it hurts like fuck but I'll get through this. As much as I might hate him right now . . . I still love him and I know me, so sadly that isn't going to change anytime soon. It would be unfair on you to tell you different and the last thing I need, however well intended is someone telling me what an arsehole Daniel is. I know he's an arsehole but I can't just stop feeling what I feel. I can't just stop loving him because he chose someone else. It's killing me that I can't but I'm not built that way." I let out a steadying breath that is holding back some rising tears. "I haven't loved like this in a very long time and I *never* got over that so this isn't going to be a quick fix but I'm Ok with that. I have a plan and you are part of that but as a friend because right now I really need my friends and one is still on holiday and one has her head in cloud wedding." I hold his warm gaze, his soft brown eyes crinkle in the corner. His smile is genuine and he lifts my fingers to his lips and kisses gently. The softness of his lips and time he takes makes me wonder whether he heard anything I have just said, well, anything other than him being part of my plan.

"You got it." He flashes a wide smile and lets my hand go to continue eating. "You sure you can't take an extra week and hang here, that could be part of the plan?" His words are muffled with the mouthful of food and I shake my head and laugh lightly, yep I can almost hear his mind running over how my plan and his, might fit.

"I've emailed work and decided to take a week unpaid holiday, *my* plan," I emphasise the possessive part, "is to have a chat with Tom. I think Marco may need some space sooner rather than later and I have a bit of clearing out to do which is going to leave my wardrobe a little bare so I might need a loan for a while." I am trying my hardest to make every step sound positive but every word, every action, every part of my plan effectively severs one more tie with Daniel and my fragile heart is having trouble embracing any part of it.

Ethan stands and fetches his wallet handing me a card while I shake my head furiously. The name on the bank card is mine but it's definitely not mine. "Dad wanted me to give you this but after we talked the other night I thought you two would probably sort this out next time you caught up. This is yours and I'm pretty sure he won't consider it a loan." I am speechless as I stare at the card in my hand. "So are you burning or dumping?"

"Charity shop." My voice is quiet and I am devastated that I didn't need him to explain what he meant.

"It's probably for the best, you don't want constant reminders." He puts his fork down and sits back rubbing his flat tummy that isn't the slightest bit round despite the mountain of food he has consumed.

"No,. .no reminders." I sigh and close my eyes, the tell-tale prickles rising and pinching behind my nose. I don't need reminders to feel like this, I just do, but I don't need to be tracked either.

The train journey was exhausting mostly because I fought my desperate need to sleep the entire six hours. Six hours of dissecting my time with Daniel, my wonderful, life affirming time with the most amazing man who captured my head, my heart and my soul and then broke me into tiny pathetic pieces. My head is filled with broken conversations, gaps in information and misunderstandings. No, not misunderstanding just complete incomprehension. "*I don't need to check anything . . . I trust her.*" His exact words and yet he can't see that she is in love with him. Does he really think that wouldn't be a problem? Perhaps that is insignificant when parried against insurmountable guilt. Maybe his guilt is the only significant thing in this wreckage. He honestly believes he is doing this to save his soul and a chance at redemption he hoped I could understand. He needed me to trust and because

the Only Choice

I couldn't, he had no other choice. He didn't choose her, he just didn't choose me. Around and around unanswerable questions bombard my every conscious thought. God I feel like my head is going to explode with doubt and devastation. I can't express how thankful I am as the cab pulls to stop outside my home.

It's only four in the afternoon but I am so ready for bed I think I might sleep through until the weekend. Climbing the hall stairs I freeze at the top at the view of neatly stacked boxes outside my front door; plain elegant black boxes towering high above my five foot six frame, two deep and three wide. There must be fifty unmarked boxes. My chest pinches tight when I peek inside the top one but I recognised them from the dressing room in Daniels apartment so I already know they would be filled with my clothes. My elderly neighbour opens her door.

"Oh Bethany thank heavens it's you." She rushes over bursting with excitement and curiosity. "These came first thing but I really don't think it is wise to keep them in the hall my dear." Its then I see a card stuck to one of the boxes, I recognise the script *Miss Thorne* and nothing else. Wow, that was quick. Efficient, clean and brutal, if only it was painless too.

"No Elsie, you're right. I didn't know they would be delivered today but don't worry they will be gone this afternoon. I promise." I take my key out and enter my apartment slowly welcoming the spread of numbness through my body relishing in the respite it affords from the utterly consuming pain. I can embrace this and function, at least numb there are no tears. I make my way to the kitchen and dig under the sink for some bin bags, not as elegant as the boxes but fit for purpose. I then pick up my phone noticing there are no missed calls or messages, turning it face down I leave it on the counter. It is like I can't bear to look at the sore reminder of the consequences of my choice. I fish around in my bag for the card I know is there. I punch the number.

"Bethany are you all right?" Peter's kind voice pierces the numbness and I have to pinch my nails hard into my palm to stop a sudden sob in my throat.

"Yes Peter I'm fine, really, thanks." I need to stop using 'fine' if I'm ever going to convince anyone any different. "I was hoping you might be able to give me a hand with moving some stuff."

"Oh sure, not a problem. I can be over in half an hour what do you need?" His voice is crackly like he's on speakerphone.

"Strong pair of arms and a van?" I tell him.

He chuckles and says in a knowing drawl. "Right. I'll be over in twenty."

Perfect. It is amazing how quickly you can clear drawers and hangers if there is little to no folding involved. It's cathartic and in just under fifteen minutes my wardrobes and cupboards' are the clothing equivalent of Old Mother Hubbard. I am pretty much left with what I am standing in, plus a few old t-shirts and one pair of jeans, all pre Daniel, when the doorbell buzzes. I press to let Peter in and go to open my front door. I have stacked the black sacks in my hallway and wait for Peter to reach the landing. He opens his arms to me as he reaches the top step, tilting his head as I hesitate. "Come on girl you know you want to?"

I squeeze out a small smile and step into his hug which is more like a vice as he squeezes my spine to crack in several places; six hours on a train will do that to you and I actually feel better when he releases me. "So what are we doing?"

"Um Ok well, this lot," I point to the boxes, "and the bags are all heading to the charity shop on Brompton Road. I called so they have been warned." I let out a deep breath.

"Are you sure about this honey?" Peter's deep voice is soft with worry.

"Was he sure when he got you to do this earlier?" I retort sadly.

"Point taken." He nods and goes to start taking the boxes down. "Good job I brought the limo." He mutters as he disappears with an armful. It only takes a few trips to clear the hall and surprisingly they do all fit in the car. Peter hugs me once more and again impresses that I can call him anytime. I thank him again and just as he is about the leave, a jumble of words escape me before I can rein them back.

"Look out for him Peter. I mean take care of him, please." I smile lightly as Peter gives a sharp nod before sitting in the front of the limo and driving away.

I pick my phone out of my back pocket and dial the number I had found on Google for after-hours security firms. This may cost a little extra but I want the apartment clean today, no speakers, no cameras, not a trace of surveillance. It's gone ten at night before the guy from the security firm leaves and my bedroom looks like I am going to need the week to make good the mess he has made. To be fair he did say he could dismantle the system one of two ways, slow and neat or quick and dirty. I collapse on my bed opting for the spring clean to start in the morning when my phone rings; having ignored it all evening I finally answer Sofia's call.

"Hey sister." I sigh and moan with an achy stretch of my body.

"Don't sister me! I've been calling all day I was worried, don't fucking do that to me Bets. Paul's just about to call off the wedding I've been so crazy!" She huffs as I snort at her dramatics. "Oh that's right laugh it up! You're a stones' throw from being bumped as Maid of Honour; just count yourself lucky you've already been fitted for the dress." She warns.

"I'm sorry Sofs. Just had some stuff to sort but I'm hundred percent back now and ready for my MOH duties. Speaking of which, you haven't change the colour scheme have you?" I enquire hesitantly, praying that my dream wasn't a hideous premonition.

"Urr No why would you say that?"

"And you didn't give Daniel a plus one invitation?" I need to clarify the specifics of the nightmare.

"Again no, why would I? He was your invite and it's not likely he'd come now anyway. You're freaking me out a little, do you mind telling me what's going on?"

I spend the next half hour giving her the PG rated version of my weekend ending with the security guy leaving and me taking her call.

"You did what?" She screams so loud I flinch too late to pull the phone from my ear and suffer the piercing aural pain as a consequence. "I mean I am obviously devastated for you Bets but seriously you gave all those dresses to charity! Are you fucking insane! What were you thinking?" She moans with fake outrage. It is a good distracting tactic and I offer up an ever so tiny laugh. I shake my head impressed she can take my mind from heartbreak to crimes against couture, if only for a moment. "Good night Sofs." I switch my phone off and pull my covers tight hoping for instant oblivion.

Chapter Two

I SURPRISED MYSELF this week. I still feel numb and I'm not sleeping so well, waking with the same bloody nightmare but I have kept busy. I managed to repair the damage to the walls the security guy made and buy a basic working wardrobe of clothes. Today is Saturday I have a lunch arranged with Sofia, her mum Vivienne and her Aunt Marie which is a much needed distraction. Vivienne has booked a corner table at the Windows restaurant on the twenty eighth floor of the Hilton on the corner of Hyde Park. The clear sky means there is an uninterrupted one eighty degree view of West London and a perfect view of Daniels apartment building opposite the park. So, despite the stunning view I only have eyes for the light and airy interior. The restaurant is surrounded by floor to ceiling glass and there is a slightly raised mezzanine which means that everyone seated will have some view over the city. The cocktail bar next to the restaurant, Sofia explains is very lively at the weekend and has the most spectacular view as the sun sets and London lights up. I don't need to go to the cocktail bar for that. I have witnessed that spectacle on many occasions, mostly with Daniels arms wrapped around my waist.

I take a sip of the chilled pink champagne and gaze again

around the room, trying to quell the rising sadness and search for another distraction. There is an impressive piece of artwork in the shape of an intertwined piece of ribbon made from rippling steel. It stretches the length of the centre of the room and hangs above the tables, reflecting the light on every bend and curve of the shiny material. There is loud laughter from a large group of people on the end table, perhaps fifteen family members celebrating. I find I can happily tune out from the memories of that view and from our own tables conversation. That is until Marie asks me outright why I don't just settle down with Marco. It wasn't just the pungent smell of the ham hock and pea volute that has me stuffing a napkin in my mouth to prevent the sudden rush of vomit. Luckily Sofia intercedes on my behalf.

"Ew gross Aunt Marie and just as likely as *me* hooking up with Marco." With a disgruntled look on her face she pushes her plate far away as if the idea has put a stop to her appetite as well as mine. Vivienne tactfully changes the subject.

"I think we will need another fitting for you Bets you look like you've lost some weight." Her sweet smile and intent kind eyes causes my nose to prickle sharply and I sniff back the instant onset of tears. I quickly reach for my water to give my body something to do other than cry. Sofia gasps, as if seeing me for the first time.

"Shit!" Sofia's mouth drops open.

"Sofia language." Embarrassed, Vivienne reprimands her daughter.

"Sorry Mama but God I didn't even notice. Bets are you eating at all at the moment? The dress is going to hang off you like a stick in a sack and that is *not* how it is supposed to look." She grumbles and I don't know whether she is more concerned for me or the dress. "Are you ok? Maybe come and stay with us for a while, Mama can feed you back up?" She holds my hand and threads her fingers through and I know she's not so worried about the dress.

"I'm good, really, just been off my food a little. A persistent stomach bug but it's still four weeks to go and I'm sure I can pack on the pounds in no time." I grab another bread roll and see both the women relax.

"Maybe just have a fitting a few days before the big day just in case. Sofia is right, the dress really does need to be fitted." Vivienne offers and Sofia agrees with an enthusiastic nod. I make a break for the ladies just as coffee and petit fours are being served with homemade marshmallow that looks amazing. Sofia is quick to follow. She grabs my elbow and manoeuvres me to sit on the silk covered high backed chair in the powder room, drawing her own chair directly in front of me. Her fixed intense chocolate eyes laced with query and concern. Shit!

"So it's really over?" Her direct approach is expected but shocking all the same like a sucker punch to my chest and I can't help my involuntary grasp to my heart at the sudden unbearable pain. I manage to nod but her gaze is unrelenting and I know she needs more. "What about the contract? I thought the rolling thing meant you always had six months to sort this shit out?"

"Well I guess I didn't read the fine print because he sure as shit invoked the six month break clause. Besides what am I realistically going to do . . . sue him?" I drop my head in my hands with the futility of such a thing. "I think I made a terrible mistake pushing like that. He asked me to trust him and I couldn't." I squeeze my eyes and fight with everything to hold myself together but everything feels wrong when he is not in my life, everything is ugly and painful. "What if he really needs this to ease his pain and I couldn't support him? What if she really needs his help to save her marriage? I can't imagine wanting something so bad, well I can, and just maybe you *would* do anything, absolutely anything . . . Even ask an ex for his . . ." I clasp my hands to my mouth to physically try and hold the sobs quiet but my shoulders judder as my body loses its battle to contain my sorrow.

"Sweetheart, don't, please don't cry Bets and I'm sorry to say this but would you just listen to yourself for a moment and then shut the fuck up." Her words are so softly spoken, kind and gentle but my head snaps up because they are harsh and hateful. "No sweetheart, I don't mean shut up I don't want to listen to your pain because I can see you're truly broken Bets. I can and it kills me. What I mean is you can't go on believing that kind of bullshit. There are at most two things happening here and both are the result of a jealous ex. One she is in love with him, anyone could see that at New Year and that she sick enough to try something like this speaks volumes for her mental state and desperation. You're probably right about the fertility thing and her original pregnancy from what you learned from Mr Wilson. But without proof you will just come across as mean and insensitive and that just isn't you Bets. You don't have a mean bone in your body." She takes my hand, threads her fingers and grips really tight and then lets go to hand me a much needed tissue.

"I sort of do for her." I sniff.

"Well it's justified, believe me. The second thing is she's fucking with Daniel's guilt and he, for whatever reason, is happy to play along. He clearly has some serious issues with his Father and Sister's death which is understandable and then to have his own baby's death heaped on top of that. You can't blame him for trying to get some peace, however tenuously it is proffered." She again cups my hands that are now clasped tightly in my lap, wringing the tissue to shreds.

"And I just abandoned him and sent him back to her. I should've trusted him more." I shake my head.

"Fuck no! Look, I think what he was asking is above and beyond what any normal girlfriend would deem acceptable interaction with an ex but if you love him there is obviously a middle ground. Its up to you to set what that is but I don't see that you should be handing him over on a silver platter either." She straightens her back and tilts her head goading me, trying to fire my spark but although I felt it heat for a moment it fizzled out just as quickly.

"I might be wrong about her you know. She may just need some help from an old friend." I have to consider the possibility

the Only Choice

that my view of the world is somewhat tainted. The result is I do, in fact, see psycho bitches when I hear clipping heels. They could just as easily be a simple pair of really nice Jimmy Choos.

"Well you think that if it helps you sleep." She pats her hand on my knee and tightens her lip. "So has he called, text or been banging on your door like he should?"

"Daniel doesn't deal that way. In fact I doubt I'll hear from him at all." I let out a deep sad gasp. "Sorry." My eyes spill with a fountain of tears that this time I can't control and Sofia is quickly kneeling beside me with her arms wrapped around my head pulling me silently against her chest.

"Oh sweetheart I'm so sorry Bets, shhh." She smooth's my hair and whispers repeatedly how sorry she is but I know in my empty heart she's nowhere near as sorry as I am.

The next day I get a boxed delivery from the restaurant with a personal but threatening note from Joe explaining he has lovingly prepared my favourite dishes and that he would be round later to check I'd eaten everything. I optimistically go through the motions of heating and dishing up the delicious food. He had packed enough for a dinner party of six, not a single woman struggling to hold down bread. A feast of still warm lemon, olive oil and rosemary loaf, cheesy cauliflower gratin with pancetta, ricotta gnocchi with creamy wild asparagus sauce, fried sweet peppers with balsamic vinegar and my favourite favourite spinach and ricotta ravioli with sage butter. For dessert there are individual pots of chocolate and amaretto panna cotta with a small tray of dark chocolate dipped strawberries. It looks amazing, it smells fantastic and even as my tummy rumbles I covered each dish with cling. I just couldn't physically bring myself to put anything in my mouth. I did try but each time my mouth pooled with water and I felt the urge to wretch but Marco is back today on a late flight so I know it won't go to waste. That in itself is only small comfort as I dejectedly nibble on my dry toast.

ProProducts is a small firm of maybe ten researchers and three directors. One of which is Christopher Taylor the Finance Director, who also has a second job as a part-time lecturer at my University. I met him on one occasion before Mr Wilson informed me of this internship opportunity just before Christmas and then I met him once more at my interview but I have not really seen much of him since then. The office is in a shared facility with many other type of IT or media companies each renting a small part of a much bigger building. As such the facilities are much better than a stand-alone office of this size could provide. There is a small coffee bar and an actual bar that opens in the evening. There are ultra-modern and high tech screening rooms for presentations to hire and there is a large chill out area in the basement, with a pool table and vending machines for the offices that hold unsociable work hours. The *ProProducts* office occupies part of the first floor and is open plan with small funky cubicles and three separate offices at one end for the directors and a small meeting room.

I take my seat at my desk just after eight and I'm pleased to be the first in the office. I am also pleased that it has been at least five minutes since I last thought about Daniel which is a big improvement on the five-second intervals of the last week. I check my email and notice an urgent appointment notification for nine thirty this morning with Christopher Taylor. I spend the next hour and half just stacking my piles of paper on my desk into manageable sections and prioritising my 'to do' list. As others start to come in I get a strange feeling that I might be missing something, maybe a significant event, maybe someone has died. There is a definite sombre feel and I have yet to speak to anyone, everyone is studiously sitting with their heads buried. Just before nine thirty I gather my bag and make my way to the corner office of Christopher Taylor; Finance Director. I knock gently. I didn't see him come but he is quick to ask me to enter and briskly asks me to take a seat. It's difficult to tell whether my sinking feeling in my stomach is portent or whether it's just this ongoing bug. I simply feel damn sick all the time so I just don't know.

His office is a mess, stacks and stacks of paper crowd his desk, the floor and the surrounding walls leaning against any and all available space. His desk is clear but I think that is because he has scraped everything on to the floor. Behind him is a wall full of shelving with reference books, codes of practice, reference material and application guidance books. All wedged and crammed so not a millimetre of space is wasted. I move the stack of papers on the only chair opposite his desk and carefully sit, mindful that he is not his usual friendly self. I have only met him on a couple of occasions but he was definitely more relaxed then. In fact he looks distinctly uncomfortable. He is a tall man, slim, attractive and he is shifting in his seat. He is wearing jeans and a button down white shirt, more casual than when he is at the University but this place is more on the informal side. His hair is a darker blonde now that he has had it cut much shorter and he no longer sports the roguish stubble. He seems nervous and bizarrely I feel sorry for him when it's me that has been called to a rather ominous meeting; I take pity on him.

"Mr Taylor is there a problem?" My voice is calm if a little shaky.

"Chris, call me Chris and why would you ask that?" His brows knit together and he leans his elbows on his desk.

"Oh it might just be me but it seems a little quiet out there and well, you look . . . um . . . tense." I try to smile some comfort and he gives only the tightest smile back.

"Right well, " He straightens his back and grimaces like he is about to do something unpleasant. He is about to do something unpleasant. "I regret that we are going to have to let you go." He rushes the words then adds as if he forgot, "with immediate effect." He sits back a little, gauging my reaction. To be honest I am not surprised, I have been a waste of space these last few weeks. Nevertheless I am still taken back, it's just that I have never been made redundant before.

"Oh I see, well I guess I understand." My voice is quiet and I go to pick up my bag.

"You don't seem surprised?" Chris's voice has an edge that makes me look up, he is cross. Why the hell should he be cross? He still has a job, no wait, he still has *two* jobs.

"Well, I know I haven't been here long and I've had to have had some unexpected time off . . . so I guess it's not a huge surprise that you made me redundant." I stand and shrug.

He stands quickly and the chair tips over, his voice is quiet but firm "We didn't make you redundant Bethany you've been fired!" He places his knuckles on the desk and his scowl is burning into me.

"Fired but why?" I slip back down into the seat in utter shock and my whispered words are enough to cause Chris to step around the desk and crouch in front of me.

"Bethany look at me." I meet his eyes but I can feel mine start to pool with liquid. "We have to take theft very seriously. This is what we do here, it's all about our research and protecting our Intellectual Property." I am nodding as he speaks. "We won't be pressing charges but—"

I interrupt before his words actually register. "—I know, of course. Wait! . . . what? What theft? Have I stolen something? You think I stole something?" I can hear my voice start to rise and large warm drops of tears hit my cheek. Chris reaches into his pocket and hands me a soft cotton handkerchief. "I haven't stolen anything Chris, I wouldn't." I shake my head and sob a little more. I can't believe this is happening. He stands and sits quietly on the edge of his desk while I gather myself and stop crying. "I don't understand." I finally manage to say without causing more tears.

He draws in a deep breath and continues to look at me and since I have nothing to hide I meet his stare. "The project you have been working on, the safety system for cyclists. The patent

the Only Choice

search results came back and it already has a patent pending." He hands me some papers and I slowly flick through. There is not much here but it is definitely my design, my outline and my proposal. I must look confused but he chooses not to elaborate his findings.

"This is my project, this . . ." I wave the paper to highlight my focus. "This is mine, how could I steal it if it's already mine?" I stifle another sob.

He lets out a frustrated huff like he is talking to an annoying child and I'm sorry I don't understand but the document in my hand is mine, I wrote it. "Look at the back, the name of the company applying for the patent, the lead partner and the date. That date is nearly twelve months before you *claim* to have come up with the idea and still six months before you had submitted this outline?" The sentence is phrased as a question but I have stopped listening. All I can see is the name of the applicant **Stone R & D Ltd**. It doesn't matter what I say right now, no one is going to believe me. Funny that they will happily believe I would hack my way in to Daniel's R & D Company and steal a project idea though. I laugh bitterly, if only I were that good, that corrupt, if only I was more like Kit. I wince at that inner thought, realisation that I may have hit a new low for me. "This is very serious Bethany." His angry tone makes me realise I laughed out loud. "This could affect your position on your course at the University. If it is found you have been plagiarising in other areas of your work."

My head snaps and I stand. "I don't plagiarise and I didn't steal shit. If you want to believe that, well that's your call and there is nothing I can do about that but don't think for one minute this ends here! I didn't steal anything and I'll prove it." I snatch my bag and turn abruptly for the door.

"Bethany." His voice is softer and I turn to see his face, his eyes seem less harsh and he is trying to smile but it doesn't quite make it. "I am sorry and for what it's worth I didn't think you did it but we just can't take the risk, well, anyway . . . I just wish I knew how this could've happened."

I snort. "That is exactly what I'm going to find out." I leave his room and see an office full of bobbing heads snap down to focus on their work, even if it is just until I leave the building.

Once outside I stagger to the nearest bench as my vision blurs and I feel lightheaded. I don't feel sad anymore, so no more pathetic tears. I don't feel numb anymore so no more wistful recollections I just feel pure fucking rage. Hasn't he taken enough? Did he really need this too? God if Chris is right and I could lose my place on my course, fuck I can't even process how angry I would be. In one hit I think I'd just have to rip his bollocks right off and smile at the knowledge that Angel would lose her sperm donor at the same time. Christ, he just brings out the best in me. I shake these foreign thoughts from my head and call someone who might be able to help. The phone rings several times, I hear it switch to an alternate line before it is answered.

"Economics Faculty can I help?" The bright pleasant voice answers Mr Wilson's phone throwing me completely.

"Oh I'm sorry I was trying to get hold of Mr Wilson. I must have dialled the wrong number." I apologise.

"—No no you have the right number but Mr Wilson's calls will be transferred here while he is away." She assures me.

"Oh right. Do you know when he is due back I really need to speak to him urgently?" It might not be life threatening urgent but it is urgent to me and it may well be life threatening to Mr Stone the way I'm feeling at the moment.

"He won't be back until the week before the new semester in October I'm afraid. It's pretty much admin staff and some occasional teaching staff but they keep irregular hours so I couldn't guarantee—" I politely interrupt because either she hasn't spoken to anyone in a really long time or she is just being super informative but she isn't really telling me anything remotely helpful.

"—Thank you, that's Ok. I'll maybe drop him an email, he might check in with any luck. Thank you though." I hang up. I will send an email when I get home but now I just have one more call to make. The first call to Daniel rings and rings, the second

the Only Choice

the same, the third gets transferred to answer phone as does the next fifteen. I can be a stalker too. I don't leave a message but just hang on long enough to register my call. The next call gets answered and I feel a sudden panic as my heart races momentarily eclipsing my anger.

"Bethany this is Colin I am afraid Mr Stone won't be able to take your call." I can hear him swallow and I know he must feel almost as bad as I do about this call, almost. "Is there anything I can do to help?"

"Can you put me through?" My clipped response causes him to sigh and the regret is evident in his gentle tone.

"I'm sorry Bethany you know I can't. I mean you know I'd love to but—" and now I feel bad for asking.

"It's all right Colin, I understand. I'm sorry for asking." My tone too softens. It is not his fault his boss is a son of a bitch and a coward. "Is he in today? I mean is he in all day?"

"You know I can't tell you that, God . . . I never thought I'd hate my job but right now . . ." He mutters.

"No that's fine Colin." I let out a heartfelt sigh and hear Colin curse.

"Look there is no way he'll see you but if you were around lunch time he maybe escorting some business associates around the foyer at that time. But you didn't hear that from me." His voice drops to a whisper.

"Thank you Colin, I owe you." I hope he can hear me smile, even if it is mingled with malicious intent.

"No Mum I've told you not to call at work. Look good luck and I'll see you later." I hear him sigh before the line goes quiet.

He hangs up and I hope he managed to pull that off, I would hate him getting into trouble. Since my hopeful rendezvous with Mr Arsehole is lunch time and it's a good two hour walk from Battersea to the other side of the city I fix my sights on the tallest building in Canary Wharf and head that way on foot. The walk will give me time to clear my head, focus my mind and plot my vengeance. Now I'm being dramatic, I don't want revenge. I just want to know why? Why he stole from me? Why he would risk my future when he knew exactly how hard I worked and how precious it was to me? But mostly I just want to know why he won't even take my call? The lump in my throat seems to be a permanent fixture. After everything we have been through and promised each other I can't believe he can shut down like he has, like we were nothing, like I am nothing. Today, at least he has made it crystal clear that I am no different to any number of others that Daniel has implemented his bullshit Total Communication Shutdown policy on.

The walk is exactly what I need and I am completely distracted by the activity along the riverbank from County Hall to Tower Bridge. Even in the relatively early morning the path is full of tourists and school children from all over the country, all over the world. Drawn to the London Eye, the Aquarium and further along The Globe; Tate Modern and the not so wobbly bridge which I cross and turn right making my way in to the business heart of the city. It takes me less than two hours in the end. Just after eleven I am standing outside Daniel's office building and just because it feels right to add to my pain I check my finger print on the entrance door to the side and my heart sinks at the not surprising red light of denied access flashing brightly. My legs feel suddenly weaker and I stumble a little backwards but manage not to fall. This is very different from our last forced split. Last time I was still able to gain access to Daniel's building just in time to escape Clive but then Daniel knew we weren't really split. He just didn't know at the time why, or why it had to be that way. But this time is not the same, this time he knows it is over and I've got the message loud and clear. I enter through the main revolving doors and make my way to the desk, where Eddie is checking people into the building. He looks a little shocked and then a little embarrassed and I guess he got the 'I've dumped Bethany memo' from Mr Stone.

"Hello Eddie." I smile sweetly. "How is Mrs Jones? Did she like the Limoncello I got her for New Year?" I know its low to try

the Only Choice

and currie favour but desperate times and all.

"Oh Miss Thorne, yes, yes she did it was perfect for the meal she had in mind and thank you she is very well." He coughs lightly and shuffles from one foot to the next. "Um Miss Thorne I'm afraid I have very strict instructions to—" I nod my head in understanding and take his hand because he looks quite troubled as I interrupt.

"—It's fine Eddie, I know, but I'm going to sit over there if that's Ok? If you would let Mr Stone know that I won't be leaving anytime soon I would be grateful." I smile again and turn to take an empty seat by the revolving door because along with nausea I am having trouble regulating my body temperature too and I need the little bits of fresh air that manage to sneak in each time the door rotates.

"Oh I'm not sure you are allowed to stay." He is frowning.

"We're you told to throw me out?" I ask sweetly. His eyes widen.

"No not at all, I wouldn't anyway." He looks affronted at the suggestion but I'm not so shocked. It is possible and it wouldn't be the first time.

"We're you told not to let me through?" I enquire kindly.

"Yes." He confirms warily.

"and you haven't so we are all good." I smile again and take my seat.

I spend the next two hours sitting, people watching and pressing redial on Daniels phone. I know it's childish but I am not leaving until he sees me and now I am no longer employed I have plenty of spare time to irritate Mr Stone, yes that's perfectly healthy. Oh fuck what am I doing? What does it really matter, if my product gets to market sooner because his company is pushing the development is that a bad thing? I'm not being altruistic just realistic. I couldn't fight this, with the resources Daniel has and his reputation it would be foolish and would probably guarantee I get kicked off my course. But I still deserve an explanation. I just reach into my bag when a shadow falls across me and

I look up into the kind but stern face of Daniel's chief operating officer Jason. He holds his hand and I automatically take it. He pulls me to my feet.

"Come with me Bethany." He marches across the reception, swipes a card and walks to the bank of elevators. He releases my hand and punches the button. I risk a look his way, pleased that I am being taken somewhere, maybe to see Daniel probably not but at least I will get to speak to someone and Jason is a good start. As Daniel's right hand man he is the closest person I have met to Daniel that might be considered a friend, particularly in light of their shared interests outside of the office. Jason is attractive in a well groomed GQ kind of way, slightly shorter than Daniel with short brown hair that is tinged with copper. His light brown eyes have golden flecks and his lips are full but currently fixed in a tight line. I guess I am interrupting his day and dealing with exes is probably not part of his job description. The elevator opens and I follow him in, he frowns at the men about to follow me and they both retreat as the door closes.

"You shouldn't be here Bethany, you know that right?" His tone is clipped and agitated.

I exhale loudly. "Yes I'm getting that impression." I rub my forehead and pinch the bridge of my nose. The tension is fast becoming a killer headache. "If it helps at all I'm here for business reasons." I hold his gaze as he looks surprised.

"Really?" He tilts his head.

"Oh don't get me wrong I would love to know why Mr. Arsewipe can't be an adult and take my calls but I'm guessing you can't answer that?" I raise an inquisitive brow and when he chuckles and shakes his head, I continue. "No well, thought as much. So I just want to know why Stone R & D stole my design and passed it off as one of their own?" I leave that hanging in the air, pleased at the utter shock on Jason's face as I step off the elevator. Jason follows quickly just as the doors begin to close and takes my elbow leading me along the corridor to an office at the end, his office.

"That's a very serious allegation Bethany." His voice is gruff, his grip is tight and I am thankful for my flat pumps or I'd be flat on my arse by now.

"Well I'm not here for the warm welcome, that's for sure." I snap.

He stands to the side and watches me enter his office before closing the door and leaning against it. He takes a moment and pushes off casually all the time he keeps his eyes fixed on me. Reading my every movement for some sort of tell that maybe I'm might be trying to trick him. He walks to his desk and slowly sits motioning me to do the same.

"So do you want to tell me what makes you think we've stolen from you exactly?" His voice is calm if a little condescending but I choose not to bite.

"I don't think. I know, and . . ." I rummage through my bag and pull the crumpled application that Chris gave me earlier. I don't have my copy but it's enough for him to get started. "This is your application and I can email my copy over later but there's little point they are identical." I lean over and he takes the forms. Smoothing them on his desk and slowly reading the documents.

"I think there must be a misunderstanding, maybe you *do* need to speak with Daniel?" He muses quietly more to himself as he shakes his head at that thought. "No, look, I'll look into it, give me your details and I will contact you as soon as I have some more information." He sits back and narrows his eyes, he is still so suspicious and yet it's not me that has stolen anything.

"Can't you get my details from Daniel?" I challenge and he smirks.

"No I don't think that would be wise, beside he's made it perfectly clear he— " He censures himself but I already feel the crushing rejection in the unsaid words. Daniel's made it perfectly clear he wants nothing to do with me and no one is to mention my name. I no longer exist.

"So he's at lunch and I'm really not allowed to see him?" I fight the rising tears, pinch my nails into my palms and focus on the growing anger once more.

"He has some business associates he is entertaining in the private dining room and no darling you are not allowed to see him." He rolls his eyes like I just say the silliest things.

"But I am allowed to see you?" His eyes widen and I catch a flash of heat as I emphasise the last words and what they might mean. I don't know what they mean but I am not above exploring any angle to get an audience with Mr Arsehole.

"Bethany." He shakes his head lightly, "you could well make me break my rule, 'shitting where I eat' in fact once I'm sure he's serious I am definitely breaking that rule but for now let's just keep this business." He fights the grin that threatens his implacable face.

I relax a little but strangely feel empowered to push this. I go to stand and make my way the door turning slowly and just before I leave say. "In that case maybe I'll see you at the club." With that and as Jason's jaw drops I walk out leaving the door to swing shut with a loud click. I barely make it to the elevator when Jason has my elbow gripped tight and is walking me to an empty room. Once the door closes he turns to face me.

"You can't go there Bethany its members only!" He voice is harsh and panicked.

"Really?" I mock. "Because I'm pretty sure I got in last time when I wasn't a member?" I pull my elbow from his hold and try for the door but he blocks me with his arm.

He growls. "You can't go there on your own, they'll eat you alive."

"I kind of thought that was the point!" I snap back. "Look," I point my finger hard into his chest and scowl because he has no right to tell me what I can or can't do, even if I don't really want to do what I'm threatening to do. "Mr arsehole up there opened that door for me and just because he's kicked me to the curb doesn't mean he or you can dictate whether I choose to walk through that door again. He stole my future; he broke my fucking heart but this body, this is mine and I will do whatever I please with it."

My words soften toward the end as I lose my fire. I realise that the best threat I can come up with is to fuck a bunch of Dominant strangers, wow this day just keeps getting better. "Look, forget I said that, in fact just forget everything." I let out a sad breath that fails to hold back a few tears. "I'll go now Jason, and don't worry about looking into my project, it was silly to think I could take him on." He steps aside and walks me in silence to the elevator. Before the door closes he hands me his card.

"Just in case. Don't go alone." His light brown eyes darken, he removes his arm as the door slides shut. I slip the card in the tiny back pocket of my skirt as the lift rapidly drops to the floor along with my hopes and dreams.

Chapter Three

I CAN'T BELIEVE I said that, what was I thinking? I know I have no intention of going back to the club. I didn't even get a fluttering in my stomach at the thought and I know it's because I wasn't lying when I said Daniel had opened that door. But what I didn't say was that he is the only one I want to walk through it with. Would I risk going? Hoping that Jason would let Daniel know, hoping he would come for me as he had before. I snort as the lift door opens at the ridiculous fairy-tale line of thinking. My wayward mind is racing, he won't even take my call, he won't see me and it's laughable to think any different. Daniel Stone will definitely *not* rescue me. I don't think I have ever felt so low, felt so worthless. I have nothing left, I'm a shell. I don't think I can make it to the main door without breaking down and drawing mortifying attention my way. CCTV is everywhere so I duck my head down and rush toward the ladies. Slumped in a cubicle, my bottom instantly numb on the hard seat cover I drop my head in my hands and quietly cry, muffling my sobs with my sleeve. God I'm pathetic. Pathetic, nothing and alone; I just need them to start pumping *Heart Will Go On* through the speakers and I think I will top myself.

My phone starts to vibrate in my bag. I wipe my face dry and

the Only Choice

let out a 'pulling myself together' breath. "Hey sister." I swallow a rising lump because the breath didn't quite work.

"What's up Bets you sound strange?" Sofia has been consumed with all things wedding recently and understandably, so I am a little surprised she picked up on my shaky tone so quickly. I give her a brief outline of my stellar morning, neglecting to mention I am currently hiding in the ladies.

"Where are you now?" Her tone hasn't softened despite my tale of woe.

"Ladies, I kind of lost it in the lift and ran to the toilets before . . ." I falter and wipe the rivers rolling down my cheeks.

"Where's your fucking dignity Bethany Edith Thorne?" She snaps.

I wince at her harsh words. She's bringing out the big guns with my middle name and I know she's pissed. "Elvis." I reply. "I'm hiding in the toilet right now, where do you think my dignity is? It's left the fucking building." I bite back

"Well for fuck sake Bets go and get it back. This isn't about standing by your man or even wanting him back because the douche doesn't deserve you but you do deserve some answers and you deserve them from him. Fuck Bethany, since when did you start believing . . . you know I can't even say it and you know Marco would throw a shit fit if he thought you were self-doubting over this bullshit. Now, I want you to go back out there, up to his office and demand some answers. It's the very least and I mean the *very* least you deserve." She huffs to emphasise her righteous indignation.

"It's not that easy—" I try to argue.

"—Don't give me that, you can be fierce when you are protecting me or Marco or anyone else you love so—"

"—No," I interrupt her rant softly because I think someone has just come in. "No, I mean you are right but it's not that easy. I would have to get past the sphincter police and I don't want to embarrass myself anymore, it's humiliating. I agree with what you said, really I do, I just don't know how I can—" She stops me with an abrupt laugh.

"There are always *ways* Bethany, you know that. You weren't always the bosses girlfriend, you were staff remember?" I can almost see her conspiratorial brows wiggling and I let out a laugh, God I love this woman.

"Of course . . . Ok who do you know in the kitchen, because that could be perfect. He has a private lunch right about now." My voice is whispered my hand cupped over the phone.

"Give me two minutes, in the meantime wipe the pandas will you?" I frown at the phone as I pull it away from my face wondering if I am speaking on a video call. She hangs up and I straighten my short black skirt and blouse, take my button up cardigan out of my bag and put it on, shoulders back, head high, I open the door and walk over to the sink. I just finish removing the panda eyes when my phone buzzes to life.

"You're in luck he's got external caterers for this lunch and he's got them from my club no less. Gaby is working over there today and she says she'll switch with you if you meet her at the loading doors by the staff entrance in five minutes. They have had the first course and they are just about to take the second up so you better shift your arse. Now boldly go, woman!" Her voice is firm and excited at the same time. "And Bets he's treated you like you were nothing . . . so don't you dare let him get away with it." She hangs up before I can get all tearful again. I grab my bag and walk quickly from the ladies across the main foyer and out of the revolving doors. I walk ahead so as not to make it too obvious I am just rounding the building. The plaza is busy with the lunchtime rush and I have to weave through the people taking impromptu picnics on the steps. I freeze when I see Daniels car but notice that Peter is in a reclined position, clearly not expecting Daniel any time soon. I can see Gaby by the loading bay waving frantically and I run to meet her. She flings her arms around me and starts to pull at her white jacket as I quickly remove my cardigan.

"Quick quick they are just loading the carts! Paula will serve the plates you follow with the sauce. I'll keep your bag but I'm going to head home, pretend I wasn't even here if that's Ok?" She giggles. "Lucky I work for either Sofia or her family because I would not want to get on their bad side." She pushes me to the elevator where Paula, I assume, is waiting with a fully loaded cart. Just as the door close Gaby waves and I mouth 'thank you.'

Paula smiles at me nervously and I wonder how much she knows. I confidently do my buttons on my jacket and shake my shoulders releasing some tension then I smile brightly at her. "No need to look so worried, I could do this in my sleep . . . You won't even know I'm there." She gives me a tight smile and I know Gaby hasn't told her anything. We push the cart to the boardroom door which I quietly open and Paula eases the cart over the threshold and positions it at the back of the room. Daniel has his back to us, he is wearing a dark navy suit and I can smell his cologne. A light infusion of citrus and spice easily over powered by the meal we just brought in if I wasn't so attuned. I am grateful he has his back to us however, because my heart is racing and my skin is tingling with a mix of fear and a result of being near him. I curse my body for these innate, involuntary and traitorous reactions. Fortunately, I have Sofia's indignant words and my raging anger swirling inside so I know that this encounter is likely to turn me on as much as a smear test would.

The room is sparsely furnished with a large oval glass topped table dominating the centre of the room. The four men are seated two each side of Daniel and he is at the head. The full height glass wall holds an invisible door that opens on to a seating area outside on a platform that overlooks the Thames and out toward Greenwich Park on a clear day. I know this, because it's the same view from Daniels office but I take no time or pleasure in the vista today. I remove the plates from the warming cart; take the protective covers revealing an elegant arrangement of the pan fried duck breast with baby glazed carrots, trimmed French beans and fondant potatoes. I hand the plates to Paula as she sets about serving the table; one of the men addresses Daniel.

"Thought we'd lost you for a while Stone heard you'd picked up some skirt." He laughs gruffly and I can feel my shoulders stiffen. "Glad it wasn't serious, still she must have been a whore in the bedroom to keep you interested for so long?" He slaps the man sitting next to him as they all fall into low dirty laughter. "You'll have to get me her details now you're done. I'm intrigued or was there more to it, did you actually love her?" He snorts and wrinkles his nose like he's just smelt something disgusting when the only thing disgusting is him.

Daniels voice is low, softly spoken so the room goes quiet and I find I'm holding my breath. "There was something more." He hesitates and I feel a flutter of anticipation just before the rot of reality. "A little R & D project that's now mine . . . and ask Colin for her details I no longer keep them." I grip the cart as I feel my knees buckle, I grit my teeth and swallow back the water pooling in my mouth. With clarity and serenity I hadn't expected after his most hurtful words I calmly walk over to his side holding the jug of hot redcurrant jus, without looking up he sits back to allow me better access to his plate and his lap. For maximum effect I quickly tip the jug completely into his lap and then let the jug go. From this height and the weight of the large ceramic container landing directly on his groin, he is hit hard. His hands grab at his prize possession, covered in hot red liquid it looks like his taken a direct hit from a shotgun not a tasty berry reduction.

"Fuck! . . . What the Fuck!" He pushes back and stands sending his chair flying but freezes when he lifts his head to meet my eyes. I walk over to him, standing as tall as I can, still dwarfed by his immense frame but no longer intimidated. I point my finger softly on his chest and watch him recoil as if I too have burned him.

"You, Mr Stone are a liar, a thief, a son of a bitch," I laugh bitterly, "but you knew that last one already. You are an arsehole and a coward." The room is silent and I turn and walk away, just before I close the door I turn my head. "I thought you were a gentleman; shame on you." I am only slightly sorry that I am leaving

Paula to clean up my mess and although my legs feel like jelly I make my way to the elevator. The doors open, I pass Jason whose head snaps in a double take and just as the doors close I see Daniel furious, looking like he's been in a blood bath, shouting.

"Jason! Stop her! Fuck don't let her leave!" His voice disappears behind the closed doors and my last image is of Jason's arm pushing for the ever closing gap with a look of pure confusion.

Fuck! I slap my hands on the rail in the lift, holding with a white knuckle grip and adrenaline pumping so hard in my veins that my whole body shakes. I draw in fast deep breaths that just make me light headed and the speedy descent of the lift makes my knees give way as it reaches the ground floor. The doors open and I am greeted by a very stern looking Eddie, who doesn't return my attempted smile.

"You left the building. I saw you leave. Do you mind telling me how you managed to get back in?" He folds his arms waiting for an explanation but I am not inclined to hang around, having *boldly gone,* I now want to timidly leave.

"You know Eddie I would love to but I might have outstayed my welcome. You can escort me off this time just to be safe." I wink at him and I see his shoulders relax and a twinge in the corner of his mouth as he tries to suppress some warmer emotion than the one he is currently presenting. I try to step out and to his side but he holds up his hand.

"Oh I'm sorry Miss Thorne but since you trespassed and assaulted the CEO leaving is no longer an option." He informs me without a hint of humour.

My mouth drops in shock. "What? You have to be kidding?" I laugh coldly. "Has he called the police? Am I going to be arrested?" I put my hands on my hips, he might be technically right but I'm not going to be intimidated or back down. He rests his hand on my shoulder and gives me a gentle squeeze.

"I don't think that's his intention but he was I little cross when he called down. I think it is best if I take you back up there so you can get this mess sorted, without the need for the police and," he fumbles and hesitates. "I'm sorry to have to do this but Mr Stone insisted." He frowns and his cheeks tinge pink under his dark tan as he reaches into his back pocket. He lifts a pair of industrial looking silver hand cuffs. I had seen them on his belt before but assumed they were for show.

"I just bet he did. Oh you've got to be kidding me? Seriously?" I almost laugh but he turns me round and as gently as possible clips the cuffs to my wrists. Stepping into the lift he presses the top floor button. We are quiet for a moment. "You really think this is necessary?" I jangle the cuffs to make my point.

"I am just doing what I'm told Bethany and I can't have you slipping through my fingers again. I need this job, so yes, I think it's necessary. I think it's safest." He nods to himself, happy I think with his justification. The lift smoothly pulls to a stop, which in mere seconds has reached the twenty ninth floor and he motions for me to step out. I turn to face him.

"Safest for whom?" I whisper to the closing doors.

"Shit Bethany what did you do?" Colin's hushed voice makes me turn again. He is walking briskly from his desk along the corridor. He peeps around my body and his eyes are wide at the sight of the cuffs. "Shit!" He whispers again and takes my elbow and leads me along toward Daniels office. It is then I notice that the other offices are empty and there are no other people on this floor. In fact it is eerily quiet.

"Extended lunch hour?" I quip with a casualness I'm not feeling.

"Ha, you're funny! No he's closed this floor and I'm to escort you to his office and then leave for the day." His voice is conspiratorially quiet.

I swallow loudly. I don't have my phone and I don't know anyone's number by heart anymore, who does? Everything is stored on my phone. Shit. I let out a puff because there is fuck all I can do about it now. "Right, well if you are the last person to see me alive, tell my best friend that's the last time I take her advice." I nudge him lightly but with my arms secured behind my back

the Only Choice

I am a little off balance and stumble. Too late to catch me Colin watches as I skid along the carpet and pick up a fierce carpet burn on my right knee, the sting is sharp and makes me squeal. "Owww Oh that stings like a bitch!" Colin helps me up with kind words and I clamp my jaw tight as the pain fires brightly from its origin. Colin pauses for a moment of sympathy while I compose myself but only for a moment, he then opens Daniels door and tilts his head for me to enter. He is not coming in and he is going to leave me, alone.

"Take care Bethany and I'd be very surprised if I'm the last person to see you alive." He smiles and winks.

My light laugh is more nervous now. "Ohhh well that's a comfort, you being very surprised. I guess I've got nothing to worry about then?"

"I didn't say that now did I?" He winks again and closes the door.

I get a sudden rush of Déjà vu, standing bound, nervous with my heart racing. I look around, his desk is the same, the seating area the same. The only indication that my desk was ever in the corner is the slight indentations in the rug. You wouldn't notice them if you didn't know to look. There is no sight or sound as to the whereabouts of Daniel so I go to take the seat opposite his desk. I have to sit straight because of the position of my arms and now I am having to raise my lower leg as the carpet burn actually broke the skin and is seeping tiny droplets of blood down my shin. I must sit for at least ten minutes when I hear some noise come from Daniels private bathroom behind his desk. I thought there was only one entrance to that room, but maybe not or maybe he has been in there the whole time. The sound is muffled but I can definitely hear the shower now. Great, I'll just sit here, bleeding and uncomfortable while he takes a shower.

I know this waiting is all part of his dominance and desire for control and as much as it pisses me off I can't deny that it is effective. I can feel subtle changes in my body with every passing minute. My breath is shallow, my skin tingles and little hairs raise on my neck and arms and dammit if I need to shift again, adjusting my position to ease the building pull and tightening between my legs. Finally, after what felt like days the door flush against the panelling behind his desk slides open and Daniel steps into the room. Holy shit I'm in trouble. I tuck my legs beneath the chair and sit up, lifting my chin trying my hardest to hold on to the residual anger and hurt; a daunting task given the image before me. His slow steps toward me only emphasise the flex and ripple of his abdomen. His shirt is open and his chest is dotted with droplets of water that escaped the towel he is currently dragging through is damp hair. His suit trousers hang loosely from his narrow hips and he is bare foot and silent walking up to me. He stops directly in front. His face, as expected gives nothing away but his eyes are dark and whether he is angry or not, I can't deny their fierce implacable heat. My throat is dry and I struggle to stop my breath from catching opting to hold it instead, biting my lips as I do.

He chuckles and strokes his finger up my throat and tips my chin up. Not that I had taken my eyes off him but he is now holding me so I don't move. "God I fucking love the way your body responds to me." He licks his full lips and I can't help my breath escape on a whimper but I quickly check myself and pull back enough to free myself from his finger hold.

"Don't flatter yourself. That's just biology, my body reacting to an attractive male, involuntary and unwelcome, I assure you. I am pretty sure my body had a similar reaction when Jason dragged me into that empty office earlier." It's brief but I notice his shock. "Animal instincts, it's just a shame my body is not so discerning or selective but I'm working on it." I narrow my eyes and keep my tone harsh, my words clipped. He smiles and leans forward his lips at my neck; his whispered breath kisses my sensitive skin.

"Mmmm." He traces his long finger down my throat and over the swell of my breasts, his thumb joining to pinch the hard peaked nipple beneath my blouse causing a shooting blissful pain to

the Only Choice

ignite deep inside. I pant out a shocked breath. "And how is that working out for you?" His tongue scorches as he licks a path from just below my neck to my collarbone and dammit if I don't lean to give him access. My skin is alive and I shiver from tip to toe.

Ignoring the smugness that is now settled on his face I rattle my cuffs breaking the intense exchange from disintegrating further out of my control. "Are these really necessary?" I snap.

His voice is deep and serious. "For what I have in mind, they are absolutely necessary."

"Daniel." My voice is a little higher pitched than I was hoping but I am on edge and trying to sound deadly serious. "I don't know what you think you are going to do, but you're not. I came here for answers, that's all, answers. You can't make me do anything regardless of the cuffs. I didn't come here to fuck!" I sound much braver than I am feeling.

He growls and I can see the tension in his jaw. "But that's the problem isn't it. I can't be near you without wanting you." He quickly corrects himself. "Without wanting to fuck you." He stands back and rakes his hand through his hair, his voice is hard and accusatory. "Regardless of what you want Miss Thorne, you broke in to my office, you assaulted me and you made some slanderous accusations all in front of witnesses. I am not inclined to give you what you want without some exchange, but . . ." he steps again to me and pulls me up holding me tight against his hard body and hot erection, like a branding iron it presses into my thigh. My neck tilts back to see the desire in his eyes. I don't fool myself that this is anything other than lust. His expression is dark and determined, and his focus and goal is crystal clear. "You do, however, have an impression of me that I do feel inclined to correct, *after* I get what I want."

"What is it you want?" My voice is barely a whisper and it is only his strong arms holding me upright. My body is trembling and I can hardly breathe I'm so confused.

"I want you to be a good little sub for me." His voice has

a desperate edge. "I want Lola." I can feel him hold his breath waiting my reply. I am speechless, turned-on, confused, turned-on, angry, and turned-on. Maybe it's because our last time together I didn't know *was* the last time, maybe because this close I can't think straight and every fibre in my body craves him. Or maybe because if this is going to be a purely physical act, as Lola, I can at least, protect Bethany's emotional heart. I don't trust my voice not to betray my fragile state so I nod. I can see his shoulders relax and he holds me at arm's length his eyes hungrily explore my body but widen in shock.

"Shit! You're bleeding. What have you done, are you all right? Sit down." His panic and concern is a sharp contrast from his aloof, impersonal demands as my Dominant. It's just what I don't need. He gently eases me into the chair but stops pushing me back when he realises my cuffed arms would prevent that.

"It's just a carpet burn, I tripped outside. It just kept bleeding but it's dried now. It looks worse than it is." I shrug because it looks bad but I know it will clean up Ok.

"Fuck it looks like you've been in a slasher movie. Stay there let me clean you up." His voice is gentle and I can't stand it.

"Don't!" My voice is sharp and catches as I swallow a painful lump.

"Don't what?" His brows knit and his voice deepens.

"Don't be nice." I can feel my eyes prickle and he shakes his head lightly, pushes up but leans in to whisper.

"I'm a liar, a thief, coward and an arsehole, remember?" He nibbles my earlobe sending a million shivers racing over my skin. "I'm not nice." He walks back toward his bathroom and doesn't hear me breathe out.

"You were nice to me." I can feel the trickle of tears and am frustrated I can't wipe them dry. I need to stop, focus and play my part. My starring role as Lola, The Good Sub. I cough and say much louder. "And a son of a bitch, don't forget you're a son of a bitch too."

He stands at the door his face a dark scowl, holding a small

the Only Choice

bowl. He steps toward me and crouches low on his haunches just in front of me. "I'm not likely to forget that." His voice is gruff but his eyes hold sadness in the brief look he flashes before his mask slips back and he is again unreadable. He squeezes some cotton wool dry and starts to clean the dried blood from my leg. He takes his time with warm soothing strokes along my shin and tender gentle massages with his other hand along my calve. I let my eyes drift close and relax in to his touch so much so that I am unaware he has stopped until he coughs. My eyes snap to his and he raises a curious brow and is suppressing a grin.

"Sorry." I gush and I can feel my cheeks heat.

"Please don't. I love it when you blush." He shakes his head replacing that gentle tone with a sterner reprimand. "It's not bad but you should take more care."

I want to laugh bitterly and tell him that, yes that's what I need to take care of, tripping and scraping my knee but not to worry about the huge fucking hole he's ripped in my chest. I decide to just bite my lip and fix my best death stare. I don't need to give him any ammunition to destroy me further. I just need to be more like him, impassive, hard and take my pleasure where I can and right now, I believe I'm owed big time. I lift my chin and meet his heated gaze, his eyes are liquid lust. He carefully removes his belt, deliberately dragging it through the loops in his suit trousers at a tortuously slow pace, his intentions implicit. I lick my dry lips, the pain in my chest soon to be replaced with a more diverting type of pain. My core is liquid heat, I can see from the bulge in his trousers and the drape of his belt that our next exchange is not going to be all about pleasure.

Chapter Four

DANIEL SMOOTHES THE long leather strap of his belt through his fingers, winding it around each palm and pulling it tight before he releases it and repeats the movement. Never taking his dark stare from me he places the belt on the desk and motions with a sharp nod and a curling of his fingers for me to stand. My legs feel heavy and unstable but my automatic response is to obey. I pivot and pull myself to stand in front of him. Every move he makes is slow and deliberate, the silence is palpable, the tension explosive. He walks round me and I follow him with my eyes. He shakes his head and makes a disapproving grumble.

"Tsk tsk eyes down sub, now I know I trained you better than that. Or perhaps this about your desire to be reminded?" He sweeps my hair from around my neck and scoops it over one shoulder. His fingers barely touching my skin but the raw heat instantly burns where they skim. I breathe heavily through my nose, lower my eyes but otherwise hold perfectly still. He strokes his warm strong hands over my shoulders, down my arms to my joined hands. "Good girl." He surprises me when he unlocks the cuffs and pockets them. He then turns me to face him but I keep my eyes down, now looking at his bare feet. He takes my wrists

the Only Choice

and uses his thumbs to gently rub circles all along the faint pink line where the cuffs have been. His strong hands move up my arms and to my shoulders, taking his time to ease the stiffness. I find I all too easily relax into his masterful massage. I don't understand what he's doing but I don't understand what I'm doing either so I sigh and drift into a sensual haze where his fingertips banish my numbness and bring me back to life.

"Strip." His deep voice sends a chill across my skin. He steps away to give me room. He sits on the edge of his desk but fixes me with a lust filled stare that is so intense I feel it pierce right through me. It's unsettling and I am glad I only risked a glimpse but now keep my eyes fixed to the floor. With trembling fingers and an unsteady breath I start to pull at my clothes. I hear him draw a sharp breath when I am finally left standing in my bra and panties. His voice husky and hard, a warning. "If I have to repeat myself, it's just going to add to your punishment." I shiver once more but quickly reach around to unclip my bra and step out of my panties. My body is flushed with a million prickles dancing on my skin, my breath now rapid shallow pants and there is no hiding how turned on I am, not now. "Mmm." He hums with satisfaction and stands so close all I can feel is heat, his smell is intoxicating; sweet and spice and it makes my mouth dry. He snakes his arms around my waist, again pulling me tight against his arousal. His hands gripping the cheeks firmly of my bottom, squeezing and scraping his fingernails along the soft skin. "I do struggle with this perfect skin, so delicate, so flawless and my desire to mark it." He draws in a ragged breath. "It's a paradox."

I can't help scoff. "You don't seem to struggle that hard." He laughs loudly and twists me in his arms.

"Oh good." He drawls. "More reasons to mark this beautiful backside. Please. . . . continue." His breath heats my neck with his softly spoken ominous words. He takes my hands in one of his and loops something softer but just as restrictive as the cuffs, firmly around my wrists. "You are right of course. I don't struggle too hard and do you know why that is?" He threads his fin-

45

gers into my hair from my neck gathering a handful and pulling sharply causing a shot of pain and a gasp of breath to escape my mouth. He is waiting for an answer.

"No Sir." I need to remember to speak not just mouth off.

"Because it's what you need. It's what I want but it's what you need. The pain helps doesn't it?" His whisper against my ear is thick with sensual menace. He squeezes my hair, pinching to the point of constant pain.

"Yes Sir." I gasp pushing into his grip. He hasn't said my name, he hasn't called me Lola and I wonder who he is talking too because as Lola the 'good little sub' pain is a by-product of the game. But for me it's much more. In fact he is spot on, I do need the pain. It does help because, even, if only for a brief moment, it makes me forget. I may not understand it but I embrace it and welcome the respite, the release and the reward. He seems to sense a shift in me and stiffens pulling away but grabs the top of my arm and walks me toward the seating area. The back of the sofa is hip height and wide and he pushes me over, my head falling over so I am not quite doubled up but my tummy is curled over the soft cushions and my bottom is completely exposed. "Don't move." I roll my eyes at this because from this angle and with my hands tied behind my back; I would have to have stomach muscles of steel to lift myself upright and my stomach muscles are more a sponge consistency since I haven't been to a Krav class in ages.

I do turn my face to see he has picked up his belt and is striding back with purpose. I close my eyes and savour the building desire and driving need swirling like a cyclone deep inside. I can feel the material of his trousers brush against my legs and his hand smoothly strokes the top of my thighs and bottom. His palm feels hot on my sensitive skin but I am instantly chilled all over resulting in an unexpected full body shiver. "Oh baby, you are so fucking ready for this." I hear the swish in the air strangely simultaneous to the smack and unbelievable sting on my cheek. Fuck! I push my head hard into the deep soft cushion and scream;

pleased the desperate howl is muffled to a more acceptable cry. Oh my God that hurts. Again, swish, slap and again and again. I can feel the welts rise and my skin tingle and burn. My breathing is so rapid I can see light spots drift over my closed lids as the strikes continue to rain down, not in the same spot but not so far apart either. My whole backside and thighs are on fire. I will my muscles to relax and I feel a wave of calmness engulf me. I am encased in a blanket of raging heat, it's comforting and diverting. All I feel is warm and floaty.

The sound of the belt hitting the floor has my consciousness peak back to this strange reality. I jump as I feel his long fingers trace between the crack of my cheeks, avoiding the burning skin but sweeping down into my sensitive sodden folds. His fingers slide and glide through my slickness and I can't prevent the involuntary roll of my hips back to try and gain more connection. He moans a dark throaty sound and continues his leisurely intimate movements. "You know I always underestimate your talent for enduring administered punishment. How could I forget how stubborn you are, but still . . ." He presses his thumbs firmly over my clit and I shudder, "It's not the only form of punishment is it?" I whimper as he moves his thumb in delicious circles.

I bite my lips together and push back against his hand as he slips a second finger inside me, swirling and curling against the sweetest soft spot. Instantly my core clenches and I can feel the spasms take control just as he stops all movement. His other hand presses me firmer onto the sofa so I can't move or wriggle against his hand for the necessary friction. A small pathetic cry escapes my throat but not my mouth as my contracting muscles ebb, along with my ill-fated orgasm. Again and again he brings me frayed and panting to within a whisper of ultimate pleasure. My body is racked and exhausted, a sheen of perspiration coating every inch and once more I bite back my begging words, drawing on my last fragments of strength. He growls as he stops once more. "Something you want to say baby?" His guttural tone is feral but I can hear the frustration in his voice and it gives me a boost to my inner strength. My body is limp, taking everything he is giving me and stoically enduring everything he denies but as he slowly pumps his fingers in and out, swirling his thumb and pressing too lightly I clench hard trying to prevent the telltale ripple of muscles signalling the very start of my journey to oblivion. A sign he is more than familiar with. His fingers continue a merciless slow torture and I can't hold a moment longer; I exhale, relax and grind hard and quickly into his surprised grip. It's enough, that tiny extra friction that he has denied me for what seems like endless hours is mine and I fall. I free fall screaming and trembling, my hips buck, my spine arches, a gravity defying feet and against every tired muscle in my body I quake.

"Fuck!" He shouts and roughly removes his hand. It's not ideal. I love it when he brings me down gently with tender caresses or his sublime tongue but I guess under the circumstance that was unlikely. I can't move. I lie wilted as short, sharp waves of pleasure ripple through me. My body blissfully drained of sexual tension. I wisely keep my face pressed against the sofa. I don't think it would do me any favours if he saw my shit eating grin right now. "Fuck!" He growls again and pulls me up sharply and turns me to face him. My head spins as I adjust to the blood now rushing to my feet. I feel woozy, really lightheaded and wobbly. Despite the furious look on his face he waits for me to steady myself. "You are *so* going to pay for that." He grinds the words out through gritted teeth but I see nothing but pure lust and desire in his deep dark blue eyes.

"I know." I hold his challenging gaze and tilt my chin in an open invitation for him to do his worst. Because frankly, he has done his worst and this now, this is a picnic in comparison. A sexy as hell, mind blowing, painfully erotic picnic. His grip on my arms is tight enough to know that it will bruise, but then given the treatment of my backside they won't be the only ones I pick up this afternoon. He positions me in the centre of the room and tells me not to move. He reaches into the draw on his desk and presses some sort on control button. I hear a whirring sound above and look up as a panel slides out at an angel holding a film projector. I must look confused but he chooses not to enlighten me as he returns and reaches up to pull at thin metal wire on a retractable pulley from the ceiling next to the projector. He unties my hands from behind me and secures them in front. He then loops the metal wire around my bound wrists, clips a padded bar to the wire and places it in my hands on the bar with no explanation. He presses a button to retract the slack in the wire, pulling my arms high above my head until I am on my tip toes, every muscle stretched tight like a bow. I can ease the tension by supporting my weight with my hands on the bar but it just brings me further off the floor and makes me swing helplessly like an act for Cirque De Soleil that didn't quite make the cut.

"God you look amazing." His breathy response has my body humming with anticipation. I take a quick glance up into his eyes and can see the hunger and pure undiluted desire. As wound as I am I think I could come from his penetrating eyes alone and his sinful grin makes me wonder if he thinks the same. He still has his trousers on although the strain in material has the seams on the very edge of their tolerance. He has lost his shirt; his bare chest is cut, defined and glowing with a similar hard earned sheen to the one covering my skin. His solid sculptured muscles tantalise as he draws deep powerful breaths. He presses his firm body against mine, holding my hips as I sway. I frantically try to grip with my toes to steady myself. I am obviously exposed and vulnerable, not a huge surprise since this was his intention in putting me in this position but I am super turned on, off the charts horny, one touch and I just know I'll lose it. "You're going to need to focus baby. I can't have you going off like that again." He holds my chin, his nose touching mine his eyes piercing my soul with their fire. "Not unless I say so, understood?" His voice is sinfully seductive and I tremble again, with his words alone. What the hell is wrong with me? He is right I do need to focus, focus on my role, my distance and my pain.

His hand cups my cheek and he sweeps his soft lips up my

neck, nibbling my ear and drawing the lobe through his teeth biting enough to make me jump. He chuckles again, grabs my hair tight. I gasp but just as he is about to brush is sweet gentle lips across mine I snap my mouth shut, pull my lips in and shift enough to the side to evade his kiss. He snarls, actually snarls, baring his teeth. He grips tighter on my hair and tries again to kiss me but despite the sharp needles in my scalp from having my hair pulled so tight, I twist my head and again successfully avoid is beautiful mouth, now this *is* torture. "What the fuck do you think you are doing? Fucking kiss me!" He shakes his hand that is gripping me tight and I wince as the hairs pinch and resist being torn from my scalp. I shake my head, not helping to ease this particular pain. He pulls harder and I cry out, he takes the opportunity to sweep his tongue across my lips and dip inside, sliding and trying to engage with mine. His lips caress and move but I just lock my jaw open, my tongue lifeless, and my head stiff and unyielding.

He pulls back like I've spat in his face and growls again. "I asked you to kiss me and I fucking meant it." He shakes his head in anger and tilts my head. "Look at me." That command I obey, instantly, his eyes are dark pools of yearning and anger. He lets out a deep breath. "Lola is not a whore, you are not a whore. Now fucking kiss me." For the first time tonight his voice sounds uncertain and for the second time his eyes are tinged with sadness.

"Aren't I?" My voice is a breathless whisper but he freezes at my words.

"What? No, never!" His face registers the shock his tone conveys.

"Really, because I am pretty sure I'm exchanging my body for information. Doesn't that make me a whore?" My voice is surprisingly calm, he sounds increasingly irritated.

"No!" He snaps angrily, his tone brooking no further debate but I press on regardless of my defenceless predicament.

"Oh because that is exactly what it sounded like in your boardroom, when you were handing out my details like you were my fucking pimp." I have lost the edge of calmness and my voice breaks as the emotions underlying this revelation hits home, hard. He recoils; my words have hit him too. Anger in his eyes giving way to softness, a softness I cherished and loved so deeply that a slew of fresh wounds puncture my fragile heart. He cups my face with his hands, his voice like velvet and his thumbs gently stroking my cheeks.

"Why the fuck would I disclose my personal life to some motherfucker just because he thinks he knows me and we happen to have lunch together?" His tone is deadly serious and his face a picture of heart-rending concern. I shake my head, I heard the words. I didn't believe them at the time but that is because I didn't want to believe them but looking at his beautiful face and his soul searching eyes I believe him now. "Kiss me." His voice is a quiet plea but I know I am struggling to keep my emotional-self safe, it tenuous at best and kissing him would be the end. This has to be physical, just physical. I shake my head, my eyes glass over with regret that I can't give him what he wants without shredding my self-esteem, destroying my heart and losing my fucking mind. He holds my stare for endless minutes waiting for my reply and all I can manage is to repeat the slightest shake of my head. He lets me go with an exaggerated exhale of angry breath; his voice is cold and harsh. "Very well have it your way."

He drops to his knees in front of me on with one sweep of his arms down the backs of my legs he scoops behind my knees and lifts them over his shoulders. I squeal and pull my weight onto the bar. I clench and tense every muscle from my tightly gripped hands to my tummy, thighs on his shoulders and calves against his back. His fingers press like individual spikes into the soft flesh of my bottom and his mouth covers my core. All in an instant, all too fast to register until it's too late and I am gasping for air. His tongue delves deep with deliciously languid strokes along my folds, swirling and pushing, dipping inside he moans and the vibrations ripple deep inside and echo through every nerve ending. I try to swallow my scream but there is no hope.

I am open and helpless and he is relentlessly devouring every intimate part of me.

"Ahh God Sir, Fuck. . . . . Please. . . . . please ahhhh . . ." The muscles in my arms are shaking, no, my whole body is shaking and he pushes on and on. I throw my head back and scream as I feel my blessed body take over and I have no will to stop it. I am grateful to step aside a moment and let this overwhelm me, because fuck it feels so good. It is driving me insane. He stills and I must look panicked as he catches my expression through his heavy lidded eyes and his impossibly long lashes.

"Please what baby?" His words are endearing but his tone is ice cold and I understand what he wants from me, but I can't.

"Please let me come." I offer but he shakes his head and blows a cool breath on my ultra-sensitive centre.

"Nah–ah. Try again baby, Please what?" He slowly licks his lips and my thighs tremble like they've just run a marathon.

"Please fuck me." My begging words are turning more hostile with frustration.

"Oh I will but nah–ah. Third times a charm baby, please what?" His lips are millimetres from my core and he inhales deeply and my whole body sags onto his shoulders.

"Fuck!" I cry. "I can't, please Sir. . . . arhhh." His lips press and suck my folds and his tongue circles my clit building the instant tremors that had barely subsided, his mouth fixes over my very centre. He sucks and draws his tongue flat across the nub of nerves, only to flick with the tip of his tongue so lightly I try to tense my thighs and move my hips to gain some much needed leverage. His hands clasp down tight and I know I'm not moving anywhere he doesn't want me. "Arghhh." I puff out aching again for release. "Please . . . please I'm begging please." I pull myself against his grip but I can do nothing more and receive an angry growl and a graze of his teeth over my sensitive flesh. He stops once again as I start to spasm.

"Please what?" His cold voice cuts me out of my haze, he looks calm and unaffected by my pleas and I realise he could probably do this all night but my body is spent.

I whisper. "Please. Kiss me Sir." My eyes are closed and I hear him shuffle and let out a deep moan. He wipes his mouth along the inside of my thigh, the slight scrape indicating a shadow of stubble not yet visible. Standing firm against my swaying, trembling body he cups the back of my head and I sigh conceding this sweet painful submission. His lips touch mine, soft and sure, sweet and tender. It's killing me, his tongue is tentative as it traces the seam gently urging me to open; my fight and resistance long departed I welcome him. Light tangled dances; my tongue strokes his and quickly turns demanding and vital, like my next breath. He pulls my hair and I catch my breath while I try to regain my focus on his feral eyes so close to mine. His jaw is clenched and the small muscle ticks wildly at the sharp edge of the curve on his face. He releases me and frantically pulls at my bound wrists, unclipping the cable and untying the restraint but without giving me time to stabilise on my feet he scoops me into his arms and carries me to the sofa. He reverently lays me flat, suddenly I'm made of glass again. His hands slowly trace my skin from my neck, along my collar bone down my torso. To my hips and back up sweeping movement until he captures my breasts and holds watching with heated eyes as my nipples tighten and my breath hitches. Shaking his head he straightens and starts to undo his buttons and zip. He takes himself in his hand stroking his length slowly, fuck I've missed this sight. So strong, so sensual, so fucking sexy.

My next words surprise me as much as him, but in a moment of clarity in a haze of passionate euphoria my inner common sense peaks through. "Condom?" It may have been quiet but it had the impact of screaming through a bull horn.

"What?" His eyes widen but quickly narrow and he seems undistracted as he continues to languidly stroke himself. I tilt my head because it wasn't a trick question but in this bizarre standoff it looks like I am the one that needs to clarify.

"Condom Sir, I don't mean to offend, but I don't trust her as much as you seem to." I try to shift away and squeeze my legs together but he pushes himself further between, not quite leaning his full weight over me but his hips are keeping my thighs spread and his other hand on my hip prevents me moving away.

"We are not doing this now." His deep voice is strained and he pushes the tip of his cock against my folds, smoothly moving up and down the slick sensitive tissue causing my thighs to quiver. I throw my head back and whimper because I need to feel him more than my next breath, more than my sanity and certainly more than my timid common sense which didn't stand a chance against this desire consuming every fibre of my being. He pushes deeper and we both exhale on a guttural moan. He moves further up the sofa taking me with him, pushing deeper, getting closer. I find my fingers gripping his hard unforgiving muscles on his back pulling him closer; needing his weight, his dominance, needing him. One hand strokes my cheek, tilting my chin firmly so he can kiss me without fear of rebuttal, not that I could. I couldn't deny him a single thing right now. I cry as he pushes deeper, changing his angle and using his other hand to grip my knee moving it higher to get just that little bit deeper and he does. Christ, I choke out a scream as he touches something so deep it sets my core alight, sending fire sizzling through my nerve endings and leaving me a panting trembling wreck.

"Oh fuck, ah . .ah yes God, yes." I exhale, limp and quivering. He looks down into my eyes with a wicked smirk.

"We are going to keep doing this until you remember to ask for permission to come." He kisses me lightly on the nose and pulls his hips back and plunges hard causing a sharp cry in the back of my throat. My breath is ragged, my skin a slick sheen of fresh perspiration and my muscles are in a constant state of nervous twitching, alert and exhausted in equal measure. He leans up on one elbow and takes one hand to where we are joined. His thumb sweeping small delicate circles on my exposed nub of nerves and sensing the instant build of pressure he drives deep again, relentless and hard. All the time he lunges and grinds, pushing my body like an expert, talented and intuitive he holds my eyes with his dark pools of liquid lust and passion, raw and real. He takes my breath away and he's going to make me come, again. I cry out this time.

"Please, please sir . . . please may I come?" My frantic plea is almost too late as I can feel the ripple of contractions begin at the base of my spine. He chuckles knowing how close I am.

"Oh you do like living on the edge." He slows the tortuous roll of his hips and I can see he is struggling too as beads of perspiration gather and fall in rivulets down his temples. "Come for me." He whispers and I let go before he finishes his consent. He throws his head back on an animalistic roar so loud. I am for the first time glad he has cleared the office floor. Following me with his own release he sinks deep and collapses onto me pushing my breath from my body with his weight.

Chapter Five

WE LAY ENTWINED and immobile for, I'm not sure how long and I would still be there if Daniel hadn't moved and carefully carried me to his bathroom. I watch silently as he readies the shower and strips the rest of his clothes. My body is too exhausted and my mind too frazzled to process how I feel but I am looking forward to that shower. Clouds of billowing steam rise and mist the glass of the shower door and the mirrors on the walls. He holds my hand and leads me in, standing, held in his arms as the hot rods of water pummel my aching bones and I sigh because I think I must be in heaven. He takes some soap in his hands and begins to massage and wash my tired body, delicately worshiping every inch and I can feel my eyes pool when I realise I am actually in hell. This is too much . . . it has to stop. He has to stop. "Blue." I struggle to mumble my safe word because it sticks in my throat and the noise of the shower muffles the sound.

"What's that baby?" He still has one arm wrapped around my waist as he cleanses me with the other and he leans his ear to my mouth. I am glad the water is hiding the tears I can now feel flow freely down my cheeks.

"Blue." I repeat and everything stops. He steps back, hands in the air like I have a gun to his chest. An interesting analogy, because he blasted my heart to smithereens when he walked away last week. His jaw clenches as does his fists but he turns, leaves the shower and leaves the bathroom without a word. I sink to the floor, my cries drowned out by the noise of the falling water. What the fuck was I thinking; that I could be that detached I could just fuck him without feeling something, without having all this hurt just heaped upon me once more. I'm not a robot and nothing's changed. He didn't even want to see me. If I hadn't pulled that little stunt would I have even seen him again, ever? He has enough gatekeepers to keep me away. Would I have found another way? Surely I can't be that desperate. God I hope I am never *that* desperate. He made his choice and I remind myself that if it wasn't for him steeling my idea and risking my future I wouldn't be here. Fuck, I don't want to make a fool of myself any more than I have already. I need to get my shit sorted and I need to get out of here.

I open the door to the office still towel drying my hair. Daniel is pacing angrily, running his hand through his own wet hair with badly hidden agitation. He stops and faces me, his face a picture of fury. "It's pretty fucking insulting that you think I would be fucking someone else, you know that right?" His angry voice is loud and as an indignant edge. "I mean, wouldn't you be insulted if I threw that in your face or asked if you'd had your contraceptive shot; treated you like some irresponsible tramp. Fuck! You'd be more than insulted you'd rightly rip my bollocks off, so why?" He swallows to calm his raging runaway temper, dragging his hand through his hair once more. His voice is softer. "How could you ask that?" His eyes are deep blue and hold a wealth of love and longing. I walk over to him and take his hands just as they are about to repeat their hair dragging journey.

"I'm sorry. I didn't mean to piss you off but not to state the bloody obvious but we aren't together so I can't make any assumptions. You can't make any assumptions. It was the smart thing to do. " I nod because in light of his accusation I have a cold tingle down my spine knowing that although I may not be a tramp, I am irresponsible. "Daniel, you wouldn't see me, you wouldn't even take my call. Why would I *not* think you've moved on?" My voice is shaky and I have to swallow back the building threat of tears. "Why wouldn't you take my call?" It's his turn to roughly pull his hands and turn away.

"I don't work that way I told you that. This way it's easier. Cleaner." His cold words are clinical and precise as a scalpel.

"Oh well that's good to know, wouldn't want to make a mess." I snap with as much contempt as I can manage.

"This whole thing is a fucking mess and that's not what I meant. It's too fucking hard. It has to be like this for now." He puts his head in his hands and I can almost hear his teeth grind then his head suddenly snaps up his eyes narrowed with suspicion. "What did you mean I couldn't make assumptions? Are you fucking someone else?" He snaps.

"Look I don't have to do this with you!" I snap right back. "We.Are.Not.Together.YOU.LEFT.ME." He fixes me with his enraged glare but unflinching I hold his contact. He shakes his head, walks toward me, takes my hand and leads me to the sofa. I pull my hand from his hold and he grabs it right back with a grumble.

"Why did you safe word Bethany?" The fury has vanished and he is again full of concern. I deal much better with the anger. After some long silent moments and some resigned sighs I answer the only way I think will explain.

"Self-preservation." He lets me take my hand this time. He huffs but doesn't try to take it back.

"I should have told you about your safety project. I just wanted to get it started, these things are often time sensitive and I didn't want you missing out. I should have told you from the start but it was easier to make the application under my R&D company banner and transfer it over to you once it was all certified. That will still happen." His calm assurance and dismissive tone is

the Only Choice

like this is just a natural way of things and should automatically mitigate any misunderstanding on my part.

I am not even surprised he never asked or that he never told me and I don't even care anymore. It was my project now it isn't. How or when it gets to market will have little to do with me so I may as well let it go now. Less I have to do with Daniel the more protected my heart will be. I don't want to come across as a martyr by walking away from something he knew was important so I will just let it go when the time comes. What is important is my course and the accusation that Chris Taylor made about my credibility.

"Fine." I nod and leave that for another day. "I don't want this to impact on my course."

His brows furrow and he looks confused. "Why would it?"

I snort and shake my head. "Well, it could be inferred that since this project is a Stone application and the date was long before I came on the scene, some may think I stole it. I can't have that suggestion shadowing any of my course work. You have a connection with the University and they are more likely to believe you. I just can't risk losing this too." My voice waivers and damn I can feel my eyes prickle. He grasps my hands again.

"I wouldn't do that Bethany, never, believe me. I would never lie to you." His voice is sincere but it doesn't prevent the bitter laugh that escapes my tight lips. He scowls.

"Well you have me there Daniel." I pull my hands again and stand. "I will have to believe you about this. There is nothing else I can do I'm just a lowly student but don't start with a lie because it really doesn't fill me with a whole heap of confidence." I walk to the door but just as I open he rushes and slaps his hand flat slamming it shut.

"When did I lie to you?" He growls. We are silent for long moments before I reply.

"You said you'd never hurt me." My voice is quiet and he freezes at my words allowing me to open the door and walk through. I am surprised that he follows me to the lifts, he is close but silent. I lean to press the button and notice something flutter to the ground. Daniel bends to pick it up.

"Why the fuck do you have Jason's business card?" He waves the card in my face and I try to take it but he pulls it away out of my reach.

"He was being kind, he wanted me to have it." I sigh, exhausted and not needing another fight.

"Oh I just bet he did." His tone ripe with sarcasm.

"How is it any different from your 'friend' getting my details from Colin exactly?" It appears I do have some strength after all.

"I told you I didn't discuss my personal life and I meant it. There is no fucking way Colin would give your details to anyone and that includes Jason. You are not to see him Bethany." His clipped demand is filled with anger.

Oh I can feel my hackles rise, my back straightens and I have fire in my eyes as I challenge. "Really? Well it's a good job it has fuck all to do with you." I jab my finger on the lift call button because it is taking forever.

"He has particular tastes . . . he—" He can't seem to finish his sentence. God he looks furious, frustrated, mixed with anxious.

"—I know Daniel, I was there remember?" At last the lift arrives I hold out my hand for him to give me Jason's card but he very childishly tears it up with a smirk on his face. I let out a frustrated puff and walk into the waiting lift.

"No matter." Turning, I smile indulgently. "Lucky for me Jason *does* take my calls." The lift doors close and I grin. Ok, now that was childish, but damn it felt good.

I didn't sleep well and I was up a good hour before my alarm was due to go off. In light of Daniel's throw away comment about my contraceptive shot I didn't want to wait for the surgery to open to call on the off chance they had an appointment. I wanted to be parked outside the front door. This was an emergency. The receptionist walks up and eyes me suspiciously and before she opens the door she turns to face me.

"You know if it's an emergency you could go to A & E. The doctors won't be here for another half hour." She has a haughty air and a clipped tone.

"No that's fine; it's not an emergency as such. I just wanted to be here when you open . . . um . . . on the off chance." I try to smile but I am a bundle of nerves and anxious worry. The last thing I am capable of now is trying to melt the resolve of an irritated gatekeeper.

"You don't have an appointment?" Her incredulous accusation would be more fitting if she had cried 'murderer!' She huffs as she jangles her very important keys and opens the door. "You can't wait inside." She adds and slams the door.

I perch on the wall beside the entrance and mumble to myself 'what a shocker! I mean because you've been so warm and fuzzy.'

"Bethany?" I look up to see Dr Ward smiling at me. She is smartly dressed in an immaculate navy skirt with bright pink silk blouse. She is carrying her doctors case and her jacket is slung over one arm because despite the early morning its sticky warm already. "First sign of madness, talking to yourself." She laughs lightly and stops in front of me with a soft quizzical look on her face. She must be in her late forties, minimal make up on flawless pale skin, light blue eyes and scraped back blonde hair.

I smile tightly, still too distracted to make small talk. All I manage is a nod and civil greeting. "Good morning Dr. Ward."

She opens the door and motions for me to follow her. "I bet Cathy told you to wait out here?" She whispers as I follow close behind.

"Well I don't have an appointment and—"

Dr Ward laughs conspiratorially. "Oh well that explains a lot. Look it's obviously important, I am sure I will fit you in. I know I'm booked but if you don't mind waiting we can sort something. Go take a seat; I'll go do the peace keeper thing with Cathy. I will see you shortly." She walks over to the reception desk and I take a seat in the far corner of the waiting room, trying my best to look invisible.

An hour passes and I have successfully skimmed through the seven dog eared copies of weekly magazines that ranged from purely gossip, fashion, cooking to gardening and health. I have resisted the information leaflets but with a morbid sense of curiosity getting the better of me I pick up a leaflet on pregnancy. Checking off the symptoms I start to feel a little better; morning sickness, that would be no. Yes I've felt a bit sick and have been off my food but given the trauma of a break up from hell I don't think that is unusual and it's certainly not restricted to the morning. I know Lili from the restaurant says it's the only up-side to a break up . . . the weight loss. Weight gain, well that's a definite no, my clothes are hanging from me and I have to have my dress for the wedding re fitted as a consequence. Sensitive breasts, the waiting room is now full so I can't exactly check that one right now but I don't think they feel any different. I hear my name before I can consume any more of the information but I am satisfied that my panic is unjustified.

"Bethany, sorry you've been waiting so long." Dr Ward smiles sweetly and points to the chair for me to take a seat. "Now what's the emergency?"

"Contraceptive shot and the morning after pill." I flush bright pink and cringe that I am supposed to be a responsible adult and here I am looking anything but.

"Right, Ok, let's see, you missed the date for your last shot. So you have been unprotected since then and I take it you've since had unprotected sex?" She scribbles some notes and glances my way.

I blow out a long held breath. "Yes, Yesterday late afternoon and a just over a week ago."

Her smile is warm and I am grateful. Doctors must practice that non-judgemental look for years to perfect it and I am super appreciative, because I want to cry for being such an idiot.

the Only Choice

"The date of you last period?"

"May 13th and and I am due on today." I suck in some air because I suddenly feel like I am going to be sick. I can feel the colour drain from my face and Dr.Ward looks with concern and squeezes my leg.

"Lets not jump the gun Bethany. It is very early to be making those assumptions but you will have to take the pregnancy test before I can give you another shot." She hands me a plastic pot and goes back to swivelling a rotating disc with dates in tiny digits. I walk numbly from the room. All these stupid sayings fill my head, *cart before the horse* Bethany, *locking the stable door after the horse has bolted, gift horse in the mouth* and why are they all equine related? I shake my head. It's stupid, I'm stupid and I can make up all the reasons in the world. I've been under stress that's why my period didn't appear like my clockwork normal this morning, my symptoms aren't really symptoms and we only did it once, or was it twice? It doesn't bloody matter, when you know, you just know and I fucking know.

I watch patiently with Dr.Ward for the results and she smiles brightly adding with a strangely cheerful voice. "You know these tests are so sensitive now they can even detect pregnancy before you missed your period!" But then her smile tightens and she looks directly at me. "You are pregnant Bethany, one to two weeks if you are sure on your dates but definitely pregnant."

"But I haven't been sick . . . I mean no morning sickness." My words fall dumbly from my mouth and I am not surprised when Dr.Ward offers an understanding smile.

"No, well that's good. Not everyone suffers, maybe you're one of the lucky ones." Her smile widens with her kind eyes.

I know my face has frozen and I absently wonder if it would be appropriate to stick my fingers in my ears and hum *Naughty Boy; La La*. My throat feels dry and constricted and I struggle to swallow. Dr. Ward passes a glass of water and I sip, liking the feel of the ice cool liquid pouring down my parched throat. I put the glass down and go to pick up my bag, appointment over. Dr.

Ward hands me a fistful of leaflets. "It's very early Bethany, read these, *all* of these and come and see me next week." I have lost the capacity for speech, but nod and smile like an idiot, and not for the first time in less than an hour I berate myself. Yes I am an idiot, a stupid fucking idiot.

I stroll in a daze, grateful my internal navigation is on autopilot as I work my way through the residential back streets of West London; all the way back to my apartment and quietly let myself in. Marco worked late last night and would probably still be sleeping. I slump on my bed, fanning out the literature Dr. Ward has given me. I pick up the one I had started to look at in the waiting room and again read the list of symptoms, noting for the first time the words *may* experience. My eyes partly focus on increased tiredness and I exhale a small laugh, well that one is right on the money. I am bone tired and succumb to the pull of my freshly made bed, falling face down, fully clothed, both mentally and physically shattered.

It's dark when I stir, my curtains aren't drawn so there is a little light from the street and I can hear voices in the kitchen. I gather the leaflets and put them in my bedside draw, deciding my rumbling stomach needs urgent attention and perhaps my head is not in the right state to take in any more information. I'm still in shock. My clothes are rumpled and twisted where I have moved unconsciously in my sleep so I quickly change into some soft grey yoga pants and one of my few remaining original t-shirts.

I peak my head through the doorway to the kitchen but am unsuccessful in staying hidden, squealing with surprise as Marco barrels towards me lifting me high and hugging me tight. We have really only passed notes since he came back and God I've missed him. I find I hold on to his hug little tighter and blink back a sudden splash of tears, tired and emotional, yep I read that too.

"Hey Boo it's been forever." He gently drops me to the floor and holds me back to look at me. "Christ you look like shit, are you sick?" His deep frown is serious but he holds back a grin. I slap him hard on his chest and he rubs the spot and stumbles back

the Only Choice

like I have caused serious damage, but chuckles and returns to the kitchen. It's then I notice Ethan who slowly stands and holds his arms wide, his bright smile even wider.

"Take no notice you look . . ." but he hesitates just a little too long and I sigh and walk to the hall mirror. He calls after me. "You look beautiful Bets, you always do. Just maybe a bit tired." He generously offers because looking at my reflection I am much more inclined to agree with Marco. I ruffle my hair so it looks more tousled than bed head and pinch my cheeks to get some colour but that really is the best I can do at the moment, perhaps some food will help. I walk back into the kitchen and go to hug Ethan, pleased that there doesn't seem to be any residual awkwardness from the tail end of our weekend together. I walk to the fridge and pour a glass of milk before returning to take the stool next to Ethan.

Just as an unsettling silence falls my stomach makes the most unladylike sound and we all laugh out and my cheeks finally get some much needed colour. Marco has just ordered pizza but I really fancy something simple and he is sweet enough to insist that I stay seated as he makes me an omelette. We chat and its very comfortable, the most normal I have felt in a while. I decline a beer when the boys open a second round or the offer of a glass of wine, sticking with the milk avoiding Marco's raised brow and curious pursed lips.

"So Dan the Dick is out of the picture?" Marco bluntly asks stopping the progression of my food to mouth and fork in mid-air. Christ, I thought Sofia was to the point. I am glad I didn't have a mouthful because he would be wearing it right now. Undeterred he carries on in the same nonchalant manor "Look he came off the 'Dick List' for a while there but he's definitely on it now. If he has let you go Boo, he is taking the top spot. I'd call him mega dick but I wouldn't want that to get misinterpreted." He takes a swig from his bottle which fails epically to hide his own amusement.

I shake my head and let out a light laugh through my nose,

just like Marco to 'call a spade a fucking shovel.' "Yes he is out of the picture." I am nowhere near ready to post mortem the cluster fuck that is the Bethany and Daniel fallout, so I divert the conversation. "So you didn't propose to Rose then?" Yes, that should do it. It's Marco's turn to lose some colour, shocked and spluttering he chokes messily on his beer, spitting his mouthful down his front.

"What the fuck Bets! Why would you? . . . What on earth? . . . Christ has Aunt Marie been plotting again?" He wipes his front with the dishcloth just making the shirt wetter and both Ethan and I are chuckling at his outrage.

"No not Aunt Marie this time, actually it was me and Sofs, we just thought, well you'd taken her to see the family. That's like unheard of and we just assumed . . ." I shrug but he interrupts clearly eager to re-establish his single carefree status.

"We went on holiday together and we stayed with the family because it was free. We're not even exclusive! She sees other guys . . . I see other girls . . . she's cooler to hang with than the others more so because she isn't hung up on relationship labels. Christ when you girls get together!" He huffs and crosses his arms over his chest. Ethan is in fits.

"Eww Marco, I did not need to know that!" I push my plate away, pleased that I had eaten half and not really put off by his revelation but not able to eat any more. "But you're taking her to the wedding, right? I mean you are still taking her to the wedding Marco?" His eyes widen as he can hear my rising panic in my tone.

"Shit no, she's on holiday visiting her sister in the States." He sounds just as alarmed. Ethan looks between the two of us, knowing he is missing something crucial, blissfully unaware of the significance of both Marco and I not having dates for Sofia's wedding.

"Shit." We both conclude.

"You have to get a date Marco!" I point my finger in warning.

"I have to get a date?" He laughs incredulously and repeats.

the Only Choice

"I have to get a date; you're funny Bets." He flicks the contact screen on his phone and a blur of images scroll in a flash of pretty girls. "Not so much a problem for me Boo . . ." He flashes a cocky smile, overcome with an over inflated sense of smugness he waves his finger in my direction. "It's you darling girl, *you* have to get a date."

I shake my head. "No no it will be fine, so long as you have a date, we'll be safe." I mutter.

"Ok Ok." Ethan halts our cryptic ramblings. "You are going to have to explain because you sound like a bunch of crazy people. Why do either of you *need* to have a date for Sofia's wedding, can't you just go together?"

"Nooooo." Dramatically and in unison we reply but I explain further. "Oh good God no! If I showed up in the dress Sofia has me in and Marco as groomsman there is absolutely no way Sofia and Paul would be the only ones getting hitched that day. Aunt Marie would see to that. In fact I don't even think she'd be the only one." I look to Marco for support and he grunts in confirmation. "Since as long as I can remember there has not been a single family gathering, outside of his mum and dad I mean, where it isn't complete torture for Marco and me. I haven't helped never having had a boyfriend in that time and Marco has been brilliant as a man-whore." I wink at him and he shrugs lightly. "Sorry, but that is the only reason they leave us alone. But weddings make people crazy at the best of times and with Sofia being Marco's twin and my best friend there is no way on earth we can go without partners." I don't think I drew breath and feel a little lightheaded. "It will be fine if you have a date though; that should be enough." I smile, nod and calm myself. Marco doesn't look so sure.

"Under normal circumstances I'd agree but its Sofs wedding we are talking about. Do you know how many single male cousins we have coming out of the woodwork?" He shakes his head slowly like he doesn't fancy my chances. "Exactly." He nods sagely as he takes in the horror that must be plastered all over my face.

"Shit." I puff out.

"I'll be your date." Ethan nudges me and I look at his face and there is not a hint of mischief just kind eyes and a warm smile. He clarifies. "Not a date date, just a 'keeping you safe date.'" He adds, "but if you call me your brother you're on your own, just warning." He takes a large pull of his beer and I try to gauge if he is harbouring any expectations but his offer seems genuine and since the prospect of going solo is truly terrifying it is extremely tempting.

"Really you don't have to—" Before I can say another word Marco rushes to high five Ethan.

"Perfect!" A loud slap resonates as their palms meet. Marco is visibly relieved. I wish I shared his sentiment and I need to make sure that Ethan is definitely on the same page.

"That's really kind Ethan but it's not a date date. Oh God this is going to be a train wreck." I grab my milk and huff because I seriously need something stronger.

"Relax, I understand Bets, really, crystal clear. It will be fun." He winks at Marco who just laughs. "Besides I can't have you married off to some random cousin before I get my shot." Same page? Not even in the same library.

I am back to feeling drained, my eyes snap to Marco and to his credit he hides his surprise well and I can offer no other explanation other than a weary shrug. Marco goes to answer the door and returns with a pizza large enough to share so I am surprised when Ethan takes the opportunity to leave. I escort him to the door.

"You've never had a boyfriend?" He stands filling the doorway with his tall sleek frame, his eyes hold suspicion and disbelief, his expression is waiting for the punch line.

"Had one boyfriend but not since I was sixteen. No time." I smile but I know it doesn't even touch my cheeks.

His fingers trace my hairline and he tucks my wild hair, momentarily taming it behind my ear. "You have time now." His words are soft and heartfelt. I hold his fingers stopping them from repeating his intimate touch.

"Ethan I can't. Please." I can't express how sorry I am for everything. How bad I feel I can't return a fraction of what he clearly feels for me. Other than friendship, I have nothing and given what's going on inside me right now I'm sad that I never will. He leans and gently kisses my cheek.

"Ok Bets, you win." He lets out a deep breath, a flash of sadness passes over his gaze rapidly replaced with a wicked grin. "For now." He swoops quickly to kiss my cheek before he turns his back and walks away. I close the door and fall with my back flat letting out a frustrated growl. I don't feel like I've won anything.

"Sooo Ethan eh?" Marco is leaning against the hall the wedge of a slice of pizza poised to drop into his open mouth.

"Not going there Marco." I sigh resignedly; his expression changes from cocky to concerned in an instant. Clearly sensing that I am tired, emotional and on the raggedy edge he puts his one free arm around me, squeezing and steering me to the sofa for a much needed cuddle.

Chapter Six

MY APPOINTMENT WITH Dr. Ward the following week was no surprise. I had read and re read every leaflet but there was never a question that I wouldn't be keeping the baby. I know living at home when I was younger my sister Kit had joked that abortion was an alternative to contraception; it chilled me then as the thought of that choice does now. It is a choice but how ever unplanned, I feel strangely settled that this is my choice and my choice alone. It's not ideal, it's not perfect and its far far away from being a fairy tale ending but I'll survive. I am not alone, I have the most amazing family that nature neglected to give me but I also have a new family that nature did. I have some security, although how extensive I am still mostly in denial but I know I will be able to provide for the two of us. My only decision has been to keep it secret until after the wedding.

Sofia has been planning her big day since the age of seven, when she hand stitched Barbie her very own designer wedding dress because the shop one wasn't good enough. Sofia has orchestrated the most amazing day and I would never forgive myself if I did anything to detract from that. She in particular has a large extended family all expected to come so both Sofia and Paul have put an inordinate amount of effort in to their day. This

the Only Choice

wedding is very much about *the* day.

    I have made my follow up appointments and am now armed with more literature regarding antenatal care, prenatal vitamins and a list of what to expect that would easily bring on sickness if I wasn't already feeling sick, all the damn time. I push these to the bottom of my bag and make my way through Green Park and on toward Piccadilly to the American Diner, where I am meeting Tom for brunch. We spoke last week, presumably because Ethan had told him of my break up. It was sweet he thought to check up on me and even more impressive he managed to ask questions without being intrusive. I told him as much and he laughed explaining that particular talent had served him well and anytime I wanted he would teach me all his secret interrogation techniques. The Diner is busy, intimate booths of dark oak line one side and the décor is tasteful Americana but not a pastiche of the nineteen fifties. It is classic, iconic, original American. Tom towers over the partition separating the booths and waves me over. I remove my jacket and slide in along the dark red leather bench, pushing my bag underneath the seat.

    We order and because I haven't actually told anyone I was fired, opting for the less shameful excuse that it was a temporary internship that proved to be a little more temporary than I had anticipated. Tom asks me directly what my plans are for the summer. I outline my thoughts, such as they are. I am working back at the restaurant, mostly covering holidays and I will do this until the wedding and then I think I'll maybe do some travelling. He smiles warmly at this because he knows this new information is directly a result of his generosity and my reluctant acceptance. I have since graciously accepted an allowance similar to the one Ethan receives. It was hard for me but made easier after my talk with Ethan and even easier when I saw the genuine delight on Tom's face. I have declined the offer of the apartment. I thought I would be taking him up on it if Marco had, in fact, proposed to Rose but I am happier to be staying with Marco. At least until the baby is born. I am not sure how having a baby would fit with the

Batchelor image he maintains and cultivates but I'll cross that bridge another day.

The waiter brings my water and Tom a cappuccino. I sit a little further back, my sense of smell has become super sensitive and I am struggling with my reaction to all things coffee flavoured but with a little effort I can hold back any involuntary convulsions. A few breaths through my mouth, the unpleasant swell of nausea passes and I can take a sip of my drink.

"You must speak with Ethan before you go off anywhere. There is pretty much nowhere he hasn't been and he's like a personal *Lonely Planet* guide when it comes to travelling alone." His tone clearly highlights his reservations regarding my plans but he is also reticent to express his obvious worry. He is still unsure the father daughter boundaries and it makes me smile, even if his concern is unwarranted. "In fact why don't you two go together, I know he was planning another trip maybe you—"

I wave my hand to stop him before that line of thinking can develop further. "I will speak to him but really with everything that has happened I just want a little time to myself. It's been an eventful year." My voice is soft as I muse aloud, "and I need some time to process." I smile to ease the concern on his face. "I will be fine but I really want to do this on my own."

"Ok but I don't have to like it." He grumbles.

I scoff. "Oh don't worry you won't be alone there, I haven't had the courage to mention it to anyone yet. I thought I'd leave it until the wedding, when everyone is three sheets to the wind." We chuckle together and he squeezes my hand but drops the subject. "But I will speak to Ethan before I make firm arrangements."

"Good but you will have to call him during the day. The evenings have been off limits since he met his new mystery lady." Tom wiggles his brow.

"Mystery lady. . . . hmmm?" I chuckle to myself. I swear it should be Ethan and Marco who are twins with their prolific and carefree dating.

"Honestly, I rarely ask anymore. As soon as I learn a young

the Only Choice

lady's name he has moved on to the next. Still you are only young once . . . as I am sure you will discover this summer. Travelling is such an adventure." His smile is bright and filled with encouragement. "Speaking of the summer, you know you could always work for me until you travel. I bet the pay would be better." He beams and I can see where Ethan gets his killer smile. There is nothing genetic there, it is just full-on confidence.

"Well, I could see why you would want to hire me, what with my in-depth knowledge in construction and all?" I quip sarcastically with a raised brow.

He laughs. "I thought interns are meant to be trained . . . you're not supposed to have an in depth understanding." He challenges, his back straightens and his whole aura has shifted from relaxed and casual to something much more formidable. He is gearing himself up for a negotiation. I can feel it, I can see it, his eyes sparkle. It's why he has been so successful he thrives on this, he clearly loves it.

"Yes but perhaps some desire to work in construction might be preferable, no?" I also straighten my back. I kind of like the challenge too, especially when I know I'm going to win.

"Not necessarily, you are bright. I am sure there would be somewhere you would fit perfectly, we don't have to put you on the tools." He can't help his grin spreading like wildfire across his rough tanned face.

"I know you think you're pretty persuasive but you're not going to win this one Tom." I lay my napkin into my lap and try to hide my humour at this exchange.

"And you are so sure about this because I've been so unsuccessful in the past?" I let him have that one because he has got his way over a number of issues regarding me but only since my talk with Ethan.

"No, in-*spite* of it." I lean forward adopting a more assertive position, which he mirrors but he is sporting a huge smile. "I promised I would cover holidays at the restaurant and if I make a promise I keep it." I narrow my eyes with finality and bite my lips to stop my own winning grin.

He sinks back deflated and defeated. "Always?" His last effort lacks heart.

"Always." I nod and only flinch internally thinking that my last promise was to marry Daniel. Right before he told me he was going to be having a baby with his ex, I don't think there is a judge in the land that would've held me to that promise. So I nod again, happy that I do, under any *normal* circumstance keep my promise. With that, the waiter serves our brunch, American size portions of pancakes with maple syrup for me and the same for Tom with maple cured bacon on the side. The steam and smells rise as does the contents of my stomach as the smell of the bacon hits me like a brick. I clench my teeth and swallow the liquid pooling in my mouth, choking back my gag reflex. I squish the napkin in my face just in case I don't quite make it to the Ladies. I scramble from the booth and run flat out, dramatically slamming through two sets of fire doors before I am safely bent double over the ladies toilet.

Tom seemed happy enough with my blatant misuse of 'women's' problems' get out card' to explain my sudden departure and since he had cleared his plate by the time I returned I was even able to eat some of my pancakes. The portion was massive but with an empty stomach I did make a decent effort. I make my apologies for cutting our get together short but I was taking the easy afternoon shift at the restaurant and had to leave. Tom made me promise to come to visit him, taking advantage of his new knowledge regarding my promises and I happily did. I also promised to bring Marco, Sofia and Paul if their diaries would accommodate an afternoon in the country.

"It's safe to come in now Bets!" Ricki the youngest kitchen porter shouts to me as I take my waitress apron from my hanger in the staff room. "All the hard works done! . . . Ow What the fuck

the Only Choice

Joe!" He cries out.

I peek round the corner into the kitchen and see Joe retrieve his hand from the back of Ricki's head. He winks at me and I laugh. It feels good to be back. "Take no notice Bets, we're always busy and besides we don't want to frighten you off now we only just got you back. So we're happy to ease you in gently." He scowls at Ricki, who actually steps back with wide quaking eyes. Joe is a big guy and I can see how he could be intimidating but to me he is just a big bear. He grabs and hugs me like one as I enter his domain.

"Hey Joe, need to breathe here." I wriggle from his arms and make my way to the swing door separating the restaurant. The smells in the kitchen are intense and I am sure they are delicious, just not to me at the moment. So in the quiet times I am lucky to be able to work the bar. As much as Joe loves me I think that bond would be tested to destruction if I kept retching every time I had to serve certain dishes. Which luckily are limited at the moment to those with bacon or any pork products for that matter. I meet Lili at the edge of the bar, she smiles but looks a little harassed.

"Oh hey Bets can you take this coffee order to the booth out back, table twelve. I really need to pee." She is hopping from one foot to the next like an infant and I chuckle, taking the tray but she has vanished before I can comment. I turn my head and take a deep breath, holding it to avoid as much of the aroma as possible. Small breaths through my mouth will help if I actually have to speak but holding my breath is better. I can see the held hands before I register the faces, well I see Angel's face first but Daniel's too as he snatches his hand back giving me space to put their drinks. My breath escapes me but I manage to avoid his eyes, irritated that my usual tingle of hairs, my early warning system seems to also be affected by my new addition. I place the sugar, cream and Daniels espresso down and I put the last cup on my tray in front of Angel. She hasn't recognised me and I watch transfixed as she leans forward and blows the steam of the Americano in an attempt to cool it, successfully forcing the rich hot flavour right up my nose. Oh Shit, my shoulders jerk and I swallow, spin and dash to the disabled toilet. The only toilet on this floor and the nearest.

My tray crashes to the floor and I grab the sink. This time, my urge to purge has already subsided. A few deep breaths and the cooling tingles and queasy tummy settles. My brow is peppered with droplets of perspiration and I rinse my hands under the cold running water, which feels really good. The door opens and Daniel steps in locking it behind him. The tingles are back, my throat suddenly dry and my heart thumping in my chest. I wish I could just feel anger, undiluted jealousy or even remain feeling sick which would be a normal reaction. But no, my body takes over and I have a raging battle with my sanity on one side, a weak opponent, against the might of my lust for the man in front of me. Is it even possible to crave someone this much and then he stalks toward me, slow, intimidating steps, radiating dominance. His eyes darken and whatever he is thinking is badly masked and sends pure raw heat straight between my legs. I try to step back as my need and desire are seriously clouding my judgement.

"What are you doing here?" His reproachful tone is a shock. Maybe it's not lust in his eyes, maybe he is just angry, angry that I have spoiled his date.

I look behind me quickly to make sure I am not going to trip and step back further. 1let out a sharp laugh. "Ha! That's good Daniel. What am I doing here? Well, since your thoughtful intervention over my patent application I was deemed a security risk and was fired. So I am here because I fucking work here! But you! You are here because let me guess . . . there are no other restaurants in London you could think of to have a cosy date?" I catch a glimpse of a smirk. I grit my teeth because it is still frowned upon, punching the clients in the face, even if his face is begging for it. I growl in the back of my throat and push my hands hard against his chest and try to push past. He is immovable and his hands grab mine and easily twist them behind me, pulling my body to his he steps me back against the wall, holding

the Only Choice

my hands in one of his. His other hand strokes my cheek and rests firmly on my throat, the movement of swallowing pushing against his palm. His eyes are on fire, his breath whispers on my skin, fresh sweet mint. "You're an arsehole and I hate you." I whisper with very little conviction.

"You're jealous and I couldn't be happier." His deep voice is velvet and his lips are soft as he kisses the length of my jaw, delicate light kisses, tempting and teasing me. A small whimper leaves my mouth on a sigh and he swoops to capture it. His tongue tracing the seam and dipping inside. I welcome him, opening my mouth a little more, willing him to take more, tilting my head and leaning into this sensual union. He pushes his hard body against mine and I can feel the heat of his iron hard erection through his thin suit trousers and I shamelessly grind my body harder into his. I don't even care that I am at work or that Angel is sitting outside waiting for him, I just want him, now. What's got into me? I am like a horny teenage boy for Christ sake. Dismissing every rational thought that surfaces and is desperate to be heard I pull my hands from his grasp and start to tug wildly at his belt. He steadies my frantic hands.

"Bethany we need to talk." He coughs out looking a little ruffled, it makes me smile that I am ruffling mister steadfast control freak.

"Actually we don't. We need to fuck!" I try again to release his straining erection but he pushes hard into me so there is no space for my hands to work his zipper. "Argg." I relax my tense, sexually frustrated body and look up into his eyes. "Look, are you seeing Angel? Is she your girlfriend now?" The amused grin and warm eyes vanish and he looks angry.

"No. it's not like that I told you before—" His voice is stern but I interrupt, really not wanting to re hash that discussion now, other things on my mind.

"—Great, so no reason to be jealous. Now if you don't mind?" I wiggle my hips and rub my palms flat down the front of his trousers. It's all the room he is letting me have but he moans when my hands pass over his thick, throbbing cock.

"Bethany." He admonishes.

"Are you on a date?" I challenge, my eyes narrow and my heart's in my mouth.

"No." He doesn't hesitate with his answer and I don't hesitate with my response.

"Prove it." I think my whole body trembles with anticipation that he might deny me and I hold my breath for the endless second it takes for him to cover my mouth with his forceful hungry lips. Our hands fumbling together to remove the barriers preventing our blissful reunion. I push his trousers and boxer pants roughly to his thighs, his slightly widened stance preventing them dropping to the floor. He scrunches my skirt up, his fingers slipping through my panties at my hip and yanking hard. I cry out wishing I had worn more delicate material that disintegrated without such necessary force. All the while his tongue is delving and consuming swollen lips, my tongue dances with his and I whimper because I can't seem to get enough. With one hand he reaches to hold my hair pulling back to exposed my neck and I try to shake my head because I know exactly what he is intending and I am not his to mark.

Breathless but forceful I cry out. "Don't you fucking dare."

He pulls back, dark blue eyes scowling with heat and lust. He stands straight, still and menacing, silent but for our deep breaths. "Soon." His voice is like gravel and he makes a guttural sound as he slowly kneels in front of me, never taking his eyes off mine. It's probably the sexiest thing I have ever witnessed. He breathes my scent in, eyes closed; taking all the time in the world and looks at me once more through his thick long lashes. His hands spread my thighs and he licks his tongue on the tender inside, high but below the apex, kissing the soft flesh before increasing the pressure and sucking down hard, pulling the blood from deep inside, swirling it along the surface. Gripping my thighs, each fingertip a mark on my skin, each sucking swirl of his tongue a mark on my body and each desperate cry he draws from my soul a mark on my heart. He moans with satisfaction and almost as an afterthought, licks his tongue deep along my core causing my legs to quake and my thighs to tense. He freezes and snaps his head to look at me.

"Jesus Bethany, what's gotten into you? It feels like you'd come if I just told you to, without even touching you?" His voice is thick with desire and with that deep timbre I know he is right and I am not particularly happy at how shaken and vulnerable that makes me. Something to process later, right now I still need to come but I'm not going to beg, like he says I'm super responsive so one touch of my hand will also do the trick. I take my hand from his hair where I had been gripping for balance with one leg on his shoulder and lightly sweep my hand over my tummy and toward my core. My fingers are snatched and squeezed painfully as Daniel growls and stands, his erection bobbing and fierce between my open thighs. "Not a fucking chance. Ok I won't mark you where I want, yet, but there is no way I am not going to be the one to make you come." He nudges his thick soft crown, sliding to my entrance and I clench in eagerness, he pushes further, deeper and we both let out a satisfied moan. He pulls back and thrusts hard, I cry out and hold his solid shoulders pulling him in, I need him close, I need him deep.

His eyes fix on mine as he pounds into me, it feels so sweet, so intense and I wouldn't fight the building pressure and blissful spasms even if I could but I do surprise myself when I gasp out. "Daniel, I want to come." I pant short breaths fighting the inevitable release. "Can I come?" It's not exactly begging, somewhere in between but we are not exactly in a place where I can trust him not to torture me with denial, and God my body needs this.

"Ah Fuck yes baby, yes, yes come for me." He steps into me even though there is nowhere left to go, just deeper and harder.

"Ahhh. .mmmmmm." The overwhelming wave of pleasure engulfs me and I am so grateful Daniel has the presence of mind to slap his hand over my mouth as I scream my release. Slowing his hips I am not sure if he finished too. I am so caught up with the earth shattering orgasm that has left me unable to speak, move or breathe. He leans his full weight against mine to stop me from sliding down the wall, not through extreme exhaustion, or sated euphoria which I am feeling but because my bones have ceased to perform their basic function. My body continues to contract and shudder with pleasant aftershocks and my head finally returns from its hiding place. Still buried inside me Daniel is the first to speak.

"Shit Bethany, that was . . . Christ! Are you Ok?" His light fingers cup my face and I feel strangely embarrassed, strange because he still has his cock wedged deep inside. Choosing to ignore the loaded question because honestly I have no fucking idea if I'm Ok, I deflect.

"Um did you? I mean I wasn't sure." I try to move and hard as he still is, he languidly withdraws and pushes back, effectively stopping me. I think maybe he didn't.

"Yes thank you. You seemed a little preoccupied, so you may have missed it." His wicked grin makes me laugh and he tenderly kisses the corner of my mouth. My libido being the untamed monster that it is, if he continues to move like that we are likely to never leave this delightfully romantic toilet. I push at his shoulders.

"Oh good." I smile still trying to push his firm frame away from me, eager to put some distance now my raging hormones have ebbed. "Right well, I should be getting back and I guess you should be too." I bite down my comments about, 'wouldn't want to keep an evil bitch waiting' for another time. After all he still has his cock in me and apparently he isn't putting it anywhere else, for now. He pulls out from me and I move to the side, my tongue swipes my own lips automatically at the sight of his still rock hard cock. He lets out a deep throaty laugh that sends a fresh wave of tingles across my skin.

"I won't say no but I wouldn't want you getting the sack." His flippant remark has my mouth dropped open in utter affront at his insensitivity. "All right, if you insist." He steps toward me hold-

the Only Choice

ing his shaft in one hand stroking sensually and offering his other for me to take. My mouth snaps and I scowl my best death stare.

"You are fucking unbelievable! I am glad getting fired amuses you and don't even pretend that you hold any concern over my employment here. You just don't want to keep your date waiting." My angry words hold a wealth of venom but they seem to have little effect, his face is impassive, his dark eyes give nothing away. He straightens his back, tucks his shirt in and zips his zip. Stepping once more up to me he tenderly tucks my hair behind my ear, kisses my cheek and whispers.

"Not my date." He opens the door and goes to leave, looking directly at me, like he is assessing his prise and with a small knowing smile on his lips he adds, "until next time." He softly closes the door.

Ah shit! shit! shit! I quickly straighten my blouse, skirt and check myself in the mirror. Wow that's an improvement, full lips and lots of colour and if it wasn't so blatantly obvious that I have just been fucked senseless I would be delighted with this healthy glow, given my recent pallor. I peek my head round the door and with shameful confidence walk back through the restaurant to the bar, thankful we have had no new customers and Lili is idly polishing some glasses.

"Hey Bets, what's up?" She doesn't look concerned so I am thinking it a generic greeting, not a specific enquiry for me to disclose that I have just got down and dirty in the disabled toilet.

"Oh you know same same, Oh! Other than Arse-Hat of an ex decided to bring his new date here for a cozy date." I nod in the direction of the booth.

"Shit Bets sorry I didn't even look, took the order without peeping up from my pad." She grimaces, breaking the golden rule of good waitressing; more friendly eye contact more likely to get a tip. "She's just ordered some wine and I think they'll be staying for food now he's back, do you want me to take this?" She offers considerately.

I huff out a steely breath because yes I do want her to take this. I do want to go and hide in the kitchen but I'm not going to. She doesn't frighten me, my uncontrollable reactions to him, however, scare the shit out of me. "No I've got this." I take the tray with a bottle of red and a bottle of sparkling water. I fix my most fake smile and sigh. "Here goes." Lili starts humming the theme from Rocky and it makes me snicker so that when I reach there table I have a genuine smile on my face. Daniel straightens and I can see his jaw tick, he looks uncomfortable and I realise he wasn't expecting me to serve. Well, I am made of stronger stuff, apparently. I place the tray down, open the water, pour and then start to uncork the wine. I pour two glasses, slip the tray under my arm and take out my pad, with my sweetest voice I ask what they would like. I know she has recognised me, she probably knew from the moment I served coffee but she chooses now to acknowledge me.

"Oh my goodness Bethany, how lovely. I didn't recognise you, what a surprise. Did you know Bethany worked here darling?" Her voice is soft her smile is slight, like a china doll and just as sinister.

"No." His abrupt curt response highlighting his unease. "I didn't know she was back working here."

"So would you like to hear the specials?" I don't want to enter into small talk. I think we are past that. I just want to be mature and professional, take their order and leave. Angel reaches her hand and lays it on my arm squeezing lightly. I can't help but flinch and I tense my muscles to prevent the instant image in my head playing out. The one with me flipping that hold and pulling her to the floor, laying her out with my knee on her throat. I love my inner dialogue sometimes.

"Bethany," Her voice dripping with maleficent sincerity. "I am so sorry *things* didn't work out. ."

"Angel." Daniels warning tone is gruff but she ignores it.

"You have to know I am hoping you two will work things out. I am so grateful to Daniel but devastated that you don't understand . . . I just pray—"

I promised myself I wouldn't stoop because I know from bitter experience how easy it is to become the villain but I can't stand it. I slap the pad down and lean my slight frame right over her, my finger in her face. She looks startled and pushes back into the cushion back of the booth. "Look bitch! You can fool Daniel with whatever this saintly desperate doting wife act you've got going on but don't think for one fucking minute I don't know exactly what you're up to." My voice doesn't sound like my own, feral and dark.

"Bethany!" Daniel shouts and slams his fist on the table

"No Daniel." I draw in a sharp breath through my nose, so much for professional and mature. "You know what? I'd like you to leave." Petty and childishness rule: I step back giving them enough room to comply.

"Excuse me?" Daniel chokes out with a laugh.

I straighten my shoulders. "I said I would like you both to leave. Daniel you are friends with Tony Junior so I won't ban you from coming again but you . . ." I look directly at a very surprised Angel. "You have no friends here so you are never welcome back!" I maintain my scowl, adrenalin and fury pumping wildly through my veins. Shit! I have never acted like this at work, Jesus Tony is going to kill me but even as I start to regret my unprofessional outburst I have to keep my steely façade for fear of looking even more foolish.

Daniel smiles and rubs his fingers along the edge of the table cloth but other than that small movement shows no other sign of leaving. "I don't think you have the authority to do that Bethany but I will accept your apology if you also apologise to my guest."

I can feel my hands shake with rage and because I don't trust my brain to censor my mouth I turn and head to the kitchen. Swinging the doors wide with a crash I effectively draw the attention of Joe, whose head was in a paper and several of the other chefs and kitchen porters. "Get your knives I need help throwing someone out, full strength if you don't mind boys."

Joe stands and waves his hands in a calming motion "Ok Annie put your gun down, why am I doing this exactly?"

I can feel my tears prickle in my eyes as they pool but don't fall. "You remember what you said you'd do to my sister if she ever showed her face?" Joe's expression darkens and he reaches for his large carving knife. "Honestly, the woman out there is worse and the man she's with, isn't much better at the moment. I know you know about what I've been through with this break-up Joe. Marco would've given you the heads up before I came back to work and I told you myself about Daniel's ex from hell . . . Well now you get an up close and personal with the bitch." I blink and a few drops hit my cheek it's like a red rag and Joe motions for the others to follow him. At his side he hesitates when he sees who I am talking about.

"Ah Shit Bets you didn't say it was Danny out there too. Tony will be pissed if this back fires." He says under his breath.

"Does it make a difference?" I look up into his face and he grins and nudges me.

"No sweetheart, none at all." He strides forward stopping beside the table, his staff forming a very intimidating semi-circle and me tucked in beside him. "I believe Bethany asked you to leave. So I think its best you do just that." His voice is calm and filled with authority or maybe it's that he is the size of a house.

Daniel pinches his lips together but fails to hide his grin, smiling he stands and pats Joe lightly on the shoulder. He nods to Angel who scrabbles to get her bag from the floor and pull her coat from the hook on the wall. "See ya later Joe." Daniel nods, winks at me and flashes a heart stopping smile. Not waiting for Angel he walks out of the restaurant; she trots to follow, tripping on her heels to catch up after him.

Chapter Seven

I FELT STRANGELY empowered by my show of borrowed strength but that vanished when Anthony Junior called me into the office. Loyalty in the kitchen is akin to a cult at times so I know no one has grassed me up so I could only assume Daniel had done the honours.' Anthony is sitting back in his chair his dark brows furrowed over his chocolate brown eyes, his hands steepled in contemplation or prayer, not sure which. He is dressed in a smart light grey suit, no tie and petrol blue and white striped shirt. He doesn't look angry which is good but I decide to pre-empt a dressing down. Because, however right it felt at the time, I was out of line and I don't have the authority to ban patrons. He nods for me to take a seat, his silence is a standard tactic for making anyone he is reprimanding uncomfortable. It is effective and I have seen it make those much stronger than I, crumble. My words rush out in a garbled apology.

"Anthony I'm really sorry. I'm not sure what came over me, it won't *ever* happen again." I bite my lip to stop myself when he raises his hand.

"Well, it's a first for you so I am inclined to believe you. Would you mind telling me why my head chef has threatened one of my best customers with a knife?" He tilts his head; his voice is the epitome of measured calm.

"Joe didn't threaten as such, he just asked him to leave on my behalf." I add, to clarify this was my decision and Joe had just 'got my back.' "It wasn't his biggest *big* knife." I smile but quickly flatten my lips at his sharp narrow eyes, not ready to make jokes, good to know.

"This is serious Bethany, Danny could take this further." He sighs and shakes his head. "I will back your decision, you know that. But if I ban Danny I think this will get ugly pretty quickly, in fact I know it will." He taps his Mont Blanc pen lightly on his desk with agitation.

"I didn't ban Daniel just the bit. .just his guest and you don't really have to exclude her. I was just . . . well like I said I don't know what came over me. If they come back I'll just get one of the others to serve." I offer a tentative smile and I am relieved when he smiles back.

"No you are right, she is not welcome. I may try and stay out of the family gossip but I'd have to be a hermit not to know what's going on, maybe not the specifics but enough." He lays the pen flat, taps his fingers nervously on his lips while he chews his bottom lip like he doesn't want to say what he is about to say. "Right, not sure how to put this exactly so I'm just going to say it. Danny has asked for your shift schedule." I let out a deep breath and rub my forehead, squeezing my eyes at the instant pressure.

"Okaay." I say slowly, "and you're not giving it to him because it's intrusive, an invasion of my privacy or just that it's weird . . . Any or all of the above really Anthony?" I offer.

He bursts out a short laugh. "Everything between you two is weird but no, I mean yes. I am going to give it to him. Don't look so shocked, Joe pulled a knife on him! He's got leverage. Beside you don't have to serve him, the worst he can do is what? Order some great food and not get served by my best waitress." I snort at his attempt to flatter. He tips his head, excusing me and effectively finishing all further discussion. "Oh Bethany?" I turn and see he is grinning. "Maybe try and keep a lid on the restaurant rage from now on?" I smile tightly, fuming as I shut his door with a little more force than was necessary.

I finish the rest of my shift in a complete state of confusion. I don't know whether to be mad that Daniel is infiltrating my life again, after I had barely started to come to terms with his exit, or be pleased by it. My stomach is tied in knots and I know I can't think straight when he is near. That has always been the case but it's made so much worse by my shocking lack of control. I don't believe anything has changed so I don't really know what he wants from me. This is so fucked up I can't think straight and I can't even ask my best friend for advice, yet. I just have to keep my distance, difficult if he shows up at work every day; not impossible, just difficult.

I thank Joe again for his help and he laughs telling me it was fun and I admit Angel did look like she was about to shit herself and that was funny. I am still laughing as I open the back door and slip my pale denim jacket over my shoulders. I stumble to a stop when I see Daniel leaning against his Bentley, loose fitted jeans, a fitted pale blue button up shirt and casual deck shoes that show a hint of his tanned skin in lieu of socks. His dark hair is a little too long to style but it flops with a rough sexy quality. Like my fingers have just pulled it just so in the heat of a passionate exchange. Dammit I can feel a liquid heat burning deep inside and I tense to stop my legs from squeezing together, because I know he is staring. Just waiting for such a blatant display of the arousal he evokes.

He pushes off the side of his car and holds out the single white avalanche rose for me to take. I just look at the beautiful flower, full open petals and a subtle sweet fragrance, strong even from just one flower. I keep my hands at my side, fighting my ingrain manors to accept such a pretty gift. "An olive branch?" His voice is tempered softness. I arch a suspicious brow and he chuckles. "Where's the trust Bethany? After all *you* did kick *me* out and I'm the one standing making an apology." He opens his arms wide, almost as wide and seductive as his smile. I fold my arms over my middle and stand my ground.

"Tell me, why are you apologising? You never apologise." My quip full of attitude.

"Exactly, so you must take my offering as sincere. Several reasons actually. I am sorry for you loosing your job, never my intention. I am sorry for bringing Angel here, I would never had I known but mostly I'm sorry for letting you go. I am unbelievably sorry for that." He steps toward me and I am frozen to the spot by his utterly unexpected declaration.

I shake my head like I hadn't just heard what he said and look in to his clear blue sparkling eyes, smiling and sure. "What's changed?" I ask, afraid of the answer.

He traces his the back of his fingers along my cheek and I curse myself for leaning into his touch. "I realised I made a mistake, rare I know, but apparently I do make them." His light tone does nothing to stop my fear being realised.

"No Daniel, I mean what has actually changed?" I take his fingers that are cupped against my jaw and gently push them from my touch.

He coughs and straightens. "Nothing has changed, but I want you back so we will sort this out."

I laugh bitterly. "Do I look like a Mormon?" I step back shaking my head incredulously.

"Angel is happily married Bethany, for Christ sake why can't you trust me." His jaw is ticking and although his voice is still calm I can see he is reining in his temper, I don't share his restraint.

"Oh My God, this is not about trust it's about the fucking obvious. If she's so happily married where's her fucking husband? Why is she draped all over you every time I see her? Why does she look at me like I'm a clueless irritant and why can't you see any of this?" I twist away from his body. Stiff and angry as his body appears, it still generates serious heat in mine.

"If I felt for a moment any of this was important I might give it a seconds thought, but I don't. I will say, her husband is flying

the Only Choice

in this weekend, his work keeps him away, but that's an end to it. I have made my position as clear as I can but I can see you will need some persuading." He steps and sweeps his arm around my waist pulling me tight against his firm unyielding body. Leaning in he strokes his nose from my collar bone to my ear and whispers. "Which I will enjoy immensely." I again curse my stupid body for shivering at his words causing a deep appreciative rumbling hum in his chest. I wait limp until he releases me to stand on my own, still only inches from me.

"If that's all?" I exhale trying to feign indifference even if all my nerves are tingling with promise. "I guess I'll be seeing you tomorrow?" I narrow my eyes but he looks confused. "You have my schedule for some other reason?" I query.

He nods. "Tony told you?" He smiles a thin lipped response in acknowledgment. "Then yes, I will see you tomorrow." He draws in a deep breath which perversely prevents me from walking away, expectant for more and I'm not disappointed just wholly shocked. "So do you want to go back to the flat or would you prefer the back of the car?" His silky smooth voice fails to hide his lust filled request.

"Eh. . Excuse me?" I stutter, pleased I managed any words at all.

"Your punishment." He speaks slowly as if I am a small child and at this moment I do feel a bit 'special' in that department. "I assume you would prefer some privacy?" He smirks when he continues, "I have no objection to over the knee right here but—"

"No!" I shout and then snarl a whisper. "You can't be fucking serious? You think you are going to punish me?" Even as my indignant words leave my mouth with righteous outrage, they fall flat as my core heats and liquefies.

"Oh I know I'm going to punish you. I have never been spoken to the way you did this afternoon. No one has *ever* been that rude." His face is stern, not a hint of amusement or irony.

I snort lightly. "Maybe not to your face." He pulls me tight once more and I can feel his steel hard erection firm against my thigh, heat pulsing from him directly into my veins.

"Oh Bethany, keep it up baby and we'll go right here. Your whole body is thrumming; it would be a crime to deny this." He drags his fingernails against my scalp and grabs a handful of hair sending electrical shots across my skin to my core.

I gasp. "This isn't fair." His eyes pierce me, liquid lust and fire, his lips brush mine and I tremble from tip to toe.

He laughs against my mouth, withholding the soft sweet taste and a small whimper escapes my throat. "I never said I was going to be fair, you know me Bethany I plan to do whatever it takes. In fact, I can pretty much guarantee that I will be anything but fair. When it comes to you I plan on being downright dirty." His tongue traces the seam of my lips and I open a little, my tongue peeking to taste his. He groans and swoops in forcing my mouth to accept the invasion. Taking deep swirling plunges, tasting and taking, my heartbeat races and I am instantly breathless. His strong arms holding me firm, secure and preventing my body pooling on the pavement. He breaks the kiss and I mourn the loss, I am comforted he seems just as breathless. "The car, I'll never make it to the flat." He stoops to pick up my bag I had dropped somewhere along the way and then stoops again to pick me up as my body doesn't seem to want to respond to any of my commands but is more than happy to succumb to his.

He pulls me to sit beside him but as the car pulls away he takes my wrist and positions me across his legs that are bent at the knees and clamped together. I can feel his hardness throbbing against my hip, twitching to join in but confined to its denim prison. He smoothes my skirt over my bottom, slow sweeping movements, rubbing with no pressure at all. His fingertips curl under the hem and he lifts, rolling the material over the round curve of my bottom. We both Inhale sharply as my pale skin is revealed, remnants of my panties still in the pedestal bin in the restaurant toilet. "Ah fuck Bethany, you are perfect. You know you were made for me." He coughs and his soft voice is replaced with a sterner, authoritative tone. "Thirty and I want you to count

the Only Choice

and I don't want you to come."

"Then don't stick your fingers anywhere near me because I can't make any promises, the way my body is at the moment I have no fucking control." My breathless voice is needy and the mounting pressure is already causing my toes to curl.

"Mmmm I know. Like I said, perfect." He traces one long finger down the bottom of my spine and continues down the crack to my soaking centre and I buck my hips and bite down a scream, my legs shaking and rapid pants try to calm my clenching muscles. "Shit! You weren't joking. This is extreme responsiveness, sexy as hell but shit, what's got your body all keyed up like this?" I have mixed feelings as he removes his finger and my body quietens and I pray he is not really a mind reader because I know *exactly* why my body is in horny teenager mode. It may not have been on the literature Dr Ward gave me but 'possible increases in libido' certainly came up when I google searched pregnancy symptoms. Strike possible and underline definite . . . I shake my head.

"I have no idea but if it's a problem we can stop this." One arm presses down on my shoulders pinning me in place while his other resumes the soft seductive strokes over my bottom and the back of my thighs.

"You want me to stop?" His hand slows and my head shakes of its own volition.

"No. Please, I don't want you to stop." I can hear the shake in my voice, my emotions maybe all over the place but my body reads like an open book. Right now it's chapter one, 'BDSM for dummies; pain and pleasure. The sting of his palm.' "Arhhh!!" I exhale and absorb the fire and burn that races through my body. "One." Again and again in quick succession, I count, he strikes, I count, he strikes and I writhe. He holds me firm but as my counting is coming to an end my need to come is unbearable and I can feel prickles as tears sting the corners of my eyes. My body glows with a slick sheen of perspiration but I shiver all over and I can't seem to draw enough breath with my shallow panting.

He strikes one last time and gently lifts me up, my eyes roll as the blood rushes from my head and my whole body trembles. "Thank you." I gasp. I'm a wreck.

He picks me up and holds me cradled in his arms, every nerve, every cell is super sensitive and screaming for release. He squeezes tighter but I can't stop shaking. "Oh poor baby, here let me help." He shifts so I am sideways, my back resting on the seat of the car, still holding me tight. His body half covering mine he takes his other hand, gently cups between my legs and presses lightly with the pad of his thumb on my nub of needy nerves. I cry, gasp, convulse and press my face into his chest because I want to scream, it feels so good, so much, too much. Wave after wave of rolling pleasure ebbing as he so gently brings me back to earth. He holds me, stroking my hair and kissing me lightly. So much for keeping my distance, I am going to need a much better plan. Perhaps a body guard or maybe a chastity belt . . . a little late for that. Besides the way I'm feeling I would've picked the lock before the key was pocketed. I think my plan for travel is my best option. Some real physical distance before I resort to begging Daniel to be my sex slave, or more likely that I'm begging him to become *his* sex slave.

I can feel the car has stopped and my eyelids flutter open. I sense the intensity of his gaze before my eyes meet his, steely dark and possessive, still urgent and hungry. He shifts and I use the movement to slide to his side. He still has his arms around me but he is rock hard and trying to get comfortable. I bite my cheek to stop my tongue from licking my lips at the thought of his taste in my mouth; my damn body is going to be the death of me. I wriggle and pull my skirt into place, straighten my blouse and check my hair in the reflective glass of the car window. Yes . . . wild, with that just fucked look, perfect. I reach to open the door but he moves with me and holds my hand over the handle.

"Stay with me tonight?" His soft voice is thick with desire but the edge of uncertainty makes my chest ache and recoil like a fully body punch in the solar plexus. I know my voice would

the Only Choice

betray me so I shake my head once and push the handle down and step from the car. He is still holding my hand and he looks from his hand to my face, a dazzling smile spreads slowly. "I want you Bethany. Look into my eyes and tell me you don't want the same thing I do?"

"It's not about what I want." My voice is soft and with every fibre of strength I am fighting the need to throw myself back in to the car and back into his fucked up life but I don't. I can't.

He chuckles and his grin is assuredly cocky. "Baby, what you want, what I want, it's the same damn thing and that is *the only* thing that matters."

"Not any more." My soft words cause a brief frown on is perfect face but I turn and scamper to the safety of my flat, feeling the relief of prey escaping its natural predator. Physical distance . . . my only hope of survival.

The next day he called my mobile, seeing his caller id I swiped reject. He called again and again. My short walk to work was peppered with call reject moments until after a short respite I took a call from a different number.

"Good Morning Bethany." I could hear the smile in his voice, I just hoped he couldn't hear the smile in mine.

"Good Morning Daniel, nice trick but you know I'm just going to add this to my address book and I won't pick up next time." I sound decidedly smug. I love technology, sometimes.

"Good to know." He sounds unperturbed by this and continues to chat about everything and nothing. He makes me laugh and I find I have reached the restaurant for work without noticing the journey. I am just about to inform him that I have to go when his voice drops and I am hovering, still outside the back door waiting for his next words. "Bethany . . . I miss starting my day inside you." His words are like a hot wire to my clit and he chuckles to hear my intake of breath. Fuck I do not need to start the day like this and I can't risk continuing this conversation because I know first-hand how effective his aural skills can be; so I hang up.

One step from the kitchen into the restaurant and I feel him. Sure enough, he is sitting in the same booth he was yesterday. He only smiles sweetly, his eyes kind and warm, crinkly all the way in the corners while he chats on the phone. My whole shift I avoid his table but he seems happy just to sit, work and eat. He even holds a few meetings much to the confusion of his PA Colin and some other employees that have been dragged across town. It is a lot of effort considering he hasn't even spoken to me and if I am honest it is pretty flattering if completely impractical, crazy and unsustainable. Still if that's the worst he can do, as Tony said, it's not so bad. I finish my shift and find him waiting by his car, white rose in hand. Today I graciously accept it because he looks so cute and his smile is genuine and heart stopping.

"Would you like a lift?" He holds the door open and I laugh shaking my head.

"Thank you but I'll be safer walking." I slip my shoulder bag over my head and fish my ear phones out of my pocket.

"Possibly, although you looked a little flustered this morning when you arrived. Maybe walking isn't so safe after all?" He starts to walk toward me and I clench my thighs at the rising heat. It's a subtle movement but it doesn't go unnoticed. "I might be able to help with that?" He raises a cheeky eyebrow, his hands slip to my waist and slide to my hips exerting pressure that is echoed rumbling at the base of my spine. A noise which is a mixture of squeak and groan escapes into my closed mouth and he purses his lips trying not to laugh. I am grateful for these flashes of arrogance because they are enough to ground me even as my body violently screams; 'what the hell, just do it already.' The traitor that it is. I step back and turn calling over my shoulder.

"I don't doubt that for a moment but so can B.O.B." I don't turn to check but I'm pretty sure he is scowling. I can't imagine he would be a fan of battery boyfriend but my body is so easily charged these days, I am starting to think I should perhaps start carrying a BOB junior all the damn time. A new essential, like one of my five a day. My phone rings and I pick up seeing a local code.

"That wasn't very polite." His gravelly voice, unexpected and potent sends a chill across my skin. It's exhausting the reactions he draws from my body. His voice alone instantaneously has me on high alert and erotically receptive. The latent threat of his tone makes my mouth dry and my panties wet. I glance furtively over my shoulder half expecting his car to be crawling behind me but I relax when there is nothing but a solid line of black cabs. Since he has no qualms about exploiting his effect on me I may as well take some pleasure of my own, on my own.

"No sir, it wasn't. Now what do you plan on doing about it?" I feel so much power in the moment I am breathless with it, well that and my increase in walking pace. I am nearly home and I kind of hope he wants to play. I hear him groan.

"Mmm what shall I do?" He sighs and is quite on the line. I can barely hear him breathing. "Are you home?"

"Nearly . . . five minutes." I am dodging pedestrians eager to reach my goal, both my goals.

"Good. Go to your room, strip to your panties and lie on the bed. I will call you in ten minutes put me on speaker. You will need your hands." He hangs up and I break into a jog. Oh good! He *is* going to play.

Lying quietly still for ten minutes has done nothing to calm my racing heart and nervous anticipation. I know I have removed the camera and I could be doing the washing up right now for all he knows but I still feel strangely compelled to obey his commands. I crave his punishment and I want to please him. I am struggling to believe these changes I am suffering are a result of what can't be much more than a tiny bundle of cells at this stage. I take a moment to do a mental check that it isn't just all in my head. My senses are ultra-sensitive, smell, taste, when I do manage to stomach food. Sight and hearing not so much, tired? Yes, emotional? Yes, raging hormones? Um yes . . . I am, after all, lying half naked waiting for some phone relief from a man I am not seeing but I can't seem to resist. That has to be a result of altered brain function as well as hormones. What about sore breasts? I lift my hands and cup myself. I know for health reasons I should but this is not something I do on a regular basis so I don't know. Yes they feel delicate but is that normal? When Daniel does it, it feels amazing, sensitive and sometimes painful but always incredible. It is like when a doctor presses on a place you've never pressed before and asks if it hurts; well yes but would it normally? I don't know because I don't go round pressing myself or fondling my breasts so I have no frame of reference.

I puff out a frustrated breath when it finally occurs to me, that I am an idiot. This *is* my punishment. Twenty five minutes waiting for something, anything . . . punishment, relief, maybe even reward but nothing. I am being denied. Well, that may be his intention but the final outcome is most definitely in my hands. I am aroused, half naked and now I seem to be gently holding my own breasts which are almost as sensitive to my touch as his. My nipples are achingly hard and my skin is prickled with a million goose bumps. I don't actually own a BOB, thought I had one from a hen party goody bag but apparently not. Still I have my fingers, a healthy imagination and the sex drive of a horny rabbit. This really shouldn't take long. I close my eyes and moan because all I can see is his eyes, his face contorted with desire. I succumb to this blissful image and in my mind replace my hands with his, my breath with his and my. . . . Shit! Shit! The doorbell breaks my dream like haze, halting the fantasy before it took its first forbidden step. I grab my robe from the back of my bedroom door and roughly push my arms through the sleeve, taking my frustrated anger out on the silky material. I am going to take that front door key and shove it where the sun don't shine. Marco has managed to get in the main door just not in to the apartment. He has not even bothered to look under the plant pot. I fumble with the main lock.

"For fuck sake Marco the keys under the—" I snap my mouth

shut when I am faced not with my forgetful flatmate but the smouldering image of my recently dissolved fantasy. He steps in through the door forcing me to step back. His hands take the edge of my robe and cross it firmly, tightening it again at the waist whilst looking over his shoulder. There is no one there and it makes me chuckle, barely a flash of cleavage was exposed and he acts like I'm Lady Cadaver.

"Please don't finish that sentence with plant pot because I will have to punish you all over again and I have plans for us tonight." His arm sweeps around my waist and he steers me into my bedroom.

"So leaving me waiting was my punishment?" I watch him walk toward my wardrobe where he frowns as he rummages through my sparse array of clothing.

"No, stopping you from finishing, that was your punishment and judging by that tone you answered the door with I would say I was successful?" He turns his head with a cocky grin. He pulls out a sleeveless black silk knitted dress with a flared skirt and a horizontal lace pattern. It is pretty much the only cocktail dress I had bought when I restocked my wardrobe. He lays it on the bed and starts to look for some shoes. I pinch my lips to stop from smirking when I hear him grumble. I know I only have wedges with any heal, not a stiletto insight. He pulls out a black wedged sandal but he doesn't look happy about it. He is just about to put them next to the dress when he grins, noticing a small folded pile of clothes near my dresser under which he has spied the telltale red sole of Sofia's patent black Louboutins with killer heels. "There, that is better." He looks so pleased with himself. "Now if you would get dressed . . . I am taking you on a date." His stellar smile disarms me but I have to protest.

"I don't think that's—" He steps up to me and places his firm finger against my lips halting my words.

"You have to let me try Bethany and I promise nothing will happen to you tonight, that you don't want to happen." His words are like velvet, a soft and seductive promise and that is exactly what I'm worried about. He chuckles, "Good to know." He kisses me lightly. His lips sweet and warm but my eyes are wide, that was in my head, did I say that out loud? "I am expecting a delivery so I will be a gentleman and wait in the hall and Bethany . . ." He pauses, my eyes are still wide from his ability to mind read. "You may wear panties."

I snort out an unladylike laugh. "Definitely a gentleman, thank you most kindly Sir." I do a mock curtsey and usher him from my room.

Chapter Eight

I PILE MY hair in a loose bun on top of my head and brush the wayward tendrils away from my face, some lip gloss and I'm done. The weather has been uncharacteristically not very British recently and this evening is no exception, warm, balmy with almost tropical humidity, hence the wayward tendrils. There is a gentle knock on my door.

"Are you decent?" His gravelly voice makes my skin dance with a sprinkling of a million prickles and I think in my current heighten state of constant sexual arousal I can safely answer 'not even remotely' but I settle for a polite affirmation. The door opens and he leans on the frame, his arms crossing his trim waist, his forearms tanned, sculpted and his eyes . . . they could scorch the clothes from my skin.

"God you are so fucking beautiful." His frown deepens like this thought has made him angry. He shakes his head at the troubled expression, replacing it with an utterly wicked smile. "But there's something missing." He pushes himself from the doorframe with his shoulders and in two strides is directly in front of me, not touching but I can instantly feel the palpable heat and tension his body ignites. He traces a finger down my cheek, I feel his gentle touch but he isn't actually touching me; my body is reacting to the nearness, to the anticipation, to the promise. This is going to be a tortuously long night. "Tonight is a date Bethany. I don't want you to think for one moment what we have is just about sex, even if that sex is phenomenal. I will not be fucking you, or making love to you tonight." His grin widens at my pathetic whimper that is strangled at the back of my throat. "Having said that, your body seems to be hyper responsive to my touch and I do intend on touching you, a great deal." His middle finger barely touches my chin to tilt it so his eyes are fixed on mine. "And I can't have you begging all night, because I'm only human and I'm trying to be a gentleman."

I sniff at his arrogance but it falls flat. His eyes darken, like he is setting my soul on fire and I can feel the heat burning fiercely in my depths, building pressure and embers of desire that will rage with the slightest fanning. His mouth is millimetres from mine and he is holding his sweet lips just out of reach. Even as I sway for contact he reacts and withdraws enough, enough to prove his point. I can feel my lips form the shape of my first begging words.

"Pl. ." He kisses me so lightly but it calms the embers for now and I sigh.

"So to help us both I'd like you to wear these." He holds his palm and my eyes are momentarily drawn from his gaze to what looks like, two small glossy black marbles in his hands. He chuckles at my frown.

"Well, this is hardly a *Pretty Woman* moment Daniel." I joke and I can feel my cheeks flush. Personally I may not be super experienced with sex toys but I've been educated by the best. Frequent awkward conversations with Marco and the boys in the restaurant kitchen left no topic taboo.

"Bethany, when I give you a diamond necklace, it won't be a rental." His serious expression leaves me in no doubt of his words but it gives way to a wickedly slow grin. "Now, turn around Bethany, bend over and place your hands on the bed." His voice is dark and hoarse and when I hesitate he asks. "Do you

the Only Choice

trust me?" I turn and follow his instruction, my actions speaking for me. He runs his hand down my spine and lifts the hem of my dress over my bottom. It is an act that makes me feel extremely exposed but when he pulls my panties to one side this vulnerability intensifies. His deep satisfied humming from his chest and the soft sweep of his finger in my slick folds instantly dissolves any unease and I find my hips move toward his too delicate touch. He dips one finger inside, pulls it slowly out and the next feeling is more intense, a change in pressure and temperature as he pushes one of the balls inside me. Before I can clench and acclimate he pushes the second ball deep, along with his finger, swirling and moving the foreign objects so I am acutely aware of their presence. He removes his finger and drags it once more along my length and up the crack of my bottom. He carefully replaces my panties and pats my dress back into place.

I stand and turn to face him, my face a flush of colour and I wobble as the balls move ever so lightly inside. The feeling is strange, not unpleasant and a little distracting. "Umm and this is supposed to help how exactly?" I hold myself perfectly still and he moves a little closer. His hands gently brush the stray hair away from my eyes, stroking his fingers lightly across my neck and down my back; his mouth brushes my cheekbone. I shiver when I feel a gentle build of pressure, moving and swirling deep inside.

"Mmm lets see shall we?" His fresh minty breath follows his whispered words as his lips trace mine, his tongue seeking entry. Trembling I gasp as a satisfying wave of pleasure gently bursts inside, nothing monumental but delicious and calming. My seemingly insatiable need quelled and abated without a single, pant, beg or torn piece of clothing. "No need for BOB." He growls, "And I get to be the perfect gentleman making sure you have the most enjoyable date imaginable without compromising my intentions." He sounds smug but he moves his hand to adjust himself and I laugh and draw in a sharp breath at the same time. Ok so no sudden movements or sharp contracting muscles and gently does it from now on, which includes sudden fits of laughter.

"I think this is all good in theory but I have a feeling it's not going to be that simple." I cautiously lean down to pick up my bag. "And what about you?" I raise my brow and bite my lips to hold back the inevitable grin.

"I promise nothing will happen tonight that you don't want to happen but I was serious about no sex. You have to understand, nothing is more important than you understanding *exactly* what you mean to me. I need to make you mine . . . again." His serious tone hangs heavy but he shrugs, "So I will have to endure the hard on from hell all evening while you have an evening full of mini orgasms. Sucks to be me right now, eh?" He winks and laughs but my tongue darts to moisten my lips at the only word I heard and he holds his hand up. "Hey, I'm not a Saint, keep looking like that and this will be the shortest fucking date in history." He cups my cheeks with both hands large enough to cover my entire face, his expression so sincere it melts my heart. "Please baby, let me do this?" I nod and he flashes his heart steeling smile, grabs my hand and leads me from the apartment. "Great, I promise this is going to be fun." His enthusiasm is contagious and has me feeling all warm and fuzzy; well, I think it's his enthusiasm.

I am very confused. We are standing outside my apartment, Daniel's car is nowhere to be seen and he seems to be leading me to a mini that is double parked. Not a new model mini like the one Ethan owns. This is an original mini, fire engine red, union jack on the roof and tiny, it's absolutely tiny. As we approach a small, wiry looking man in his late twenties, with light blonde hair and a wispy ginger beard gets out of the front seat and rushes round to open our door. He is dressed smartly in trousers, shirt and black tie, he probably ditched his jacket because of the heat or more likely because there's no room for it in the car.

"Hello Mr Stone, my names Billy and I am your driver for this evening." He sweeps his arm in the direction of the back seat. "Welcome, if you would like to make yourselves comfortable, we'll get started." His voice is bright and energetic. Daniel moves to allow me to step, fold and wedge myself into the back seat. I shuffle back, the seat is actually quite comfortable and I have enough leg room but then I'm only five foot six. I can't help but laugh as Daniel, at just shy of six four attempts to squeeze his frame in beside me. He laughs too but shuffles and moves so his large arm is around my shoulders and his legs are more on my side, either that or they would be tucked under his chin. He holds my hand with his free hand; lifting it to his lips he kisses the fingertips. Billy gets in starts up and announces that he is going to guide us through London on an original *mini* tour. The biggest smile stretches across my face. I love London but like many that live in this city I am ashamed to say I don't take the time to enjoy it. I have probably visited all the major sights at one time but I take most for granted and have never been on a guided tour. Not even one of the many open top bus tours and they practically pass my front door every day.

I squeak as we hit our first pot hole that feels like the Grand Canyon in this car, you forget how lovely suspension is until there is none, or very little in this case. My muscles automatically tense and I get an instant warm rush and gentle wave of pleasure that causes me to let out a surprised breath. I hear Daniel chuckle. I turn to scowl but he is looking out of the window. Billy is giving a lively commentary as we pass Big Ben and the Houses of Parliament. The constant ebb and flow of pleasure from every bump in the road and every stroke of Daniels soft fingers on my neck or gentle kiss on my cheek is sublime but it does mean I pay little attention to the tour. We pass Buckingham Palace and St James, weaving our way across the city via a web of tiny back streets. Who knew there where that many cobbled streets left and who knew a mini would fit down them or that this tour would drive every single one of them. We drive across the river past The Globe and finally stop near The London Eye.

Daniel thanks Billy as I regain my composure. He takes my hand and walks me toward the river, and out on to a private pier where a large speed boat is tied. I halt and he turns looking at my feet, maybe he thinks my heel is stuck in the wooden boarding. His eyes travel slowly up my body and his smile gets wider with every inch covered until he meets my eyes and sees that my head is shaking. He steps to my side and wraps his strong arm around my shoulder pulling me to him and toward the boat.

"I promise you'll love it." His intonation fails to hide how true he believes his words to be and he has the cheek to wink as he holds his hand to me to follow him on to the sleek polished luxury speed boat. I slip out of my shoes and take his hand and steady myself as I step on and sit straight down. I know very little about cars and even less about boats but this one is very smart. On closer inspection the glossy black exterior is actually a midnight blue with a slight metallic sparkle, the plush seats that curve around the back of the boat are cream leather with dark blue piping and every surface is either super shiny chrome or polished wood. There are two large leather swivel chairs one behind what looks like a dash board and the wheel. Daniel sits beside me and lightly places his hand on the skirt of my dress, half touching my skin, his hand is warm and firm and although I feel a tingle all over it is manageable. The desire and need is there but it's not all consuming. It is just normal and I am so grateful because for the first time in a while my brain can function. "You look so fucking beautiful, you look like you do when you've just—"

"—All clear to go Sir?" The voice interrupts and I giggle. Daniel kisses my nose and turns.

"All good thank you Mark, maybe not to the barrier, just the Dome and back?" Daniel clears his throat and flashes me a quick heated look.

"Very good Sir." Mark turns and starts the very loud engine, the rumble sends a storm of vibrations through the boat and through me and I find I grip Daniels knee and the seat in anticipation of I know what's coming. Because that would be me. This city is most incredible when the sun begins to set. I adore the riverbank vista and I love the varied skyline with its endless sea of sparkling lights. I love that Daniel wanted to show me this and I love that this is a proper date. We didn't really date first time round. We just were and then my sister put an end to that and then we were again and now Angel has put an end to that. Maybe this time, dating is a better way to start, less drama more fun. The boat is fast and we speed and bump and jump our way up the Thames. Daniel holds my thigh as my body lifts and plummets with each wave and drop. The speed is exhilarating, the wind whips my hair loose and instead of fighting to keep it contained I loosen my tie and shake it out completely. I must look like medusa but I don't care, it feels amazing, I feel free and I can't fight how happy I am right now. I start to laugh with the next sudden drop and Daniel swings his arm pulling me close as I am tossed about unable to contain the fits of giggles. It is hard over the noise of the engine but I think he's laughing too, he is certainly smiling. He is right, this is fun but like with most things too much and it very quickly stops being fun. I am just about there as one more wave of pleasure gently erupts and rolls away as we pull alongside the pier once more. I can feel my thighs tremble and I am exhausted and slightly queasy. Daniel takes one look at me, concern etched on his face.

"Are you all right, you look a little pale do you need me to. . . . Um help?" He shifts and my eyes flick to the distinctive bulge in his jeans. "Not that." He adds quickly and I stifle a laugh because I can't take any more tensing of my internal muscles.

"I think maybe I have had enough pleasure for one night." I smile and see his shoulders relax. "And I would kill for some chips." I smile, a little shy and he laughs loudly.

"No need to resort to murder, but chips? Are you sure? I was planning on taking you to The Berkerley." He pulls me up to stand and I wobble but he steadies me with his hands firmly on my hips.

"I'm craving chips." My mouth snaps at my slip but I quickly add. "I wouldn't want you thinking I'm after your money. I don't mind being a cheap date and I really fancy chips, something simple and soon." I prompt.

"You've never been about the money baby. I'm truly sorry I ever said that." He adds absently, " but not really an issue anymore when you have your own—"

I step back with a frown. "What are you talking about? I don't have my own. Well, I have a bit thanks to Tom but he really wanted—" I am getting flustered, fuck, but just as I start to get all agitated at the turn this light banter has taken Daniel pulls me to his chest and kisses my hair.

"Baby, stop sweating the small stuff. By the time you turn twenty-one you won't give it a seconds thought." I know I am confused but he doesn't elaborate. "Now, I believe you are wanting to return some item of mine?" He wiggles his brow and I look around at our low but exposed position given that we are less than twenty five meters from the London Eye and all its entire occupants. He takes my hand and leads me to a hatch near the driver's seat that I hadn't noticed. I climb down following him, his hands rest on my calves and slide up my legs as I descend, lifting my dress as I go. A few short moments, an intimate adjustment and a passionate kiss later and I am climbing the few vertical steps back up to the deck. I can hear his groan and he mumbles something about 'fuck being a gentleman.' I laugh when he reaches the deck and holds my hand once more.

"If you were a gentleman you wouldn't be blatantly staring at my arse as I climbed that ladder." I grin with mock outrage.

"It is because I'm a gentleman that I was only *staring* at your arse." He leads me back to dry land and we make our way the along bustling riverbank path. With County Hall, The London Eye, The Globe and Tate Modern all within easy walking distance this area is rightly, heavily packed with tourists. I nod to a patch of grass near the County Hall next to the hotel entrance and Daniel lays his jacket for me to sit while he hunts and gathers. I take my shoes off because although I haven't walked far, they are really not made for anything much more than standing still or better yet, in a display case with a spotlight. I lie back and relax,

the Only Choice

taking in the sounds and smells, no distinct conversations and no distinct smells until I feel movement next to me and sit up to Daniel sitting down. "Sorry no chips but I know you love these and it is simple so I_" He has handed me a large bacon bap and the rancid smell assaults my nose like a grenade causing a violent instant heave of my stomach. I push his hand, turn and scramble away. Thankful I no longer have my shoes as I run flat out into the foyer of the hotel and quickly spot the ladies. Just in time I dry heave into the toilet. So so grateful I made it and although it hurts I am glad I had an empty stomach because I don't think I would have made it this far.

There is a loud crash and a lady who must have been at the sink shrieks. "This is the Ladies!"

Daniels voice is calm but forceful. "I am aware of that. My girlfriend." He offers as way of explanation. It doesn't explain anything but it is all she is getting because I can now feel his hand gently resting on my hunched back. My hands are still gripping the seat and I am still swallowing back all the moisture in my mouth waiting for the next heave. Oh God how am I going to explain this? I can't say it was the boat, he'll feel bad. I can't tell him I don't love bacon when he knows I do, normally I do and I can't tell him it's the same bug I have been using as an excuse all week because he'll have me seeing a specialist in the morning and then I'll be really embarrassed. "Hey baby, can I get you anything?" I heave just at the thought of what he got me last time and continue to do that for endless minutes. My tummy hurts but I think I have finished I can still feel his warm hand gently massaging my back.

"Some water, please." My voice is raw, husky and if it wasn't for the fact I'm probably drooling it might even be a sexy voice. I wipe my face on the crumpled mass of tissues he hands me and make my way to the sink. He nods and I expect him to leave but he just stands staring, eyes filled with worry and as crappy as I feel I need to ease his concern. "I'm fine, sorry, clearly not fine fine but I'm Ok. I think it was a combination of bumpy rides, empty stomach and seeing a greasy bun. I've had a bit of a tummy bug and I think I'm just a little sensitive." I laugh lightly, deciding a combination of all my excuses is probably more believable. "I wasn't kidding when I said simple." I let out a breath and grab his clenched hand, smiling. "OK?" His jaw is tense and his eyes darken but he nods and threads his fingers through mine. "Wait! Where are my shoes and your jacket?" I am looking him up and down like he might have secret pockets or something. He shrugs and leads me to the bar. He sits me in a semi-circular booth in the elegant piano bar, orders my water and goes back to retrieve our things. I notice him speaking to a waiter but returns empty handed. "Um shoes? . . . Jacket?" I enquire.

"I would like to say I have had them sent to the room I have booked for us here tonight." He sits beside me his thigh pressed against mine.

"And have you?" He strokes his long finger along my jaw, his expression infuriatingly neutral.

"I have booked a room. I have not had our things sent there." I let out a frustrated puff I don't know whether to be irritated at his arrogance and his presumption or furious that he's being so obtuse.

"So my shoes have been stolen! No sorry, Sofia's shoes have been stolen and your jacket?Great!" I sit back sharply and he just laughs louder.

"Small stuff baby. I'll replace the shoes and the jacket wasn't a favourite or anything special, so it too can be replaced." I am about to challenge him on his flagrant disposable attitude when the waiter brings me a delicate basket of chips and can't help the huge smile that invades my face.

"Thank you." I whisper to Daniel, as the waiter carefully sets a knife, fork and condiments.

He whispers back "you are most welcome."

"I'm not staying here tonight." I reply just as softly back at him with a grin. I pick up a chip with my fingers a pop it in my mouth wishing I had blown on it first as I am left to huff and puff to cool it in my mouth, not very good manners. He leans over and takes one too, blowing and arching a brow, like he's teaching me basic laws of physics. I smile lightly and take another, they are piping hot, obviously, but crisp, fluffy and delicious.

"Really, and what makes you think that?" He pops the chip in his mouth and I can't take my eyes off the way his lips move so slowly savouring the taste or savouring my reaction.

"Because you said this was a date, and since we are not actually together." I point out and he narrows his eyes at this but I continue. "This is our first date yes? So, I don't put out on a first date and as a gentleman you shouldn't have presumed I would."

"You did put out on our first date though." He grins.

I can feel my cheeks flush pink and the sultry tone has my hairs prickling like an electrical current has passed through them. "Pretty sure that wasn't a date either but um yes, I did. You are kind of . . . well . . . It's hard to say no to you." My voice is soft and I can hear my own hesitancy.

"Good to know." He holds the cooled chip to my lips and I open on instinct. "So how is it you don't seem to have the same compunction now?"

My mouth is suddenly dry, his fingers have worked their way to the nape of my neck and are entwining into my hair, twirling and gripping and it makes me gasp. These words I am about to say sound ridiculous to my ears so it's impressive he doesn't laugh. "I'm stronger." I know I *have* to be rather than I know I am.

"I can see that." His dark blue eyes fix on mine and he looks deep inside me but there is no irony or amusement. He releases his hold and allows me to finish my food, still idly stroking my thigh or my neck. Always touching, it's nice, it's wonderful, this is really hard. He wants to order some wine but I manage to persuade him that herbal tea would be better. He has been quiet for some time as I let my tea seep. The silence is heavy and I glance his way occasionally and each time his intense gaze is fixed on me. His expression is implacable, he could be holding something back or he could be wanting the date to end, he could be so full of lust he wants to bend me over this very low table. Honestly, I have no fucking idea because he gives nothing away. I turn and sit to face him creating a bit of space, his hand drops from my thigh to the seat between us.

"Should I go?" I could've slapped him for the shock my question has caused.

"Why the fuck would you ask that? Do you want to go?" His voice is flat angry.

"No I don't want to go but you just . . ." I sigh heavily. "What do you want from me Daniel?" I rub my fingers at my temple. I know where this evening is rapidly heading.

"Marry Me?" His voice is a whisper but my laugh is a lot louder and again he looks shocked but also hurt and I hate that, but I did not see *that* coming.

"Daniel, it's a first date remember? Talk like that is likely to scare a girl off and if it doesn't that should scare you off." I cup his face and he is trying to smile but I can see he is really saddened by my words. "Daniel I do love you, but this is complicated and despite the trite words, it very often isn't 'all you need.' What about Angel?" I really didn't want to do this tonight. I really wanted the date but it's such a huge fucking white elephant in between us, it is inevitable.

"She has what she wants, my commitment is done. I have paid my dues there is nothing more I have to do." His cold clipped response is shocking but not because of its delivery.

Oh My God! This actually breaks my heart that he believes that. I trace my fingers through his hair with one hand and hold his cheek with the other. "Oh Daniel . . . God I wish that was true." He pulls back; brows furrowed his eyes angry and confused.

"What? It is true, I have a contract signed. You don't believe me?" His jaw is ticking and I can hear his teeth grind.

"I believe *you* believe that, but no Daniel I don't believe this is over. Not even remotely." I place calming hands on his thighs

the Only Choice

because he has moved his hands to his side. "This isn't about a contract because we both know that any contract can be broken and given the right circumstances you would break it in an instant . . . you have before." He was about to interrupt but the timely sore reminder about our recent contract dissolution, the one he promised would give me comfort and security, has his lips pressed into a thin line. "Suppose one day Angel changes her mind, or more likely reveals her true colours. No, don't scowl. I'm allowed to have a low opinion of her, she's fucking up *my* life." It may be my gut reaction with no evidential proof but to me that is as good as fact. However, I am under no illusion Angel has been so forthcoming with Daniel as to reveal her true intentions. I shake my head because this isn't about me either. "Ok so she changes her mind and wants to tell the child about the father, the *real* father, would you deny that? No, of course you wouldn't. It's no more the child's fault than it is mine and you would never exclude yourself from a child's life like that. Not your own child and I wouldn't want you to." I know I am asking questions and answering for him and I know it sounds like I am rambling but from the look on his face I don't think he has even considered what I am saying. He seems to have frozen, maybe he agrees. I sort of hope he does given what I am carrying inside me. "But that leaves Angel and I know you don't believe me but I don't believe her motives are entirely pure?" I am astounded at my own restraint but I really don't want to be the villain, again. He scowls but I raise a finger to protest his protest. "Daniel, it would still mean she's in your life and that means she's in my life and I really have to think if that's best for us." I have to stop my hand from resting across my tummy but I know I am not talking about Daniel and I anymore.

He is quiet and I can feel his mind racing, "So if I had had a child prior to meeting you, we would never be together?"

My jaw drops, my restraint weakens. "Wow, that's what you heard from that! No Daniel I didn't say that. I wouldn't care if you had a whole football team of children before me, but this isn't *before* me is it? It's *with* me and you made this decision without me. She doesn't just want your baby Daniel, she wants you. Arghh!" I don't care that people are staring he makes me so fucking mad that he can't see this but all the air in my rage escapes when I see such sadness in his eyes.

"We're broken." His hand reaches for mine and I grab it like a lifeline.

"No Daniel, we're not broken. We're just not fixed." My smile is brief as I feel his sadness consume me too. He lifts my fingers to his lips and kisses softly.

"Yet." He exhales.

Chapter Nine

"TWICE!" SOFIA SCREECHES in my ear. It is two weeks until the wedding and I am having my dress re-fitted at her parent's house in her bedroom. Sofia's mum has just left to get more pins and has been caught on the phone with one of the many relatives making their way to London in the next few weeks. So I am standing like a mannequin getting harpooned every time I breathe. I hadn't told Sofia of my encounters with Daniel at the weekend away or the more recent ones. Only because I don't need to be under a microscope right now but she's been relentless and I cave.

I push my fingers to her lips and quieten her down. I am so not having this conversation in front of her mum. "Yes Sofs twice, well twice, actual intercourse, but a few other near misses." I shake my head and flush bright red with shame.

She laughs loudly. "Listen to you, 'intercourse' you sound like a biology text book. So you fucked him twice and x-rated on a few other occasions . . . get you!" She fans herself but it's me that's over heating with embarrassment.

"Oh God I'm a slut!" I cover my face with both my hands but she peels the fingers back laughing with tears in her eyes.

"You're hardly a slut for sleeping with your boyfriend." She quips raising a brow and crossing her arms.

"But that's exactly what I am because he is not my boyfriend. He may have walked away from me but I wouldn't have stayed. Not when he's hell bent on being sperm donor to Angel. No scratch that, not now he has *become* her sperm donor. Nothing has changed . . . it's just I can't seem to resist him. I'm barely functioning on my own. I'm not sleeping, I cry all the time, I'm all over the place emotionally. I'm a complete wreck but if he gets me alone I can't keep my hands off him, it's pathetic, shameful and I'm incapable of stopping myself." I sigh exasperated.

"It's fucking hot is what it is." She crawls to the end of the bed and sits crossed legged in front of me, her brows knit with consternation. "Don't get mad but I have to ask, is it so wrong he wants to help her out, if she is not lying that is? I mean if I couldn't conceive and I asked for your help, wouldn't you help or at least consider it?" The serious turn in the conversation was not what I was expecting and I am quiet while I consider her words.

I take her hand. "You know I would sweetie but then I don't want to steel your husband. If I thought for a moment she was genuine I would, maybe be a bit more understanding, but let's not forget I didn't get that chance." I pause because I would like to think I am being objective about this highly subjective situation and satisfied I continue. "Look this just fucking stinks. I can't be certain about everything but I am certain that she wants him. If he can't see, won't see what she's up to there is nothing I can do." I pause when I think of his expression, distant almost desolate eyes and I sigh heavily with my own sadness before I continue to explain our last encounter. "He did look sad though . . . when I gave him a different end scenario where Angel wants to tell the baby who the daddy is. It was like he hadn't actually thought about it. I know he'd never turn his back on his own child but it was like this was a revelation that . . . . . . Ow!" I try to sit but the few pins Vivienne managed to poke in effectively prevent that.

"You love him. I mean all that passion and insatiable lust aside you really love him?" She smiles softly still holding hands.

the Only Choice

"Too much." I can feel my eyes prickle and I fight the spill of tears as Vivienne re-enters the room.

"Right now." Vivienne bustles around me prodding and poking. "You've lost some weight around the waist but it seems to have gone to your boobs, lucky you." She winks playfully and I chuckle. She quietly pins my dress and Sofia goes to fetch some drinks, I ask for a herbal ginger and honey tea. It's my new favourite as it seem to really help with the nausea. It causes a raised brow or two but I just declare I'm on a health kick for the wedding. "How are you feeling sweetheart?" Vivienne whispers just as soon as Sofia is out of earshot.

"I'm good thanks Viv. It's not been the best time I'm not going to lie but—" I chatter on but she interrupts.

"No sweetie, I heard you'd not been feeling well and I need to know you're taking good care of yourself; extra care I mean." She holds my gaze and I suddenly want to be wrapped in her arms and tell her everything. Her kind smile and knowing eyes nearly break me but Sofia opens the doors and we both resume our positions. "Well, that should do. I've left a little room for growth." My head snaps and my eyes are wide with alarm. "I am sort of hoping your appetite returns. You are looking way too thin darling, bones are for dogs, men like some meat." She gives a generous jiggle with her gorgeous curves to emphasise her point.

I change back into my jeans, skinny black spaghetti strap top and soft grey hoodie. Sofia starts to stuff her overnight things into her large pink leather Tote with the care of a seasoned backpacker. She declares that tonight, with the help of the girls, we shall formulate a plan. A last minute sleepover for a few that couldn't make the hen weekend will turn my apartment into headquarters for 'Operation Get Daniel's Head Out Of His Arse.' Sofia is at saturation point with the wedding and needs another focus. I would quite like a quiet night in but as Maid of Honour, it's my duty to make her wishes reality and fixing my love life is her current wish. She is not the only one at saturation point.

I have seen Daniel every day at work since our 'first' date but he has kept himself to himself. He looks contemplative and distracted most of the time but he continues to work from the booth in the restaurant and meets me outside after each shift from work. I have resisted the temptation to accept a lift but do talk to him most of the walk home. My heightened sex drive is completely manageable when I am not in close proximity to him. It's not like I find myself dry humping inanimate objects for relief. It is just *him* that dissolves any self-control and since our date we have both kept a little distance. It's disconcerting that I hate the distance but need it at the same time. I can't think straight when he's there and I miss him when he isn't. I need to sort my head, my heart and my future and I am sick of my passive acceptance of Angel's interference. I am actually pleased about tonight, excited that at least some plan of action might be born.

We stop at the restaurant on the way back to mine to pick up some antipasti and other nibbles, a couple of bottles of wine and a few flavours of gelato. I leave Sofia to set up while I take a quick shower and change into my PJ's. We are only expecting Gaby, her partner Saskia and Sam from, well from a few places but my overriding memory of her is when she took me to Daniel's club as Lola. I physically shiver at my recall, Daniel's commands were harsh and calculated, his dominance was so cold, his touch left me empty and desolate. So different from his dominance with me alone, in the flat when we play or anywhere else for that matter; every command I tremble to obey, alive and sentient to his pleasure. His intuitive sensuality, his raw passion and attentive touch ignites every nerve in my body and I crave him like I need my next breath, he is my oxygen and fuck if I'm not selfish enough to want him to myself. It would appear that I don't share either.

I have fixed a pitcher of Virgin Mojito but add the rum to everyone's drink but mine, with the brown sugar and strong mint flavour I can hide the fact I'm not actually drinking alcohol. Besides the way we have all been laughing and messing around you would never know I wasn't three sheets to the wind. I have

the Only Choice

filled everyone in on the basic information and as if I would anticipate any different everyone is rightly outraged at Angel's unreasonable demands and are incredulous at Daniels unreserved acceptance. They all ignore my attempt to give a balanced view and agree that at the very least, I should have been part of the decision making process. I can't argue that. Gaby is trawling the internet for information about Angel and her hubby just to give us some visuals to vent our outrage. I feel all fired up but no actual plan has formed. I grab a pen and pad, determined to get something tangible out of this rapidly deteriorating drunken evening.

"Guys, come on now focus, what is my actual plan?" They all cough and frown trying to look serious and pensive. Sam slides in behind Gaby and watches the screen over her shoulder. Sofia sits tightly next to me looking expectantly at the blank note pad and Saskia just looks at me with an encouraging smile. "Right, so bottom line, I want my man back, to myself and I would quite like Angel to show her true colours to Daniel, that is. Yes?" I am faced with a flurry of excited nodding so I continue. "Right, so how do I do that?" And like a conductor silencing the orchestra with a skilful stroke of his baton; all movement ceases; all nods stop and smiles are replaced with frowns.

"You need evidence!" Saskia shouts and puts her hand up at the same time which makes us all laugh but it's a start.

"Yes, good, Daniel won't, for whatever twisted fucked up reason entertain that Angel has anything other than the most innocent of intentions, so I need to prove otherwise." I tap my pen on the pad, which is still blank but maybe not for long. "What evidence would prove she's a lying, manipulative—"

"You could ask her?" Sofia offers but clarifies when I just raise a brow. "No I mean she might just tell you, like gloat . . . some people are *that* stupid. I have a friend who's a cop and sometimes, he told me, they have little evidence but the criminal or whatever, will just confess after just a few questions. It's like they can't help themselves." She shrugs. "But you could tape her if she did. That would be proof." She sits back with a satisfied smile and chinks her glass with Saskia.

"I don't actually relish getting that close but I could ask her uncle Mr Wilson about the actual fertility issues. Get some details on the genetic likelihood that she can even have children, that might be a start." I nod and write that down as number one.

"I don't know Bets, however you put that it's either going to sound super creepy or mean and insensitive." Sofia knows my fear of being the villain and I nod because she has a point.

"I know but there might be a way of asking without really asking, I don't know . . ." My voice trails off because it doesn't sit well and I feel hideously uncomfortable delving into what could be just a terribly sad scenario if it turns out I'm wrong. But then Angel had no qualms letting Daniel blame himself all this time and manipulated that guilt to her advantage. I think I have some leeway here.

"You could ask her husband?" Sam offers and I look over to see a sneaky smile creep across her face.

"I don't know her husband." I reply.

"No, but *I* do." She turns the laptop round and there is a picture of Angel beside a dark haired man with dark features and a permanent tan. He is only slight taller than her and stocky. He is dressed in a tux and she is in a long red silk evening gown. The picture isn't recent because her hair is much shorter in the photo. Sam closes the lid of the laptop and coolly swirls her drink. We have all fallen silent waiting for her to elaborate and she does. His name is Sebastian, he is a member of the same club Daniel belongs to or belonged to. I have no idea if he is still a member and Sebastian or Seb always visits when he is in town and always asks for Sam, well always asks for Selena. She has known him for five years, three of which he has been married to Angel. Sam doesn't knows the specifics of their relationship but as far as she knew Angel had never been to the club so Sam would assume she either doesn't know, doesn't want to know or doesn't care.

"Why would he tell me anything?" I am intrigued enough to ask.

the Only Choice

"He wouldn't. But me on the other hand . . . Oh believe me honey. . . . he would tell me *anything* you want to know and I guarantee he wouldn't lie." She winks at me and I feel a flush of heat. She giggles, "I'm his Domme." We all breathe out a knowing 'oh' but the looks flying between us are anything but knowledgeable. Her lips curl in a warm knowing smile. "Look, it's simple, what I do, what he asks for . . . I could ask him for his pin number for his Swiss bank account number and for his first born and he would agree. All I'm saying is if you want truth, that is your plan A. Hell it should be your plan A through to Z." She nods to the laptop. Images are flashing like a strobe across my mind, the club, those rooms, crosses, whips and chains and I know how successful Daniel was at getting my truth. I don't doubt Sam for one minute but it's not like I can confirm that I completely understand without revealing a little too much information to everyone else.

"Plan A?" I almost regret asking.

"Plan A; he is flying in this weekend and I'm seeing him Saturday. You can be my partner, I will still ask the questions. You can tape it all and voila!–Proof, evidence the whole shebang." I heard Sofia's sharp intake of breath, she asks.

"Partners?" Her voice is shaky on my behalf but Sam eases the subtle tension with a loud laugh.

"Relax would you, this is actually perfect. He rarely wants sex and well, you would be long gone if he did. It's more of a show, a rather dramatic show of power, that type of shit. He is a masochist." She hums a little in thought. "But you would have to get a second sponsor to get in the club in the first place." She wiggles her fingers over her lips while she is weighing up some key information only she is privy to. "Seb can nominate you as my partner but you'd need another. It's not like the Christmas party, this is a very very exclusive club. You need two sponsors; I don't suppose Daniel?" I laugh out at this and she joins in. "No, I guess not . . . still the offers there honey and you know I'd keep you safe." She leans over and wraps her arm protectively across my shoulder and I tip my head into her hold.

"I know that Sam but I'm not sure I'm that good an actress to pull off an act like that?" I squeeze her hand. "So I think I'll go with *my* plan A." I shuffle and stand looking down at the one and only plan on my pad. A visit to Mr Wilson it is then. I offer to get refills before we huddle on the sofa together to indulge in an ultimate girlie flick. Dirty Dancing; happy to ignore the obvious age differences between sixteen year old Baby and middle aged Jonny, we all succumb to the innocence of romance and a great soundtrack.

I wake up early the next day, pretty much the only benefit from a sober girls' night in and it did mean I was able to fire off an email to Mr Wilson. There was a slim chance that he checked his emails and a slimmer chance that he would be in University at all in the holidays but I had to try. I wasn't sure how successful my plan A was going to be but I did also have the matter of making sure my place at University hadn't been jeopardised by Daniel's misguided assistance in gaining a Patent on my behalf. I really wanted to speak to Mr Wilson about that before the next semester. I was surprised that after my shower I had a reply and not an out of office notification either. He was only briefly back, in fact could meet me this afternoon as he was flying back out in the morning. I called Joe and switched my shift to this morning and spent the next fifteen minutes doing my best impression of a headless chicken.

With my change of shift I found it was strange working without Daniels ever present striking form as a recent but permanent fixture in the booth. He may not engage with me while I work but I am so attuned to him that I feel his absence like a physical hole in my chest. Unsettling as these feelings are, they are the driving reason I feel compelled to attack this situation, seek out confirmation and proof, indisputable proof and hopefully not piss off the man I am trying to convince in the process. It's a delicate balance and I can see that no one will benefit from an 'I told you so' situation. I just want this over so we can move forward,

Angel and baggage free. I am making the huge assumption he is not going to freak at my 'proof' but if I'm honest I can't even think about that right now, one drama at a time. The restaurant is unusually quiet and Joe lets me leave early so I don't have to rush and can enjoy at least part of the walk to the campus. My phone rings just as I round the corner from the restaurant.

"You changed your shift?" His clipped tone sounds irritated and it matches mine now I've taken his call.

"Is there something you want Daniel?" My tone is equally irritable.

"I thought you didn't mind the arrangement at the restaurant?" His voice softens clearly adjusting to my frosty response.

"I don't mind." My voice softens too and because I need to start making my intentions clear I decide to tell him a little more. "Honestly, I like you being there and this shift, I missed you."

"Ah baby, you made my day." I can hear his smile. "So where are you walking to?" His light casual question makes me stop in my tracks. I am quiet for some minutes as I scour my surroundings because there is no way he could know I'm walking. I can't see his car and I can't see him but I do now have an eerie feeling I am being watched. "Baby, you still there?" I don't answer but decide to slowly walk back to the restaurant because if it isn't Daniel, then whoever is reporting my whereabouts might still be there. I see the shadow move behind the darkened window and not that I see him but after several months of having him as my shadow I just know it's Patrick skulking behind the wheel of the blacked out Audi. I stand directly beside the door, staring at my distorted reflection. It is either the curve of the glass or I do, in fact, look that pissed. "Bethany?" His voice is no longer playful but has an edge.

"Daniel." I grit my teeth and I am sure he can hear the grind. "I don't need to tell you where I'm walking Patrick can do that for you." My voice is surprisingly calm.

"Ah." He breathes out a heavy breath like I have caused him a minor irritation.

"Ah!" I snap at this major violation. "You just can't help yourself can you! Christ Daniel I can't believe I actually thought you trusted me and that you were giving me some space. Why the fuck is Patrick following me? God, I'm such a fucking idiot—" My breathless rant is interrupted by his stern voice, deep and serious.

"—Are you finished?" I'm not finished but there is something in his tone that wisely prevents my verbal vomit. "I didn't want to do this over the phone Bethany. I wanted to tell you when I could be with you." He pauses and my anger has flipped a one eighty to anxiety in a second.

"What is it Daniel? You're scaring me." He is silent for an unbearable moment as I hear him draw in a deep slow breath. What scares me more is that Daniel, above anything, cares about my safety and this tone I recognise and I kind of wish he was here too.

"Kit flew into Paris last week and I have had Patrick keep an eye on you since then. I didn't want to tell you because you . . . well you were dealing with enough shit. I was hoping to wait until after the wedding, maybe take you away for a bit." I hear him swallow and I mirror that but my throat is too dry, my legs don't feel so stable and I lean against Patrick's car. He has got out and is just looking at me with a small kind smile which I try to return. "But I was going to have to tell you tonight because although she hasn't checked out she hasn't been back to her hotel in four days."

"But she's in Paris?" My voice is barely a whisper, I feel sick and shaky. I hadn't thought she would ever come back or maybe I just hoped she never would.

"It's still too close." He sounds frustrated. "A two hour train journey and difficult to trace."

"You think she's in London?" I can hear the panic in my voice and Patrick steps around the car and wraps his beefy heavy arm around my shoulder. He doesn't look entirely comfortable with the position but I am grateful for the gesture. Daniel lets out a

the Only Choice

heavy sigh.

"Baby, I don't know but I would really appreciate if you would let Patrick take you where you need to go." I find myself dumbly nodding which he obviously can't see. "Bethany?" His tone not really a question.

"Yes, of course, yes . . . that's very kind." I am mumbling, my head is a fuzzy daze and I would probably not make it to the end of the street without getting lost. So with absolutely no resistance I sit in the passenger seat when Patrick opens the door; my phone is still to my ear. "Thank you Daniel."

"Don't thank me baby, it's my job." His voice is firm and decisive and at times like this I love that he is so sure about us.

I tell Patrick where I need to be and try to process this new information. I think Kit would have to be pretty stupid to try anything, even coming anywhere near me and Kit is a lot of things but stupid isn't one of them. I wonder if it's me, that I am a magnet for crazy women and I shudder at the thought that Kit and Angel would ever cross paths. Regardless of my knowledge and experience of the crazy bitch genre I would never survive their combined evil force of nature. I persuade Patrick that I will be fine at the University and he agrees not to accompany me, on the condition that I let him take me home straight after my meeting, no deviations or detours. I walk the length of the corridor in the oldest part of the main building without seeing a soul. The polished wooden floor reflects like glass and is evidence of the lack of footfall during the holidays. I knock on Mr Wilson's door but there is no answer, the door is locked but I am a little early so I turn, lean heavily against the wall and slide down to sit on the floor and wait. I close my eyes and drift off to the haunting sound of Ellie Goulding Halcyon Days, feeling a surge of emotional tingles of track six, *Figure 8*. I snap my eyes open blinking back the rise of water behind my lids only to see a pair of sage green corduroy trousers.

Mr Wilson is smiling down at me as I fumble to remove my earphones and he fumbles to put his key into his office door.

"Hello Mr Wilson . . . Thank you so much for seeing me in your holiday. I am really grateful." I certainly sound grateful. He offers a generous smile in return and I follow him inside. I take a seat while he shuffles some papers on his desk and opens his computer, frowning at the screen as it takes its time coming back to life, whirring, clicking and moaning as if disgruntled to be disturbed from a deep slumber. I try to read his face as his eyes dart over the screen picking up salient information and dismissing what isn't. He sits back and looks intently at me. He looks well, his silver grey hair is a little longer with an unruly wave that looks rougish and suits him. He has a warm tan and his more casual polo shirt makes him look relaxed and approachable. Not that his more formal attire makes him unapproachable, his kind amenable nature makes that impossible.

"Bethany you don't need to worry, this misunderstanding over your patent application has been cleared with the very extensive report Stone R & D submitted. A copy was sent to Chris Taylor at ProProducts but I am afraid they have filled your position." His concern is genuine like this was somehow his responsibility.

"I couldn't go back there but thank you." My voice is quiet.

"There is nothing to thank me for my dear. It would seem Daniel got you into this mess but it would seem he's bent over backwards to get you out of it." His smile is wide and his sigh suggest it's 'whats to be expected,' this is Daniel Stone after all. "It is all sorted this end I just hope it's not caused too much trouble. You know I believe he would've had your best interests at heart. I have never seen him like this. He just isn't very good at not doing everything *his* way."

I sniff out a light laugh. "I had noticed. I am relieved it's sorted, really, it's almost all I could think about. I am so glad you could see me, I think I would've been a wreck if I had had to wait until October."

"I wouldn't have let you get kicked off the course and neither would Daniel." He nods and grins. I feel a sense of relief but it is only fleeting as what I have to ask next is above and beyond

the Only Choice

our professional relationship. I just pray it's not too much because I really value his friendship. I am just desperate. He sits forward. "There must be something else because we both know this could've been accomplished with a well constructed email or with a telephone call." He sees me swallow and it's loud enough to be audible even to his sometime selective hearing. "What can I help you with Bethany?"

I shift in my seat under his intense gaze and start to chew my lip. "It's not about my course." I return his stare trying to gauge whether I am wholly out of line.

"I gathered as much but really I think we are a little beyond the professional student professor relationship; well I would like to think so. I would like to think you consider me a friend and someone you could trust." His kind words are just the encouragement I needed to hear.

"It's about Angel . . . I need some information . . . personal information." He sits back with a frown but he raises a brow for me to continue. I don't know how much to reveal. I don't know how much he knows about the details of Daniel and Angels relationship. I know he doesn't hold his 'niece' in the highest regard but that doesn't mean Daniel would thank me for airing all his dirty laundry to someone he respects like a father. So with the care of navigating a minefield I try and explain why I need his assistance. "I believe she wants Daniel back and she is using their past and not in a good way."

"She is married Bethany are you sure about this?" He leans on his elbows his expression full of concern. I just widen my eyes and tilt my head in an expression that screams 'yes pretty sure.' He nods with understanding.

"I think she is trying to use a tactical pregnancy to her advantage. It's manipulative and cruel." I can feel my voice shake.

"Manipulative and cruel certainly sound like Angel and I know I am the last person besides Mrs W to think well of her the but even I would have trouble believing that she would do something so insidious as use a pregnancy against him. Besides being unlikely, why would Daniel go along with anything like that?" He lets out a puff of air and shakes his head in disbelief.

"He thinks he owes her and won't or can't see beyond that. I've tried, believe me." I emphasise these last words to try and highlight my exasperation. "I have tried to make him see what she's doing is wrong but he is stubbornly blinkered when it comes to her."

"Ha! Yes that does sound like Daniel, stubborn to a fault." He snorts but I interrupt him picking up on his last statement.

"Wait, why would it be unlikely?" I lean forward and I can see the internal struggle flash across his face as he decides whether this question is one question too far. I panic because I don't want to put him in that position and jeopardise this precious balance of friendship and trust. "Sorry Mr Wilson, I shouldn't have asked. You don't have to answer that." I reach for my bag feeling suddenly intrusive and uncomfortable.

"No, Bethany, it's fine, really. It's just that . . . she can't have children." He lets out a painfully heavy sigh. "I told you about Angels mother. She knew the infertility was genetic and despite the miracle of falling pregnant with Angel herself there were many many years of unbearable heartbreak and pain. She wanted to save Angel from that uncertainty, so she had Angel was tested when she hit puberty. Her mother didn't want her to go through the anxiety of years of false hope." He pauses, "I suppose with modern medicine, there is always the possibility of another miracle but I'm afraid it would have to be a miracle." He looks sad and I don't know whether that is because the story is sad, which it is or whether he is sad he told me.

"Daniel doesn't know this?" It is more of a statement than a question.

"Very few people do and I would appreciate it if it remained that way." I nod but I am trying to think how I can use this information. This changes everything and without the appropriate filter, I blurt out.

"Do you have proof?" I screw my face up and cringe as I hear my harsh words and recoil at his shocked expression. "I'm sorry, God I'm so sorry Mr Wilson . . . forgive me but Daniel needs to know this and he won't believe me, you have to tell him, he has to know." My voice pitch rises with each desperate word not helped by Mr Wilsons slowly shaking head.

"Bethany, I'm sorry *that* is not my tale to tell." I can see the sadness in his eyes and as much as I want to shake him and beg and plead for his help I can see he feels remorse at telling me this much. My only small comfort is that *I'm* not crazy and my spiddy senses were spot on. I just have to find another way to prove it. I lean down to pick up my bag and walk round to his side of the desk; I lean down and kiss him lightly on the cheek.

"Of course, I'm sorry I asked, please forgive me. I love him Mr Wilson, it clouds my judgement and my sensitivity. Thank you for all your help and I promise I won't betray your confidence but if you do find a way . . . I'd appreciate Daniel learning the truth, before it's too late." I walk to the door and turn on the threshold, my soft words drift as I leave the door to close. "Because it's not just about him anymore." My brief moment of elation from discovering the truth is surpassed by the realisation that nothing's changed and Angel still has Daniel exactly where she wants him, guilt wrapped around her bony finger.

Chapter Ten

MARCO HAS BEEN working extra shifts for the last few weeks because he too wants to go travelling after the wedding. He has only just come back from his holiday with Rose so he really needs to earn some serious brownie points if he was going to be allowed more time off. The result is that I hadn't seen him since our brief drink with Ethan, which made me think I hadn't seen Ethan since then either, just a few texts and the odd phone call. I had spoken to him after Tom's advice, specifically about my travel plans, as vague as they are. He has convinced me that travelling alone isn't such a great idea but my options are limited. Ethan had agreed to start his travels to coincide with mine, beginning with a few of the more obscure European cities. I would really like to visit Malmo in Sweden because I have a new found love of Swedish TV crimes, maybe then head down toward Vienna, Budapest and then on to the Dalmatian Coast before heading further East. My original thoughts had been along those lines but now I think a few cities then a peaceful beach for a week or two would be heaven. So I will need to speak to Ethan about how that might fit with his plans. None of these plans have I mentioned to my non-boyfriend and significant other but at least his mention of taking me away means

the Only Choice

we are on the same page regarding needing a break. He is just unaware that I am intending paying a single traveller supplement when I go. I know he might not like it . . . who am I kidding, he will completely freak that I have kept this from him.

My phone buzzes as my doorbell chimes.

"Were your ears burning?" I chuckle as I answer Daniels call.

"You are talking about me?" His deep voice flares my skin with a sprinkling of light standing hairs. "You have company?" He sounds confused and I realise Patrick must be outside. Something that only this morning would've had me spitting feathers but now I find gratefully comforting.

"No company, just talking to myself." I let out a light nervous laugh. "I haven't lost it but I'm getting there. Can you hang on I just need to get the door?" I tuck the phone against my shoulder and cheek.

"Sure, knock yourself out." I hear the echo on the call as the open door reveals his tall frame leaning against the banister on the landing opposite my apartment. His grin is infectious but it doesn't make me smile, it melts my core to liquid lust. I am acutely aware I haven't been alone with him since our 'first' date, something my body reacts to rectify. I step toward him, holding my breath and sucking in my bottom lip like I can already taste his intoxicating scent on my lips. My fingers twitch with residual memory of his smooth rough skin over tight toned muscles, his eyes bore into me and I have to exhale to expel the building heat in my body. I know my libido has not exactly being playing nice but this is so much more and I feel it in my bones. When I took his call this morning I became enlightened. I understood with absolute clarity that above all, for him, *it's* about me and that is utterly seductive and sexy as hell. I want to be consumed by him, I want his passion, his obsession. I want him to own me, mark me, and marry me. That is what I want now and I feel giddy with this self-discovery but unfortunately for the first time in my life I can't count on the one person I need to, me. I just don't trust myself. So for my sanity I just have to make sure this decision is the result of my brain and heart and not generated from somewhere lower. Until then I will have to keep this monumental revelation, to myself, for now.

He pushes himself off the banister and meets me in the centre of the hall, towering and firm, radiating heat and power and I pool before him. Ironic but true, I try and remind myself only time away will give me the clarity and peace of mind to marry this beautiful man but right now, I just want to wrap myself around every inch of him. This is us, we have our own *normal* and we belong together. I am beyond frustrated that I still need proof of Angel's deception but at least *I* know the truth. It is a start and what we have is worth fighting for. The intensity of his gaze sears my soul and I know in my heart he won't ever let me go and I don't ever want him to. As scared as his call this morning made me, I feel safe now. As perverse as his loyalty to Angel is I feel cherished now and as respectful of my wishes to keep his distance . . . I want him now. His hand cups my neck and tilts my head moving my face so his lips brush mine, his hold tightens and all air rushes from my lungs. Every hair, every nerve, every molecule crackles with latent lust and desire, poised to explode with his next touch and my heart hurts it is beating so hard.

"What do you want Bethany?" The timbre of his deep breathy voice is pure and raw.

"You." My words are stolen from my lips with the force of his unyielding mouth. He pulls me roughly against his rock solid frame exerting enough pressure in his fingertips to mark me and I tremble with the pleasure this thought alone evokes but I want more. He sucks, pulls and bites my now swollen lips. His tongue dances and plunges, urgent and demanding, fierce, possessive and I love it. I return his passion and grip him just as tightly. He pinches his fingers into my hair and pulls me back breaking our connection, I gasp for breath. His eyes are feral but his grin is deliciously wicked.

"Good answer." He stoops and sweeps me up high on to his shoulder. His hard muscle and bone winding me as I fold over, dangling and hopelessly trying to steady myself with fistfuls of his clothing. His loud slap on my arse echo's in the sparsely furnished hallway and I would be surprised if there wasn't a person in the building that didn't hear the noise closely followed by my surprised yelp.

He kicks my bedroom door open and slams it shut with such force the lock rattles and a sharp crack of wood fracturing is heard but with surprising restraint he bends and plops me gently on to my bed. I fall back onto my elbows, my knees slightly bend and my legs tremble as I hold the semi closed position fighting my wanton need to spread before him. He stands motionless but his eyes move slowly from my toes up my body, scorching with the blatant desire and my skin reacts in his wake as if teased by his feather light kisses, sensual and seductive. I wonder if I will ever cease to be shocked by his ability to draw such violent erotic reactions with barely a single touch. He slips his jacket from his shoulders and carefully folds and places it on the corner my bed and with a deliberate measured pace he starts to un button his shirt, with each pop I feel my heart beat jump a little faster, my panting breath a little sharper and a little more moisture pools inside.

"Still need a little space?" His voice is deep, his tone is light but I can see the seriousness of his words in his slightly narrowed eyes. I shake my head. We still have a heap of shit to deal with but one thing I am certain of, at least at this moment, is I do *not* want a little space. I want no space, I want negative space. "Answer the question Bethany?" His dominant growl causes a delicious shiver to flash across my skin.

"No Sir." I swallow and lick my dry lips, my voice is a raspy whisper. His shirt is open and he has unclipped his belt so his suit trousers have dropped to hang low, revealing the dusting of dark hair that gathers to from a slightly darker line of hair dipping below his belt. My eyes are fixed on his hovering hand, just at his zip which is curved with the bulge of his straining erection. His light chuckle makes me break my hypnotic gaze and meet his heated stare.

"I'm going to make you beg." He starts to draw the zip down and a small whimper escapes into my throat.

I laugh to try and hide some of my desperation. "And I thought you liked a challenge." He raises a curious brow. "Because that really isn't going to take long." Before he can make another move I sink back onto the bed and sigh, shamelessly pleading. "Please, please Daniel, please Sir, please, please fuck me." My knees straighten and I drop my hand to rest on top of my panties with my middle finger just tucked under the elastic. I hear his groan and sneak a look to see him shed the last of his clothes. This is different, it is usually me naked whilst he is fully clothed. But he looks far from vulnerable, he looks potent, hungry and indecent or maybe I'm projecting. He kneels at the end of the bed, my toes touching his skin. This first skin on skin is all I can feel, this contact is the source of a wave of pure heat that ripples then spreads like a wildfire through my body.

"Oh baby, that's not begging." His gruff voice and veiled threat is like a touch-paper to my incendiary desire. "Spread."

I hear his deep throaty groan as I spread my legs wide and he hears my higher pitched cry when he places his firm hands on the inside of my thighs, his fingertips pressing the crease where my thigh meets my most sensitive skin. His touch feels hot and solid and he presses the heel of his hands hard pushing me wider, holding the tension as my muscles rebel against the pressure. I squeeze my eyes shut absorbing the sensory overload, pain of muscles stretched to unbearable tension, sensitive folds spread wide, open, vulnerable, cooled with exposure and heated with his breath. So intimate and so fucking sexy I know I am going to shatter as soon as he touches me, however he decides to touch me. His dominant mode is unmistakeable. I decide to play it safe, I am in no state to endure his blend of sweet torture and I am not stupid enough to test his endurance. I would break in half before he would even break sweat.

"Please Daniel may I come?" My voice is shaky and I curse

that my body is so fucking sensitive and more so, that I can't tell him why. He looks up with a curious expression and I shrug as if I am just as curious.

"Really?" His surprise is genuine, mine is more resigned.

"Really, I'm sorry but really, please may I come?" I can feel my face flash with colour and I am glad that my body has the grace to be embarrassed at how easy I am. He laughs and his breath blasts my core and causes me to jump his fingers grip in reflex, holding me immobile.

"Interesting . . . but no need to apologise. I will try and not let it go to my head." He quips but I laugh at his lame pun. "And since you remembered to ask, you may come. But don't get used to having your own way baby because the rest of the night is mine." He disappears low and I feel the electric pulse of his sweeping tongue as he drags it steadily along my folds and purses his lips over my core and sucks, deep and swirling pressure. My hips dig into the mattress and my back arches off the bed so far I am sure it is a perfect semi-circle. My fingers grip the sheet and my head is pressed into the pillow, all in instant, all shocking violent reactions to this cresting onslaught of pleasure. He holds me as my body shakes, shudders and falls, spiralling and riding wave after convulsive wave of exquisite erotic indulgence.

"Fuck Bethany you are amazing, you taste amazing, *you* are so fucking amazing." He pitches up and puts his arms either side of my torso leaning on his elbows so he is only barely above me. His heat almost as intense as his perfect blue eyes.

I let out a deep satisfied sigh and snicker. "Having trouble with your adjectives Mr Stone." I tilt my head and look around my room. "I know I've got a thesaurus somewhere, arghhh!" I squeal and wriggle as his fingers dart to my side below my ribs and dig and wiggle, ultimate torture.

"No." His lips are a hairs breadth from mine, his serious eyes penetrate and he stills, holding me secure. "My tongue has just been better employed fulfilling pleasure rather than forming eloquent words that would still fail to describe you or what you are to me." His smile is breath-taking and he looks rightly smug; his words far exceed any compliment, they are flawless. I tense my tummy muscle and pull myself to meet his lips but he smiles wide and shakes his head. "Ah ah Miss Thorne. Since you offer no challenge where begging is concerned let's see how long before you are screaming for me to stop." He grazes his teeth along the shell of my ear and down my neck before his sinks harder into the soft flesh. I let out a sharp cry of pain and a shiver of luxurious bliss that only comes with acceptance, I am his. His to torture, tease and tame, his to make beg, scream and his to mark. It's hedonism, it's heaven, it's hell and I want it all.

If I ever doubted he was a man of his word, it was proven irrefutable that late afternoon and early evening. He played my body like an artist bringing me to levels of heightened ecstasy I hadn't the imagination to even dream. Every millimetre of my skin was stroked and teased, delighted and dazed I fell again and again, insatiable at first, demanding and needy morphed into docile assent as utter exhaustion crept into my muscles and bones. He moved inside me with brutal passion and tender adoration in equal measure holding back his own release until my muscles finally gave up there tentative hold of my bones and I sank limp but managed to mouth out the words, my begging words to stop. Our bodies once slick with heated sweat had cooled with his measured strokes but warmed again after my plea, he picked up his pace once more and with a few final deep thrusts and a unexpected change in angle and grind he threw his head back and growled as I join him in what I pray is the end of this marathon session.

I don't remember how he took my dress off. I do remember him tearing my panties down my legs and I am grateful I am naked now as I relish the feel of his sticky skin against mine. Our legs are entwined and his strong arms hold me flush against him. I would be holding him too if my muscles were responding to my brain but they are not. I would've have offered to fix a drink or run a bath, but nada, a jelly fish has more rigidity than I do. My body is useless and my mind isn't much better; a mush of climax inspired euphoria, mixing with the inevitable dampening doses of reality and fucked up visions of my future. I reflectively squeeze him as he shifts to move because I don't want to lose this feeling, because right now I feel perfect, we feel right and I feel safe. So just for one more moment please don't move. Somehow sensing my silent plea he relaxes back pulling me tighter and kissing my hair. I let out a shamelessly satisfied sigh and he laughs.

"How are you feeling?" His voice is deep but he sounds sleepy, to be fair I am impressed he can speak at all. I know I will have to communicate in a series of grunts and sighs. I repeat my satisfied sigh followed but an equally gratified moan, muscles not quite responding to my desire to stretch. He chuckles, "Good to know." His sigh sounds like mine. I hear his phone ring again, it was what caused him to move last time but this time his shift is more determined and he slides from under me. "Looks like someone's keen to test my temper." He picks up his trousers and fishes his phone from the pocket. He frowns but only briefly, he swipes to take the call .He strides out of the bedroom without glancing my way but not before I hear him say Angel's name in a soft tone that makes me so fucking jealous I forget it's his release currently running down my leg.

The bedroom is dark and I have closed my eyes but moments before sleep steels me a painful bright light assaults my lids and I pinch them tighter. This isn't the light from a doorway. Daniel has switched the main light on and I can hear him picking up his clothes and treading with deliberate heavy steps. I roll onto my side and wince at the stiffness of my muscles and soreness of everything else. Blinking to adjust to the harsh light I shield my eyes with my hand and try to focus on the movement at the end of the bed. He has his back turned and he already has his trousers and shirt on. He is bent over slipping into his shoes and I can see his jaw is clenched but even if I couldn't I can feel the tension.

"Daniel? What is it?" I am more awake now and carefully pull myself up to sit against the headboard. I tuck the sheet under my chin, a flimsy barrier but one I clutch when he turns to face me his face dark with fury and rage. "Shit Daniel what is it?" I want to ask what's happened with Angel but I don't want to know anything about her poison and she is poison.

"I'm so fucking angry I can't even look at you!" He grates and snaps his head away from me. He reaches to grab his jacket. I quickly scramble to the end of the bed and hold his wrist before he pulls away. He looks with disgust at my hand and I feel like I have somehow infected him and let go.

My voice is quiet and he won't meet my eyes. "Daniel what is it? What have I done?"

"You have no fucking right! My decisions. My choice. My life. It has nothing to do with you!" He spits these words like daggers and they slice straight through my soft flesh, leaving chunks where my heart should be. He lets out a heavy sigh. Someone has clearly just informed him not only where I have been this afternoon but also the content of the meeting.

"'Nothing to do with me'? Am I hearing that right? 'Your life, your choices' and that has nothing to do with me?" He shakes his head and I know he is fighting to rein in his temper, he is clearly not a fan of *my* stalker talents. "I'm just trying to get some answers for you." I don't want a screaming match and to go over and over the same shit. He knows all my arguments but blindly refuses to acknowledge any part of them.

"No Bethany, I don't need answers. I need you to stop. Stop this now and I would appreciate your pathetic attempts at playing detective to stop before you hurt anyone else." Since he doesn't look hurt he just looks pissed I can only assume he is referring to Angel. I doubt she's hurt but she will be delighted that I have just royally fucked up. I don't know how to get him to understand.

"I'm sorry you find my attempts to secure our future pathetic but since you don't seem to give a shit I thought one of us should try, but you are right, I don't want anyone getting hurt. I'll do anything to prevent that." I try to keep my voice calm and not reflect the building despair I feel inside. His shoulders relax and he runs his hand softly over my cheek.

"This has nothing to do with you baby, you have to leave it to me. I don't want you getting hurt." His face is impassive but his eyes hold something and I can't tell if its sadness or regret but for the first time his words give me a little encouragement. I know his primary concern is me but he just said that I should leave *it* to him. Maybe he is already investigating my suspicions, he certainly looked troubled and pensive enough when I first talked about the future of Angels child.

"You'll look into it?" I can't hide my hopeful tone but it's misplaced. His cold eyes shut down and his jaw locks frozen.

"There is nothing to look into. Now fucking drop it. I mean it Bethany . . . you need to drop this." He snaps and I recoil with the understanding of his words. He turns and walks, out of my bedroom and out of my flat.

I throw myself hard back on to the bed with pure frustration. I can't let this go when I know she's lying but will I lose him in the process? The thought alone is enough to crack my heart in a million pieces. If I do nothing she will undoubtedly work her way back into his life one way or another, because she is determined and desperate. She may be calculating and cruel wielding guilt like she does but that is irrelevant if Daniel can't see it and more over he has told me explicitly to stop. If I manage to get proof, how do I give it to him in a way that won't break us? Honestly, even if that is the case I would rather he was with someone else than trapped by her. There is always the slightest chance that he would be so grateful of his narrow escape that he would forget my deception and forgive my interference. I have to hope for the possibility that he will forgive me. My head is spinning with unknown outcomes and broken hearted scenarios but one thing is crystal clear, I still have to get proof. I pick up my phone and scroll through my recently dialled numbers.

"Bets, had fun the other night we should—" She answers my call with a bright cheerful voice, happy to chat but I cut her short as politely as I can.

"Hey Sam, I need help with Plan B." The line goes quiet and

I can hear the sound of high heels clipping along a floor, then a door suction shut.

Her voice is still hushed but she sounds excited. "Oh Bets, it'll be fun but are you sure?"

I don't share her enthusiasm and her definition of fun and mine are probably not in the same ball park but I am certain this is now my *only* plan. This is my last ditched attempt, balls to the wall and a winner takes it all showdown. If this fails I have nothing left because if it comes down to my hunch against his history with Angel I know how *that* fairy tale ends and Disney have yet to set the music to the 'ditched lover single mother movie.' "One hundred percent." My voice is determined but I can see my hands shake a little.

"Tomorrow night then, come to me for six because you will need some extra time to get used to the outfit." She doesn't hear me struggle to swallow as my mouth dries. "And you still need a sponsor honey . . . I could ask one of my clients but if they are there they will expect to . . . well—" She hesitates and I jump right in with panic in my voice.

"—No No, that's fine. I know someone." I offer but at the same time challenge the wisdom of my 'better the devil you know' approach.

"All righty then see you at six, don't forget the recorder. Gotta go babe can't wait. Always wanted to be a Bond girl." She giggles and hangs up and my mind races to picture the Bond girl that was a Domme, like my brain has time for trivia. My next call is a little more tricky. I slip a T-shirt over my head and walk to the kitchen, next to the phone is a basket full of crap, vouchers, pennies, hair bands and business cards. I easily pick out the one I want; it's thicker, slicker and elegant like the companies owner. Two cards had slipped into my skirt pocket that day at Daniel's office, only one of the cards Daniel had destroyed. I type the number and save the contact to my phone. It rings for several seconds and I glance at my watch unaware it had gotten so late, eleven thirty is a bit late to be making a non-emergency call. I

the Only Choice

shake my head because to me, this is an emergency.

"Sinclair." Jason's voice sounds deeper than in person.

"Jason, it's Bethany Thorne." I pause but he makes no sound, so with a false sense of confidence that I know I will be drawing on frequently over the next few days I continue. "I need your help."

"Why do I get the feeling I'm not going to like this?" His laugh has a light rumbling quality but he is not wrong.

"Oh I know you are not going to like this but I'm going to ask you anyway." I draw in a deep breath and I can hear him do the same. "I need you to be my sponsor for the club." I hear him expel a sharp laugh but he is still quiet, waiting, so I clarify. "It's only for one night, tomorrow night." As if that makes it all right.

"I never thought I looked that stupid but clearly I do. Why on earth would I do that Bethany?" He snorts with amusement.

"Because if you don't I will have to ask a stranger." My clipped response has him cursing. It was a bit of a leap to assume he would agree, he doesn't really know me and he has a vested interest in not getting involved. But when he handed me his card at Daniels office he looked genuinely alarmed at the prospect that I might visit the club alone. I was just hoping I hadn't read him wrong.

"Aw Fuck Bethany, you can't do that." His voice sounds resigned and I can't help a small satisfied smile creep across my lips. "Aw shit!" He curses as he recognises his own defeat.

"And I would appreciate if you didn't tell Daniel." I add, at this he laughs loudly.

"Oh yes, because that was definitely my next call, 'Hey Daniel I'm taking the love of your life to the most depraved sex club in London.'" He mimics.

"I didn't say you had to take me." I correct him on this but not that I may no longer be the love of Daniel's life.

"You think I'm not!" His voice is incredulous. "Why the fuck are you doing this Bethany? Apart from wanting me to lose my job."

"You won't lose your job if he doesn't find out and I have no intention of telling him. Do you?" I need to make that clear because I lose everything if he finds out. I need to let him learn the truth in a way that doesn't irrevocably break us but that's for another day, first I have to get the proof.

"Fuck no! But why Bethany? Seriously, what are you doing?" We both know he has already agreed but he needs something more. He might be risking more than his job if Daniel finds out.

"The right thing." I exhale before I put the phone down. God I hope it's the right thing.

Chapter Eleven

DESPITE THE UTTER exhaustion I feel in every part of my body most of the time, I am unable to have an uninterrupted night sleep. Last night I thought I would tear my hair out I was so restless; mind racing, twitchy legs, itchy hair and random hot flushes filled with anxiety. I would put this worst night to date, down to the day and evening ahead but regardless, these sleepless nights are a consistent recurring struggle. I decide to go back to Dr Ward because this doesn't feel normal. The waiting room is chaos. There is some sort of flash crowd gathering of new mums and crying babies or 'baby clinic' Dr Ward enlightens me with a warm smile. My face must look like an impression of Munch's The Scream. I'm not ready . . . I am so not ready . . . I am never going to be ready.

"Bethany . . . what can I do for you?" She only glances up momentarily before reading her notes on the screen. "You have another check up in a few weeks . . . so what seems to be troubling you or is it nothing to do with the baby?" Satisfied with her scan of my history she turns her full attention to me, a shadow of concern flits across her kind face.

"I don't think its the baby. I just feel so tired and I'm not sleeping. I feel sick all the time and recently I have felt anxious

". . . you know unsettled. Last night was the worst and I was hoping you could perhaps give me something to calm me or help me sleep?" Dr Ward sits back. She starts to unwrap the cuff to take my blood pressure.

"I see." She starts to pump the air into the cuff. "Have you been taking your vitamins?"

"Oh . . . well . . . I did buy some but maybe not everyday." I bite my lip and cringe.

"Are you eating regularly and well . . . a good balance?"

"I haven't felt much like eating but when I do it isn't junk. I just feel sick so its hard."

"Yes I understand but lack of food will affect your energy levels. Your body will divert its resources to the baby so you must make sure there is enough for you. It could be why you are so tired." She lets the air deflate. "Your blood pressure is a little low. Pregnancy takes a lot out of your body. You need to make it your priority. I know this was a surprise to you but it is happening now and you need to take it seriously." Her words may sound like a reprimand but they act like a wake up call. "Your friends, I am sure are thrilled and will be happy to help if you ask . . . It is not a great time to go it alone Bethany when you don't have to." I wrinkle my nose and she raises her perfect brow. "You haven't told anyone have you?" I shake my head. "Not even the father?"

"Especially not the father . . . not yet." I add at her sudden sympathetic expression. "I will. I don't have a problem with telling him. It is just the timing is a little off. Same goes for my friends." It is too complicated to summarise so I simply shrug it off.

"I see. Look Bethany considering the circumstances it is entirely normal for you to feel anxious, unsettled and exhausted. I would consider it *not* normal if you weren't. You know I can't prescribe anything to help you sleep?" She smiles as I nod my acknowledgement. "There is nothing wrong with you or the baby. The anxiety I believe will lessen the more people you can share this with but I can't promise the exhaustion will get better without you taking better care of yourself." She puts her pen flat on the desk because common sense seems to be the only thing she is dishing out today.

"I will . . . I promise." I reach for my shoulder bag and although she has told me nothing exceptional I do feel better just knowing feeling like shit, is to be expected. I am, in fact normal. My shift starts soon and I find I have to jog through Green Park or I will be late. I forgo my earphones and listen to the steady fall of my feet hitting the pavement as I find my rhythm. I know I am not going to manage to jog the entire journey my body is fighting me with every step. I have even cut across the grass to shorten the route. I practically collapse at the railing just outside the park entrance. I easily spot Angel leaving Daniels building. I no longer feel the burn in my muscles from exertion but I do feel sick at the sight. She is fresh faced and flushed. I drop my head to my knees, I didn't make eye contact so I don't think she saw me, another few minutes to catch my breath and we will have both moved on.

The wheels of the taxi stop directly in front of me and I look up to see the open window and a knowing smile on Angel's face. "You look like you are struggling would you like a ride?" Her tone is kind and I can't see anything particularly sinister in her eyes so I guess now is as good a time as any, to try and uncover her true intentions. Besides, in the light of Dr Ward telling me I need to start taking better care of myself, her offer is appreciated.

"Actually that would be very kind, thank you." I stand as she opens the door and I slide in next to her. "I'm not usually this exhausted. I think I might be coming down with something." I give a weak smile and inwardly cringe at the state I must look, sweaty, out of breath and I probably stink too. Whereas she is immaculate, serene, perfect and has just left Daniel's apartment in the middle of the day. He is unlikely to be there at this time but she obviously has complete access.

"You do look pale are you keeping well?" Her lips try to curl in a smile, I think, but it looks more like a smirk and now I am starting to get that gut feeling again.

"Angel, this is kind but I'm sure you don't want to do small talk. Is this just a coincidence or do you have something specific you would like to talk about?" I fail to hide my own irritation. She sighs as if this meeting is equally tiring for her.

"Well, it is a coincidence, but I did want to speak to you. Lucky for me your subtle attempt to stalk was so obvious. Daniel isn't staying here by the way I just came to pick up some post." She frowns when she notices my whole body relax and now she looks irritated that she has unintentionally eased my mind. "I doubt it was your intention but thank you for pushing Daniel." She draws in a deep breath and seems to enjoy the enforced pause a little too much, a satisfied expression spreads across her face. She finally turns to me and her smile slips and her frown deepens with seriousness. "I don't think I have ever seen him quite so angry. I want to make sure you stay away. You have hurt him enough . . . now it is my turn." She stops herself, cruel amusement curling her thin red lips. She shakes her head and whatever image away. "So I just want to be sure." I am speechless so she carries on. "Daniel wants me. He just doesn't know it yet, but he will, we have history." She tips her head and whispers. "Do you really think you stood a chance? Look how close we've become, it's been what? . . . a few months and he's already going to give me his child."

"Can you even have children?" I ask bluntly because she set the precedent for the cruel tone of this confrontation.

"Miracles do happen Bethany, after all look at you. I mean you can't possibly think he was serious about a long term relationship with you. I am astounded you lasted as long as you did but like I said . . . miracles." She simpers out a light laugh filled with mockery. "Even if you were really still together, how long do you think you would have? I am his first love Bethany you need to think of that before you make more of a fool of yourself." She reaches to comfort me with her tiny fingers but hesitates and wisely withdraws.

"Do you really love him?" I manage to ask but my words are

the Only Choice

barely audible above the diesel engine of the taxi.

"Would that help? Would you keep away if I did? Would it make a difference to the outcome? Will it stop him coming back to me? Not in the least . . . Ah look we're here at your little place of work." She nods toward the restaurant but I am afraid she has answered all her own questions with that one answer. *No not in the least.* "This has been nice Bethany." She smiles sweetly like you would to a dear friend. "I hate to repeat myself but I will make an exception, you would be wise to keep away Bethany. Do yourself this one favour and forget about him. It is so undignified to chase." She smiles with pity this time.

"Isn't that what you're doing?" I exit from the door she holds open.

"No Bethany I don't chase. I catch." She slams the door with more strength than I would credit her tiny frame. It makes me jump with the finality of the gesture.

I didn't get a call from Daniel all morning and he didn't come to the restaurant today. I miss him every minute but I am not surprised and it is probably a blessing in disguise given how distracted I have been since I spoke to Jason and Sam. My nervous sickness today at least has nothing to do with my growing peanut in my belly. I haven't actually checked but I think six weeks should be about that size. No, today is all about my debut as a dominatrix. I'd laugh if I wasn't so scared and didn't have so much riding on my performance tonight. I spoke to Patrick when I saw him outside my place and before I got the cab to Sam's apartment. I draw huge comfort from Daniel's constant protective nature, so much that he would keep Patrick watching over me, regardless of how pissed off he might be. I told Patrick my plan to visit a friend, I'd share a cab with her to drop her at work before heading back to mine. I assured him he didn't have to watch me but I could tell by his smile that, that wasn't my decision to make. At least he had a rough idea how the evening would look and hopefully he wouldn't look too closely.

I wave to Patrick as Sam lets me in. She is wearing a fluffy pink onesie with tiny white bunnies, her skin is flawless rich coffee without a bit of make-up and her hair is wrapped in a towel fresh from a soak. I laugh as I follow her into her apartment and straight into her bedroom. "And this outfit would be the 'dominatrix for pacifists' option, what would they call you dressed like that?" She laughs too, critically regarding the super cute, polar opposite to the BDSM image of clothes, she's wearing.

"Hey sweetie I could be dressed like Mary Fucking Poppins but they would still call me Mistress Selina when I have a whip in my hand." She picks up her glass and jiggles the ice. "It's early so this is just tonic would you like something stronger?"

"Oh no I'll be fine, tonic will be fine." I may sound a little uncertain but my smile is forcing confidence that is obviously convincing.

She shrugs and smiles back. "No Dutch courage this time Bets, maybe you're a natural at this after all?" She winks and heads to the kitchen to refill her drink and grab one for me, I shout after her.

"Oh no I still need the Dutch courage I just need so much I won't be able to function. Tonight I am going to pretend I'm on stage, that this is a play and I'm having an out of body experience." I take the glass and smile at her confused face, she shrugs again.

"Hey, whatever gets you through." She starts to pull out some dull matt bin liners and a fist full of straps and belts. "You'll be fine, Jason signed you in and I spoke to him. I wouldn't tell him why you're there or who you were playing with but I did tell him you'd be safe, that you were a dear friend and my responsibility. I nearly told him I'd have you back before curfew he sounded so much like a damn father." She scoops up her collection of materials and drops them in my lap, she laughs loudly at my look of shock. She's expecting me to wear this? "And he said he was meeting you directly after and I mean *directly,* you are not to leave the room unaccompanied. He made me promise." My look of shock has turned to horror. She turns unfazed and sits herself

the Only Choice

in front of her dressing table that looks more like a Sioux science lab, with lotions, potions and scalps. "Get your arse in gear girl we still have to go over the questions. If you've showered already you can just put that on and I'll do your make-up and hair when I'm done." I am speechless but her commands and tone have me moving to obey and I realise we are both naturals, she's the dominant and I'm definitely the submissive.

I actually have a hundred questions but I had to pick just a few so he wouldn't get suspicious and Sam didn't want a script just a general area of interrogation. She explained that there is a flow of information, a rhythm with every demand and yield and if she had to stop to check her notes, well it's just not very professional. I am not surprised she prides herself in her work, she always looks exquisite and there is a reason she is sought after and can charge what she does. I may not share her skill set but I do share her work ethic and tonight I will endeavour to be just as professional, just not a true professional. We had agreed on three questions. I want to know why he was here in the UK, that question may answer either his business intentions or indicate his relationship with Angel. I want to know how 'happily' they are married, although I know from her perspective the relationship is over I am curious whether he has any idea. It is possible he is unaware what his wife's plans are exactly. The last question, and I have no idea how Sam is going to integrate this into a sexual scenario but I want to know whether he is aware of the infertility pretence she is asserting.

I still haven't changed and now my nerves are bubbling in my tummy and are making me twitchy. I finger the slippery material in my lap, not bin liners after all but a black rubber vest. Sam assures me it's a dress but there is no way that is stretching over my arse let alone reach my knees. She has lent me a thigh high pair of black leather stiletto lace up boots and a little draw string leather sack with, she tells me, my props for the evening. I take my bundle and make my way into the bathroom where I quickly strip down leaving my panties on. I take the vest, it is cold, slippery and doesn't stretch as much as you would think. I put both my arms through the bottom and try to slip my body through the tiny gap, using my elbow and hands to grip and stretch. I don't think I have ever felt less sexy and more fat as I have to pinch and fold my skin into the material which snaps viciously back punishing my body for its intrusion. Like an over stretched rubber band I pull the material out at my widest point easing it over my hips and rolling it down as far as it will go. It smells funky, looks a mottled grey colour and barely covers my butt; but I'm in, a feat in itself and I let out a victory breath.

The mirror in the bathroom is small and I can't really see myself and I am going to need to sit to put the boots on so I return to the bedroom. Sam is dressed in a red PVC cat-suit, skin tight and shiny. Her hair has been scraped back and is slick and smooth, pulled high on her head in a long swishing pony tail with extensions for added volume, it's spectacular. She winks at my dropped jaw and stunned gaze and licks her finger, touches her jutting hip and makes a hissing sound. Damn right she looks hot. I nervously look down at the inner tube I'm currently sporting and wonder how we are supposed to pull off a double act. She laughs at my expression but doesn't comment she simply takes my hand, sits me at the dressing table and starts to work her magic. But I am going to need a bit more than Bibbedy Bobbedy Boo if I am going to pull this off.

I could kiss her, no mice or pumpkins necessary but the transformation is amazing just swap Cinders for *Underworld* Selene. My hair has been slicked and tucked into a net and I am wearing a blue black sleek wig, cut short in a sharp angled bob. My skin is pale in comparison and she has my eyes heavy, dark and sultry. I declined the blue contacts as unnecessary, I have no intention of letting anyone get that close and besides I have tried them before and I'll end up crying all night. She finishes with a nude lip gloss and motions for me to stand, holding what looks like industrial sized hair spray she drags me into the hall and proceeds to spray me down with a silicone gel. I squeeze my eyes shut and hold my breath as she turns and turns me, making sure every inch of my dress is covered. I gasp for air once I am back in her room and before I can ask 'what the fuck' she points to her full length mirror attached to the back of her door.

"Wow." I mouth the words because no sound comes out and she giggles. "No seriously wow, Sam!" She puts a protective arm around my shoulder and hugs me.

"I know Bets, what can I say, I had good source material but you look smoking hot, even if I do say so myself." She lets me go but I am still staring at my reflection. I don't recognise myself; the dress is no longer mottled grey but ultra-shiny, sleek and super tight. My waist looks tiny, the tight material emphasises the curve of my hips and slope of my backside, even I can't resist stroking the tempting curves. Christ! My breasts look massive, pushed high and squeezed together, a precarious balcony of soft flesh ready to tip as the material of the dress warms, stretches and loses its tautness. It looks like I've been finely coated in a slick of sexy oil. The leather boots cling to my legs, the laces look like a ladder up my thigh and the band of exposed skin separating the dress from the boots looks smooth and delicate. A stark contrast to the harsh polished rubber and all the more tantalising for being exposed.

"Sorry Bets but you need to lose the panties, can't have VPL in rubber, it's just wrong." She snickers as I turn to assess her comment. She's right the lines do look wrong against the smooth finish everywhere else the dress touches but shit I didn't bring a g-string or anything that small. I admonish my misplaced conservatism. It's not like I have to broadcast the fact and it's not the first time I've gone commando. It's just the first time I've gone commando without Daniel. I shimmy out of the offending article and tug at the hem of the dress's resistant material, which snaps back a little higher as if to mock my attempt at modesty.

Sam hands me my coat and after reluctantly refusing a 'on for the road' drink we head out. Sam's flatmate is posing as me tonight and I have given her my jacket and keys. She is a little older but similar build and has long dark hair and if we bundle into the cab together hopefully Patrick won't notice and will follow her back to my flat. She said she would wait there for an hour before changing and heading back. I tried to apologise for all the trouble but both girls laughed off my concerns, loving the intrigue and deceit, declaring it was all very 'James Bond.' As the cab moves through the busy late night traffic and the sun finally gives up its hold on the evening I take a moment to look into my bag of tricks. I palm the small recording device I borrowed from Marco, he loves his gadgets and I just knew he would have some sort of spy recording device. It's shaped like a bullet and is similar size too, small but with a USB connection. It's cute and compact which is lucky because there is absolutely only one place I can comfortably hide it in this outfit. The other object has a small black lacquered handle with a button end, pulling it discreetly the ends fan out on my hand, twenty or thirty strips of velvet soft suede. My fingers twist the material and I pull the strands through my hand. I can't imagine this being anything other than sensual to the touch, its light feathering kissing the skin would be exquisite, even wielded with a heavy hand I can't imagine it would hurt but maybe that's the illusion. I fold the tentacles back into my purse wondering if I will actually have to use them tonight.

"It's a training flogger . . . I thought you might like something to keep your hands busy. Chewing your fingers raw might give you away as not a natural Domme." Her laugh is lightly musical interrupting my thoughts, but I am pleased she thought about these practicalities. My fingers were already nervous twiddling the delicate strands before I hid the flogger away.

We reach the door and a wave of panic washes over me, cooling my skin and draining the colour from my face. I have tucked the recorder between my breasts, hidden from view and pretty damn secure unless I melt from the heat I'm generating. Which might be a real possibility because although this material is natural it's not exactly breathable. Sam turns me around and slips a soft blindfold over my eyes the only problem is I can see through

the Only Choice

the holes. I let out a nervous laugh. "Sam this blindfold is broken." I whisper and she giggles. "Not a blindfold Bets, I just thought you'd appreciate the anonymity, might help you relax because you look like you've got a six foot spike wedged up your arse." She whispers back.

I know she is trying to make me feel relaxed with her friendly jibe and her effort is appreciated, even if I don't actually feel relaxed. But she's risking a lot and I don't need my apprehension rubbing off on her. I nod and try a light laugh that almost sounds natural and I flash a bright 'game-on' smile. "Let's do this. I won't let you down." I slip my hand into hers and I am grateful for the comforting squeeze she gives me.

"I know that Bets and I'll keep you safe. Who knows you might take a trick or two back for your Mr Stone." She wiggles her brow and I almost splutter and choke. "No,. . maybe not." She pats my back affectionately. "I can no more see him submitting, as I can see you demanding he submit but I guess tonight you might get to prove me wrong." The imposing black gloss Georgian door opens ominously and I take a deep breath. Showtime.

Chapter Twelve

SAM HOLDS MY hand as we check our coats and she continues to hold it as she leads me across the darkened room toward the bar. The instrumental music is loud with a sensual slow heavy bass. The booths that edge the richly decorated social area are all occupied with couples or small groups. The scene is really no different from other exclusive private clubs, other than the dress code and the lack of personal space exhibited between patrons. Sam orders two white wine spritzers because now I am here I really do need some bottled courage and I figure a spritzer is better than a neat glass. Some women might not even realise they were pregnant this early and no matter how many other justifications I ponder I still end up only pretending to sip my drink. Sam informs me her client has arrived and she will come back for me in half an hour because he should be ready to talk by then and it will spare me a little of the show. She runs through some basic safety tips repeated from the first time she brought me here. She tells me not to accept drinks and if anyone asks anything, to be polite and answer something along the lines of, 'thank you, I'm flattered but I'm afraid that's not possible tonight' and if it gets too awkward to hide in the ladies and she'll find me there.

the Only Choice

I think the ladies sounds like a great idea but then I glance furtively around the room and as everyone seems more than occupied I am happy to stay at the bar. I chat a little with the barmaid, it is quiet and she seems friendly. She enjoys her work but added little detail, discretion is golden and even with my slim mask I am grateful it is. A deep voice I recognise as Jason, asks me from behind, if the seat next to me is taken and I get the sudden rush of excitement and fear. I turn to face him, he returns my smile but I know he hasn't recognised me from his expression. Not that this situation isn't extremely awkward as it is but to prevent any irrevocable faux pas, where he asks me how much for the night or he whips his dick out and suggests I might like 'something in his size,' I pat the seat next to me and break the ice.

"Jason, you know you didn't have to come, I just needed your sponsor." I lean in and whisper the last bit.

"Holy Fuck Bethany! What the hell?" He is stuttering and his eyes are on stalks. "I mean shit, look at you. Fuck! I didn't recognise you!" He slaps his hand over his mouth to stop the curses and to shut his jaw closed.

"That would be the general idea." I tilt my head and raise a brow.

"Yes, of course. Well, good job. Sorry I'll stop staring in a minute." He laughs. "Well maybe I won't but I'll try at least." He nods to the bar and orders a whiskey and another for me although my glass is still full. I ask for a tonic instead and he furrows his brow.

"Need a clear head." I smile tightly as the nerves start to return.

"I'm not happy about this Bethany and what the fuck are you doing alone at the bar? You're lucky I'm the only freak man enough to approach but I can see them circling." His voice is deeper than Daniels but just as stern. He takes a quick look and I follow his gaze, noticing for the first time some men at the end of the bar and on the edge of the dance floor looking our way.

"Sam's um . . . setting up. She's going to come and get me in a few minutes and if I was uncomfortable I was going to hide in the ladies but I'm fine and this is just a bar."

He sniffs dismissively. "At the moment it is and don't think for a second you'd be that safe in the ladies." He takes his glass and raises a toast against mine. "Here's to doing the right thing." He doesn't sound remotely happy about the toast but he clinks his glass against mine and takes a sip. Sam appears at his shoulder and orders another for herself. I start to move from the stool when she waves me back to sit.

"No rush Bets." She takes a sip of my wine while she waits for hers. "He can wait." She smiles at me and gives Jason a full on wicked wink that makes his back straighten and a deep cough form at the back of his throat. I bite my lips together to prevent a childish giggle escaping but it is impressive the reactions she evokes in men, even a hardened alpha which Jason definitely is. After what feels like an hour but is probably no more than ten minutes Sam is motioning me to follow her. I slip down from the stool and Jason holds my hand as I wobble on the high heels.

"I'll wait for you here. Don't leave without me or I'll worry, OK?" He smiles but it doesn't reach his eyes and I can tell he is almost as anxious as I am.

"I will, I promise and thank you for this Jason." I squeeze his hand to draw some comfort and add with borrowed confidence. "I'm doing the right thing because he didn't give me a choice. Failure is not an option Grrrr." He laughs loudly at my attempt to appear dominant. I am pretty sure he can spot a fake I just hope Mr Angel isn't so intuitive.

The room Sam leads me into is dark with a few dimmed sconce lights and one spotlight aimed at the chest of the man kneeling in the centre of the room. Sam motions for me to walk around the perimeter of the room slowly and I do. Happy to follow any instruction that doesn't involve me having to speak or think, because my heart is in my throat and my brain checked out when I crossed the threshold. I make my way around the front of the room, I can see the man is gagged with large red rubber ball that stretches his lips thin and shiny, with saliva dripping down his chin. My feet falter and Sam cracks her whip which makes us both jump but my eyes meet hers and she smiles and nods for me to keep walking. Sebastian is blindfolded and his hands have been secured to his ankles, he is still wearing his boxers but he looks uncomfortable as he strains against his restraint and his erection strains against the gaping material in his shorts. His breathing is surprisingly calm and he lets out the occasional satisfied groan as he twists and moves against his bindings. His back is laced with fierce red welts and I get a strange tingle at seeing these familiar marks. I don't believe my marks were any less red and the heat they generated I can feel again in my core as if they are fresh on my skin.

Sam unclips his gag and caresses his cheeks where the straps had creased his skin he leans into her touch like a kitten. He looks up to where he assumes her face is and asks if there is someone else in the room but before he finishes the question she swipes her hand across his face and quickly smoothes the sting with her palm and soft words.

"You don't get to ask the questions pet. You know better than that." She pats his red cheek and draws her long fingernail along his jaw bone, scratching the slight stubble and leaving a feint line. "Now why are you here pet?" She draws in a sigh that sounds like she is bored already with his answer, "and if you lie." She leans in and whispers in his ear making him visibly shiver. "I won't let you come." She steps back and he shakes his head roughly at that unpleasant idea.

"I won't lie Mistress Selina, I would never lie to you." He is quick to respond. She draws her fingernails through his hair and pulls it roughly back tilting his head back and exposing his throat. I recognise these moves and my body is reacting in kind, my heart beat is picking up and my skin glows with a light cover of perspiration. "I have just been fucked over with a deal and I've come to make sure my wife keeps her end of our arrangement." He pauses as Sam remains silent. "And to see you Mistress Selina." Sam looks over to me and mouths 'Oh My God" and I just nod numbly, shocked at this open disclosure but keen to hear more.

"I like that you came to see me but business deals bore me." Sam walks round to stand directly in front of him and tips his chin up as far as it will go with the tip of her whip. I wonder what she's doing, she needs to keep him talking about the deal not tell him she is bored, surely?

"This one would have interested you. It was worth millions but fucking Stone wouldn't bite. Fucking due-diligence and now I've got to wait until Angel can work herself back in to get my money, but it will be worth it. She's promised me and for the fucking shit I have to agree to I'm earning every penny. Arhhh!" Sam has circled him once more and brought her whip down sharply on his backside and he cries out again with each stroke. The sound rings in my ears and my mind is racing with too much information thanks to Sam and that is why she has the whip and I can only look on in awe.

"Arhh poor baby." Sam croons stroking the whip tenderly across his inflamed back. "Don't you love each other any more." Her lips curl with heavy sarcasm.

"I love her Mistress . . . I have always loved her but she is incapable of loving anyone. It is her own brand of sadism. She makes you fall in love and then she withdraws: her affection, her touch, her time. I'm a masochist but even I have trouble taking that much pain." His voice is raw and I falter at the honesty. "She doesn't want me anymore but she needs me for a little while longer. Then she will cut me loose and she will be free to pursue Daniel Stone in earnest . . . She told me once he was the only one that got away. He is a challenge to her now and he *will* fall in love with her. She doesn't lose . . . ever." Sam yawns loudly and barely breaks her stride.

"How interesting." Her tone perfectly bored. "What's the nasty lady getting you to do? Do you have to pretend to be blissfully, happily, married." Her mocking sarcasm is perfectly punctuated

the Only Choice

with careful strikes of the whip on his inflamed rear.

"No, I only have to pretend that for a few more weeks." He is panting rushing his words, giving Mistress Selina what she demands, trying to please her, trying not to get punished. "But I have to say I'm firing blanks and I have to say that until I get my money. I hate that shit, people thinking I'm not a real man." His whiny voice only emphasises his position as pathetic rather than submissive.

Keeping with her demeanour of disinterest Sam asks. "Well, it might not be a lie and you aren't a man you are my pet." She grips his hair once more tilting his head at an uncomfortable angle, the muscles in his neck taught and strained. She leans down and licks his face from chin to ear.

His laugh is ugly. "My two kids in Mexico would prove otherwise don't you think? I'm not the one firing blanks." Sam retrieves the gag from the floor beside him and informs Sebastian that she is so tired of his voice, he is to open his mouth once more. Once the gag is secured she motions me to the door. On the other side of the closed door I throw my arms around her and we both jump tiny excited jumps together desperately wanting to scream our success but not wanting to be heard.

"Oh My God Sam, you were amazing, that was . . . I'm speechless." I hug her once more.

"Just tell me you've recorded that?" She whispers and I pat my tightly packed breasts which are concealing the recording device. "Give me five minutes and I'll meet you at the bar."

"Five minutes?" I challenge.

"Hey I'm a pro . . . five minutes, tops." She giggles and gives me a sexy wink disappearing back into the room. I let out a deep breath filled with relief and excitement. I can't believe it worked. I mean I hoped and prayed it would but that it actually did. I am shocked. I have proof that Angel has lied to Daniel. There was other stuff there too but I can't process that now. I will need to listen again and again to get it all. He sang like a canary but then I don't know why I'm surprised, Daniel always got the truth from me in a similar fashion. I make my way to the ladies my heart is still racing and I need to stop shaking before I return to the bar.

Sam is at the bar by the time I leave the ladies. My hands wouldn't stop shaking and I was sweating so much I had to towel dry myself. I think it was mostly the cause of the rubber dress rather than my nerves but it was pretty gross. I look around for Jason but can't see him, he may have gone to play. Since Sam is staying for the evening she can let him know I've left so he won't need to worry. I want to hug her again but she looks guarded as I approach and I decide to just give her my best and most grateful smile. I decline a drink and realising I didn't bring any money for the cab I graciously accept Sam's loan. God I owe her big time. I give her a kiss on the cheek and walk around the edge of the room to the entrance. I just step past one of the booths when a tight grip holds my wrist and spins me back to face the direction I had come. Standing like an impenetrable wall is the towering frame of Daniel Stone, impassive face and ice cold eyes. His eyes drift down my body but there is no hint of heat, if anything he looks disgusted and I feel both cold and sick.

"Interesting career choice." His voice drips with distain and I can't quite believe I'm hearing the gravity in his words.

"Sorry you can't be serious? You think . . ." Words fail me so my head just shakes incredulously.

"Think what? That you're dressed for work? That you're here in a sex club with your professional friend in a professional capacity? Now why would I think that?" He doesn't leave me space to answer which is good because he has left me speechless. He tugs at my wrist. "Now shall we, I believe you know I'm good for the money." He pulls me forward and I stumble, his loose grip allows me to fall on to one knee. I look up into is glacial expression I can feel my eyes prickle but I fight to not let the building tears fall. I pull my hand from his grip and steadily get back to my feet, straightening my back I tip my chin and scowl.

"I'm not—"

He growls his interruption. "—Not what? So that wasn't your

friend paying you for your . . . assistance?" He smirks but it's not sexy. It's cruel.

"No!" I snap back "That was my friend lending me the cab fare home because," I motion up and down my outfit, exhibit A of my explanation. "I have nowhere to carry money." He might be justifiably upset finding me here, but he is, in fact, here too. I struggle to hide my own anger. But remarkably manage to keep my overwhelming hurt under control, for the moment. But I need to get out of here if I am to keep it that way.

His lips form a thin tight line as he considers me. "In that case I'll get Colin to transfer your fee directly." His sneer is just as harsh.

"God you're such an arsehole in this place." I snarl at him but still keep my voice at a normal volume.

"And you are a *whore* when you are in this place . . . It would seem we are a perfect match after-all." His words are whispered smooth and he even tucks my wig behind my ear. I shake free of his transparent false affection and try to step away.

"Fuck you." I whisper my voice cracking. He steps to close the distance and pulls me tight, squeezing my shoulders, his strong arms securing me against his side. Striding toward the back rooms my feet barely touch the ground.

"No Bethany. Fuck You."

I turn my head and see the worried look of both Jason and Sam but I shake my head to stop them assisting. They've done all they can. This is my mess and it's going to get a whole lot messier.

Chapter Thirteen

HE SPINS ME into a room that is a carbon copy of the one Sam and I had just vacated and I stumble to the middle but manage to remain standing this time. He closes the door and turns the lock and I struggle to swallow the lump that has risen to the back of my throat. My mouth is dry and my breathing is rapidly rising shallow pants. He doesn't make eye contact but moves me to the centre of the room and he doesn't need to tell me not to move, the tension and dominance is radiating of him in tidal waves. He unhooks a wire from the wall and drags it to the centre of the room. There are cuffs on the end and he wastes no time securing my wrists and pulling the wire tight lifting my arms high until I am on my tip toes. He has held me in this position in his office and I tremble at the memory both painful and tortuously erotic but I feel none of that now. This false supplication leaves me feeling isolated and exposed. My dress rides up so the cheeks of my bottom are clearly visible. He takes the mask from my eyes and I desperately wish he would stroke my face with his fingers so I can lean into him, like Sebastian had leaned into Sam but he has no intention of giving me comfort. I can see that in his cold flat eyes. My heart plummets. What have I done? Last time I was here it was self-sabotage, this

the Only Choice

time it's more like self-destruction.

He stands in front of me and runs his hand over the swell of my breasts and down my sides over my bottom and down my thighs. He rolls the hem of my dress that is only too eager to retreat on itself, winding up to my waist with the snap of an overstretched rubber band. His hand smoothes down my tummy and pushes between my legs despite me trying to keep them pinched together. He looks me in the eye and as much as I want to look away I hold his emotionless gaze.

"So which part of this is you *not* being a whore, the rubber dress, the no panties at a sex club or you . . . dripping wet?" He presses his middle finger deep in my folds and he moves the abundant moisture around, down and along the folds and up over my clit. My body responds, trembles and shudders. I grit my teeth, he is angry and lashing out but I won't dignify his accusations. He knows my body responds to him. I am always wet for him but since I can't tell him why I'm here, dressed like this I just have to let him be angry. "Oh come on Bethany, if you aren't here in a professional capacity then why are you here? Mmm? Who was your sponsor? I know you've been insatiable of late but are you really just here for cock?" My head snaps up, my eyes meet his, which are narrow and sharp at his suggestion. He shrugs and continues to move his fingers along my sensitive core, stroking and teasing, building the pleasure but not pushing too far. "No I didn't think so. So tell me Bethany was it worth it?" He sinks two fingers inside and I gasp and drop my head to his shoulder. "Got what you needed, did you?" His soft deep words are said with menace and I get a chill that he must know, somehow. Jason wouldn't have told him and Sam was as surprised as I was to see him, maybe he saw Sebastian leave.

"What do you know Daniel . . . why do you think I'm here?" My voice is breathless but my tone, unrepentant. I sink a little as he swirls his finger hitting the sweetest spot deep inside. I want to hold him as my body sways, held steady by his fingers alone.

"Oh no ba" He checks himself before he calls me baby, that

stings. "That is not how this works. You don't get to ask the questions." His breath is a fresh breeze of mint and whiskey, kissing my neck and the irony is not lost on me that not half an hour ago I was vicariously in his position. He leans down, his mouth covers mine with angry possession and I pull at my restraints desperate to hold him. His tongue plunges deep, swirling, his lips are soft and sweet, he sucks on my tongue as he pulls back only to sweep back in capturing my head with his other hand, pushing me hard against him. When he pulls back the next time he draws my bottom lip between his teeth and I flinch at the anticipated bite. I cry in the back of my throat as the coppery taste floods my mouth; my lips are sore and swollen. He kisses along my jaw up to my ear and down to my collar bone, tender featherlike and cherished. He reaches my neck and I brace for the inevitable bite and draw on my flesh that will mark me but it doesn't come and I feel its absence in the pit of my stomach.

His fingers move in a tortuously slow pace, his thumb circles my clit without the necessary pressure to drive me over the edge but even so I recognise the clenching and tension in my core that starts to build and so does Daniel. "Why are you here Bethany? Who is your sponsor?" My body starts to quiver and he stills his fingers, breathing heavily in my ear and waiting until my own breathing has quietened. He does this several times, each time a little closer to my release and I can't help the sobs escape each time he denies me. "Well, fuck Bethany if you don't want to come I might as well." He removes his hand from between my legs my hips buck involuntarily at the loss and scramble to get purchase on the tip of my toes. He unzips his suit trousers and lets them drop to his mid-thigh as his legs are braced wide; he holds his heavy cock loosely stroking its length. I fight the urge to lick my lips but I can't help the whimper in the back of my throat.

He sweeps his strong arm around my waist and drops it just below the cheeks of my bottom pulling me toward him. I try to keep my legs together but he growls a command for me to spread and I do. He lifts me up and positions the thick head of his cock at my entrance. In one smooth continuous movement he sinks inside me and I relish the feeling of being completely full, even though I know he isn't all the way in. He nudges me with his arm, pushing deeper and my breath catches. I wrap my legs around his waist and I'm grateful he is supporting my weight, easing the ache in my arms even for a moment. My sensitive core clenches around his thick thrusting shaft like its afraid to let go and I am so desperate to let go I move my hips and meet each thrust with needy desire and desperation. His fingers pinch my hips holding me firm and preventing my movements, preventing my grind against him, preventing my climax. He stills and again with herculean control stays off another climax and judging by the tension in his jaw it's not just mine.

If I could just hold him with my arms I could get the necessary leverage. I try to wriggle again but he just holds firm and I cry at the sharp pain from his fingers and the frustration at his refusal to grant my release.

"Please Daniel, Please Sir, please, please please . . . please I need to come." My mindless litany goes unheeded. He is never going to let me come and I can hear the desperation in my voice but still he doesn't acknowledge my plea. He holds me still and takes a few deep breaths and rolls his hips once, moving deep inside and grunting loudly he throws his head back before relaxing his hold. Fuck, Oh I hate him right now. I can't believe he did that, he came and leaves me hanging, literally. Right now I don't know why I bothered, fuck him if he wants to believe her. If he wants to let Angel and her husband take him for millions or worse get sucked back into a hollow, deceitful relationship well fuck him. They deserve each other. He pulls back from me and I take a moment. It doesn't take even that to see him, all of him, my perfect. He makes my heart stop. All I ever see when I fall into his bottomless crystal blue eyes is the man I love, completely, utterly. My love for him is all consuming, a 'I won't survive without you love' and I know I won't. I also know that it is worth fighting for, it is worth any cost because he doesn't deserve her.

He deserves me and *we* deserve an Angel free future.

He tucks his still hard cock into his trousers and I am distracted by the ache between my legs at its absence. I take a deep breath before I let him know why I'm here. "You needed to know the truth. You needed proof, I got proof." My voice is breathless, evidence of my unfinished erotic ordeal. He hadn't really moved away but he is only a hairs breadth from me now, holding my chin with a firm grip.

"I needed you to trust me. I told you I needed you to stop Bethany and you did it anyway. So I hope it was worth it." He spins and steps away raking his hands through his hair. His agitation and the expression of resignation in his face is like a slap to mine, utter panic engulfs me.

"No Daniel, no no . . . but I got the proof Daniel. I didn't do it for me and it's worth it if it means you don't have to carry all that fucking guilt and pay for a debt that wasn't yours to pay." My voice breaks into a sob but his eyes are cold, unmoved by my distress.

"Don't you fucking dare tell me this is for my benefit. You did this for you, so you could have your future all neat and tidy. Perfect and happy and fuck anyone else and their suffering." He paces the room before turning, his expression is a picture of barely contained fury. "Proof you say?" His condescending tone holds so much disgust I want to howl. "So, am I to believe what you and your *friend* heard during a scene with Mistress Selene? It's laughable Bethany. It's just your word against his." His blatant contempt is like full body punch and I feel the oxygen leave my body in a painful rush. I can't believe he thinks that but it's not just my word.

"Oh I know that and I know exactly what my word means to you but I have other proof, I have a recording. So it's not just my word." I try to sound assertive and indignant as I dangle from the wire. I can't argue whose suffering he is talking about, I can't argue his beliefs they are so ingrained because he's so fucking stubborn but if he can just hear the truth . . . Whether he forgives

the Only Choice

me after that or what he chooses to do then, is out of my hands.

"Oh really?" He steps forward his face so close I can feel his lips and I struggle not to lean into them. I can't give him any more of me. I drop my eyes to my cleavage indicating where he needs to look and he fails to hide his smile at the prospect of delving in there. "This is the only upside to this." His fingers easily slip between my breasts, the dress doesn't breathe and I appear to glow like a pig in rubber. He pinches the device between his fingers and pulls it free but I can see as he holds it before me that the device is wet. Dripping in fact and my heart sinks that I didn't think to check if it would work in wet conditions. I mean why would I? It's not like I anticipated having to do this underwater. He shakes the excess water off and rubs it dry against his trousers, pulls my dress back down to cover my bottom and then leaves the room.

He returns only moments later with a laptop and Jason. Our eyes meet briefly but mine must reflect the horror I feel. I shake my head so slightly but enough, hoping to indicate that I haven't said anything about him to Daniel. Daniel fiddles with the computer and plugs the device in, a few clicks and I can hear the recording. I breathe a sigh of relief, it worked. A few minutes pass but all I can hear is muffled sounds, very muffled sounds. I can't make out a single word. My head drops and I feel the tingle in my nose first then the prickle of water in my eyes. All for nothing, the device had been so embedded, insulated in between my breasts, tight in the dress that nothing got through. He snaps the laptop shut and walks slowly back to me. He prises my fisted hand open, places the device in it and slowly curls my fingers back around it.

"I know you must be disappointed but really people say all sorts of shit when they are being whipped and tortured." He words are soft, comforting but deeply sarcastic. His eyes hold none of their fire and all of his pain. I know I have lost him and I am instantly chilled to my soul.

"I always told the truth." I manage to breathe out.

His hand strokes my jaw and he tilts my face to meet his eyes, mine are now streaming but he is unaffected. "Yes you did." He hums, "in fact, I am counting on it." He steps away from me and walks to one wall that holds racks of whips and floggers. He picks up a stubby short crop with a flat end, he slaps it menacingly against his palm and I jump at the sharp sound. "I thought I made myself clear. I thought you understood the consequences Bethany but I know now that is not the case. An error I will rectify immediately . . . So there is no misunderstanding about our future . . . to be crystal clear Bethany . . . we have no future." His enunciation of each word like a blunt nail in my broken heart. "I brought Jason here, just so you know what that means, exactly. Sharing, is no longer a problem." He waves his whip toward Jason and he swirls it round as he attempts to list everything I've lost. "Total Communication Shutdown but this time there will be no breaches. I will block your calls, you won't be able to contact me, *ever*." He spits these words like bullets before drawing another breath to continue his devastating withdrawal from my life. "Patrick will cease to give you protection, no more proposals. I won't pursue you. I am done." He taps his fingers pensively on his jaw. "I know there's more but to quote you *baby,*" he pauses. "'No-more.'" He draws the whip under my chin, my cheeks are streaming and I am struggling to gasp for breath. My arms are screaming in agony and its nothing compared to the pain in my heart. "But I do want to know who sponsored you, so for old times' sake let's play the truth game, one . . . last . . . time." He spins me so my arms are twisted and I am barely touching the floor. I face Jason but his eyes are downcast. I hear the swish and feel the strike at same time, hard on my rubber clad backside.

 The noise echoes and the sting feels like a knife has sliced at my flesh, instant furious heat and a pain so sharp I cry out. Again and again and I draw in ragged breaths letting the fire and agony consume me because it will always be a fraction of the pain inside my chest. "Just a name Bethany and I'll stop and you'll never see me again." His cruel words just make me want to hold on as long as I'm conscious. I don't want to never see him again. He draws back striking the tops of my thighs and I cry out, screaming, that is so sensitive there, Christ! That hurts. I look ahead with watery eyes. I can't focus on Jason but I know he is there, my head feels heavy and I drop it as I take more strikes to my backside. I can no longer feel the individual strikes I just feel like my body is encased in flames. I lose track of each blow, I lose track of time, there is just endless enduring pain. His hands cup my head, pulls me close to his face and my heart breaks completely at the utter desolation and sadness in his eyes and I can't bear a moment more pain in our hearts. I whisper my safe-word, dragged from my memory, "blue." My voice is raspy but by the narrowing of his eyes I know he hears me.

"Ha! Nice try Bethany but you don't get to safe word me. I want a fucking answer. Who sponsored you?" His voice is raw, angry, and so cold but honestly, I don't even think he does want an answer. He just needs to punish me for this pain I've caused. That's why I need it to stop, I can't stand his pain. Strike, strike, strike. . . . then stop. There is a scuffle of shoes and some grunts and harsh breaths.

"For fuck sake Daniel! She safe word, back the fuck up man! It was me, I sponsored her because for some fucking reason I thought you would rather I did it, instead of some arsehole stranger but looking at you now, I'm not so sure." Jason is panting as he struggles to hold Daniel back.

Daniel shrugs his hold and steps to me, cupping my face his tender hold finishes me off and I sink limp and sobbing uncontrollably. "Baby, I loved you so much, I loved you so fucking much." His voice is barely a whisper, his words pure agony. "I know I never deserved someone like you, never deserved to just be happy but I didn't think I deserved this either. You broke my fucking heart Bethany." His forehead touches mine and I hear the break in his voice, his eyes are a bottomless pit of sorrow mirrored only but the depths of loss I feel in me. "How could you do this to us?" This is a messed up fucking tragedy. "You should've trusted me." His last whispered words feather the damp skin on my cheeks.

"And you should've trusted me." I mouth back but my mouth is too dry to speak. He lets my head fall and walks away nothing but raw pain and betrayal in his eyes."Wait!" My cry is broken with an uncontrollable sob. "Daniel . . . wait! Angel . . . she warned me to stay away. She said you love her but don't know it yet and I just need to stay away." Each word is laboured with deep steadying breaths. "She told me to stay away Daniel . . . why would she do that if she didn't want you for herself?" He steps back into the room, closing the distance but not entering my personal space.

"She told me Bethany . . . she told me she warned you to stay away . . . and then she apologised to me for interfering. She was just being a friend to me . . . She couldn't stand to see me in pain . . . Whats your excuse Bethany?" He leaves his accusation hanging like a noose before he silently turns and leaves the room.

The wire is loosened and I collapse into myself. Jason is at my side unclipping my restraints. He gently rubs my wrists which are raw and numb. "Why didn't you just tell him?" He helps me to my feet and I use his arm for much needed support, wincing with the smallest movement.

"I didn't want him to leave." The tears are still falling but the sobs have subsided as the familiar numbness begins to creep back in. Jason looks confused. "He said if I told him he would leave and I'd never see him again."

Jason snorts at this. "Twisted logic, well I hope it was worth it."

I open my palm at the useless device; Jason takes it and puts it in his back pocket. "I doubt even if that had worked it would've made a difference but I had to try. She's lying and I wanted him to know the truth, even if *that* cost." I draw in a very shaky breath but manage not to sob before I continue. "I know I've lost him but he doesn't deserve to live the life she has planned out of guilt. He has nothing to feel guilty about." I flinch as he places his jacket on my shoulders and the edge skims my thighs.

the Only Choice

"He does now." Jason opens the door and I tentatively follow him through.

Jason drives me home and I silently welcome the creeping numbness that moves through my body like a lethal dose of anaesthetic. I wish the last few months had never happened. That I could erase the healing and go back to enduring the crippling pain of Daniel walking away the first time because I have that now but I also have the image of his beautiful face contorted with utter sadness and betrayal, etched in my mind. His suffering is unbearable. I try to justify that I had no choice, desperate to cling to the notion that I did the only thing I could to save us. But the fact is, he had made his choice and I just couldn't accept it and the only person I have helped, the only person that comes out of this unscathed and happy is Angel. When his sadness dissolves, when the betrayal fades the only thing left will be hatred and I can't bare it. I shiver as the rivulets of sweat trapped in my dress cool my body; in my peripheral consciousness I am aware that Jason has turned the heat up in the car but the chill I feel is in my bones and a thousand suns won't warm me. The engine sinks to a quiet hum and I recognise the steps leading to my apartment. I go to open the door but Jason's quiet voice stops me.

"I'm sorry Bethany." His deep voice sounds strange and I look to see intense concern in his eyes.

"You have nothing to be sorry about Jason, I'm grateful for your help—" He is quick to interrupt.

"He wouldn't have been there if it wasn't for me."

"You told him?" The shock clear in the volume of my voice.

"Fuck no . . . No he called and asked where I was . . . I swear I had no idea he would want to meet me there. I was stuck, I couldn't meet him anywhere else because you would've been left there alone . . . I didn't have a choice Bethany but I'm really sorry it played out the way it did." His face is filled with a dark shadow of concern.

"Me too." I feel unbelievably sorry for myself but I feel just as bad for putting him in this situation. "Jason I am . . ." I swallow a sudden unexpected sob back. "I am so sorry if I've got you in to trouble. I wouldn't have told him you know?" My voice is shaky but sincere.

"That's what I was afraid of." He tries to laugh but his face shows no relief at the attempt. "Look I'm a big boy I can handle Daniel, besides I'm fucking good at what I do and he's a business man. I'll be fine." His hand hovers somewhere near my knee but seeing the exposed skin he opts to hold my hand, squeezing and pulling it into his other hand. "Are you going to be all right?" I look at our hands clasped together on his lap and I know there is comfort there but I can't feel it and several long moments pass when I pull away realising the absolute heart rending truth in my answer.

"No." He lets my hands go and I open the door and walk up my steps. I don't look back.

Chapter Fourteen

I AM GRATEFUL for one thing and that is that Sofia's wedding is on Saturday and as such everyone close and dear to me is so consumed with that day that my drama and despair is going unnoticed. Partly because of the day itself and partly because I have drawn on all my acting skills to push aside my devastation for a few more days. I can cry myself to sleep but I don't sleep and I can put drops in my eyes to hide the bursting red capillaries and I can pretend to eat and toast at the pre wedding lunches and other gatherings. At the spa treat for Sofia and I the day before the big day I can focus every bit of attention rightly on the bride-to-be with enough genuine enthusiasm and a fake smile that would shame a pageant pro. I can do all this because it needs to be done. I love Sofia and her family and my shit is my shit; a few more days and I can go away and sort it all out. With a little time and a little distance I can think about my future, our future, a future without Daniel. I know in my heart he will never forgive me and I have to live with that and as much as each night I want to curl up and die to ease this pain, I don't.

Sofia's last night as a single women and we are staying at her parents. Marco has managed to get a date after all, a close friend of Rose who is willing to play the date game or more likely act as chaperone. They are staying at our place because of the early start. We have just had a Chinese take away and are about to settle for a cheesy film, maybe a musical we're not sure and Sofia is flicking through the library of DVDs. My mobile rings and seeing its Ethan's number I leave the room and head toward the kitchen.

"Hey Ethan, you get your suit OK?" I fiddle around the kitchen tidying and picking at the food I wasn't able to eat earlier.

"Oh yeah about that . . ." He starts to mumble an apology but it doesn't matter, pretty much nothing does at this point. "You know that girl I've been seeing well, I've kind of made a commitment to her and it would feel wrong, you know?" He pauses waiting for my reaction. We haven't talked in a while but I do recall Tom, at our last get together, mention something about Ethan meeting someone. Then again, this is Ethan and I really didn't pay it too much attention but this has been a few weeks now.

"It's fine Ethan, really not a problem. Marco has a date so the big panic is over." I try to laugh it off but that type of sound feels unwelcome in my mouth.

"But you can ask Daniel right, you guys are back together?" I can hear he feels bad for letting me down and is trying to make sure I am really Ok but this hasn't helped. I try to swallow now my mouth is suddenly dry. I haven't told anyone that the almost reunion is back to a non-reunion, permanently this time.

"Oh sure but I know he's busy. Look its fine really, thanks for offering in the first place." I try to divert the conversation. "So getting serious, that's good right?" My tone is teasing and I am surprised by his sincere response.

"Yeah it's good, really good. It's strange, I mean she's a whole heap of crazy but there's something about her. She tries to be this super tough bitch and even down-right nasty but we talked one night for hours and she's not so tough. She's just had to *be* tough." He lets out a contented sigh and I smile because I can hear it in his voice. He is really taken with her. "Anyway, I really like her so . . ." He pauses for a few more seconds when I click and interrupt.

"So you won't be travelling with me either?" I conclude.

"Ah sorry Bets, but I just don't want to leave right now. She's got this job that's going to keep her here for several months and I'd like to use that time, you know . . . Anyway we thought we'd go travelling after. She'll get paid for this job and then we can see a bit of the world together. I really like her Bets." His usual cocky tone is somewhat sheepish.

"I'm happy for you Ethan." My voice is soft but I hope he can hear how genuine my sentiments are; even if happiness isn't in *my* repertoire at the moment.

"Are you still going to go travelling? I hate you to cancel because of me but then I'd hate for you to go on your own." He hesitates.

"No I'll still go and don't worry I'm a big girl. Had self-defence training from the best and everything. I'll be fine. I'll probably tag along with Marco anyway." I added the last bit to ease his mind but I am more inclined than ever to do this on my own.

"Oh that's good, really good. I think Dad would kill me if he knew I'd bailed and left you to travel alone." He laughs and now I feel guilty that I'm lying, well maybe I'm not lying. I might still go with Marco, at this exact moment I haven't decided. So not technically lying and so no guilt. We finish the call arranging to meet sometime before I leave. A tentative lunch with his new lady where he plans to go over my travel itinerary, adding it's the least he could do and I have to let him because it appears to ease his conscience.

Exhausted by the weight of recent and future events I just want to curl up and hibernate, which I must admit, is an improvement. Instead however, I take my warm milk from the microwave and curl up next to my best friend on her parents sofa. Together we are wrapped in the softest blanket and settled down to watch the 'not at all cheesy but tragically romantic,' Moulin Rouge.

"You're gonna Marry Me!" His eyebrows are pinched together and he looks angry almost mean. I slap him hard on his shoulder and he steps back rubbing the hurt and mouthing an over dramatic 'Ow' following by his cheeky grin. It's one of my favourite dreams and it couldn't be more timely to have it the night before Sofia's wedding. Immediately after his statement of fact John had effortlessly scrambled up the twisted branches of the Damson tree in the churchyard and was shaking the smaller branches. It was late summer and we were both starting new schools in September. I was heading off to the girls Grammar and he was heading to the mixed Comprehensive school. I didn't want to go, I wanted to go to his school. My mum wouldn't let me but it was John that convinced me to go to the Grammar in the end. He got angry that I could be so stupid and then he got sad that I would waste this chance and I hated it when he was sad. He shouts down again. "I said I'm gonna marry you!" I look up in to his soft brown eyes, his dark hair flopping, way too long for school but perfect for the summer. His cheeks are dirty from the climb and his grin reveals his bright white teeth but the falling fruit has me shielding my head for cover.

I hear the thud of his feet as he jumps down beside me, his eleven year old self still the same height as me so we are eye to eye. I can't explain the feeling I have swirling in my belly when he stares at me with such intensity but I have felt unsettled for a little while now. "You're worried about changing school and not seeing me every day." I scoff at his words which sound like a brag. He can be so full of himself but I bite my lip when I see in his eyes he doesn't mean it that way, not at all. "You will see me every day, your bus gets in after mine and I'll be waiting for you." He picks the end of my t-shirt and pulls it out flat and I hold the ends tight replacing my hands where his have been. He starts to collect the fruit and put it in my makeshift basket. "And you are worried about a whole bunch of other stuff that you shouldn't not when you need to study. So I'm just saying, I'm gonna marry you and take care of you and stuff so quit worrying."

"Why are you going to marry me?" My T-shirt is filling with fruit and stretching the material beyond probable recovery. He holds one of the damsons in his hand carefully looking it over and gently rubbing the surface dust to reveal a deep purple gloss, turgid and juicy. He walks back to me and he looks in my eyes.

"We're both alone Bets but we don't ever have to be lonely." He hands me the fruit and I take it.

"You have a huge family John." My words are soft and they falter when I understand what he means. "I'm never lonely." Because I'm always with John, even when I'm not. I take a bite of the delicious fresh fruit still warm from the tree, juice dribbling onto my already ruined t-shirt and hand the rest to John.

"Me either." He puts the small fruit in his mouth pip and all. This moment I feel as warm as the sun beating on our backs and as young as we were it was this moment our friendship changed.

"Do you love me John?" I know he does but I would really like to hear the words.

"No Bethany, I told you. I love Lara Croft." He spits the pip from his mouth and grins but he wraps his scrawny arm around my scrawnier shoulders and we giggle and laugh together as we make our way back across the graveyard and home.

It's really early, the sun not quite peeking through the curtains in the guest room and I stretch luxuriously forcing my muscles to the point of pain before recoiling in satisfied exhaustion at the effort. Closing my eyes once more to try and hold the tender dream for a few moments longer but it slips beyond my desperate grasp leaving me just a little sadder than before, as if that was possible. I hear the click on my door, the soft swish of wood against deep pile carpet and the brief light streaks across the room and my closed lids. I feel the dip in the bed and feel the body crawl as close as possible without touching, as if that would prevent me waking up. "What's up Sofs?" In the dark I turn my face to hers just making out the darker shadow.

"Sorry Bets I didn't want to wake you." She whispers and I sniff a light laugh because we both know that's not true. "It's just that I've got cold feet." Her words are softly spoken but I snap upright and twist to turn the light on. We are both blinking like a couple of moles in the dessert but when my eyes finally adjust I calmly ask her. "What!" It wasn't calm, it was frantic. Her face is a picture of cool but her lips start to curl in a mischievous grin at the same time I feel the ice cold rush of her feet as they plant firmly against my legs. "Arghhh!! Fuck!" I squeal and jump back sliding to the edge of the bed away from her offending limbs, her feet are fucking freezing and she is giggling uncontrollably. "What the fuck Sofs!" I cry out as I rub warmth back into my legs and shiver at my unsuccessful effort. "Not funny!" I hate being cold but the sheer panic that raced through me actually stopped my heart. "Jeeze you scared the crap out of me. My life literally drained when I thought you actually meant . . . you know that you were having second thoughts" I hold my thumping chest as she looks at me like I am the mad one. "Seriously, if you had doubts about a match which was clearly made in heaven what chance would I have eh?" She continues to chuckle.

"Ah come on Bets that was funny." She rubs her feet vigorously on the bed, before snuggling back down tucking my quilt under her chin her big brown eyes smiling and sheepish.

"On so many levels that was not funny." I laugh and snuggle back too, leaving the light on because it will be light soon and the day will begin in earnest.

"Sorry." She yawns and her smile is so wide there is no way she believes her own words of apology but this is her day and so it begins for Princess Sofia.

"Trouble sleeping?" I don't know why I decide to whisper but it feels like our conversation might, in fact wake the household.

"A little but not because of today." She pauses.

"You're not worried about today sweetie because you know it will be perfect. I promise." The planets have aligned and all the work and behind the scenes activity will guarantee it.

"Oh no I'm not worried about today, I'm really excited . . . it's going to be fun." I can feel her excitement like it is a physical thing pulsating around her so I have no trouble believing her. "I've been a bad friend Bets. Marco told me Ethan bailed and that Daniel hasn't been around much and I . . ."

"—Hey!" I stop her. "You're my best friend." I waggle my head from side to side to indicate the fact that she is half of my best friend and she smiles, "and you are not to make any part of this day about me or I'll be pissed and Marco will push you off the podium of joint best friend." I warn.

"Ok but as it's my day, I want just this one conversation then no more Ok?" She pulls the 'her day' card like a master and I think this is going to be the longest twenty-four hours.

"Ok but not much to tell." She arches a brow at my lie and I wonder how much I can get away with telling her to appease her stubborn curiosity. "Ethan was only doing Marco and me a favour but Marco has a date so it's no biggie. Besides Ethan has a girlfriend now and by his own admission it would be weird." She nods at this but her penetrating eyes fix me at my obvious unfinished disclosure. I closed my eyes and draw in a deep breath but the air hurts my lungs and the ache of pure agony rushes through my nerves in waves and my eyes water. The visual verification of my sorrow is too much and Sofia shuffles and awkwardly wraps her arms around me kissing my hair and shhing my building sobs. I had been so proud that I had held my fragile state together in front of everyone and I am mortified I break today of all days. "I'm so sorry Sofs." She pulls me tighter muffling my words against her.

"You will be if you keep apologising." She mutters and I sniff trying to rein back the onslaught of sadness. "So, no Daniel?" She pulls back to see that although I have held back the sobs the tears are still falling as I shake my head. "And you don't want to talk about it?" I shake my head in absolute agreement. "Well, I'll let this go today, but only because I'm selfish and don't want my Maid of Honour red eyed and snotty in the photos." I love that she can make me laugh even if she is serious. "But before I leave on honeymoon we are talking Ok? I'm away for nearly two months so we have to work your shit out before we go or you're coming with us." I nod because I really need to talk to someone and I can finally tell Sofia about the baby, my baby. The thought causes a shock to my system like a slap to my face. I need to get my shit together. I can't be a blubbering mess, because once again I will have someone totally dependent on me and me alone. Sofia is looking at me intently as she assesses the grief laden emotions flashing across my face before the more familiar ones of resolve and determination settle. "You won't be alone today Bets, I guarantee that." She yawns and closes her heavy lids. I am thankful she has because I don't have to pretend to smile. I thought I'd be sharing this day with Daniel. He was never just my plus one, he was my only one and without him I feel so fucking lonely.

The morning is a blur as people fuss and gather; tweak and pamper, a steady stream of well-wishers dropping by before heading off to the church. Sofia is a picture of calm sat wrapped in her silk gown with 'The Bride' scrolled in sparkly diamontes on the back, sipping on champagne as her cousin fixes her hair and make-up. I sit beside her as Aunt Marie fixes my hair in a half up mess of rich chestnut curls with tiny pearls sprinkled in the main swirl of hair. My makeup is light but I have had to use a calming concealer to hide the redness around my eyes and industrial strength waterproof mascara if I am to survive today without resembling chi chi the panda. I nurse my sparkling elder-flower in the champagne glass and watch the scene around me. It is like a time lapse movie where everyone else is a distorted haze of movement but I'm just still and slightly out of focus. When did my life get so out of focus? Why did I let it get so out of focus? Stupid questions, stupid rhetorical questions because you do stupid things when you love someone so much you can't focus on anything else. You make stupid choices and make stupid mistakes and some mistakes, some choices are unforgivable.

The room has gone quiet and I look up to see Sofia standing with her mum. Vivienne has her handkerchief pressed against her eyes and is holding her daughters hand with the other, smiling, utter love expressed openly on her face and I feel my first real pang of loneliness. God I'm so selfish and I reprimand myself that I won't forgive me either if I do anything to make Sofia sad on her day. I shake my head and physically pull myself together. I stand and walk over and take Sofia's other hand.

"Come on sweetie, let's get you in that dress." She nods and I can see her eyes pool with water. "Hey no tears you told me no puffy red eyes or snot remember?" I admonish her with a gentle nudge that has her laughing.

"All right girls I'll leave you to it and go and get Milly ready. She is fighting her mother every step of the way." She sighs with exasperation. "I thought every little four year old girl would love to be a princess for the day, but not Milly. I swear she'll be back in that God awful Chelsea junior football kit before the days through." She grumbles as she leaves the room. I grimace because I am in charge of taming the tomboy, at least for the ceremony as Milly is the only other bridesmaid. Sofia decided that choosing the youngest niece was diplomatic and saved having something like sixteen bridesmaids. I take her new dress from the doorframe and gently unzip its protective cover. Its ivory lace fitted bodice is delicately decorated with fine handmade lace and the skirt is full length riot of organza and silk, ruffled, scooped and folded in on itself. It's stunning. She has a fine lace veil that clips in the back of her hair with a diamond hair clip, both handed down from her mother's family, old and borrowed.

I stand back and we both stare wide eyed at each other trying to force back the inevitable tears. "Sofs you look—"

"—Don't you dare Miss!" She bites her lip and I mirror her move as I can feel mine tremble. I take a steady breath.

"You're right. Ok, well let's just say you scrub up well." We both laugh and the emotional magnitude of the moment dissipates instantly. "You ready?" She arches her brow and drags her eyes down my body with a disapproving scowl. I am wearing my pyjama bottoms and a skinny vest. "You don't like my outfit?" I mock but I step out of her reach just in case she's not up for jokes and judging by the continued scowl I was right to move. "This will take two minutes max. I needed to make sure you were already before I send your Dad in. So one last time got everything?" I watch as she does a quick mental list.

"Shit!" Her eyes display genuine panic.

"What? What's wrong?" I step up to her because with all that material it's an effort for her to move to me.

"Blue, I don't have anything blue, Fuck!" She snaps and I laugh but slap my hand at my mouth as she narrows her eyes at my insensitivity.

"Sorry, but you do have your language, that's pretty blue." I snicker and she slaps me hard on my arm but laughs out too. I look at my hand and twiddle the tiny ring on the little finger on my left hand. The one with the small silver band with a heart shaped twist with tiny blue stones that never pretended to be anything precious but was more precious than any stones. John gave me this ring on my sixteenth birthday, a promise ring not an engagement ring he said because an engagement was a period of time and this ring was a promise of a lifetime. I have cried a lifetime of tears, and because of me that promise went un-kept. My unbearable sadness I hide today though, is that deep down I always thought that I would make that promise to Daniel and now I have ruined that too. I twist the ring from my finger instantly feeling its absence and hand it to Sofia, even as she shakes her head she holds her hand out. "You should wear this." I try to smile but I can't make my lips cooperate with the false emotion.

"Bets I can't." She holds the ring in her palm. She knows I have never taken it off, not in four years, not once.

"Don't think you have a choice, Miss 'you have to be at the church in forty minutes.'" I raise my brow as a challenge because faced with this, there really isn't a choice for the sometime superstitious Sofia.

"It's a borrow though, a blue and a borrow. I can't keep it." She is adamant and I'm pleased because I couldn't really bare to let it go.

"I'll pick it up when we meet before the honeymoon and before I leave on my travels." I wink and head for the door.

"Your travels? Well, you are definitely not travelling without telling me every detail young lady!" She shouts after me and I shout back passing her Dad, stopping to give him a brief peck on his pride filled cheek.

"Wouldn't dream of it!" I reply and dash into my room for my two minute turnaround.

This wedding is very much a mix of traditional to appease her older relatives and modern to appease the bride. She wanted a new dress in favour of the traditional handed down gown and looking at her on the arm of Paul as they walk down the aisle toward the priest, she definitely made the right choice. She is stunning, breath-taking and all those other adjectives that fall short on such occasions. I stand at the front just beside Marco, his Mum and Dad and without exception we all have watery eyes. I squeeze Milly's hand not sure why when she gives me a look that is confused and judgemental but she smiles when she realises my hand had nothing to do with a reprimand. The small church is crammed to the trusses with family and friends, standing room only at the back. Every exposed column and beam has been knotted and entwined with miles of ivory silk ribbon; flowers thread the aisle and fragrance the room with a subtle sweet scent. Paul fails miserably at his only job, to be the blank canvas for the bride because he looks sharp and elegant in his navy Armani suit. He also fails to hide is pride and pleasure as he escorts his future wife to the altar sporting the biggest smile I have ever seen.

The ceremony is simple and once the glass is broken, the applause and cheers are deafening and the chaos and planned mayhem flows, a confetti storm outside the church, releasing the doves and walking around the gardens. The reception area is set for the cocktail hour for the guest while the family disappear for the photos. There is a very visible subsidence of tension once the ceremony is over, Sofia and Paul are all smiles and are now comfortably relaxed enough to really enjoy their day. I haven't been to a wedding before but if they are all like this I can easily see what the fuss is about; a true celebration of coming together, family, friends and lovers. To have someone to share your life, just one person, to share all the joy, all your loves and fears, heartache and happiness; who wouldn't want that? I stop myself before my raggedly emotional state gets carried away. I walk over to Marco who is equally dashing in his navy suit.

"My sister must love you very much. You look stunning." He leans in to kiss my cheek and takes my hand and holds it out to take an exaggerated look at me. My fitted silk court dress is very flattering, if a little tight across the bust now and the halter neck does nothing to soften my expanding chest. Still I'm grateful it fits and isn't tartan because I know from my dream I looked hideous in tartan.

"She was very kind, yes, maybe she was hoping to get me hooked up so I won't be her spinster friend for too long." I nudge him and he tilts his head ignoring my joke. "Where's your date?" I ask and he senses the panic as my eyes flash over to a gaggle of his Aunts all looking our way.

"Don't panic, she's in the main reception with the other guests. We're heading over shortly to the main welcome area before Sofs and Paul make their entrance." He nods in the direction of the glass conservatory where the reception has been set up. I can hear the traditional band playing already in the distance.

I sigh in relief all the same. "Phew! Just a quick panic. You know you did make it sound like there was going to be an army of single cousins for me to fight off but everyone's coupled up. I'm not complaining, I'm glad but I had no idea these things were like this. I think I'm the only single one here." My jokey quip falters and I hear the hitch in my voice. He wraps his strong arms around my shoulders but it's not enough and he turns me and

the Only Choice

gives me a much needed full on hug. I sniff back a sniffle and breathe out a deep breath. "I'm sorry. I'm pathetic. I just didn't think I'd be on my own."

"You're not." He reassures me and I nod into his chest.

"I know, I've got you guys but I—"

He holds my shoulders and pulls back. "No I mean you are not on your own. Your date is here." He turns me a full one eighty and I gasp. Daniel stands, dark and dangerous and right in front of me. I step back into Marco's chest and he steadies me with his hands on the tops of my arms, my heart is racing and I struggle to breathe. I know Marco can feel me tremble because he gives me a reassuring squeeze. Daniel steps forward his eyes penetrate mine and sear my soul but his face gives nothing and I am filled with confusion, confusion and need, confusion and want, mostly want and need. "This is my sister's wedding Daniel. I hope I don't need to remind you are here as a guest." Marco's voice rumbles and I can feel some tension in his grip but he relaxes, which makes me relax too.

Daniel nods addressing Marco over my shoulder but not taking his eyes from me. "Your sisters call to me this morning expressed as much. She is the bride and her wish is my command . . . I have no intention of being escorted from your premises,. . . . again." He fights back a grin but gives in when I bite my lips to hide mine.

"Very well." Marco steps beside me and holds his hand out for Daniel, who reciprocates. "In that case I hope you have a great day. I'm heading over to the main room, see you over there Boo. The reception to receive the happy couple will be soon Ok?" He winks at me I nod numbly trying to process the image before me. Daniel takes my hand and leads me to the very edge of the garden away from the family, my hand tingles at his touch. I wanted him to be here so much and now he is I'm terrified. I don't want to let him go again and I'm terrified that that is no longer my choice, so despite the need to hold on I try to pull my hand away, essential for my self-preservation, but he holds tighter.

"Daniel, I don't understand what are you doing here?" I whisper even though we are far from any eavesdroppers. I really can't believe he is here, did he come for me; my heart squeezes tight as if an invisible fist is holding it firm preventing it from bursting all over my ivory silk dress.

"It is as I said, Sofia called and—"

"She pulled the 'i'm the bride card' didn't she? Did she say her whole day would be ruined or something?" I shake my head at my lovely over dramatic best friend.

"Something along those lines yes . . . You look very beautiful Bethany." His eyes darken and I can see the tension his thoughts are causing course across his face. "You take my breath away, as always." He dips his head to maintain eye contact as I try to look away. "You haven't told anyone about us? We're you hoping I would change my mind?" His words chill me but they are softly spoken. I don't think he means to re hash and hurt me I think he just wants to understand.

"No Daniel, I know you won't change your mind." I blow out the painful breath and flinch at the real pain curling around my heart with my own admission. "I didn't tell anyone because today is about Sofia and they love me enough that if I had told them that I . . . that we . . . what I'd—" I swallow because as much as I know this is my fault I can't say it out loud just yet it's too fucking painful to admit just how much I fucked *us* up.

"I understand." His smooth calm voice stops my fall, stops me breaking further. "I just needed to know. Ethan called me too, he felt bad for letting you down and tried to guilt me into dropping whatever was so important that I could leave you alone on such a day." His thumb traces circles on the back of my hand. It's distracting, he's distracting. "And he was right nothing, nothing is so important that you should be lonely today."

"I'm hardly alone." My words are barely audible because I don't believe them and I know he won't either. Being lonely is more than a feeling, it's a crushing weight that suffocates a

the Only Choice

fragile heart, my fragile heart.

"I know you're not alone, but that isn't what I meant. I wanted to be with you today." He emphasises the last word and his teeth grind audibly.

"Today." I repeat softly.

"Today." He repeats firmly. "I have a proposition." He waits expecting some response but I just gaze at his beautiful face getting my fill because I feel I understand the reality of his ominous use of the repeated word. "For today, we forget everything and just enjoy the celebration for what it is. Your best friend's wedding and a special day. You and me. No past, no future, just present." I can see the uncertainty in his eyes and I wonder if he can see the devastation in mine at his proposition. But what is really pathetic is that I am going to agree because I know any amount of time with him is better than no time and that is ultimately what's on offer no more time.

"A Cinderella scenario if you will." I offer to clarify his proposition.

He smiles, its breath-taking. "Exactly." His voice is light with hope.

"And what happens at midnight?" I hate that my voice sound so tentative, that I can't accept an end even when it's offered on a silver platter.

"At midnight, everything changes." He steps to me his hand sweeps smoothly around my waist. I have to tilt my head back to maintain my eye contact.

"Ok." I breathe out my pathetic acceptance. I would like to think that I am so mature and that this is simply a terribly civilised break up. Or that, given the chance, if you knew this was the last time you were going to see someone, someone you loved like no other before, wouldn't you choose to spend the time just like this. Laughing, loving and entwined in each other but the truth is, knowing this is the end is like a punctured artery and the slow internal bleeding will ultimately be the end of me. But I'm not going to back track, I am going to take the scraps that are offered because for one last night I just want it to be us, and even if it isn't real it's still better than the alternative.

Chapter Fifteen

WE STAND FOR a moment and I am trying for the life of me to understand why he is really here, his face gives me nothing but his eyes are filled with sadness that punctures my heart. His lips curl ever so slightly into a tender smile and I decide then, I can do this. I decide that this day is going to be our day too. A wonderful day to share with someone I love, suspend all reality and immerse myself in the fairy-tale of the happily ever after because I understand my happily ever after is going to be more Grimm than Disney. I blow out a sharp breath to strengthen my resolve and with a surge of uninhibited determination to embrace and take whatever pleasure I can from my last day with Daniel. I step against him pushing through the tangible barrier of instant heat our bodies create. My hands cup his face the slight stubble scratching the soft skin on my palms. Tingles ignite across the surface of my skin and I smile at the intake of breath he forces as I cover his mouth with barely contained passion, holding him firm as my soft lips move with purpose and possession. His immediate shock and tension is instantly replaced with a firm but relaxed reciprocation, his hand carefully threading into my hair, gripping and pulling me further into the kiss I initiated. I gasp and he moans pushing his tongue deep inside and I wonder if every sensation I experience with him today will be just as intense, just as explosive. God I hope so.

I pull back and place my hand on his heaving chest and gently tap my fingers as I feign calm I am definitely not feeling and I fight the smirk I want to express at his wide eyes and ruffled countenance.

"Shall we?" I ask with a light carefree tone.

He coughs and shifts a little but fails to hide the bulge distorting the clean line of his suit trousers. "Shall we what?" His voice is raspy. I laugh out, shaking my head and take his hand to lead him across the manicured lawn to the period glass conservatory to join the line forming to welcome the wedding party. Sofia's family gene pool dominates the room with their strong dark features and stronger characters. My feet barely touch the ground once I enter the room as brothers, uncles and cousins hug and pick me up and pass me along like a party game of pass the parcel. I finally find my feet at the end of the long line of friends and family and instantly a pair of strong arms wrap around my waist and Daniel pulls me so I am cloaked in his body. He whispers. "Please don't tell me I have to watch you dance with all those people that have just manhandled you like you were crowd surfing?" His breath feathers my skin but his gruff tone is clipped and I twist to see his tell-tale jaw ticking. I lean up and he obliges by returning my offered kiss.

"I would have to be confidant that that would even have an effect on you if torture was my plan." His eyes fix on mine trying to see my game plan, but I don't have one. "And I'm not confident and it's not my plan. My plan is to enjoy you today. So no, none of these people will be dancing with me later. I have you for one day, so I won't waste a minute." His eyes widen, perhaps a little shocked at my revelation but given that nothing is at stake any more I have no reason to be cautious, no reason to lie and no reason to walk on eggshells. It's liberating. "You're mine and I'm not sharing." I smile but have to bite my inside cheek to keep it there when he adds, 'for today,' but I manage and even laugh to ease the little tension that has crept between us.

There is a loud cheer and a sudden surge of movement as Paul and Sofia begin to make their way down the line and Daniel holds me a little tighter to protect me from being jostled. It takes a little while for the couple having greeted, kissed and hugged their way down the long line but finally I get the chance to hug the most beautiful bride, ever. She holds me so tight and I hear a little sob which sets me off and we pull back, both with full wet eyes she cups my face and because of the noise she mouths 'I love you sister.' I nod with her hands still clasped to my face and mouth back the same but take a steadying breath before I break. Her eyes widen as she spots the man behind me and I shake my head almost imperceptibly but as she looks again at Daniel with narrowed eyes I hug her once more and whisper that we've sorted everything. She leans back with the biggest smile and I don't feel at all bad for the lie and technically it wasn't a lie, we have sorted everything, for today. It is just that Sofia is programmed to decode in a positive light, her glass is never half full its always overflowing.

We follow the wedding party into the main reception room where the tables are set under the impressive fifty foot high art deco glass conservatory with a domed centre that draws the sun's rays and reflects shards of rainbow lights across the room. The tables are white linen, with crystal, silver reflecting more light and sparkles. The tall stemmed vases in the centre of each table are elegantly bursting with lush bouquets of pale coloured avalanche roses, sweet peas and carnations. The top table is oval and I am on the far end next to Milly. Daniel is seated on the table next to mine and right in between Fia and Pip, Sofia's twin cousins that came on the hen weekend. Sofia had settled on ten courses in the end which was a fight given the family business and that her mother had had fourteen courses at her wedding but Sofia was adamant she didn't want to feel too fat to dance. Even with ten it is going to be a long time and with Daniel just out of reach which it will make it that much longer. I settle Milly back down and tuck in several napkins to try and protect her cream dress. Not that she cares but the photographer is still eagerly snapping away and the pictures would be spoiled with olive oil dribbled down her front. Sofia's grandfather is seated on my left. He speaks very little English but from past experience that doesn't stop heated conversations it just makes them more entertaining. I top up his champagne, I can't help the waitress in me from waiting but when I turn back to Milly I nearly drop the bottle when I see that Daniel has switched and without a word he simply winks and tips his glass to me for a refill.

I laugh because I don't even know why I'm surprised but I am surprised Milly was so quietly coerced into the exchange. I laugh again when Milly runs back over to me and whispers that she's sorry but the nice man is going to buy her a brand new Chelsea kit. That makes much more sense because as charming as Daniel is, I think his stunning good looks are wasted on a four year old, but apparently not when she adds that he also promised her a dance. She giggles as she returns to her seat and I lean in to Daniel and whisper. "Heartbreaker." My smile is met with sadness when he replies. 'No, that is your title Miss Thorne.' I take a moment. I'm sure there are going to be a few 'moments' but I refuse to look away from his deep blue eyes. They hide a wealth of emotion and probably reflect mine but no matter what they are hiding, we have this one day and I'm not going to ruin it with any more sadness. Neither of us need to fill the comfortable silence because just as the first of many courses is being laid the speeches begin. There is no formal break for speeches and the room doesn't really fall silent because the food is being served and drink is flowing. It is all very relaxed and fun. It is traditional though that anyone that wants to say a few words to the happy couple will get the chance and I believe there are many here that wish to do just that.

The microphone is handed from the closest family to start with and as the meal progresses so less familiar faces take over. Some only speaking in Italian and others really only saying the

the Only Choice

odd word of congratulations but it's all so heartfelt and filled with so much love my cheeks start to ache with smiling. I lean into Daniel to give him as much background information of those that are sharing this day. I have met most of the family at one time or another and there is always a story to tell. I love it that he laughs so freely and that rich belly laugh does things to me that make me want to keep him laughing. His eyes crinkle with pleasure and he looks truly happy; God I could look at him forever. When he laughs like that it warms my soul and when he looks at me, he sees me and for that moment I'm the only woman in the world. I find I have finished my story and am dazzled by his face to the detriment of my awareness of my immediate surroundings. Even the hushed room doesn't alert my attention to the fact that the attention of the room is now focused on me. Daniel gives a smug grin fully aware of what has me so distracted and I feel my cheeks heat and turn to face the room only to be faced with a spongy black ball inches from my face. The microphone! Oh No! The microphone! I feel a tight reassuring squeeze on my leg that is now a trembling mass of jelly. I look with utter panic at Sofia and Paul. Sofia flashes her sweetest smile and has nothing but encouragement in her eyes, Marco just a little further along winks and nods but when my eyes flicker back to Sofia I see the trace of uncertainty. I haven't moved, my hand frozen inches from taking the microphone. Not wanting to let her down, I take what courage I have that has been hiding behind my ever present sadness and man the fuck up. I stand and my chair is pulled slightly by Daniel to stop it scraping. I brush down my dress, pull my shoulders back and let out a sigh.

"Oh crap." I exhale in a whisper but straight into the microphone. There is a ripple of laughter. "Ok, if I said I knew anything about this, it would be a huge lie and since I'm a terrible liar I won't start this *little* speech with one and because I want you to believe every word I'm going to say about Sofia." I cough a little to clear my throat. "I met Sofia on my first day of college where in the space of five minutes I knew, but wouldn't recall accurately for some years to come, all the names of her many brothers and cousins, where she lived, what she loved, what she hated. I knew what she dreamed of and what secret she hid from her Dad." I grin and hear her gasp and her wide eyes flash to me and it's my turn to laugh. "Hey, you wanted me to have the microphone." I giggle and continue. "She was open and honest and I was honoured and overwhelmed when she welcomed me into her family. I went from having one person in my life to having, well looking around today, I'd say just a few more than that." There is another ripple of encouraging noises and nodding heads and I take a quick sip of water because I can feel my words start to break in the back of my throat. "She has been one half of my best friend from the moment we met but I honestly feel like I've loved her all my life. She has the biggest heart of anyone I know and if I could find a fraction of the happiness she has and rightly deserves with Paul, then I would count my blessings every day. I don't have regrets because even the bad choices lead us to where we are today. My only regret would be that if I wasn't here to share this day with you." I feel my eyes water and my hands are starting to shake when I feel comfort and warmth as Daniel threads his fingers through my hand hanging at my side. "There is a spoken song that speaks of the perfect day and how you wish everyday could be like that, well this is a perfect day and each day can be like that . . . you just have to choose the right person to share it with." I draw in a shaky breath and grab my champagne glass raising it to Sofia and Paul, "Evviva gli sposi." Sofia's eyes mirror mine as tears trickle down our cheeks and everyone joins in the toast; hurray for the newlyweds.

I quickly take my seat and lay the microphone in front of me. Sofia's Granddad picks it up and there is a not too subtle groan followed by lots of laughter from the guests. Daniel is still holding my hand and I can feel his gaze on me but I need another one of those moments before I can brave his eyes.

"That was a really lovely speech Bethany." His soft words make me look up. His smile is warm and genuine but all I can focus on his how tempting his soft full lips look. I swallow the dryness once more and take another sip of water.

"Thank you." I shake my head in an effort to push the last five minutes from my mind. My cheeks are still burning and I can still feel eyes on me even though Sofia's Granddad is doing his best to captivate the Italian speaking part of the room. The speeches may have ended but he is just a little reluctant to let go of the spotlight. The room starts to fill with more noise as people begin to mingle from table to table. "Stolen lyrics, hardly original but—"

He interrupts. "—No it was perfect, from the heart . . . from your heart." Something flashes across his face but it was so quick, maybe sorrow, maybe anger but it's gone and his killer grin is back in force. "So no regrets?"

A sharp laugh leaves my mouth with my look of astonishment that he seems happy to dive into such a potentially volatile topic of discussion but maybe he thinks the venue will prevent me from answering honestly. He is very wrong, if anything this whole situation is liberating. I have no need to lie or sugar coat and with no future with him to covert and protect. I have no consequences to fear from full disclosure. "Yes Daniel." I laugh again feeling relaxed and comfortable, happy to tell him anything he wants to hear. "I have no regrets, because I meant what I said, good or bad, my decisions meant I spent part of my life with you and no . . . I don't regret that. But that's not the question you really want to ask?" I fix him with my eyes and notice he looks a little wary maybe he senses the change in my tone, in my confidence. "You want to know if I accept I made mistakes." I take another sip of the water I have cradled in my hands and notice his eyes widen just a fraction. "Oh I made mistakes, huge mistakes. I fucked up but I'd do it again in a heartbeat if it meant protecting you from a life of . . . well, let's just say I don't regret trying to protect someone I love." I smile and chuckle as his mask slips, his jaw twitches and his throat takes a slow swallow of his champagne. I never said I would make it easy either. I know my words won't change his mind but there is no reason I have to keep them inside like an insidious poison that erodes me from the inside out.

"A little over dramatic don't you think?" His tone is flat and I can see he is withdrawing. My declaration has made him uncomfortable but really should it come as a surprise I love him that much; enough to risk my own future with him. Well, if he didn't know that, he should fucking know and I'm pretty sure he does now. Even as my heart beat races and I feel tension and hurt building my soft voice is nothing but calm and measured. I lean over and speak closer to his face.

"Not when it's your heart that is at stake Daniel." I place my lips on his cheek, the stubble is rougher than normal which only indicates that his intention to attend is very last minute or not planned at all. He turns his face, my lips graze the rough hairs before they are covered by his soft urgent mouth, steeling my breath. His lips capture and consume and the guests noise and music of the band blur into white noise when all I can feel is him, with every nerve and fibre. All I hear is his heartbeat and his deep breath. I sigh contentedly and smile against his lips as he pulls back.

"It sounds like you are reconciled—" I shake my head on a tight smile before he can finish that sentence.

"—Not reconciled." I roll my eyes like that is even a possibility. "Resigned is more apt. I know you Daniel and I know I hurt you, betrayed you and that is unforgivable." I notice he flinches at this because his pain coincides with the tear in my heart but I press on with a surprisingly level voice. "So no, I am not reconciled and yes it hurts like a motherfucker!" I place my hand on my chest but try to keep the serious sadness at bay with light shake of my head and a smile much bigger than I am capable of genuinely producing.

"But you'll survive." His eyes pierce mine as if this is the lifeline he wants me to throw. I can see the pain and feel the desperate need, but for what? Acceptance, agreement, absolution? I don't think so, but that's what happens when you have nothing left to lose, a reckless regard for yourself and those around you.

"I will exist . . . and for now that will have to do." I take a look around and notice that the tables have started to empty and the band is playing a little louder. Daniel gives a strained laugh and I look to see him straighten in his seat.

"Bethany you will survive. You will thrive and find—" But his confident words falter and it is my turn to interrupt.

"—Please don't belittle what I feel with a trite statement like 'I'll find someone else' because that is never going to happen. I'm not *that* stupid." My voice is a little sharper and I take a minute to calm my inner turmoil from spilling because despite my slightly raised tone, at this moment no one is looking at me, only Daniel. I bite my lip and force another smile, my fucking jaw is killing me. "Twice bitten, well I'd have to be a fucking moron to risk a third, don't you think?" A rhetorical question, I rub the indent in my little finger at the absent reminder of my first someone. Silence ensues when I say under my breath, "besides it's a little more complicated now." I stare into his crystal clear blue eyes and wish I had a photographic memory so I can recall them in the future when I know I'll struggle to remember their fierceness. "So," I draw out the word slowly to not so subtly change the subject, "How's your mother?" I again bite my lip but fail to hide my laugh when he barks out a loud throaty laugh.

"Nice Bethany, very smooth." He continues to catch his breath and he grabs my hand and pulls my fingers up to his soft lips, kissing the tips gently. His eyes still holding my gaze but I close mine and try to shake the residual intensity. "I'm not sure how to take the 'no filter' Miss Thorne and you are not even drunk." He nods toward my sparkling water. "And why is that? You barely took a sip at your own toast and I know you were nervous enough to probably want a whole line of tequila shots." He raises his brow and I get a twist in my tummy but force myself not to place my hand across my mid-section.

"Oh, I'm on a health kick, you know, want to look my best for the big day." His lips form a tight line.

"Hmmm. Is that so?" He pauses, his brow raised in disbelief

but he says nothing more. He traces his finger down my neck and along my collar bone, hovering at the dip at my throat before continuing down my chest and over the swell of my breasts. My breath hitches, my heartbeat frantic as my eyes dart around the room. "No-one is looking at us Bethany, although I can't think why anyone would be looking anywhere but right here." He drops his hand to my hip and wraps his fingers, curling them into my flesh and pulling me toward him. His eyes burn with heat and desire; his lips part and are a whisper from mine. I can't help my body lean into his impossible draw. I catch myself and pull back, my face I hope is expressing my confusion at his intimate display. He places his index finger on my lips to stop me from speaking, although I don't think words are in danger of escaping my mouth any time soon. "I know this body Bethany and I assume a health kick would be about losing unnecessary weight and although it may have shifted, you have definitely not lost any weight. In fact if we could exploit your secret of gaining weight in all the right places I think we could make a small fortune." His sensual tone and desire in his gaze lessens the sting of him telling me I'm fat. I know he hasn't said that, he said all the right places whilst scrutinising my breasts but I'm a woman and I definitely heard 'you're fat.' I push my chair back and he tips forward not anticipating the sudden move.

I see the confusion flash across his face but not giving him any more time to digest and draw conclusions that are for another day, I offer my hand and ask him to dance. The band plays traditional Italian music for the first dance and the same into the early evening. Daniel holds me close and I rest my head on his chest and listen to his heart. We dance with a slow beat and I sway in the comfort of his strong hold regardless of the rhythm of the band. He is surprised when I decline every interruption to dance with any others inclined to ask and he hums his approval and holds me tighter, when I whisper like the song, 'I don't want to miss a thing.' Unfortunately promises have been made and when Milly's small body wedges between us and she looks up to Daniel with a deep frown and her hands on her hips I am not going to be the one to ignite that tantrum in waiting. I step back and watch as Daniel scoops a delighted Milly onto his dress shoes and starts to step around the room. I am about to step away from the floor when Marco appears, takes my hand and sweeps me lightly across the dance floor.

I throw my head back in a loud laugh as he dips me dramatically and does and elegant turn and lift. "You're brave." I argue but despite Daniels obvious scowl I don't mean him, I mean the gaggle of smiling Aunts that follow our every move.

"Not really, even *they* know a losing battle and looking at you two I'd say it's a losing—" He stops when he feels my body tense and looks shocked at my sudden water filled eyes. "Hey Boo, God what's wrong?" He sweeps us, almost seamlessly to the edge and holds my shoulders as I try to get a grip.

"Sorry big emotional day." I let out a breath and I am relieved the tears that threaten do no more than threaten. "I'm fine, you really can't expect me not to break on a day like today." I laugh and nudge him like he is making a big deal over nothing. He dips to meet my eyes and I know he doesn't believe me but he also knows not to push and it's one of the reasons I love him. "Where's the bride? . . . They haven't left already? I know she told me that my duties were done for the day but I didn't think she was leaving already." I am searching the crowd and looking outside to the lawn peppered with evening guest still arriving.

"No . . . don't panic. She is hardly likely to leave without telling you . . . come on seriously where's your head Boo?" He rolls his eyes.

I breathe a sigh of relief, "No, I guess not—"

"But she is likely to want to wear as many outfits as she can . . . She has headed off to change or some shit . . . I don't get it . . . She said she'll be five minutes so maybe she'll surface again in an hour." He offers with a shrug but my eyes are drawn to the man behind him. Marco stiffens when Daniel places his hand in mine and pulls me past him to continue our slow dance in the midst of mayhem. With each passing minute I feel the tiny ache of unbearable misery grow a little bigger spreading from the pit of my stomach and with almost four hours until midnight I need to lighten the all-consuming gravity of the inevitable end.

"So Daniel." I have to tilt my head right back to look into his eyes because he has me flush against his chest and his arms like a vice around my waist. "What was the best thing about us?" I laugh at the sudden tension in his body but then he lets out a loud belly laugh and I can't help but join in.

"No fucking way am I touching that one." He shakes his head looking at me like I have completely lost it, he might be right. "That is right up there with guess how old I am? Or does this make me look fat? No answer is the only answer." I can feel him shake his head as he rests his chin on top of my head. I continue to chuckle. "What was the best thing about us for you?" He asks, the arrogant tone makes me think he doesn't believe I will answer but this is too much fun not to.

"Sex." My voice is throaty and completely serious. He pulls back and I smile at the utter shock on his face and then he slaps his hand over his wounded heart but his grin says he is anything but wounded. I laugh. "Like your ego needed any confirmation in that department but, the sex was pretty fucking phenomenal so for the purpose of keeping this conversation light, yeah I'd say the sex. Especially when you take me *really* hard." My voice gets soft and breathy and he dips his head to hear. "When you pin me down and spread my legs like you can't wait a moment longer, fuck that's hot!" He has stopped moving and I can feel his chest draw in slow steady breaths. "What?" I ask with all the innocence I can muster, well aware of his massive erection rubbing against my tummy. The thick heat radiating with an urgency I feel pooling between my legs; in for a penny. "So Daniel, are you going to do something with that rock hard cock you've got digging in my side or am I going to have to beg . . . because I know you love it when I beg." I fix my eyes on his and see the lust spark and rage. His jaw clenches and he hisses out a curse as he releases his hold, grabs my hand and strides out across the dance floor, along the corridor and out the main entrance. I nearly tell him that I also fucking love it when he is all cave-man like this but the fire in his eyes is fixed on scorching my soul and I just want to let it burn.

Chapter Sixteen

JUST OUTSIDE THE main door Daniel turns and I slam into his immobile solid frame, he steps me back and I hit the wall behind me with the strength and force of our two bodies colliding. I would be winded but he sweeps in and sucks the air from my lungs with lust driven urgency that is just as effective at leaving me breathless. He stops and rests his forehead against mine as we both race to control our breathing. His strong hand grips my jaw and slides down to my throat, his firm fingers and soft hold has my body trembling. He lifts his head, his eyes darken with untamed desire and his voice is deep, rough and rasping.

"You like choices Bethany so I'm going to give you a choice." His fresh warm breath kisses my skin he is so close and I struggle to swallow the dryness in my throat. "I can take you here. Hard. Fast. Down and dirty." He slowly emphasises each word and grins as he feels my body shiver at the words. "Or I can take you to my room in that hotel over there and fuck you nice and slow." Although his eyes are consumed with a need mirroring my own I still notice a glimpse of apprehension and his body tenses waiting my reply.

"Can't we do both?" I breathe out. He narrows his eyes and growls a string of curses under his breath as he steps back and

the Only Choice

pulls my hand roughly and I have to jog to keep his pace. He doesn't say a word as we practically sprint across the car park, through the foyer of the exclusive boutique hotel and stop only to wait for the lift doors to open. He nods for me to enter the lift first and I stand with my back braced on the far wall, my eyes fixed on his. He steps slowly, stalking toward me and as the doors glide to close his gaze is fixed, fierce and feral and I suddenly feel like I am in the lion's den. My heart thumps so loud it drowns the ambient music in the small box. The carnal tension obliterates any other thought in my head and I am so thankful for this moment but not as thankful as I am for the moments that I know are going to follow. He places his hands either side of my head, his impressive muscular body effectively trapping me but it's not necessary, there is nowhere else I would rather be. "Fuck." He breathes out and I know he is struggling with the right thing to do. His concern how this could complicate things is sure to be racing across his mind but this is just us, our passion and our chemistry and if everything changes at midnight then I want to grasp *this* with both hands and take.

"Yes Please Sir." I suck my bottom lip to stop the shit eating grin spread across my face when I notice the exact moment he chooses to ignore his doubts. His lips crash into mine, bruising and biting, hot swollen tissue sucked and teased, devoured and revered. A deep groan escapes his throat as the doors open and he has to stop. He pulls away a fraction and I blindly lean into his vacant space missing the contact, not realising the lift has stopped. I stumble after him as he leads me along the corridor. Cursing and fumbling with the key card, his obvious urgency makes me giggle and I try to hang on to these light moments because at every turn, at every crack and hesitation my mind is filled with my endless lists of 'will I evers? Will I ever feel this wanted again? Will anyone ever make me feel this alive, this cherished, this loved? This fucking list is endless. I blink furiously to stop the water from spilling and I manage to mask my sudden sadness just in time as Daniel slams the door open and in one swift move he has me pinned against the back of the closed door.

"Right, hard, fast, down and dirty coming up." His grin is pure wickedness and I gasp as he thrusts his steel hard length against my soft centre. His fingers grab at the hem of my dress and start to wrinkle the material slowly up my thighs but with a huff of frustration as the material resists he yanks with one sharp pull up to my waist. I close my eyes tight at the pinch on my skin but cry when I hear the material tear. "Sorry," he grins.

I roll my eyes. "No you're not." I reprimand but he has his head buried in my neck taking strong deep pulls at my skin, sucking and marking It feels delicious and I struggle to catch my breath. He tips his head back to meet my eyes and smirks.

"Not even remotely. You're lucky I don't tear the damn thing to shreds." He moans as his hands race every part of my aching body, like they are determined to cover every inch and remember every touch. I want to remember every touch.

"You wouldn't?" I pant.

He raises a brow and that cocky grin has me worried because I do have to go back to the wedding at some point. "Not the dress, but these mmm." One of his hands slides up my thigh and skims my silk clad bottom and I feel his fingers curl round the material. There is the sudden bite on my skin as he snaps the seams and my panties disintegrate in his skilful fingers. I drop my head back and hit the door with a thud as heat coils deep inside and blazes through my veins at the same time a million prickles chill me as tiny hairs cool my skin. His mouth moves from my neck along my collar bone and sears a scorching path between my breasts which he cups aggressively as he works his way down my body. I flinch at the pain shooting from his gripping hands torturing my over sensitive breasts. He stills for a split second but when I exhale a deep sensual moan he continues and I welcome the pain, something I can hold on to. Something familiar as my emotions run wild and dangerously out of my control.

"Daniel!" I cry out as he drops to his knees and holds my hips with brutal force. The guttural sound he holds back escapes

the Only Choice

when he lifts one of my legs and pushes it back against the door. Spreading me wide, the cool rush of air on my exposed sensitive flesh causes a full body shudder. I gasp his name once more, barely a whisper but I want to say so much more. I hold my breath, the anticipation is a sensory overload to my heighten libido and fragile state and I tremble and start to mumble incoherently as he presses his lips to my soaking folds. Liquid heat courses through my body from this point of contact and I shake my head, my attempts to evade and ease the intensity are futile against his iron grip. His tongue drags one long sweep up from my very centre to the very centre of my nerve endings and I cry out in panic and desperation. "Daniel . . . I . . . I. . . ." I pant as my brain tries to find suitable words, well, any words at all because all I can do is emit random animalistic sounds from petted house cat to huntress lion. I look down because Daniel has pulled back and is looking at me with heavy lidded eyes through his impossibly long lashes. He slowly licks his lips and drags his lower lip between his teeth like he is scraping and savouring my taste.

"Do I need to gag you?" He tilts his head and grins and he may be joking but I think it's a perfect solution. I am raw, emotional and vulnerable and liable to say anything, promise anything and beg for more than *this*. I don't want that because he won't want that, so I nod. I know he understands when he closes his eyes, nods too and pauses for a few seconds before removing my leg and slowly dragging his body back up, tight against mine. His fingers slip into the knot of his tie and he eases it loose, his eyes gleam with mischief and his smile is breath-taking. He slips the tie from his neck and holds it up stretched between his hands. "Your wish, my command Miss Thorne." He holds the silk tie against my lips and I shake my head so he pauses.

"No Daniel no wish and *you* command *me*." It's all I manage because the instant I open my mouth he has the tie doubled and pressed against my tongue, deftly securing a knot at the back of my head. It's for the best, this way I can keep my bleeding internal and all I get to share is the pleasure he draws from my helpless body. He presses his lips firmly against mine, my tongue helpless to join his as he traces along my swollen lips. He takes my hands and lifts them high above my head and captures them in one of his fists. He moans into my mouth as he fumbles with the zip on his trousers and releases his straining cock free and I hum my own longing as I feel its weight press against my naked skin. He lifts me with one arm tucked under my bottom and I secure my legs around his trim hips supporting my own weight while he positions himself at my molten slick core. No more pausing, no more anticipation, no more as he drives his full length, hard, fast, ferocious again and again, deep and deeper still as he angles and pushes to my limits and beyond. I scream into the cloth gripped in my teeth as he pounds relentless thrust after delirious thrust, steeling every breath from my body.

My body starts to shudder and I am desperate to hold him or push him away. I don't know, it's too intense, too much, overwhelming. My body quakes as the immense pressure deep inside begins to convulse and contract around his unrelenting lust. My skin glistens, my heart hurts from racing and my mind dissolves from trying to absorb the mind blowing pleasure mainlining through my body. He draws back and meets my glazed eyes and I hold back a sob as panic whips through me that he might choose now to punish me with denial but from the heat and urgency in his eyes it would be just as much a punishment for him. His jaw clenches and he fights to maintain control of this moments' hesitation. "Come with me." The timbre of his voice sounds almost tortured and I feel his whole tense body relax when I vigorously nod my agreement. He rears back and plunges harder, deeper and I can no longer make a noise as all oxygen needed to carry the sound is pushed far from my body with each thrust of his hips, grinding me hard, fast, down and dirty. He throws his head back but I am already falling, gasping and rolling in waves of sublime pulsing pleasure. Forceful crashes of euphoria hit me hard and shake my core and my body takes over squeezing and riding the very last ripple of this monumental climax until I hang like a lim-

the Only Choice

pet from Daniels body. My arms cling over his neck, gloriously impaled on his massive cock unable to support the weight of my legs and only his strong frame pressed against me prevents me crumbling to the floor.

I open my eyes but the black fuzzy dots still float across my peripheral vision and my breathing is ragged, just as laboured as the man I hang from. He bends his knees and clasps his hands firmly on my backside lifting me with ease and pulling me further onto his still hard erection. I try to look down between our bodies but he has me pressed tight to his body as he pushes off the wall and walks us as one to the bed, where he turns and sits. With slow deliberate moves he carefully unzips my dress and pulls it over my head. I can feel him shake and works his trousers off his feet and with a look of concentration that makes me chuckle he works he shoes and socks off too. I am staring at his shirt covered chest and my fingers twitch to undo his buttons and finally feel his skin on mine but I can't take my eyes from his. He slips his hands behind me unties his tie at the back of my head , freeing my mouth and unclips my bra but I can't help laugh when the serious hot tension is broken because he breaks our gaze to take a quick peek down. He chuckles, shrugs and coughs.

"Where's that famous control?" My mocking tone is accompanied with a slight wiggle on his cock which thickens at the movement and he groans in appreciation.

"Mmm. I have control." His voice rasps deep and gravelly. "But I'd have to be a fucking robot to not look at these fucking amazing tits." His hands scoop my weighty breasts and he reverently cups and massages as his eyes flicker from his ministration back to my eyes. His grin is infectious and I laugh at his eloquence.

"You have such a charming way with words." I fan myself to highlight my sarcasm.

"I don't need to be charming I already have my dick buried so deep in you I'm gonna need the rescue services to dig me out." He tilts his hips and hits a spot so deep I can't help the cry at the back of my throat. His hands grip my hips and he pulls me slowly, deeper onto him. His gaze is again fixed on me, it's just so intimate, so intense and I can feel every part of him inside me. I let out a shaky sigh and I can feel my eyes tingle. I breathe out slowly and blink to stop the water pooling but when his lips cover mine, gentle and possessive the tears fall. I struggle to speak, wanting to say so much but not wanting to say too much. "Gag?" His soft words and kind eyes are going to test me to destruction but I shake my head this time. "You sure?" I can hear the uncertainty in his voice but I don't want anything between us this last time. "Ok." He whispers against my lips and my breath hitches with this sweet contact.

"Fuck me nice and slow." I exhale and shiver absorbing the pleasure I feel from the inside out with him just there, deep inside me and wrapped around me but he shakes his head and I frown and hold my breath waiting for his withdrawal.

"No Bethany, I'm not going to fuck you at all. I'm going to make love to you; nice and slow, one last time." His most dazzling smile follows the words that both lift my heart and break my soul but I nod and tuck my head into his neck to hide the tears the trickle down my cheek as I exhale a quiet. 'Ok.'

Added to my endless list of 'will anyone ever make me . . . ' is definitely, 'will anyone ever make me come like that again? Because as emotionally raw and sensitive as I am, I seriously doubt it. I have had to take refuge in the bathroom to gather my fragile self together after the most earth shattering experience of my life. Nice and slow are insults of the English language in this instance, cherished, worshipped, erotically teased and delighted. My skin burnt from his touch and my soul soared, again and again. I had no limits because I couldn't even manage to speak to beg him to stop. My hands are still shaking and I've been in here for a good ten minutes. I don't take a shower because I don't want to wash

the Only Choice

his scent from my body and I will treasure the swollen lips and marks on my skin for the short time they cling to my exterior. I will nurture this broken heart because it will remind me that I have lived all the time I loved this fiercely. It is less than an hour to midnight.

Daniel is dressed when I leave the bathroom and I can feel the shift and change in him. It's understandable. It's necessary. I brush myself down and hope everyone is, by now, too drunk to notice our prolonged absence and my 'she's been fucked by a train' appearance. I decide to tackle the awkward silence head on; we still have an hour after all.

"Am I that predictable?" I grin trying to ease the burgeoning tension but he just frowns with confusion. I wave my arms around the room and point at the bed in disarray. He flashes a wicked grin but shakes his head.

"Not at all, I flew in this morning and needed somewhere to change. It was never my intention . . . I mean *this* is not why I came today." He doesn't sound regretful but there is a heavy weight of sadness to his tone which needs to be lightened.

"So midnight?" My voice attempts to be cheery but the hitch in my breath at the end means it fails.

"Midnight?" He repeats and opens the door for me to walk through, talking and walking is easier, less intense.

"Well, my life may turn back into the proverbial pumpkin but what about you?" I take his hand because I don't like the cool distance creeping in between us. Even if it is inevitable, I can still fight it until the last second of this day.

"I don't think . . ." He hesitates but clearly decides he isn't in a sharing mood. "What about you?" He flips the question but his tone is almost an accusation.

"Oh well, pumpkin aside." I nudge him and smile desperate to lift the gloom. "I'm going to disappear for a bit. I have a bit of money saved and Tom has helped so I'm going to travel. See a bit of the world before, well you know 'get my shit together.'" I laugh but it sounds flat and falls flat as I turn to look at where

Daniel has stopped walking.

"Who are you travelling with?" His dark brow furrows and I can see tension gather at his jaw.

"No-one . . . I'm kind of looking forward to some *me* time." I am not sure this is entirely true but it is the situation I am in and I am not going to cancel.

"I don't like it." He crosses his arms and I laugh out loud and turn to walk away shouting over my shoulder.

"Well it's a good thing it has fuck all to do with you then isn't it!" I walk through the main door and can hear the wedding party still in full swing but before I can make it into the main room Daniel has grabbed my hand and spun me to face him. His scowl still makes me recoil but I check myself when I remember my ticking clock as far as Daniel is concerned.

"Bethany!" He growls and I can feel the anger vibrate through his frame.

"What Daniel? Tell me was I wrong? Do my decisions have fuck all to do with you?" He straightens his shoulders and narrows' his eyes but doesn't reply. "That's what I thought and how fair do you think it is to say something like that to me, with less than an hour to go before 'everything changes.' Tell me! Because I don't think it is fair, not by a long fucking way." My voice breaks and is muffled when he steps and wraps his arms around me, my head is buried against his chest but my sobs only come harder.

"You are right, forgive me. It has nothing to do with me . . . I am sorry." His clipped tone softens with the last few words. I shake my head with stubborn determination and refuse to waste these last precious moments with futile tears. There is a crowd gathered and I can see Sofia waving her bouquet around and searching the crowd. Her eyes meet mine, hers filled with playful mischief but I can't play along. I hang back and shake my head. I watch as she throws the flowers high and smile at the surge and squeal of giggles from the gathered ladies. Once it is safe I walk over because Sofia and Paul are about to leave for the evening and I take my turn in hugging and wishing them . . . well, wishing them *everything*.

"You looked so beautiful today Sofs." Her arms are wrapped tight around my neck and I can tell from the sway of her body she is a little worse for the free flowing bubbly.

"And you look beautiful every day . . ." She pulls back with an exaggerated pout. " I am sad Marco is going travelling tomorrow and you said you are too . . . what about me? What will I do?" She hiccups and giggles. Ok so maybe a lot worse for wear.

"You'll be on your honeymoon Sofs—" She collapses in silent laughter.

"Oh yes!" She straightens herself and tries to look sober. "And you will be travelling the world with Daniel. I am so glad you worked it out . . . This has just been the perfect day, hasn't it?" She squeezes me once more before Paul drags her away and bundles her into the waiting car.

"Perfect." I say, waving the happy couple Bon Voyage.

I turn to see Daniel regarding me from the edge of the gathering. He looks restless, he looks like he is about to leave. I walk up to him. "Dance with me?" My voice is just as shaky but I manage to smile and he manages to nod and once again takes my hand and leads me into the throng of dancing wedding guests.

The vibrancy and chaotic flailing of arms is evidence enough that the alcohol has continued to flow and the room feels fit to burst with happiness. It is timely and distracting and I quickly find myself jumping and shaking some dubious shapes to the belting sounds of Pink's *True Love*. Pip and Fia throw their arms around me and we jump together singing at the top of our lungs *'I hate you, I really hate you, I want to wrap my hands around your neck. . . . So much I think it must be True Love . . .* ' Glad the DJ has the music so loud our tuneless voices can't be heard but it doesn't take a whole lot of lip reading for Daniel to know what I am singing right at him. He pulls me away and holds me tight against his strong body resting his head on mine and slowing my moves to sway with his, ignoring the thumping beats the crowd is dancing to. The blend and mix of love songs begins to seep into my conscious despite the remix and up-beat tempos and when Ellie Goulding's *Figure 8* lyrics filter in '*I need you more than I can take, you promised forever and a day and then you take it all away,*' I have to fight with all my strength to push from his hold. I break free, stumble back as my eyes blur and I turn and run for the door unable to breathe, pushing passed the guests, remaining family and waiting staff. So desperate for air I almost collapse as I cling to the pillar just outside the main doors.

I feel him before I hear his steady steps close in behind me and I shake my head and draw in a deep healing breath but it's useless. I know I'm broken because I can't stop the fucking tears from free falling. My breath stutters as I try to speak. "This is brutal." I push out a sharp breath of utter desolation as I turn to face the man I broke and the man who chooses to break me. This is so fucked up. "I know we can't all have the fairy tale ending but that doesn't stop me wanting one wish." He steps closer but doesn't reach out to touch me even though I can see his fingers move with residual memory of that connection. I tilt my head to meet his beautiful eyes unashamed that mine are unable to contain their sadness a moment longer.

"What would you wish?" His voice is tentative; I have never heard it quite like that before now. I let out a sad laugh but I am surprised he asked given how ridged his body is, how uncomfortable I am making him right now.

"Groundhog Day." My voice falters again but he nods in understanding but I still want to explain. "You know in the film Bill Murray spends all his time learning new stuff, playing the piano, learning to make ice sculptures, saving lives, that sort of thing." I hiccup and suck back, muffling the sobs so I don't sound as desperate as I feel. "I wish today was my Groundhog Day but I wouldn't change a thing. Not a single thing." Silence falls for endless seconds before he breaks it.

"Thank you for today Bethany. I will cherish the memory." His soft quiet words so filled with finality. I have to hold my

the Only Choice

mouth to stop the heart wrenching cry just waiting to escape and embarrass us both. But the sheer panic consumes me and my heart beats a deafening tattoo so loud that I think I will have to shout out to be heard.

"Daniel . . . I . . . I . . . I am so sorry. You must know . . . I'm so sorry." I fail to keep the genuine fear from my voice.

"I am sorry too." The quiet in his voice does nothing but send an eerie chill up my spine. His face is blank of any emotion. His lips are tight and I can see him start to pull away, I grab his hand and hold it in both of mine.

"Daniel, I'm sorry. I'm so fucking sorry but its midnight so what's actually changed, it's still just you and me. You're here with me . . . Can't we? . . ." My mind is messed up, frantic for the right words. Any words that will make him change his mind. He has to change his mind, my question sounds like a pitiful plea. "What's changed?" I don't actually finish this question because he interrupts and rips my heart from my chest, throws it on the ground and drives his pristine dress shoes into the mass of lifeless muscle.

"Angel is pregnant." His voice is hushed; his jaw ticks but there are no words left. I have no words and I have nothing left to stop my tears from drenching my face and drowning my soul. His voice so quiet I strain to hear. "I'm sorry you were wrong." I can see his eyes through my haze and I believe he is sorry. Maybe he is sorry I was wrong, maybe he is sorry he was right but everything has changed. My knees buckle but just as Daniel steps to catch me he is pushed aside. Marco swoops and scoops me against his body, his older brother Anthony flanking him and his father just behind them.

"I think it's time you left." I have never heard that tone from Marco before and Daniel wisely holds his hands up in retreat and starts to step away from the carnage. Just before he turns I call out.

"Daniel!" My voice is raw; the pain expressed is reflected in his face, for once an open book of absolute ruin. "I hope I continue to be wrong because you don't deserve that life if I'm right."

"You can't help yourself can you?" He shakes his head in frustration or maybe its resignation.

"Not when it comes to you." He has already walked away so I don't think he hears my whispered words but Marco does and he huffs with indignation. But he stops his judgemental tirade when he sees my face because you would have to a callous arsehole to kick me now and he's not an arsehole, he's my friend.

Chapter Seventeen

I HAVEN'T SLEPT. I didn't want to dream. I have lay naked in my bed going over every moment of the day in every possible detail. Closing my eyes tightly to hold the memory a little longer, each glance, each touch and each heartbeat I shared with him. It's been a long, painful, wonderful perfect night of pure hell. I can feel him on my skin, under my skin and every part of me feels because of him. But from this moment I have to start the unbearable process of letting go and endure, as each vibrant nerve ignited by him fizzles and dies. I know it will take more than the day I am allowing myself to wallow in self-pity, I know it will take longer than forever. Even though he wasn't my first love he was my true love and I know I will never get over that. I knew I would never survive Daniel Stone but I fell all the same. Today, I feel battered, bruised but alive and alive I feel too much. Too much pain, too much sorrow, just too much. I yearn for the welcome return of the inevitable numbness.

I know it's gross but as I drag my sorry arse out of bed and gaze at my puffy face and red swollen eyes I still can't bring myself to wash my skin of his scent. I do rinse the dried sting of tears with a splash of ice cold water and pat my face with a soft towel. I look, at least, a little more human even if I feel nothing.

I notice Marco's rucksack is all packed and leaning stuffed to bursting against the hall table and as I wander in a trance like state into the kitchen I think that I should start my own packing. I have an open ended train ticket to cover most of Europe and some ideas but nothing fixed about exploring further afield because I would really prefer having a little company for that part of my travels. I pour myself a herbal ginger tea and just as I am thinking about calling Ethan to talk through my plans my phone starts to vibrate on the counter. My heart jumps and a rush of nerves tingle and flare. My hope still in denial of my reality, but it dies just as quickly as it was raised when I don't recognise the number the text message is from. Ethan has lost his phone and is using a crappy pay as you go, could I meet him at his flat to catch up. I can't quite manage a smile but I do feel better now I actually have a plan for today and after seeing Ethan I should a sufficient 'to do list' to keep me busy and or at least distracted, until I leave.

Ethan's apartment is just back from the river Thames. A modern development of around fifty flats and from speaking to Tom I understand that I have one of the flats just waiting for me to move into but I can't think about that now. Maybe when the baby is born and Marco has had enough of sleepless nights, maybe then but that's what I will use my time away to think through properly. I walk over the Chelsea bridge and realise I must have walked passed Ethan's building every day on my way to work during my brief period as an intern. I just didn't know it at the time. Its late morning and the main revolving doors are open and I walk into a light open white marble foyer, with gleaming chrome and white leather sofas, full glass walls to the front and a small unmanned concierge desk. My soft flat ballet pumps are the only noise to disturb the quite as I squeak my way to the elevators. I press the button below the light displaying Ethan's name and start to unpick my ear phones. Only then as the door opens, do I wish I'd done that sooner because then as I step back from the vision before me I might've heard the footsteps of the large body pressed against my back and tightly gripping the tops of my arms.

"Kit?" I question myself because I know it's her but I am not wrong to question her appearance here of all places. Daniel had said she was in Paris but why is she in Ethan's apartment? Does he know her? Does he know she's my sister? I stand transfixed as question after unanswered question clogs my brain. She looks different too, her clothes are classy and understated. Her hair a soft golden brown falling in long loose curls around her lightly made up face but her eyes are just as clinical, just as cold and the lifeless smile and sneer that spreads across her face is unmistakably the Kit I remember.

"Hello Bethany, always a pleasure but I'd rather not do this in the hallway and we don't have long before sweet Ethan returns." She steps back and waves her hand for me to enter. No fucking way am I going in there, even if I do want some answers. I try to shuffle back but find my feet skid for a moment before I am lifted from my feet and walked into the apartment. "Thank you Clive." I twist to see the no neck ugly scowl and dark features of Clive. His dark dead eyes cause my body to shake uncontrollably as I remember with crystal clarity him trying to force himself inside me, a violent attack I managed to escape. I try to swallow my nerves because I need to remember what Patrick had taught me, I'm not defenceless and I am getting out of here. The instant I feel the pressure ease from Clive's ape like grip I turn but before I can evade, I feel the hammer impact of his fist slam into the side of my skull and see the flash of white flooring before the blackness, before I hit the floor and I pass out.

The humming in my head is mind numbingly intrusive, pounding through my skull leaving no chance of peace. I try to open my eyes but the pain that shoots through my head causes me to still even this small movement. Everything is screaming in agony and I feel like I have been dragged feet first, down forty flights of stairs with my head cracking each tread. The silence of my surroundings is eerie and it forces me to push through the pain and open my eyes. I know I am lying on a platform, maybe not a bed but certainly not the hard unforgiving surface of the floor I hit before I blacked out. The room ceiling is dark grey and a single old style bulb hangs in the centre giving off a harsh bright light. My right hand is pulled above my head and I look to see the cuff clipped tight around my wrist and the small chain attached to the cuff is fixed at the other end to a metal box where the chain disappears. The box is fixed to the bar on the wall effectively securing me to this spot. I shuffle up the platform and notice the sheet covering the platform is clean and there is a blanket folded neatly over the end, it may not be comfortable but this is definitely supposed to be a bed, my bed.

My eyes feel swollen and I don't know if that is from the remnants of my endless tears through the night or from more physical abuse while I was unconscious. I take a silent inventory of my body but as stiff and sore as I feel I don't think anything is broken, just a killer headache and an overwhelming fear for my future. I take in my new home; I'm thinking bijoux fixer-upper for the more psychopathic minded professional. It is small, dank with no natural light and the period detail around the dormant fireplace makes me think this is an older property, maybe Victorian. Which would fit because not so many new builds have cellars or dungeons as in this case. There is a table beside me with a jug of water and a plastic cup. I lick my dry bloated lips but don't have enough moisture for the task and because my right hand is pinned uselessly to the wall I struggle clumsily to pour a cup of water, spilling precious liquid all over the table. I don't know how long this is supposed to last but I do know that if Kit has gone to the trouble of bringing me here it's unlikely she would poison the water. It is still possible but unlikely . . . I hope. The cool water feels delicious as it trickles down my parched throat but my cracked lips sting as they touch the cup. I suck in a sharp but quiet cry and my fingers gently pat the point of pain, looking down at the streak of red on my fingertip and now tasting the

the Only Choice

copper tinge to the water. I know I must have split my lip when I fell or maybe Clive took another swing for old times' sake.

I continue to take small sips, look around and try to think. I may not understand why I'm here but at least I can try to figure a way to use something in this room to escape. The bed is sparsely covered, the table has no drawers and the chain holding my arm is so short I couldn't use it to wrap around Kit's neck even if she was sat on my lap. The wall to my right has a flat green screen, not a television just a printed green screen that covers the whole wall and at the end of the bed is a cross trainer. It is possible this is someone's home gym but it's so creepy you would have to be a serial killer in training to enjoy working out in here. I shiver at my own macabre musings, because isn't that what Kit is, a killer; not serial as such, I just happen to be her own personal re-run of the same episode. I pour and drink another cup of water, the silence at first oppressive is now tiring and I find I sink back down, shuffling and finally getting as comfortable as I can on my side with my hand strung up like I still want some answers, which is fine because I do. I close my eyes and fall asleep, waiting for my answers.

The movement on my wrist alerts me and I feel the stretch in my bicep as the small chain contracts and my hand is brought flush to the wall. I shuffle to allow the retraction without pulling my arm from its socket. The locks on the door click and I can hear keys jingle. The time between that initial noise and when the door finally opens makes my heart sink, at least three locks and two sliding bolts by the sound. The door looks heavy as it moves slowly open and Kit steps in carrying a bucket, a paper bag and an irritated look on her face, like I am causing her some huge inconvenience. She stands beside the bed and I notice she keeps enough distance that if I were to swing my legs out I would miss her but only by millimetres. She puts the bucket on the floor by her feet; my understanding is instant as is the sudden urge and discomfort from immediately bursting to pee. I frown at her static position and wonder if she is just going to stand there while

I squat on the bucket dangling from the cuff on the wall. She fumbles in the paper bag and rips the packaging and throws the white pen on the mattress beside me. I feel my colour drain as I recognise the pen and the package of the pregnancy testing kit she holds in her hand.

"Piss on that!" She crosses her arms and curls her lips like the words taste fowl, not as fowl as hearing them. I shake my head.

"I don't need to go." I offer with little conviction as my toes start to curl at the very thought of having to hold on much longer.

"Oh I'm sorry Bethany you seem to have mistaken me for someone who gives a shit what you want. Mistaken me for someone that won't ask Clive to strip you naked, hold you down and press on your bladder until you piss all over yourself as I hold that stick between your legs." She snarls the words and I swallow back a small cry in my throat and blink back my building tears. I can't let her see how this is effecting me, how broken I am right now because I know it would just make her day. I bite the inside of my cheek and dig my fingernails into my palms giving me some tangible pain to focus on. I draw in a fortifying breath and with more bravado than I can possibly be feeling, I straighten my spine and fix her emotionally barren stare with my own fiery glare.

"Fine, but you might want to loosen the leash or I will end up pissing in my jeans and then you'll not be able to get your little test done after all." I cross my ankles and put one arm across my tummy trying to protect my little secret for just a few minutes more. Kit walks back to the door and opens it enough to slide her arm through. I hear the whirring of a small motor and my arms starts to fall from its elevated position. I wriggle my fingers as the blood starts to flow back, pins and needles prickle the digits and I fist and release my hand for relief. She steps back inside and makes sure the door is closed until it clicks and she keeps her back to it and well out of my new range. I stand and squeeze my eyes at the sharp shooting pain like an ice pick between my brows and I have to bend to hold the mattress as a wave of nausea makes my legs buckle and my stomach heave. I swallow back the liquid pooling in my mouth and take a steadying breath. Let's get this over with. I pull at the buttons and roughly push my jeans and panties to my knees. My vest hangs to my mid-thigh to cover my nakedness but as I flick an angry glance at Kit she isn't even looking my way. She is inspecting her immaculately manicured nails.

I grab the stick and hover low over the bucket, my legs tremble with the tension of holding my weight at this strange angle but my fingers are trembling for an entirely different reason. I lightly hold the absorbent end of the plastic pen, angled down and in the mid-stream. I stand instantly I'm finished, empty but not relieved and pull my jeans back in place holding the stick like a weapon.

"Here you are." I wave it at her, my voice is clipped and angry because in minutes this stick is going to be screaming my secret and I am furious the first one to know is going to be the one person I hate. Well, the one person I hate the most.

"Nice try sweetie but I'm not coming anywhere near you and your ninja moves." She barks out a bitter laugh and nods to the floor. "Just put it on the floor and step back." I fight a smirk because I have to admire her memory or her research and that she's smart enough to learn from it. I put the stick face down on the floor and take a half step back. She smiles too and opens the door once more and once more the motor stars to whir and I have to keep step with the retracting chain that is now pulling my arm back to the wall and far away from Kit. Once I am secured with no give on the bed, kneeling, arm pinned above me, my face fixed with a scowl that I only wish could kill, Kit moves to retrieve the stick. She paces the room slowly, wiggling the stick in her fingers but she doesn't look at me and she doesn't speak. My mind is racing, how did she know? I mean how the fuck did she know? No-one knew except my doctor. Maybe she hacked my records, that seems a little farfetched even for Kit but there has to be something. Maybe she has been following me, seen me throw up all those times but she wasn't in my flat or at work when that happened.

She stops with her back to me and in a dramatically slow turn she fixes me with a knowing evil grin and narrow callous eyes. "Well, well. She was right after all." She quirks her pristine brows and shrugs her shoulders like I am supposed to know what the hell she is talking about, like I am supposed to know who *she* is.

"Kit?" I ask my voice shaky and desperate as she walks with purpose toward the door. She opens it and flashes me a tight indifferent smile before the door slams shut. I don't hear the locks turn and I panic and shout after her. "Kit! Kit! What are you talking about! What the fuck are you talking about! Who was right?" My voice wavers as I scream in frustration but my throat is too sore to hold the strength of my anger. "Who the fuck was right?" I cry out in exasperation not expecting to be answered when the door flies open and I suddenly wish I never knew the answer. The perfect storm of evil bitches; Kit and Angel; Angel and Kit. I suck back a silent strangled cry because crying won't help. Whatever they have planned, I won't survive but what chills my soul is that I know this isn't about me anymore.

"Now Bethany we can't have that sort of language around the baby, can we?" She smiles so sweetly at me I find my automatic reaction, ingrained manners, has me returning her smile before I physically shake my head at my own stupidity.

I tighten my lips to a thin smile and just as sweetly say. "Fuck off!"

She steps into the room rapidly crossing the small distance and slaps me hard across my cheek. My head snaps forward and is yanked back with a sharp pull of my hair, her face inches from mine her venom seeping from her lips and crawling over my skin. "I said I won't have that sort of language in front of *my* baby." Her grip tightens and I feel the hair tear from my scalp but that is no pain compared to what she has just said. I gasp in horror, my eyes flood with water and I turn my head away and my body starts to shake and convulse physically repelling the notion that I would ever let her have my baby.

She releases her grip with a violent push that smashes my head against my own knee, bruising my lips again, more swelling to my already swollen lips. She huffs and steps back. "Now look what you made me do, how can I take pictures with you looking like that?" She sighs and lightly shakes her head before carefully sitting on the edge of the bed. She is in reach of a one off kick from me but I am so fucking scared right now I just curl up a little tighter into myself. "Look we should probably go over some rules or this is going to be a unpleasant for all of us. There is really no need or any reason why we can't have a little fun." I hear Kit snicker but I don't turn her way. My widened unbelieving eyes are fixed on this vision of pure evil, perched in a neat elegant Prada package at the end of the bed. "Right." She takes a moment to compose herself when she turns, her face is masked with a sickly smile and emotionless eyes. Angel is the most terrifying person I have ever met. "Mostly, if you do what I say . . . if you behave and don't cause any trouble you will be left alone. You will be fed the best nutritional meals of course and either Kit or I will come in once a day to make sure you take the proper exercise, none of that Kung Fu nonsense." She nods at the cross trainer. "I will need you to give me some personal details to put on your social pages. Don't misunderstand me, I know everything there is to know about you from Daniel. What I need in this instance is outside of that, you know typical things you might comment on just to aid authenticity. I should caution, before you think this would be an opportunity to drop some hints or put out a cryptic cry for help. It isn't. It would be extremely unwise to treat it as such." Her detached tone and ice cold delivery actually stop my heart because it's too fucking scared to beat. Her deliberate pause is heavy and ominous but she breaks it with a wholly out of place brilliant smile before she continues with the rules. "If you prove you can follow these simple rules I will bring you something suitable to read, but no Television and no

Radio. I won't have my baby infected subliminally with all sorts of uncensored media. Books I approve will be fine but you have to prove to me you can be trusted." She smiles and sighs patting her knees before she goes to stand. "I think that covers it don't you Kit?" I don't hear Kit speak so I guess she has nodded her agreement.

"Why?" I manage to ask.

She chuckles lightly, like it's such a silly question and perhaps it is. "Kit was surprisingly willing to help with any plan that involved hurting you. For her this is very personal. You know, I even think she would've done this as gratis but she does love money and there is a great deal of it in play. Honestly Bethany, hell hath no fury like your sister." She shares a knowing grin with Kit before continuing her speech. "Me, specifically . . . hmmm . . . Well, I could give you many answers to that one Bethany, because you have something I can never have, because I want Daniel. No" She shakes her head. "Let me correct that . . . because I want Daniel to love me and he will, by the way." She laughs and places her hand where her heart should be like it's a funny joke to play with lives like she is. "I really enjoy this game and I never deny myself anything that brings me joy . . . But mostly Bethany, it's because I can." She sniffs and looks down her perfectly sculptured nose. "You will never know how easy you made this. You just didn't know when to quit. You practically gift wrapped him for me." She laughs lightly.

"You can't keep me here forever. You'll never get away with it." I scoff but my words are hollow because tied to the wall in some basement cellar, 'get away with it,' is exactly what she has done.

"Really?" She walks and stands beside Kit. "Who is going to miss you Bethany? It is actually pathetic how few people will even know you are gone. But what is really incredible, is that I didn't even have to worry about that because *you* told everyone that you are travelling, *alone,* going to get 'your shit together.' It is perfect, really, I couldn't have planned this better myself. And

I have been planning this for some time, ever since I stumbled on your file in Daniels office. Oh don't look so shocked you know what he's like, he is so very careful with the things he lo—" She shakes her head unable to say the word but I snap out the word like a personalised bullet hoping to wound.

"Love . . . what Daniel is like when he loves." But my words have no visible impact she just fixes her impassive face with another fake smile and continues to torture me with her speech.

"The file was mostly about Kit but it did have some background information regarding Ethan and your father which has proved a useful added incentive for Kit and her insatiable greed." With disconcerting hubris she smiles at Kit. Kit is a statue seemingly unaffected by the insult or maybe she took it as a complement, either way I couldn't tell. Angel turns back to face me with a deep set frown. "*You* dared to question me, interfere with my relationship with Daniel . . . threaten my plans and my future! But you under estimated our history, Daniel is so very loyal. He will never forgive himself for killing our baby. It haunts him so much that I knew you couldn't possibly win. Besides I am his first love, he will love me again. I can see he wants to and now he can."

"Your husband said you knew Daniel never loved you . . . that he was the one that got away. That's not first love . . . thats a narrow escape." I brace myself for another lunge and strike to my face but she remains standing in the doorway with Kit.

She taps her fingernails on her lip and looks to the sky as if she is trying to get answers to questions she has long since answered. "Even so," She muses like she hasn't heard a word I said. "That still wouldn't get me what I want and then you got pregnant." She huffs out her revelation with mock pleasure but I can see the envy and hurt flash in her eyes. "He doesn't know of course but he does talk and every little detail he threw my way I stored. I guess if one wasn't so sensitive to such a topic one might not pick it up but I. . well, let's just say I have a vested interest. But I do have to thank you for making this so fu—" She slaps her hand over her mouth and shakes her head with a wry smile. "You've just made this so very easy for me and even easier, because of your sorry excuse of a social life, to make you disappear." She sniffs, her expression a mix of pity and distain.

I struggle to hold the staggered breaths and my voice is so shaky I know I won't be able to hold the tears back much longer. "But they'll still know . . . they will still look for me. Marco, Sofia even Daniel might—" My voice breaks and I let out my first broken sob.

"Oh Bethany, now this is heart breaking, really it is. Marco I believe is traveling and Sofia is loved up and off on an extended honeymoon so I don't think you will be featuring on their radar for some time. So no, they won't. When they do return the answer is still no, they won't come looking because they will know exactly where you are, having the best holiday and falling in love. I will keep them updated with Twitter and Facebook, photos and snippets enough to stop anyone coming looking or suspecting anything for at least, mmmm, seven months?" She raises her brow as a question and I instantly wrap my hand across my tummy. "Yes around seven months should do and then you will . . . Oh, I don't want to spoil the surprise. I just hate it when people give the ending away don't you?" She giggles again but then her face falls and her expression is ice cold. I feel the temperature drop. "Daniel is broken. You broke him and when he sees how quickly you got over him he is going to be devastated. But you don't need to worry because I will be right there comforting him as he comforts me when my own marriage disintegrates and my tummy expands with his child." She backs out of the door closely followed by Kit and all of my hope.

I double up, my head in my lap with the enormity of what I've just heard. Pain slices deep inside and I swear if I pull up straight there will be an open wound the width of my abdomen. I rock and shake to ease the agony; but the unprecedented pain consuming me is overshadowed by the fear for my baby. What am I going to do? I can't think straight as her words slice away at my wafer thin courage and dwindling hope. She's right my best friends are away, at least for a month and maybe they won't question my absence if I'm not really absent. I don't know how she is going to show I'm sunning myself on a beach when I am pallid, fearful and held captive in a basement. This room is hardly a tour brochure photo opportunity and I am far from looking the picture of a happy traveller. I cry out loud and forget trying to remain stoic as I let the tears fall when I think of Daniel and how I wish I was fucking wrong now. I can't stop the images flash behind my closed lids of the sadness in his face when he told me Angel was pregnant. He knew then that it changed everything but he didn't know how much. He would've taken my tears at the time as resignation, confirmation that I believed we were finally over. Why would he come looking for me when we are over.

I don't know how long I cry for but my sobs are now dry, steady and constant. I clearly have no more liquid to spare. My head still throbs from the blow I took from Clive but the fuzziness and jumble of thoughts is crowding and making it really difficult to think. All I seem to generate is more confusing questions but it's when I start to figure out solutions I realise I might be slipping into some sort of post traumatic psychosis. I mean, I ask how she is going to pass off being pregnant. Well, Bethany, she could just use a bit of padding and not let anyone get too close as long as no one sees her naked. I get a sickly taste and retch in my mouth at the thought but she has a few more weeks before she will start to really show. So there is actually plenty of time to get naked now and just cover up later. What the fuck am I thinking? She isn't going to start to show at all! And what about the scan, how is she going to fake a scan? How is she going to give birth without anyone there? Wait, how am I going to give birth without anyone there? Fuck I need to get out of here. Kit and Angel, Angel and Kit . . . my rock and a hard place. My chances of getting either one on my side are laughable. I hate to acknowledge how utterly desperate my choices have become that I am even contemplating Kit as a viable collaborator in my escape plan. But after hours of futile internal dialogue that is what I am left with. Kit is the lesser of two evils. I know her, she may hate me but she knows me and we have history. We were family once. I need to start praying that blood really is thicker . . . I am just not so sure it's blood that courses through her veins because up to now it's always been poison.

Chapter Eighteen

I TWIST MY neck to try and relieve the tension. I roll my shoulders because my right one has set like concrete supporting my suspended arm. I am going to look like one of those crabs with the one huge claw if I have to hang like this for seven more months. Oh God! My heart just plummets like a dead weight through the dusty threadbare carpet on the floor, at the thought of the next seven months. I let out a scream of undiluted anguish mixed with anger, frustration and hatred. The sound bounces off the cold walls with no soft furnishings to soften the edges it sounds raw and acrid. It scrapes my sore throat and leaves me breathless; it accomplishes nothing and makes me feel more helpless and alone. I jump at the sound of the locks on the door and wonder if loud noises, along with harsh language are not acceptable and would constitute breaking the rules. Kit steps inside and pushes the door closed with her backside; her hands are balancing a tray with a covered plate and a fresh jug of water. She narrows her eyes and approaches me slowly trying to gauge whether I have any fight in me but she needn't worry I have nothing, for now.

She carefully places the tray and steps back just far enough, her hip jutting with one side dropped, her arms crossed making a balcony of her perfectly pert and paid for breasts. Her lips form a thin line and I can see her jaw twitch as she grinds her teeth silently. I make a show of how difficult it is to move when I am fixed to the wall. Eventually I sit back and with my left arm lift the lid on the plate revealing what has to be the blandest selection of food known to man. One small portion of lightly grilled chicken breast, ridged barely warmed broccoli and brown rice but I must be hungry because my mouth actually waters at this depressing dish. No cutlery to speak of, just one chubby plastic child's spoon which I hold up with a raised brow toward Kit in query. She shrugs like I should be surprised that I am not given implements that could be used to attack or maim. I shake my head and laugh as I roll the smooth chunky spoon in my hand, yep not going to be able to use this to escape. I doubt I will be able to use it to cut mashed potato. After several unsuccessful attempts at trying to spoon the chicken into smaller pieces I give up and pick the rest of the meat with my fingers, tearing it in to smaller pieces with my teeth.

As small as the portion was I still couldn't finish it all but I idly move the remaining food around my plate because I understand Kit will stand there as long as I do. My head is racing with how to get Kit on my side and I puff out a loud breath when I come up with absolutely nada. She has been an impenetrable ice queen bitch for as long as I can remember but maybe that's the problem. Maybe I have to look back further, was she really always like this? Did she really have the capacity for such cruelty at the age of five when I was born? I don't know. I seriously can't remember any good times. But I am going to need to remember because I need to get some real connection established between us, something more than what Angel is offering. I shake my cuffed wrist to get her attention. "Do you think this could be loosened? At least when I'm on my own? It's fu. .it's . . . It is hurting my shoulder." I stutter and notice her smirk as I censor my own language.

"I'll check." Her clipped tone is edged with something and I see the irritation in her face. So she isn't in charge and judging by that non-verbal disclosure she's not happy about it. Well that's a start but I need more information I just wonder if she will be as forthcoming as Angel.

"Why are you doing this Kit?" I try to keep my voice neutral, not judgemental or patronising just casually curious.

She walks forward and snatches the tray even though I have been pushing the leftover rice into a small heap that I might still eat. "I think Angel gave you all the information you need, a little too much if you ask me." She grumbles but hasn't turned away.

"She did and I know why she's doing this but I don't understand, what has she promised you? Why would you trust her, you don't trust anyone." I snort and she smiles in agreement.

"I don't trust. I don't need to. You are going to give me what I want." She blinks her eyes slowly and the snide smile spreads slowly curling the thin line of her lips.

I can feel my brow furrow as I try to think, what it is she wants, what is the only thing she has *ever* wanted. It takes a little longer than it should but I think I might still have concussion, it can be the only excuse for not seeing the bleeding obvious sooner. She isn't complicated at all. It really is exactly like Angel said . . . money. She is insatiable for money. "But I don't have any money and Daniel . . . we're not together so—" I don't get to finish because her bitter laugh cuts me off.

"And I don't need Daniel either which is why my new partnership with Angel works so well, for now." She places her hand over her mouth like she is trying to hold back uncontrollable laughter at my stupidity. "You don't even know do you. I should be so fucking angry at how easy all this is for you but it's just so pathetic it makes me laugh. No Bethany you don't have any money but you will. In six weeks' time you will have a lot of money and lucky for me we will have reconciled long enough for you to bequeath it all to me." She pauses for these words to sink in. "Oh no. Now I've gone a ruined the surprise ending." She lightly reprimands herself with a tap on her wrist because it's all so fucking funny.

The door closes and I sniffle back a whimper. The bolts slide across and the keys turn but this time the motor starts to release my chain and I curl up with my hands tucked under my chin, hands clasped together almost like I'm praying. She didn't have to do that. I have to take comfort from that small act of kindness, I have to. The light goes out and I start to think of my impossible task of changing a leopard's spots because I just know it will take forever and I only have seven months; it's not going to be long enough. I close my eyes and feel the water pool and trickle across the bridge of my nose into the other closed eye and tap tap tap as the tears fall onto the slim lumpy excuse of a pillow.

The first week was a nightmare almost on par with the ones that break my sleep each night leaving me exhausted, drenched in sweat and hoarse from screaming but the end of the second week the music started and I truly believed I had died in my sleep and was in Hell. My routine is just that, routine; dull, frustrating and surreal. I mean who does this to someone and just how sick do you have to be to actually go through with it? I am served three of the blandest meals from the school dinners book of cooking. Each day they are the same but at least I am fed and enough that I am not hungry. After four days of being half dressed as I was unable to thread any clothes over my secured arm, Kit releases the chain from the wall once she leaves the room on the condition I secure it again when they bang on the door. On my third day Angel wasted no time in making me change into a variety of outfits from my apartment because with no Marco and my front door key to hand she pretty much has the free run of the place. I would mind if it wasn't for the hope that she might get caught by Marco's family popping round to water the plants and pick up the post.

I spent an uncomfortable hour playing dress up in a depress-

the Only Choice

ing montage of my travel wardrobe. I had to pose in front of the green screen with arms placed over imaginary friends, laughing and pulling faces because I am just having the fucking time of my life. I know if either Sofia or Marco saw whatever she does with these images they would know. My face may look carefree and full of joy but the sheer horror I feel must show in my eyes. If I was a normal twenty year old with a normal social media presence I would be optimistic that this ordeal would soon be over because my friends would know. But I have no social media presence so my friends wouldn't even think to look there for up-dates, they would call or text. Something they are not likely to do when they are themselves on holiday. She is perched on my bed, chatting like we are the best of friends, what she's done today, what she's going to do tomorrow, lunch with Daniel and his mother and it's so nice to be welcomed into the family once again. I think she is going to have to put photo-shop through its paces to get rid of the green colour she induces, not jealous, just nauseous. She throws in the odd remark about my hideous chunky curves and how vile to have such large breast and it takes everything I have not to shout that they're big because I'm fucking pregnant.

I don't because it may have only been nearly two full weeks in this prison but it really only took a second or two with Angel to understand she is crazy. She is not a little bit crazy, she is clinically insane, unpredictable, a little slap happy with my face, and yes, this one is new . . . she has a gun. She has a fucking gun, in England! She always has it with her and she waves it like it's an extension of her bony fingers using it to emphasise an elaborate a tale, never treating it like the dangerous firearm it is, often pointing directly at me. So I do as I am told. I eat my three meals, I wash in the bucket of lukewarm water that is brought with my porridge each morning and I do my exercises. I do a lot more exercise than she knows about because I want to make sure if that door ever opens long enough that I am fit and able to make the most of it and at the moment I could run a fucking marathon. Unfortunately, even with the press-ups, sit-ups, yoga and the treadmill I am feeling more like a hamster on a wheel than a captive ready to break free and I am behaving like a well-trained house cat only my litter tray is a portable camping toilet.

Angel came in the next day and sat excitedly beside me, she still had the gun pointing at my side as her hand was across her own tummy and she balanced her laptop on her knees. She motions for me to sit beside her, patting the bed impatiently but it is difficult to get that close because I am attached to the wall. The stretch is uncomfortable but with a tight, fake smile I shuffle next to her, closer than I'd like but exactly where I'm told. She opens up 'my' Facebook page and I can see she has been busy. She has a selection of pictures that I have to lean in closer to double check what I am seeing. Crowded party scenes, dimly lit, colourful lights, smiling people, drinks and cigarettes in hand. There I am, right in the middle with my arm draped over the shoulder of a half-naked Abercrombie model look alike; like I would be that lucky. I can't help the snort that escapes my mouth and immediately regret it when she lashes out her backhand, the one with the gun, across my cheek. The extra weight and surprise of the strike catches me of guard and I fall forward and hit my other cheek on the corner of the bedside table. I quickly steady myself and press the sting on one side and then the other; I can feel the heat and swell instantly. My fingers are tipped with blood, it's not much and on instinct I just suck them clean. Angel throws the laptop to the floor and hurls herself headfirst into the stubby portable toilet in the corner and proceeds to heave and curse. I want to remind her about her 'not in front of the baby rule' but given the throbbing of my cheek I choose to keep that smart remark to myself.

She sits back on her heels and wipes her mouth before she turns her demonic gaze toward me. God! She looks deranged, and I don't know if it was my snort or the blood or well, she's insane it could be anything. I hold myself still, having tucked my legs up to my chest so I am now a sturdy impenetrable ball. Her face changes expression and she laughs lightly, the speed and transition from fury to placid is unnerving. She slowly picks up the lap top and snaps it shut. She snarls at me through a tightly lipped grin.

"You know I thought we could have a little fun here. I was going to show you all the places you are going to visit. I have done a journey plan and everything but you have to go and spoil it." She haughtily admonishes my appalling behaviour.

If I wasn't speechless before I am now because she actually stamps her foot like a petulant child. "And I can't have you bleeding. I hate the sight of blood. That is utterly unacceptable and as a punishment you will . . ." She pauses because I am pretty sure there is not much she can threaten me with because everything I do is for the good of the baby and it's not like I bled on purpose. "Mmm, it's tricky maybe I should let Clive come in and decide what is the best way to punish you?" I can feel my hands start to tremble and a gut wrenching roll in my stomach at the idea of being trapped in this small room with that man.

"Angel I'm sorry." I blurt out but I'm deadly serious if it will stop that horrendous scenario unfolding. "I'm sorry for laughing, it wasn't because of the page, really, the page is great. I mean, it looks great you've done a really good job. I look like I'm having the best time, honestly. It's just you have obviously gone to a lot of trouble and that picture with me and the hot guy, but . . ." I am rushing to speak and pray I am making sense not sealing my fate with cruel and vicious Clive. "Well, you want it to be believable and I just wouldn't be lucky enough to get a guy like that." I let out a deep breath and try to gauge her reaction as she seems to take in what I have just said. She walks back over to me and sits, her eyes narrowed on me like she is trying to see if I'm lying. I'm not.

"True." She elongates her words with a pensive drawl. "I mean you are nothing to look at so I guess it would be pretty ridiculous for someone that attractive to want you." I can't believe I'm nodding to encourage her line of thinking. "And this does have to at least *try* to be believable." She smiles but then scowls and my heart jumps. "But what about Daniel?" I swallow the sudden dryness because she is right. There was Daniel and he is smoking hot and the fact that I wondered why he chose me doesn't negate the fact he did choose me, at first.

"Yes there was Daniel, but he chose you Angel." I struggle to say this aloud and am proud that I don't break as the truth of this rips me from the inside out but it seems to work. Her smile is pure poison but she at least looks satisfied.

"Like that was ever a real choice." She laughs and standing she walks toward the door. "But I think you are right so no Clive today, and not because I don't want to risk the baby. I think there are plenty of ways he could punish you without hurting the baby. You might want to bare that in mind." She closes the door behind her and the light goes out. I am glad I am not afraid of the dark because it is pitch black, I can't even see my fingers when they are pressed against my nose. I wait for the chain to lengthen but shake my head at her petty cruelty, because she isn't going to release the chain, not tonight.

I have read the only fiction book that has been brought to me and I'm sure the irony was intentional; The Handmaid's Tale. I comfort myself because even with everything Offred endures, in the end she did get away, with her baby. Not that I would know this from this copy but I have read this tale before so the missing pages are just evidence of Angel's disturbing mind games. I can't bring myself to read the pregnancy books because I don't want to make this nightmare any more heart-breaking by reading that my baby has fingernails, toes and a fully formed heart. When I lie very flat and hold still I can feel a small bump, no bigger than an orange. Well, more like a Satsuma but it's there and *that* is definitely too real. I lay my hand on the tiny mound and make promises I'm not sure I can keep and sing songs that make me cry and not just because all I can remember are the saddest

the Only Choice

songs but because I really miss music. I never knew how much I would miss it until it just wasn't there. Something so normal, background noise to everyday . . . gone like a chunk bitten clean off my body, gaping and sore. I never realised how much I listen to and for how long until I am deafened and driven mad myself by the never ending silence.

The end of the second week and I have changed my mind . . . completely. I don't miss music now and I definitely prefer the silence. I wake with a jolt to the blaring voice of Whitney Huston being pumped into the small room from God knows where. The noise so sudden I jump and look to see if someone had come in with a kick arse sound system without me noticing. At first I lie back with a smile; my face feels strange like the muscles had forgotten they could move like this. I can't say I'm a huge fan but music is music and she does have a killer voice. That was the first day and apart from a small respite while Kit sat with me during my meal times it has been constant throughout the day. The next day it was the same but with Mariah Carey and the third back to Whitney and these alternate throughout the next week. I am loosing track of the actual days and I actually love the time when Kit stays, we don't talk and the silence is blissful. When Angel stays she talks and talks and unlike the music which is now like white noise I can't block her out in the same way because she throws random questions at me and if I don't respond quickly she bitch slaps me.

One lunch time Kit is just as surprised as I am to see Angel storm through the door. I glance at Kit and it is odd because there is a little panic in her eyes but also something else, something fleeting, something that looked a lot like hatred. It's me, however, that physically retracts. Tied to the wall I have no option than to take what she's dishing but what I wouldn't give to have five minutes alone, untethered.

"What the fuck did you do to him?" Her voice is screeching at me, eyes furious and she is suddenly right in my face.

"Him?" I question but try and say it in a soothing way which isn't easy when my whole body is shaking.

Slap! "Like you don't know who I'm talking about" Slap! She snarls, spittle spraying from her distorted lips. "You little whore. I want to know what you did to him because now he wants to come to the scan with me." She grabs a fistful of my hair from the side and jerks it pulling my face into hers.

"Angel," I whisper. "I'm right here, what could I do? He's probably just excited. You said you two were getting close" The tears trickle out of the corner of my eye, but the pain from my tortured scalp and stinging cheek, I would endure a thousand fold compared to the pain of hearing about Daniels treasured gift to her. Just one week from the wedding and Daniel has given her a necklace. But when she showed me, it wasn't any necklace, it was my necklace, it was my collar. My heart did race, at first, when I dared to think that he was suspicious after all and this was his way of tracking her and finding me. That was over a week ago and if he was using the necklace to find me he would've found me by now because she never takes the damn thing off.

"We're having a baby of course we're close but why does he want to see the scan? Why doesn't he trust me now?" She sounds incredulous that anyone could think such a thing but lucky for me she pinches tighter and a cry escapes instead of my own incredulous laugh. "What on earth am I supposed to do?" She is calming down, her grip loosens as her control over her burst of colourful language tightens and her voice is heavy with uncertainty and concern. I have my own concerns, part of me is pleased that he isn't just taking her word for it this time but part of me is terrified. If she is pushed into a corner will she pull the same trick as last time and hope guilt is enough to keep them together without a child. The outcome is bleak for Daniel but where would that leave me, pregnant and surplus to requirements. My precarious future affords me suitable motivation to offer some help.

"Angel, why don't you hire an ultra sound machine, take some pictures of my—" I draw in a sharp breath when her head snaps to mine. "—Of the baby and arrange to meet Daniel at your doctors but give him the wrong time. You can be there for him in the waiting room with your picture in your hand." I hold my breath while she remains silent, still only inches from my face.

"Don't the scans have names and dates on them?" She mumbles but I release my breath because I know she is going to go with this plan. Her body is relaxed and her lips curl into an ugly smile. If anyone can pull off barefaced lying its Angel, well, it's Angel and Kit.

"The dates you put in manually when you do the scan I would guess and the same with the name." I offer because I don't really know. I just assume it's like any other procedure that involves a computer, you still have to input information. The scan will just reflect that truth, not the actual truth. She lets me go like I am suddenly offensive to touch and wipes her hand on her tight pink skirt.

"Right, well, I hope that works for your sake." She snarls at me and I don't know whether she is disappointed that I seem to have dodged another bullet, literally. She waves her ever present gun toward me and leaves the room. I slump back and exhale a deep breath; the tension visibly evaporates but not just from me but from Kit too. She sits beside me and bites her cheek like she is preventing herself from sharing something. I decide to bridge this impossible gap. I know she won't be happy taking orders like she has. I have seen signs, flashes of discontent nothing concrete but I do feel us both relax when Angel left the room. That was real . . . it's a start . . . it's something and it's all I have.

"What's with the f—" I stop mid curse but her laugh interrupts my question and she tells me its fine to swear, that she doesn't give a fuck and again that niggling feeling, that tiny grain of hope start to tremble with the first signs of life. I smile, hesitant at this very fragile relationship. "What I was going to say was what's with the fucking music? I love music, I miss music but if I hear another soulful rendition of 'I will always love you' I swear I'll . . ." I shake my head and rub my free hand through my hair limp and thick with dirt. "Well, we both know I won't do jack shit because I am trapped in a room where everything is either nailed down or made of marshmallow." I exhale but manage a frustrated smile.

She snickers and the sound is sweet, genuine and I try not to stare. I quickly close my dropped jaw. I don't want to spook her by making it so obvious that her reactions are so far from 'typical.' It's like I'm sitting next to an alien. Kit is smiling, losing a battle with her need to laugh. "She doesn't want you talking to the baby and she believes listening to the 'best' vocals will make the baby musical. Oh fuck, I don't know." Her shoulders start to shake and she can't keep her laughter contained any longer. It's ridiculous, the whole thing is bat-shit crazy so I do the only thing that helps and laugh with her.

"She really believes listening to a singer with great vocals will make the baby a good singer?" I manage to draw in enough breath to speak but it is stuttered with proper belly laughs. I must look disbelieving at this because unable to speak she nods, holding her tummy and curling over. I wonder from this reaction when the last time she really laughed. "That's crazy." I state the obvious and she buckles again.

"I know right!" She draws in a breath and straightens like she is trying to compose herself. Taking a moment she checks herself, reins back in and gives me a tight smile before the familiar cool fixed; detached expression falls back in to place. The chill is instant and harsh now that, for the first time here, I have felt some indisputable warmth flow between us. Sadly I can't think of a time that happened before now. She picks up the tray and I get a surge of panic at her sudden but inevitable departure. I grab her arm and the tray wobbles but my sudden hold is soft so she doesn't drop the tray. Her eyes fix mine and her frown just highlights her own confusion at our exchange but she pulls away and narrows her brow, stern, cold and angry once more.

"Kit, please, don't leave." I beg for more than the reprieve she affords from the damn music. I beg because I want her there, I want her laughing and I want her warming a little but looking at her face now I know that that time, as fleeting as it was, is passed.

"So that's what that feels like." Her voice drips with malice and she continues as I must just look confused at her statement. "To be needed. To be needed by you." She tightens her lips and sneers before she opens the door and leaves. I am no more enlightened with her follow up statement because she didn't sound angry she sounded upset. Is she upset that I need her, because I definitely do or is she upset that I have never needed her until now, because that isn't true. I needed her for most of my life but I needed her to be the sister I can barely remember, the one before this one, the one I saw a glimpse of today. That grain of hope just sprouted its first root.

Chapter Nineteen

THE SCAN WENT well, certainly better than I wanted. I managed to help Angel input the details according to my own dates and with the help of some on-line images we managed to print off something that looked like the right type of grainy pattern. The only thing that was really uncomfortable was that I had to drink litres of water and then wait ages for Angel to set the bloody machine up. The image didn't really spark anything in me and I am starting to worry that I am deliberately distancing myself because I am finally beginning to accept the hopelessness of my situation. When she returned from meeting Daniel parading the latest gift, I realise I am not distancing myself I am biding my time because there is no way this bitch is going to have my baby. She went on to explain how excited Daniel was and proud that she was handling the break-up of her marriage so well. You know that she was so determined to not let it affect the baby. He had bought her the ugliest watch I had ever seen. It wasn't ugly but it was oversized, gaudy, encrusted with diamonds with a large mother of pearl face and a chunky silver, probably platinum chain link strap. I didn't care if it cost hundreds of thousands, it was ugly to me. She was delighted my plan had worked and I was delighted that after that, she left me alone for nearly two weeks.

The music has continued to be piped every day but on the days where Kit is caretaker she turns it off and on days when Angel was obviously around Kit gives me her iPod but told me to only listen with one ear so I could still hear the door. This small act of kindness gives me such hope and each day I lay on my bed drifting off listening to a different playlist Kit has made. Loving that she has such great taste and thinking for the first time that perhaps my taste in music was maybe influenced by her, years ago, maybe. Whether that is true or not I love the fact that I can now hit repeat on some of my favourite bands, drown out Whitney and Mariah and pretend I am not going to end up dead in less than seven months. My hand rests on my abdomen and drifts to where the hard bump is just starting to grow proud of my pubic bone. I am loosing track of the days now but I know that this weekend it is just me and Angel. I wanted to ask Kit where she was going but I am still not comfortable with how much I need her and how much I miss her when she's not there. I am not sure how telling her will do anything but make my situation that more vulnerable, as if that's even possible.

Angel has left me to eat my last meal of the day alone and when she returns she looks angry, immaculately groomed and dressed for an evening out but furious and I brace myself and my face for impact. She paces a few lengths of the room which doesn't take long before she spins and points her gun waving hand at me with a face like thunder.

"Why would he want to eat here?" She stomps and paces some more and I watch silently because I know that look; she is going to aim her venom and I am a sitting duck. "We never 'eat-in,' why does he want to eat in? I don't cook he knows that. You are up to something!" She spits at me and suddenly stops waving the gun but holds it steady. My heart beats like a rapid fire rifle and I try to calm her agitation with a soft smile even though my jaw is clenched so tight my teeth hurt.

"Angel, I'm here. I'm up to nothing but doing what you tell me. He chose you." She likes to hear this as much as I hate to say it. "Perhaps he just wants some alone time, in private." My voice is soothing but it serrates my heart when she smiles a knowing smile. That flash of understanding in her eyes makes me think that up until tonight maybe she hasn't had any time *alone* with Daniel. The slight flush of happiness of that thought is dashed when like her, I realise that he is going to be with her tonight, alone and in private. She giggles.

"Of course, how silly of me. You know I think it's all the hormones making me a little crazy." I think I just cracked a tooth, bat-shit doesn't even come close to defining this woman. I need another category of crazy. She takes the tray and before she leaves turns with what she assumes is a naughty grin. "I guess I'll see you in the morning?" The light goes off and I wonder how I am going to find my way to the toilet because now I really need to be violently sick. I leave it what I think is about an hour before I start screaming. I figure if Daniel is having a cosy night in with Miss Crazy as Fuck, and I scream loud enough he might hear me over all her lies. After I have screamed my throat raw and can barely make a whimper as I curl back on the bed and try to close my eyes without picturing Daniel holding Angel, Daniel kissing Angel . . . Daniel . . . Just Daniel.

I would scream but the air needed to make the sound has been forced from my chest with the sudden weight on my stomach and before I can move to protect myself I am inundated with a rain of flying fists and hysterical screaming. The room is still dark but the slight light filtered through the open door casts a shadow across Angel's face that only enhances her demonic behaviour. I try to shield my face from the blows; her tight fists pummel my face relentlessly. She is surprisingly heavy and my attempt to shift her is unsuccessful, if I could leverage myself up with my one free arm I might be more successful but I need that to protect my head. All I can do is hold my breath and wait for her to stop using me as her own private punching bag. My head is ringing and she catches my lip with one of her rings but I am quick to suck in the swelling, bloody tissue before she can freak out even more. She finally stops but I think that is more to do with exhaustion rather than intention because from the glare of her eyes she is in no way finished. I guess her evening didn't quite go to plan. Glad I am sucking my lip right now because I am sure I would be smiling if I wasn't. As Daniel said 'I just can't help myself.'

"He says he's over you. He says you are nothing. He even says he can't believe he ever deserved a second chance with me." She thumps her chest in earnest, before she throws her head back and barks out a bitter laugh. "Then why won't he take it? Mmmm? Why doesn't he stay the night? I thought he was going to stay the night. That's what you said!" She narrows her eyes and I feel instantly chilled to my bones. "*You* said he wanted to be alone with me. Do you think he doesn't? Do you think he still wants you?" Her eyes are cold, wild and her voice is something less than human,more like an animal snarl. I shake my head vigorously and start to protest but she slaps her hand on my mouth and holds me still, her strength is a little shocking because I know from my own exercise routine that I have built up some muscle tone but I am rendered useless against her adrenaline induced super strength.

She sits astride me, her face inches from mine and I can now see in the darkness she is wearing a long dark silk robe that has fallen open and now only partially covers a full ensemble of awkwardly sexy lingerie. Delicate black lace bra and panties with stockings and suspenders; and Daniel chose to go home. Well, at least I can understand why she's pissed but that is hardly my fault. Her breathing is frantic, whilst I am scared to breathe at all. She sits up and shifts up my body so she is not directly on my tiny bump and even though she is almost naked straddling me I can focus on nothing but her lifeless, empty eyes. She reaches her right hand behind her and after a moment of subtle movement she brings it back into view but this time she is holding a knife. Where the fuck did she keep that hidden on her almost naked body! The room maybe dark but the blade gleams with ominous intent and I swallow so loudly it would be comical but I'm not laughing. I'm terrified. The knife is so much scarier than the gun, intimately violent, it offers no possibility of a quick end. There is no such luxury with a blade. Oh Shit. Shit. Shit. I never thought I would wish that Daniel had fucked Angel but I really wish he had now because nothing holds fury like a knife wielding Angel spurned.

"Do you think he still wants you Bethany?" Her contempt is enhanced with her sickly smile.

"No Angel I don't." I don't know how I am keeping my voice so calm when I want to scream hysterically too.

"Mmmm but you think he might one day? Mmmm?" She tilts her head like she is trying to visualise this and I don't want her to visualise anything other than her and Daniel blissfully happy. Blissfully happy with my baby because only with that image firmly fixed in her crazy head, am I likely to survive tonight.

"Angel, he wants you. Only you, he is probably worried it would hurt the baby if he. ." Even as I am trying to pacify her I can't actually finish that sentence. I let out a breath but it's hard to draw another one in because of her weight on my chest.

"You know he loved your hair." She muses but her voice is too calm and that's the moment I start to tremble. "When he first told me about you, he went in to quite the detail . . . nauseatingly detailed actually, about your exquisite. . . . hmm. ." Her eyes glaze and narrow with unpleasant recollections.

"Angel please." My voice fails to remain calm like I need and the panic only makes her laugh but I beg over and over. The tears start instantly she grabs a handful of my hair and attacks with the blade. As much as I want to fight, the knife edge flashes so close to my face, my neck, nicking my skin that I freeze and only small sobs and gasps for breath escape my lips. Chunk after chunk of my hair falls from her hands and in the end I resign myself and close my eyes. It is only hair, it will grow back, that's if I am ever given enough time to let it and if she wasn't so afraid of blood it could be a lot worse. That is what the rational part of my brain is trying to say to the other part that is curled up in a corner sobbing

the Only Choice

its heart out and praying for the end, however it will end; I just want it to end.

My lips are swollen and my left eye won't open all the way but I don't need a mirror to know I must look like I've been hit in the face with an anvil. Angel was relentless last night and if the bruises up my arm are any indication of what my face is like I don't actually want to look in a mirror. I don't have to because the look on Kit's face tells me everything and more.

"Holy Shit! What happened to you?" She places the tray down and sits beside me and I wince when I involuntarily raise my brow with a sarcastic roll of my eyes at her stupid question. She has the grace to look a little embarrassed and that in itself eases the sting. "Ok my bad. I know what happened but do you mind telling me why?"

I close my eyes like I am trying to answer the meaning of life because I'm fucked if I know what goes through that crazy bitches head. I shrug because I have no idea why, I just know that this particular day, this particular trigger was Daniel. In fact, if I think back to most of her outbursts they can be traced back to something Daniel has said or done. "Bad date." I offer my explanation and take a sip of water while I mentally prepare myself for another bowl of porridge. I used to love porridge now I don't care if I ever see another rolled oat.

"Fucking men, why couldn't he just fuck her?" She grumbles and for a moment I think she's talking about Daniel but I am kind of glad he didn't 'just fuck her' even if my face is a picture of contradiction to that sentiment. She continues. "He couldn't just shove his dick in and get it all over with . . . he has to be charming and sweet and seem like he actually gives a crap." Her eyes snap to mine and she straightens her back and looks away. "Fucking men." She mumbles again and I want to ask her what on earth she is talking about when I remember she's had a weekend away.

I have finished my breakfast and she goes to take my tray but before she picks it up I stop her with a heartfelt plea.

"Please Kit, don't go." I suck in my swollen bottom lip as her face processes my request and fights all the reasons why she shouldn't and all the reasons why she might, this time.

"Why? Are you going to try memory lane one more time?" Her snide comment is only partially meant to wound because her tone is a little softer but I recoil all the same. My feeble attempt at connecting was more damaging than anything as I trawled through my memory bank. Kit had sat with me last week when I tried to get some connection going, tried to get her to remember better times. Like the time we talked our mother into playing hide and seek. *Mum had never really had the time or inclination for these type of games and after I had begged for a good half hour she agreed. But when it came round to her turn to hide I had found Kit easily and then Kit and I had gotten distracted by the television and had promptly sat down to our favourite programme. I don't even remember what it was now but I do remember the banging sound coming from our bedroom as the final credits rolled on the programme. Not only had we given up looking for Mum but she had gotten herself wedged down the side of Kits bed and had to wait until the television was quiet enough for us to hear her cry for help, she was so mad.* I had started to laugh at the end of the story but Kit remained impassive, giving a tight smile she then asked me if I remembered what happened after that. When I shook my head she proceeded to tell me how Mum had sent her to bed with three strikes from the wooden spoon on the backs of her legs and I had just been sent to bed because it was my bedtime.

Undeterred I tried another, one where I remember Kit had cared for me. *Like the time when we were asked to pick the raspberries in the garden and I ate so many I got really sick and because Mum was working Kit had made me drink my medicine for the ache and had run me a bath, rubbed my back and stayed up with me until mum got in from work. She can't have been much more than ten years old.* I hold my breath as a small smile creeps across her face as she remembers but I let the breath seep sadly out as she recalls the aftermath when she was screamed at for being irresponsible and letting me eat all the fruit. Her pocket money was stopped for four weeks to pay for more raspberries because the ones I had eaten were supposed to be for jam. I think I have another story but I can't bring myself to speak, sparse as they are, every tale I fondly remember is a nightmare for Kit and I can't help think that maybe every tale would end this way. The consequences themselves aren't horrendous but I guess, as a child herself, she must have felt she couldn't do right for doing wrong. It didn't take long before her hatred focused clearly on the one person causing all the problems. So using our shared history as a common bond, is likely to alienate her further. I can see that now, so my only other hope is to try and build a new history, hopefully one with a future.

"Oh yes because that worked out so well for me last time." I roll my one good eye and try to smile but my lip stings; she laughs lightly and relaxes to sit back beside me.

"Yeah." She draws out her sympathetically spoken agreement. "Not your finest work Bets."

I sniff out a snicker. "Maybe I'm like you after all." She cocks her head and brow and looks at me in need of clarification. "Survival Kit . . . I just want to survive." I hope my honesty won't scare her off and I freeze just waiting for her to disappear but when she doesn't move I let out the breath I was holding. I look at her and notice a slight nod followed by a shake. I need her to have this obvious inner turmoil but if it's too hard I also need her to just not leave and if I make her uncomfortable she'll leave. "Sorry." I add quickly to change the subject. "So how was your weekend?" My carefree joking tone makes her laugh out.

"Really Bets? Small talk?" She tilts her head but smiles and that encourages me that she is Ok with this, for now.

"I'm Ok with small talk, any talk really. I missed you." I she her straighten and her eyes widen but I chuckle.

"Don't panic, I'm not going all 'Stockholm' on you and I don't think we're ever going to be braiding each other's hair any time soon but it's boring in here and that fucking music, arghhh! So yes I missed you this weekend and look what happens when you're not here!" I lift up part of my mismatched mop that clings to my head in greasy clumps. I must look delightful. She shakes her head but I can see her shoulders begin to shake a little and it's not long before she is giggling and holding her mouth to stop proper laughs. I don't hold back because, I want to laugh too, I am so sick of crying.

"Ok just no falling in love with me!" She nudges me and I laugh again.

"Fat chance of that bitch!" That does it, she curls over and laughs into her hands. The laughter dies naturally after a little while. "So the weekend?" I prompt because she didn't actually answer me.

"We went away. He took me to a strange little hut on the South Coast." She stops and I can see she is nervous, uncertain because her fingers are fiddling with the sheet. Kit is never uncertain about men.

"With Ethan . . . You're still seeing him?" I haven't asked her about the two of them because I have had other things on my mind. She purses her lips and I can see her clench her jaw.

"What of it?" She snaps and I raise my hand in surrender and apology.

"I didn't mean anything by it really. I just thought you were with him to get to me and . . . well you have me." I shrug because my logic is sound.

"Yeah . . . that was the plan. That was certainly Angels plan." Her tone is tinged with bitterness and I draw comfort again from the little signs of discontent in the kidnap camp. "She's not entirely happy about me still seeing him . . . She thinks it's an unnecessary risk but I'm careful and she doesn't—" She censors herself before I can learn what Angel doesn't do or like or permit.

I may be wrong in feeling a shift between us but I am also

the Only Choice

worried that I may not survive the next time Daniel fucks up. I need to push a little harder with Kit. I pause while I try to think because however I say what I want to say is going to sound like a lie to get her on side. Even I wouldn't believe me and I pretty much believe anyone, except Kit or Angel but I just might believe Kit now. "He took you to his mother's hut by the sea?" She nods and I notice the sweetest smile flash across her face before the scowl returns and her fingers nimbly pick up the agitated moves on my sheet.

"What of it?" She is chewing her lip and I am struggling whether I should tell her what Ethan told me. I don't have anything to gain by telling her how important she obviously is to him but I have a lot to lose if she thinks I'm trying to play her.

"You are not going to believe me if I tell you, mostly because you don't trust anyone but also because you'd be an idiot to believe me in your position and you are not an idiot, never have been." I quip and hesitate even though she is smiling.

"Spit it out Bets." She narrows her eyes but her features are anything but harsh.

"Look I don't have to tell you this but I'm so sick of games. Ethan likes you." She tilts her head and sniffs like I haven't just told her something she already knew. "No Kit, he really likes you. He blew me off as stand in as my chaperone for the wedding because he met some really cool girl and it would feel weird to even pretend to be my date. He said and I quote 'she's all kinds of fucked up but there's something about her, something special.' He really likes you and he took you to his mum's place, he never takes girls there. Never." I sit back and gauge her reaction and just when I think she is going to be typical Kit and rant or dismiss all my lies she quietly asks.

"Why would you tell me this Boo? I don't understand." She uses my oldest nickname and this time I don't mind. She shakes her head and for the first time ever she looks vulnerable. I want to put my arm around her and that's a thought I never thought I would have. I don't because at the moment she's like a dear in

249

the open, completely out of her comfort zone and liable to bolt. "I really like him." Her honesty seems to surprise her and she looks a little uneasy that this foreign expression has come from her.

"I didn't have to tell you and like I said you don't have to believe me but you shouldn't let what's happening here stop what you could have with Ethan." I shrug my shoulders because I don't know what else to say. I don't know if she believed me or if it will make a difference. "He was really kind to me and I know I don't really know him that well but he is genuine, smart, funny, smoking hot if you're into reformed playboys." She snickers and I am glad I am not revealing anything that Ethan hadn't obviously already disclosed. "He's one of the good guys Kit. Maybe it's time you let yourself have a good guy for once, maybe it's time you believe you deserve a good guy." I can see she is nervously nibbling her lower lip and her expression is a mix of confusion and sadness.

"I can't stop this Bets. You know I can't and even if I could how could you ever . . ." She looks over to the door, her eyes wide and she swallows hard like she is trying to take back what she just said. I hope she doesn't, I hope she says more.

"I know you can't Kit, really I get that. You couldn't trust me any more than I could trust Angel but you're wrong if you think I couldn't forgive you. Because if you saved my life, saved my baby's life, how could I *not* forgive you?" I take a breath to stop the surge of emotion and blink back the water that pools instantly in my eyes and I can see it's too much. Kit stands abruptly, walks swiftly and without a backwards glance, opens the door and walks away. Leaving the tray behind, leaving me sore and exposed and praying I haven't pushed too hard.

I don't know whether it is deliberate but Kit only comes in to my room accompanied either with Clive or with Angel. She hasn't spoken directly to me, actually she hasn't spoken at all and she hasn't let me use her iPod either. I spend the next few days alternately cursing myself for pushing too hard, too fast and cursing Angel for the fucking relentless music. The next morning Kit

the Only Choice

comes in alone but her brusque manor means I am not inclined to try and bond again. She places the breakfast tray down and on it is a large brown envelope. As I pick at my food Kit opens the envelope and places it on the bed with a pen. I glance over the legal document with Last Will and Testament scribed in an elegant font on the cover page . . . my heart sinks. Why on earth would I think she would help me, it's always about the money with her, life is irrelevant, well, *my* life is irrelevant. I pick up the pen and don't make eye contact as I sign where the brightly coloured markers indicate. I place the pen down and continue eating the tasteless food. She hovers by the door, I am not sure what she is waiting for now but I just have to keep trying to chip away at her.

"I don't understand Kit, you don't need this money . . . Ethan loves you . . . he would take care of you . . . you would have money . . . and I would give you every penny . . . I promise—" She laughs but it sounds flat.

"Bethany you know I have never relied on anyone but me . . . I am not going to start now, even if you are right . . . Besides it is out of my hands." Her face holds all the resignation I feel and the ensuing silence cloaks the room.

She hesitates before walking over to pick up the papers but then shaking her head she stuffs the documents back in the envelope and seeing I have finished she places it on the tray and picks it up to leave. She stands in the doorway looking directly at me, her eyes look sad but I swallow back the laugh just itching to escape, why the fuck would she be sad.

"I called the ambulance." Her voice is soft but her words are shocking.

"What? What ambulance? An ambulance is coming?" My confused garbled words are rushed but I stop when she shakes her head.

"No no . . . not now." She draws in a breath and pulls her shoulders back like she is bracing herself to deliver a blow. She is. "I called the ambulance that night John died, I did it straight away. I hated you both but I never wanted him to die. It was a stupid fight that got out of hand you know . . ." She mumbles her excuses. "No one knew I'd made the call but I did it as soon as I could. I didn't know you were coming but but . . . I am sorry they didn't get there in time." I can hear her voice hitch but my ears are fuzzy with overloaded information. "I'm sorry Bets . . . I'm . . ." She snaps her mouth shut when her eyes meet mine, all I see is a fuzzy haze of an image of someone I don't know at all but who might have tried to save the boy I loved. What the fuck, why tell now?

"I don't understand, why tell me now? Like I'm not fucked up enough?" I stand and walk as far as I can to get to her, she stands her ground, her eyes fixed on mine. She looks over her shoulder and then closes the door, stepping closer to me.

"I'm sorry, that's not why I told you." She sucks in a deep breath and I brace myself again, just how much more am I supposed to take. "I . .I. . Look I just needed you to know that. I didn't want him to die Bets, it was an accident. He just had to protect your precious reputation, he couldn't just walk away but but he didn't deserve to die."

"No he didn't." I whisper.

"You were with him?" My head lifts to meet her curious eyes and I can barely nod and I can feel the plump tears burst on to my cheek. Her eyes look just a little glassy too. "He loved you so much. I think he did from that first day at school. He took you from me then, you never needed me after that and I was jealous. I hated him and I hated you. I hated that you had each other and I had no one."

I can feel my legs start to tremble and I am having trouble containing the gut wrenching sobs needing to be heard. I swallow the largest lump in my throat; my face is streaming but I can't find any words.

"I'm sorry Bets." She drops her head and her words have such finality that I force myself to beg once more, but not for me.

"Kit please, thank you, you didn't have to tell me that and I'm sorry I never knew but mostly I'm sorry I never knew you. I

the Only Choice

was five when I met John and I still needed you but you weren't there, you were never there." I shake my head because none of that matters and I think she can see that too. "I know it's too late and you can't change what's going to happen and I might just be a huge dumbass to believe you would if you could." I shake away the building sorrow because I may be the world's biggest fool but I think she would help me if she could. "But I am going to ask, I have to beg you for something and I need you to promise me. My baby . . ." I suck in a sharp breath because this hurts more than my limited vocabulary could possibly describe. "My baby doesn't deserve her. Please find a way, after I mean, to let Daniel know. DNA, whatever, it doesn't matter, if he knows the truth then the baby will be safe and I know he'll be a wonderful loving father." I swallow through the intensity of this conversation. "Even at your most cruel you wouldn't knowingly put an innocent child in the hands of that crazy bitch." I let out a tight laugh and smile when Kit's eyes smile back at me. She doesn't say a word only the slightest nod of her head and I don't know if she has agreed to my last request but I can hope, it's all I have left.

Chapter Twenty

I FEEL DISGUSTING, the lukewarm water does nothing to remove the grime I feel layering on my skin after weeks of being held prisoner and with no shampoo my hair feels no different once its dry so I have stopped wetting it in the first place. What I wouldn't give for a steaming hot shower, no no a deep bubble filled bath. Yes, lying in a luxurious bath wrapped in soft fragrant bubbles and encased in strong firm arms with dextrous fingers massaging the knots and tightness from my aching muscles. Daniel's talented fingers. Mmm I wouldn't care that the massage would end too quickly because I would love the fact that he can't wait a moment longer and judging by the deep sigh that escapes my mouth I can't either. His hands would drift down from my shoulders slipping swiftly over my silky soapy skin, delicate featherlike touches until he moves up to cup and squeeze my breasts. A little too firm and just enough to make me arch away from his chest, pushing my head harder into his neck and moaning as my nipples pebble hard and he rubs them between his thumb and forefinger until I cry out and beg for more. He loves it when I beg. The burning ache I feel deep inside starts to build and I try to twist so I can face him, I need to see his face. I need to see how much he wants me because I can't hide how much I want him. One of my arms is trapped by his and I can't move, the thumping of my heart is racing like my ragged breaths, louder, louder, thump, thump. Dammit, the first decent dream I have had in this hellhole and my fucking breakfast arrives to ruin it.

Kit enters the room and I can't help but scowl at her even though I haven't seen her for a few days and actually I am really pleased she's here. I really missed her. It is too easy to miss a lot of things and because I have nothing but time I now have a depressingly long list;— the sky, the rain, the noise, the smells, the sounds, simple things like salt in my food and fizzy drinks, a decent cup of coffee, hell a crappy cup of coffee for that matter but the list, as endless as it is, leaves me devastated when all my items are surpassed by how much I miss Daniel. Up until that morning I hadn't been able to touch him in my dreams. Kit looks a little shocked and quickly places the tray which today is covered by an opaque plastic dome. "Are you all right?" She places her hand on my forehead and I can feel a fresh blush flash across my cheeks, which adds to the flush from my dream. I nod and after she is happy that I am fine and the baby is fine she tips her head excitedly toward the tray. She clasps her hands and is biting back a tell-tale grin. I am a little curious now, this is very strange behaviour for her, unprecedented. She doesn't do giddy with excitement. I am touched she has started to ask about the baby but I can't help fear every small change is leading to a fatal case of false hope. I tentatively lift the lid, my mouth drops, my eyes widen and instantly pool with water but not as much as my mouth does at the sight of pure heaven laid on the plate before me.

"Oh my God! Oh my God!" I cry out and bounce on the spot with unbelievable joy. "Kit is that? . . ." I pick up one quarter of the white bread sandwich; it crumples and crackles in my fingers.

"Yep." Her smile is brilliantly wide and genuine and if my arm was free I would hug her but I can't actually take my eyes of this sandwich. Who would have thought I could be rendered speechless by such a simple food but it's not an ordinary sandwich. It's my long forgotten favourite, clearly one of the memories that we shared which didn't have negative connotations for either of us. Because she giggles too as I moan into my first bite of the gourmet breakfast of cream cheese, cheese and onion crisps and butter sandwich with a glass of full fat milk. I'm in heaven and I don't say a word until there is nothing left.

"Thank you." I lick my lips even though there is no longer a trace of flavour left as I have inhaled every bit. She reaches behind her and holds her hand out shyly. The dainty iced cupcake has a single candle and I suddenly understand the significance. Have I really been here over a month because that would definitely suck. It would also mean that today is my birthday. I take the cake because it is a sweet gesture and as crappy as this is for a twenty-first birthday Kit has risked herself by doing this and Kit never risks herself. The cake looks delicious and I realise I haven't had anything remotely processed for so long I could eat the paper the cake is wrapped in just so as not to waste a morsel. I peel back the paper and take a big sniff, the utter sugar rush from the smell alone makes me smile. I tear it in half but she shakes her head.

"Please Kit, Birthday cake is for sharing . . . pretty sure its bad luck to eat it all myself." She tilts away with a raised brow and pursed lips at my attempt at a bad joke but she smiles and takes the piece I'm offering. I savour the way the moist cake and sickly icing coat my teeth in gooey clumps and close my eyes as my tongue delights in this new burst of artificial flavour. Forget about the tasty dream I was having because this is culinary eroticism and the fact that I am comparing cake to an orgasm with Daniel just shows how far I've fallen. How deprived and depraved I have become. I pick the few crumbs from my T-shirt and suck them off my fingers. "Thank you Kit. Best Birthday ever!" I sit back and laugh.

"Well now I just feel shitty because that is *sooo* pathetic if this is the best." She shuffles to sit beside me and I jump a little at her unusual closeness but quickly relax because it feels nice and feelings like this are rare. I would be stupid not to take it where I can get it.

"OK not my best but it's definitely up there." We are silent for several minutes when she sits straight and I wonder if the intimacy is too much and she will bolt again.

"What was the best?" She looks at me and her big brown eyes are softly smiling, her face is softer too and she looks more comfortable, more relaxed and the fact that she is asking about me, wanting to learn things about me I can't help but think this has to be good.

"My sixteenth birthday." I say without hesitation and she jabs me in my ribs.

"Ew I do not want to know about you and John making the beast with two backs on the day you became legal." She chuckles but I can only reflect how I wish that was the case. I drop my head and rub my finger where the ring I lent to Sofia as her 'something blue' has been for the last five years.

"No we didn't." I suck in a stuttered breath and I can't believe this still hurts so much. "I mean I wanted to but he wanted to wait . . . didn't want it to be because of a date where someone else had deemed it Ok and legal. He didn't want it to be anything other than for us. Special and and . . ." My throat is dry but I carry on. "He worked, like me and had commitments but was trying to save, he wanted to take me out, you know nice meal, fancy restaurant that type of thing. No matter how much I begged he wouldn't budge until he had the money to 'treat me right.' It's pretty much why I don't give a crap about money. I mean I needed it for Mum but now, I don't need so much. You can have it, really. I know you think I take it for granted now but it's just not important because it meant I never got the chance to . . . I just loved him so much and I . . ." I feel the few tears trickle down my cheek but I wipe them away. I cried enough back then and I remind myself that the day itself was amazing. "Anyway, it was the summer holidays and John had left me clues to find each silly gift he had hidden around the village. I was mad at first because

I just wanted to be with him but each gift was special, my favourite sweet, a CD of my favourite band, my leather belt which was his and I constantly stole, silly things I don't remember them all now but all the clues lead me to our gravestone. I know that sounds weird but it was kind of our thing. We loved to read the headstones, all the people that went before, reading them aloud, remembered and some of the inscriptions were beautiful. Anyway this particular one was so lovely. Just a simple dedication from a husband to his wife.

Jake and Mable,
A thousand choices in one lifetime,
When there was really only one:
Us,
Always.

He was sitting there with a small blue velvet box. I already knew we weren't going to have sex and I already knew he was going to marry me. He told me that when I was eleven years old." I add because she looks shocked at my presumption. "The box held a promise ring and I knew his promise would never be broken . . . that he would love me and care for me and be my everything." I can feel my tears but I don't feel so sad and I am smiling remembering that wonderful day, because it was the very best birthday. I know she feels uncomfortable so I make a joke about crazy emotional hormones and she laughs easing the sombre mood. I lean forward and try to stretch my back out; sitting bunched up hurts my back and squishes my bump.

"Can you feel it move?" She is actually pointing to my heart but I know that's not what she means.

I shake my head and she looks disappointed. "No, not yet, it's a little early. I think it's supposed to be around fifteen weeks. You can't even really see the bump with my clothes on." We both fall silent and my mind races with a million requests. The most prevalent is the one I think she has promised already and I don't want to give her the opportunity to retract it but there is one thing

the Only Choice

that is praying on my mind and scaring me shitless. "You will be here, for the birth, I mean?" I can see her eyes widen but she can also hear the fear and panic in my voice at the thought of being alone or worse. She shifts off the bed and takes the tray; she turns and holds my heavy gaze full of desperate need and smiles at me. "It is just that if Angel can't stand the sight of blood . . . I mean you didn't see her when I bit my lip . . . if she reacts like that to a drop she is not going to be able to help me . . . besides I don't really want her here at all if that is an option but I don't want to be alone either." My voice trembles.

"I'll be here." Her soft words are like a warm blanket and I can't believe the comfort they afford. "See you later."

Chapter Twenty-One

SHE DIDN'T COME back at lunch time and she didn't appear at dinner. It wasn't like she had promised to return today and it's not like either of them keep to any particular routine but I just feel really sick that something is wrong. I chase my dry grilled chicken around my plate as Angel sits at the edge of my bed picking imaginary lint from her tailored trousers.

"Um Angel, Kit said she was going to be there for the birth and . . ." Before I can ask her intention regarding the event she snickers and quickly places her polished nails against her lips but her eyes meet mine for the briefest of moments. Unfortunately that moment is all I need, an instant ice chills my soul. "Angel. .whats funny?"

"What is funny . . . is that you think you are so clever. It is quite pathetic your attempt to manipulate Kit, quite pathetic." She raises her hand to stop my attempt to deny her suspicions. "Don't insult me Bethany . . . you have done enough . . . and so have I." Her cold eyes look less than human and I feel my world drop away and any hope I had fostered that my baby would, at least be safe, die with that one look. I get the feeling Kit isn't coming back and I am terrified to process what that means for Kit but I know what it means for me. It means my time is up and

the Only Choice

I have to do something drastic. I have to get out of here.

I can't let her see that I know something bad has happened. I can't let her see how scared I am and I can't let her see that I am just about desperate enough to try anything. I shake my head to change the subject because I think my best play is ignorance. "Never mind, actually I did want to ask for something."

She sniffs and looks at me down her nose. "Really? Quite the demanding little bitch aren't we?"

I grit my teeth to stop my agreement, that *she* is, in fact ,quite a demanding bitch. "I have this killer craving for some Tahini." She frowns at my request and I wonder if Kit told her of my allergy. "It's really quite healthy, with carrot sticks."

"That sesame seed hummus? You're craving that?" She laughs and wrinkles her nose. "I'll see what I can do." She moves to take my tray but leans in to whisper, her eyes narrowed with malice and utter hatred. I wonder if they match my own. "But you will owe me." Her thin lipped smile doesn't touch her eyes as she backs out of the room. I gasp for air holding the sudden pain in my chest too terrified to cry anymore I just need to get out of here, even if it kills me.

After the light is switched off I run through my very limited options. If I eat the hummus with the sesame seeds I will have a reaction, not sure how strong and not sure Angel would even bat an eyelid as I struggle for breath. No, it needs to be more. I need to bleed, the baby needs to be in jeopardy, but not actually in jeopardy. Fuck! How do I make myself bleed enough to make her take me to hospital and that's assuming she cares enough to want to save the baby. This whole room has nothing harsher than my language to cut myself with and even the cutlery an infant would struggle to injure themselves. I nibble on my thumb nail as my mind works through a number of scenarios until I think I am happy with my plan. It's not a great plan and I could very well slip into a coma before she decides to help, *if* she decides to help but it's all I have now that Kit is gone, is probably gone. My body makes an involuntary shudder because in my heart I can just feel

261

the truth, Kit is definitely gone.

Of course I may not have to pretend to bleed if she keeps coming in here in the middle of the night and hitting my head with the heel of the gun. Slam! Her fist connects hard with my cheek bone and slam again with the back of her hand. I try not to cry out but, fuck it hurts. She holds my face flat against the pillow with the gun in her hand and drags her nails down my inflamed cheek. Not enough to draw blood but enough to score the skin and make my eyes water. She leans in, her venomous words spit into my face. "Why the fuck does he keep coming here Bethany? What is he looking for? Is it you? Does he think he'll find you? Because he won't, I have you too well hidden in here." She pinches my face and holds it between her bony fingers with one hand and holds the gun to my temple with the other. My shallow panting breath can barely escape because of her weight on my chest. "He would never be happy with you. I saved you that. You should thank me. How could he ever be happy knowing he killed his own child? What kind of man could live with himself? Only I can make it bearable for him, because only I can forgive him. He needs my forgiveness to be happy, understand?" She smiles at this, because in her crazy mind I guess that makes sense but it just makes me fucking mad.

"He'd forgive himself pretty fucking quick if you told him the truth." I hold my breath expecting the full force of her rage but her eerie laugh is so much worse. She is silent for endless sadistic seconds.

"Did you honestly think your sister was going to help you? Did you honestly think I would let her?" She looks me dead in the eyes and I can't breathe as her next words destroy me. "Did you think I wasn't listening?" She throws her head back and laughs. "You might've thought you had a future. You might have thought you had a future with Daniel. It is laughable, really it is. You just don't get it do you? Only I hold his past, *me,* he has no future, will never have a future without *me.*" She pats my cheek and strokes my hair like you would a wounded animal and perhaps

the Only Choice

that's what I am to her, a pathetic, helpless wounded animal. She leaves just as silently as she came and I curl on my side, knowing she can hear I refuse to cry out but the silent tears fall, unstoppable and I let them. I cry for Kit, I cry for Daniel, and I cry for me and my baby but the tears will stop eventually because what I need is a much more potent mix of emotions. I need my anger and rage. I need to encourage and embrace the hatred that swills deep inside, fury like a fire needed to purge that vile excuse for a human. Now I am focused, now I have a plan and now I can't wait for tomorrow to come because tomorrow this ends.

I barely sleep but I'm not tired. I am determined to end this today and if my sudden illness and blood loss doesn't work I am just going to go old school and beat the shit out of her one handed. She might get a lucky shot and I might not be so fortunate but in the end she wants me dead. She wants my baby and I am under no illusion that the minute my baby is lifted from me my time is up. She's going to make sure of it, so technically I have nothing to lose. Angel swings into the room bright and cheery, polar opposite from the dark twisted demon snarling in my face last night. She chats away moaning about how much more work she has since Kit let her down and Clive is no longer employed. She even pats my back as I choke on the food stuck in my dry throat. I close my eyes to stop myself from breaking in front of her and I even try to look sympathetic to her plight. She takes my tray and just before I can ask again for the hummus she turns her head and sighs dramatically.

"I'm just off to the deli to get *your* treat. But don't make a habit of this." She waggles her finger at me like I'm a naughty child putting her to so much trouble. She also pauses long enough for me to know I should say something and I guess it's not 'fuck off and die bitch.'

"Thank you Angel, it's really very kind of you to go to so much trouble and I promise this will be my very last request." I am hoping it's just my last meal *here* and not my actual last meal. I would hate to die with the taste of hummus burning my throat and Angel looking down her nose at me with irritation that I have spoiled her day. She nods, smiles and turns to leave the room. Once the door is closed I sink back against the wall and let out a huge sigh, relieved that it is going to be today after all. I need the combination of all of these things to work together in my plan for the best impact and to ensure success.

I secure my chain to the wall hopefully for the last time and wait for Angel to loosen the chain enough for me to sit comfortably but with not too much free rein. She flounces in and puts the small brown paper deli bag on the table and sits beside me waiting for me to gush with appreciation. She looks annoyed that I smile tightly and open the bag. My skin tingles even as I remove the small pot and plastic container with the carrot sticks but I know that's just in my head. I am really not that allergic that I would react to the seeds' mere presence. I waste no more time and pick the lid off and scoop my finger in and lift a substantial heap of pinkish grainy paste and suck my finger dry, quickly repeating until I have eaten half the pot. I hesitate for a fraction of a second contemplating whether I will need to finish the pot because whether or not I was allergic this stuff tastes pretty nasty but I instantly feel the first hit of heat on my tongue.

I draw in a deep breath and can feel my rapid heartbeat thump harder in my chest and now the tingles on the skin of my throat are red hot scratches and my tongue feels puffy and swollen. Water is pooling like a lake in my mouth and I can feel it dribble out of the corner of my mouth as I try to pant in some cooler air. All of this I am managing to keep to myself and in my peripheral vision I can see Angel is still inspecting her nails or it might be the material of her skirt. With one sudden sharp movement I stab the soft plump tissue in my left palm, where my thumb joint is, with the bitten sharp point of the thumb nail on my right hand. I stab hard and rip and wriggle deeper into the flesh despite the excruciating pain because I need blood. I bite my teeth, my head feels dizzy, my mouth is on fire and now I can feel my chest tighten. The warm sticky liquid is collecting in my clenched palm and

I instantly cup myself at the crotch of my white leggings and continue to pump my fist urging my blood to run from my hand.

"Angel!" I cry out suddenly but I hardly recognise my voice, my tongue is fat and doesn't respond to my instructions. My words are slurred but the look on her face, is shocked enough for me to not have to go into detail. She slaps her hand to her mouth at the first sign of blood. "I need an ambulance, please Angel!" I look at the blood seeping down the inside of the top of my leggings and watch as she spins her head away with a hunch of her shoulders and a hand at her mouth. She doesn't move so I cry again. "Please Angel you have to get help, the baby, you might lose the baby!" Still she doesn't move and although I don't think I have lost a lot of blood I feel really dizzy, hot and I am struggling to catch a decent breath. She doesn't turn but her voice is perfectly calm.

"Well that would be unfortunate . . ." She hums and taps her fingers idly against her thighs like she is pondering what to eat for dinner. Fuck!

With a surge of pure hatred and energy I really don't have I lunge toward her but stumble as all hell breaks loose. The loud sudden bang and crash as the locks on the door disintegrate leaving the door broken and hanging from its' hinges. Patrick bursts in throwing a large metal bar to the floor and pushing Angel hard, fast and face first against the wall opposite. My knees buckle and I fall but there is no pain, before impact with the floor, I hit Daniel's outstretched arms. He holds me against his chest before he gently sits me back on the bed. His hands feel cool against my fevered skin, his soft caress starts at my face and sweeps my cheeks, down my neck, over my shoulder, every inch of my body is being traced. He is checking with his hands while his eyes refuse to break from mine. I am panting now and I can't swallow quick enough to get the air I need and get rid of the water in my mouth. He pushes me to lie down and I have no energy to resist. He starts to pull the waistband of my leggings but sucks in a breath at the blood stained clothing, his eyes dart back to mine but I shake my head and hold up my hand with the gaping tear.

He looks confused but continues to tug at my clothing, a little rough and hurried. I must look such a state he wants me to change before we leave. I can't think of any other reason to be stripping me so urgently. He fishes something from his back pocket and quickly presses a hard kiss on my wrinkled brow. "I'm sorry baby and this is going to hurt too but then I'll make it all better, I promise." He pulls back and in one swift move rolls me onto my side, stabs me hard with a needle and plunges the contents into my twitching thigh.

"Fuck!" I grab my leg and try to rub but my hand snaps back with the restriction of the chain. Daniel grabs my wrist and takes the chain and with a single rough jerk of his hand pulls the chain from the wall in a cloud of dust. With this freedom I can rub my thigh again and whatever he has pumped into my bloodstream is starting to clear my head because, my breathing is less laboured and I don't feel like I am burning from the inside out. I can focus as the fuzz dissipates and like a mirage, the clear lines of Daniel's handsome face begin to fill my vision, steel the breath just as I had got it back and pool my eyes with tears just as they had regained the clarity of vision.

"Adrenalin for your allergic reaction." He motions to where I am rubbing and I nod because I don't know what to say any more. We stare at each other for what seems like endless minutes then his hand lifts and he tucks a wayward spikey strand of my hair behind my ear and I see him struggle to swallow. He still looks so heartbroken. "I'm so fucking sorry Bethany, I'm so sorry." He drops his head and when he lifts which only takes a moment his eyes sparkle deep blue with brimming water. "I couldn't find you. I . . . I tracked her but it made no sense. I searched her place myself, I didn't understand and when I finally got some audio sound with the watch I knew you were close but I still couldn't find you. When I heard what you wanted her to get for you . . . Fuck! Bethany what were you thinking? If it wasn't for Patrick seeing her use this entrance this morning I would never

the Only Choice

have found you, do you understand!" He sounds so pissed at me and I am so fucking happy that he's pissed, I'm so fucking happy he's here. "It's nothing to smile about, you could've died. Jesus Christ Bethany look what she's done to you!" I laugh at this because the reason I look like I have been in a bar room brawl with a bunch of bikers is because she flipped every time *he* questioned her. The reason I'm here at all is because she is a crazy psycho bitch for *him* but none of that matters now. All that matters is that we are getting out of here today, safely; me, Daniel and our baby.

He scoops me into his arms and I gladly rest my head against his chest and hold my arms around his neck. What a difference a day makes, I have gone from feeling isolated, terrified and without hope to feeling safe, cherished and full of promise. "The baby?" My question sounds uncertain because I honestly don't know what to expect but I am seriously confused when at first he frowns then he smiles a knowing smile.

"There is no baby." He kisses the tip of my nose but he stops when he feels my body tense. "What? What is it?" His voice is raised and he looks stern so I shake my head because this is obviously not the right time to break the 'happy' news.

"Nothing." I smile and can feel him instantly relax. "You got her gun though, right?" He turns to face the door, Patrick is looking at us with one hand on Angels shoulder keeping her pinned to the wall. We both look at them then Daniel looks back at me.

"What gun?" He turns his back on Patrick and Angel and stepping toward the opened door his question is drowned by the ear shattering crack of gunfire, Angel's gun. There is a crunch sound of breaking bone, a soft cry and a muffled sound of Angel crumpling on the floor. Thank God Patrick took her out before she took aim, thank God she didn't manage to hit anyone, thank . . . Wait. Why are we falling? Daniel folds so slowly to his knees with me protected in his arms it's almost graceful, we both look down between us, the shadow of the tiny space between our bodies darkens as his T-shirt starts to discolour. No. .no. .no. Please no. He can't be shot, no. .no . . . no. I look into his eyes, the panic, the pain. I can feel it. God I can feel it too. So much pain, so much fucking pain. Why does it hurt me so much? I press my hand against his side and feel him wince but I wince too. I take my hand and press where I feel his pain, my side mirrors his but there's so much blood, too much blood. I sigh and though the pain is unbelievable I smile because I will gladly endure. I think if I can take some of his pain, he won't look so sad. I close my eyes and think maybe now is a good time to sleep but he is going to have to stop shouting at me. I can't sleep if he keeps shouting.

"Don't you fucking close your eyes! Don't you fucking dare! Do you hear me?"

Chapter Twenty-Two

I CAN FEEL the cold in my knees as the damp ground seeps through the thick denim of my jeans, its making them numb. I like the feeling because the pain of feeling him slip through my fingers is like a knife inching its way slowly through my side, under my ribs and piercing my heart; ripping and severing every vein, every nerve ending, tearing through the muscle and flesh as it goes. It's unbearable, its heart breaking. I am heart broken. I pull my sticky fingers from his hair but I'm confused at his soft smile and when John whispers that I will be fine I want to scream 'How can I ever be fine?' but my body won't respond. I look at my fingers that are no longer coated in blood and back up to his now deep blue eyes and Daniel is smiling now, the words he says are the same but they offer no comfort because I don't believe him. I can't believe him. I saw him bleed, I heard the gunshot, how can I be fine if he's not . . . if he's . . . I sob but no sound escapes my mouth. My body is an empty shell, my skin feels numb, and deep in my soul there is nothing, just numb. I drop my head and watch as his shirt turns from pale to dark, the rapid absorption of his blood sparks utter desolation in my soul, I scream and scream, breaking through the crippling numbness to release my pain.

"Shh shhh sweetie. It's all right, you're gonna be all right

Boo. I'll get a nurse for the pain. Shh shh don't cry, please don't cry." I hear the catch in her voice and I know she too is crying. I try to open my eyes but I can't. I know it's Sofia, I recognise her troubled voice and I so desperately want to see her face that more tears fall out the corners of my closed lids. Her soft hand wipes my cheek again and again. I hear movement and when she informs whoever has arrived that I need something for the pain I shake my head. I can shake my head, that's something and I try to speak but my throat is so dry and raw it feels like I am in mid sword swallow. I want to tell her I can't have pain relief. I don't want pain relief. I don't want to hurt the baby but the fact that I feel a cool trickle in the crook of my arm makes me think I didn't make myself clear. I hope that's the case because I don't want to think it might because I don't need to worry about the baby any more. God I'm so tired. I don't want to be tired, I want to wake up, I want to see Sofia. I want to see Marco and I want Daniel. More tears fall over my cheeks and I think that the pit of my stomach feels the way it does because I won't get what I want.

The room is dimly lit but I can see its daylight outside. The slatted blinds are three quarters shut, muting the harsh light from outside and making it bearable to open my eyes. I can open my lids but when I see the utter sadness and devastation on the faces of those I love I wish I hadn't. No one looks that sad for no reason; maybe if I close my eyes for a little longer I can avoid the horror of the truth that is going to destroy me, again. Marco meets my gaze and his face lights up. He is at my side in an instant clutching my hand and calling to Sofs. Side by side they beam at me but just behind them Vivienne and Tony look more concerned than happy. I lick my lips and although my throat is parched I manage to speak.

"How was the honeymoon?" I croak. Sofia gasps and slaps her hand to her mouth then they all let out a huge stifled laugh filled with relief.

"Oh my God Bets! You don't honestly think we went do you? As soon as I saw that first post on Facebook and then the second

the Only Choice

Daniel called . . ." She stops mid-sentence as they all flash wide eyes at each other. I can hear the increase tempo of the monitor recording my heart and it is just getting faster now I know they are hiding something.

"Tell me Sofs." I try to wet my lips but I have no moisture and I look to see if I have any water to hand. Marco lifts the glass to my lips and I take a tiny sip.

"Bethany I don't think it's a good idea to do the detail right now . . . you've just woken up and you've been through so much." She tries to placate me but even as she does she casts a worried glance over the rapidly flickering needle scribbling away beside me.

"Tell me!" I want to ask lots of questions but I am stuck with one or two word phrases for now and I am going to get more than frustrated if I have to keep repeating them.

"Tell you what?" The unfamiliar but friendly voice appears just behind Sofia. He is quite young, wearing a white coat and carrying a flip chart. "Welcome back Bethany, you gave us all quite a scare. I'm Dr Young and you are a very lucky lady." He continues to read the chart and then raises his eyes to meet mine. His smile is kind and makes him look younger still. I smile but not because he is trying to be friendly, I am smiling because of the irony, do I feel like a lucky lady, no.

"He died?" I don't care if I've been lucky and I don't care if it's not the right time. I have to know when my life ended and why I'm still alive. Strangely my question seems to have confused all of them so I just clarify. "Daniel . . . he died." My eyes water but I blink the tears away and an inappropriate chuckle ripples through the room.

"Mr Stone?" Dr Young looks to the others for confirmation as I am frozen holding my breath for what's coming, although why that would be funny is lost on me. "Oh no . . . no he didn't die. He fared somewhat better than you. The bullet hit him but went straight through, unfortunately it lodged in your spleen. Which is why you spent several hours in surgery and have only just woken up and Mr Stone has had some repair work and is causing a considerable amount of trouble on the next floor." He chuckles again but his face changes when he sees that I am not smiling and my tears seem relentless. "I'm sorry Bethany. I thought you'd be pleased to learn this news?" He steps forward and takes my hand I am shaking my head because he's got this so fucking wrong. Of course I'm pleased, I can't believe it. I thought with my dream that he had died for sure and my sub conscious was preparing me for the worst. My tears which won't fucking stop are tears of utter relief and joy. Sofia pats the doctors' shoulder and explains that I am probably a little overwhelmed and I am actually happy with the news. Under-fucking-statement-of-the-year. "Oh good, well like I say he has been more than a handful. It's all we could do not to have him restrained to the bed to prevent him coming down here but he needed his rest too and since you hadn't regained consciousness. Anyway he is due to be discharged in a few days and I am sure he will be down to see you just as soon as he is. You however, have a little longer in here I'm afraid."

Dr Young smiles as he checks the notes and asks me some standard questions. Given that no one has asked and it is the only other question on my mind I try for a five word question this time.

"Is the baby all right?" My voice is barely a whisper but he hears me perfectly and so does Daniel standing in the doorway.

"What baby?" His deep voice sends a welcome chill down my spine and even though he still sounds pissed, I don't care.

Sofia leans in and whispers. "The baby's fine. No one told him Bets, we only found out because we told the hospital we were next of kin." She kisses me on the cheek then scowls. "And I am so fucking mad at you for not telling me but lucky for you . . . peril trumps pissed and I'm just so—" She starts to sob and Marco has his arm over her shoulder whilst rolling his eyes.

"Sorry." I smile and nod my head to Daniel. "Alone please." I hope I can manage a few more words when we're alone or this conversation is going to take forever. I suck in a steady breath because I like the sound of forever. Sofia nods and ushers her parents from the room once they have very carefully hugged and kissed me.

The room is cleared and Daniel closes the door, pulls the blind over the window pane in the door, closes the blinds on the glass panel partition and the windows to the outside world. He grins as he walks toward me and I get a flutter deep in my tummy. He sits carefully on the edge of the bed but I wince at the movement, he narrows his eyes and bites his bottom lip. I tap my throat with the one hand that isn't hooked up to the tubes and croak. "Hurts to talk."

His smile is wider now and he draws in a deep breath. "Perfect . . . because I want you to listen. Since you are still in considerable pain lets hope you are less likely to argue with me or be stubborn. It might prove a little difficult to have to spank you while you are still in recovery . . . difficult, but not impossible." His lips curl at the sensual tease of punishment.

I snort and immediately regret the searing pain, as muscles I never knew were involved in such a simple non-verbal display scream in agony. I still tingle deep inside at his threat but it's also funny that I could feel remotely turned on, looking like I must and feeling like I do. But this is Daniel and there go my senses.

"Bad things happen when we aren't together." He takes my hand, turns it in his palm, his thumb traces circles on the soft skin of my wrist. "Bad things happen when I try to protect you without telling you that is what *I* am trying to do and bad things happen when you try to save me without telling me what *you* are trying to do. But mostly bad things happen when we don't trust each other. I knew Angel and Sebastian were up to something but I didn't know what and I couldn't bring myself to believe it was Angel." He closes his eyes with obvious pain and I squeeze his hand because I understand.

"First loves," I whisper and although it hurts to say it, if this gets everything out in the open and we can move on we have to face the ugly too.

"What?" His dark brow is knitted with confusion and his tone is filled with shock.

"First love Daniel" My voice is gaining strength the more I try to speak but it still sounds scratchy and fragile. "Angel said she was—" I gasp as he silences me with an urgent kiss before he pulls back shaking his head assuredly.

"She wasn't my first love Bethany. Fuck she wasn't even a Hallmark moment but she was a friend and I trusted her." He draws in a heavy sigh, "I trusted her more than I trusted you and I will never forgive myself—"

"Stop." I interrupt as sternly as I can, "Stop please, you saved me, again. There is nothing to forgive." He holds my sincere stare and I watch as his eyes soften but I start to chew my lip to prevent myself asking the question that is now burning my tongue.

"Ask me?" He softly demands and grins at his open book in a hospital gown. I shake my head.

"You think I won't spank that question out of you?" He straightens his back and adjusts his loose lounge pants. I am hit with a full wave of instant heat, raw and tingly. His gaze is fixed with lust and mischief. I try to wriggle to ease the ache but am shocked still with the very distracting and very real pain in my side. His hand reaches for my cheek and he cups it tenderly, his smile is wide and heart stealing. "Bethany, you are my only love, first, last . . . everything." He leans in to deliver what I know will be an amazingly passionate kiss to seal his desire but my lips can't hold the seriousness a moment longer as I let out a snicker. His eyes widen and he looks a little stunned. "What?"

"Barry White Daniel, really?" I hold my lips with my fingers flat against them to stop a full laugh escaping.

"Hey there is nothing wrong with borrowing lyrics from the master, besides it's a classic." His smile widens and he again leans in to ever so gently kiss my bruised lips and cheeks and brows and nose. He holds my hands silently for a few moments and I can see he still has much he needs to say so I wait patiently enjoying the comfort of his nearness. "At first it was exactly as I told you at Ethan's place that weekend. I felt this was my chance at redemption for causing so much death. This was my chance to make amends and Angel would forgive me, she would finally be able to be happy but some things didn't quite add up. I had to do this myself because whatever they were doing; well, I didn't want to put you in danger. He deals with some pretty nasty individuals and I needed you out of the picture. I think I could have kept us together if you hadn't been so stubborn but because you . . ." He takes a deep breath and sighs. "I made the decision it was safest to hurt you, push you away, make you hate me to keep you safe but you . . ." He sighs again as he tries to find the most delicate way to insult me. "You couldn't help yourself and you were likely to say something to Angel before I could learn the truth. I can't blame you for that, she had me so fucked up I didn't know what to believe. She got me thinking that you would never really want me after learning what I had done. You could pretend for a while but how could you possibly want a life with me, want to be with me, want me after I . . ." He drops his forehead on my thigh and it's my turn to trace my fingers through is thick hair. "I was so close to learning the truth. Jason had been investigating Sebastian's business in South America and Jack Wilson had managed to get some family history that had been buried. I was so mad after the club that I needed time to cool down. That you could be so reckless? I know I hurt you. God I wish I could take that night back. I had arranged to meet Angel on the Monday after the wedding, after seeing you, being with you. I didn't want to wait any longer, I thought I had enough to tackle Angel and end it all but then you disappeared." His soft lips sweep gentle kisses across the back of my hand and I can feel the scratch from his unkempt stubble.

"Sofia called me on the Tuesday and I knew something bad had happened. We met and I talked her through our options none of which involved letting Angel know we suspected her. Sofia was fucking mad at me but not as angry as I was with myself. I let you down. I didn't protect you and I couldn't find you. Five fucking weeks! I tracked her but she spent all her time at the apartment and I had searched that myself. The tracker wasn't sophisticated enough to pick up which floor she was on. I had the recorder in the watch I gave her activated and I knew she had you but it still didn't click you were in her building just buried under someone else's flat in the basement. You nearly fucking gave me a heart attack with the hummus shit and it's only because she got careless and Pat saw her go through a door that didn't belong to her that we were even there at the right time. Fuck Bethany you could've died!" I know he is angry but the love in his eyes makes my heart burst and a smile so wide it cracks my lips spreads across my face.

"I didn't think you were coming. I saw the necklace and I hoped . . . but then after so many days and nothing. I lost hope that you were coming and after she . . . and Kit." I squeeze my eyes and rub the painful tingle in my nose, "I knew I was alone . . . it didn't matter if I died, I just couldn't let her win. I couldn't let her have our baby." There I've said it.

"I will always come for you, always. I will always come for both of you, always." He slowly moves his hand and slips it under the sheet, over the top of my 'sexy' hospital gown and lays it flat on my bump. I get a flutter in my tummy and the monitor beside me picks up its staccato beat. The flutter starts again and Daniels eyes widen. He pulls the sheet back and smoothes the gown flat. He lifts his hand and places it gently once more on my, much larger than I remember, bump. Flutter again, and again, butterflies are definitely felt higher and there is no way I'm nervous. I smile and gasp and laugh all at once but he has just frozen. He shifts and removes his wallet from his back pocket; he flicks through some notes and picks out a crumpled piece of paper. "So this scan, this here . . . is our baby?" I nod and laugh as he grabs a pen and scribbles over Angel's name, leaving no trace. "I'll want a better picture, when you are recovered. We will get another one yes?" His excitement is infectious and he just keeps staring at the picture but I shake my head because it still just

the Only Choice

looks like a grey swirly pattern to me. The fluttering in my pelvis is much more heart stealing.

"You're not mad?" He looks shocked at the worry on my face and the uncertainty in my voice.

"Oh baby, I am way beyond mad. Putting yourself in danger like—"

I interrupt. "No no, I mean about the baby?" He tucks some hair that won't be tamed back around my ear and drops his head slightly, his hair falling into his eyes. He looks up through his lashes and blows the hair away with a gruff exhale of breath.

"Yes I'm fucking furious you didn't tell me. I'm fucking furious I didn't pick up the signs but no baby," he gently cups my cheek and I lean in to his touch. "I am not mad that we are having a baby. I can't quite get my head round it all yet and I don't think I will until you are fully recovered but I'm stoked I get to be a Dad. That you are carrying my child does crazy shit to me I can't begin to describe and I fucking love that you are going to be a Mum." He is quiet and I can feel him processing everything, so much information, so much drama. I feel him shudder and look to meet his gaze. "Fuck when I saw Kits body and thought it was you . . . I died a thousand deaths in that one second." He stops at my soft sob and looks utterly confused. "Don't you dare feel sorry for that bitch she got—"

"Stop!" I gasp shaking my head, he does but he looks shocked at my outburst, which has just scored my throat raw. "She was going to help me."

He tilts his head with a suspicious raised brow. "You sure about that? She was the one that got you there in the first place."

"I know but yes I'm sure." I shake my head because it's started to throb. "She promised to tell you about the baby, after, so she would've saved the baby at least." I say quietly.

"After you died you mean, after they had murdered you! Oh she's a fucking Saint." He barks out with unconfined bitterness and fury.

"No Daniel enough. I mean it. I know she wasn't a Saint but

she was going to save the baby. That's why Angel killed her and that alone cuts her a lot of slack in my book, besides it doesn't matter now does it." My voice breaks with the strain of speaking and the emotion I feel, because however twisted our relationship, she was my sister and it may be naïve but I choose to believe she *was* going to help.

"Ok baby, I didn't mean to make you upset, if anything I'm just so fucking angry at myself for letting you out of my sight." His tone is deadly serious, his jaw is clenched and his eyes fix with mine.

"Yeah coz that's healthy." I quip.

"Fuck healthy! I nearly lost you and trust me that is *never* going to happen again." He huffs through his nose and I half expect him to beat on his chest and drag me by what's left of my hair to his cave. But I also understand he was probably just as frightened as I was. I am just so glad that he cares enough to be a little bit crazy. "And you're going to marry me right? I mean that's not negotiable now?"

"Well how could I refuse such a romantic proposal." I think I manage to hiss this because despite this being my dreamed of reunion he is starting to piss me off. He drags one hand through his hair and takes a calming breath obviously noticing my new tension and clipped tone.

"Christ! I'm fucking this up. Look . . . It's just . . . it's . . . I can't lose you again Bethany." He takes this moment to cup my face once more, his fingertips gently secure and angle my head so he can brush his lips across mine. I can feel his body vibrate as it fights to keep the kiss soft for fear of hurting me, when he clearly wants to do anything but keep it soft. "Will you marry me? It's the right thing to do." His soft words started so well but the ending falls flat in my ears.

I pull back and close my eyes. This is hard because I can hear the uncertainty and longing in his voice in equal measure but I don't need a knee jerk proposal. "Daniel you don't have to ask me to marry you just because of the baby or because you suddenly feel responsible in some way. We've been through a lot but I don't . . ." I falter as his eyes flash with fury and if I didn't endure searing pain at the slightest move I would try and pull myself away from the intensity of the rage currently radiating from his body. His jaw is ticking wildly and his tried and tested release of dragging his hand through his hair has been tried, tested and failed.

"Fuck! You are unbelievable you know that! And just so as you know, I am storing all this shit you keep spouting. I am making a list and it is *not* going to Santa. Once you are able to walk out of here you are *not* going to be able to walk for a week or sit down for a month." He pulls his lips through his teeth and my eyes flick to his mouth then back to his feral eyes. "I have been asking you to marry me for months. It has fuck all to do with the baby and has everything to do with me wanting to spend every day of the rest of my life with the one person in the world I can't live a day without. The only woman I have ever truly loved, the only woman I know I don't deserve but the one I'm going to spend every waking minute of every single day, trying to prove otherwise. Yes, we've been through a lot, but it's all relative, it's our normal. That's not to say I would like our normal to be a little less horror movie and a lot more X-rated movie but what it definitely isn't is a fucking tragedy. This is our normal and *our* movie has the fucking fairy tale ending. So, I'll give you the romance, you know that baby but for right now, you have to give me my answer." He is kneeling beside my bed, empty handed but holding my one cable free hand in both of his and my eyes have been trickling with a series of tears since he said 'Fuck' with the utter frustration of a man consumed with love, love for me. I nod but he shakes his head, his lips curl into a breath taking grin. "No baby. I need to hear the words."

I sniff back the tears with a laugh and continue to nod. "Yes Daniel I'll marry you."

"Yeah you will." He stands and covers my mouth with his sweet soft lips and for now I am glad he is back to treating me like I'm made of glass because there is not an inch of me that doesn't hurt. Well, except my heart because that only hurts because it wants to burst for the first time in a long time. I don't remember him pulling away, I must have fallen asleep during the kiss. It felt so good I just let myself drift and fall knowing he was there to catch me, would always catch me. When I open my eyes the room is much darker, I don't have the disorientation I did when I first woke up. I know exactly where I am, I know exactly what happened and I know exactly who is lying in a tiny made up bed beside me. His on his side facing me, his dark hair flopped over his face, his eyes closed but even resting and covered in shadow I can see the exhaustion and seriousness edging his handsome features. His eyes open and instantly the smile that creeps across softens and lightens his face and my heart. "Hey." His deep voice soothes and tingles. He lifts his head a little and tucks his arm under to rest it at an elevated angle.

"Hey." I whisper back not sure who I am trying not to disturb. My voice sounds less croaky and doesn't feel so raw. "Shouldn't you still be in your own bed, you still have a band on your wrist so I assume you haven't actually been discharged yet?"

"There is nothing they need to do to me that they can't do right here. I'm a little sore but I haven't had major surgery or lost nearly my own body weight in blood." He grins and flashes his killer smile. "They had a fucking fight not letting me see you sooner when you were still unconscious so I'd like to see them try and keep me away from you now."

In that case I pat the bed for him to join me but narrow my eyes when he shakes his head. "I think you said something about *'not keeping away?'*" I try to shift over but stop and take a sharp breath at the first attempt at movement. He is instantly at my side.

"Ok Ok you win but don't move. I'll just wrap around you." He lets out a defeated sigh but smiles when he sees my smile.

"It's not a game, I don't care about winning. I just want you." I lean my head into his chest, his arm awkwardly resting over my head and him rolled on his side, his heat and body just the right

the Only Choice

kind of medicine. He kisses my hair and whispers.

"No more games, just you and me and a shit load of trust." I can feel his steady thump of his heart and his soft breath against my hair. The calm makes me think he has fallen asleep but then he speaks again. "Just to clarify, I didn't mean no more games in the bedroom—"

"Ow ow," I cry out because my sudden laugh hurts like hell.

"Sorry baby." He chuckles, deep and throaty. "But there is no way I'm giving up playtime with you. I fucking love playtime with you." His gravelly tone has just ignited a surge of nerves previously numb with pain killers and by the feel of his smile against my head he knows it.

When I wake next it is because the nurse is changing my IV, the room is bright. Daniel is sitting beside me looking fresh, clean and a little too hot to be good for my recovery. I feel better, I mean I feel like I've been hit with a truck but I feel better despite that. Once the nurse leaves Daniel is again by my side and I get the feeling it has been like that whether I am awake or not. He leans in to kiss my cheek and steps to the side, still holding my hand. My eyes meet Ethans' and his sadness stops my smile before it takes hold. Tom is beside him with his hand on his sons shoulder for comfort. I guess I must still look pretty shocking, I can see Tom push Ethan forward and I am so confused. Daniel leans in to whisper that Ethan blames himself for Kit and now I'm really confused. Daniel excuses himself and I reach my hand to Ethan which he takes reluctantly.

"Hey." I exhale and smile but it does nothing to ease the obvious tension.

"Bets, I'm so sorry. I didn't know. God, I didn't know who she was . . . I thought . . . I believed she—" His eyes are liquid brown and the tears fall and break my heart for him and for Kit.

"Ethan, please," I grip his hand tightly. "It's not your fault and she *did.*" His eyes snap to mine, angry and hurt with betrayal. I just hope I can make him understand, make him believe. "Kit . . . she really liked you. I know she did, she may have had a different agenda to start with, but that changed. You changed her." He just shakes his head with disbelief. "Ethan listen to me, if she didn't really like you . . . if you hadn't made her see that there was *more* she never would have tried to help me. She never would've changed her mind. Please don't believe she didn't have true feelings for you because for the first time in her life I believe she did and I am grateful you made her happy and she *was* happy. For a little while she was my sister and I never thought that was possible."

He wipes his eyes on the back of his hand. "But if it wasn't for me she wouldn't have got to you." His voice breaks and Tom steps up and rests his hand on his shoulder again.

"Don't flatter yourself" I try to laugh lightly and manage a little noise before the pain. "Kit was very resourceful; she really didn't need you for that. I'm sorry if you think you could've prevented what happened but believe me you couldn't. Ask Daniel, Kit on her own is . . . was a force to be reckoned with but with Angel . . ." I sigh and let the enormity of my timely escape wash over me. "I know I'm lucky to be here." Tom steps beside Ethan and takes my other hand. I hold Ethan's sorrowful gaze. "I'm sorry you got caught up in this because I can see how upset you are and that kills me, but I'm not sorry you fell for Kit. If you hadn't been you and you hadn't shown her how you felt about her, made her feel the same, I know I wouldn't be here, my baby wouldn't be here. So don't beat yourself up for saving me and don't beat yourself up for having feelings for Kit. She may not have deserved you to start with but she risked her life for me and she definitely deserved you in the end. She deserved a better end." He closes his eyes and I hope he is taking in my words of comfort because they are all true. I can see by Tom's expression that he is just as upset but his shoulders relax a little as I finished speaking. He squeezes Ethan's shoulder and his warm eyes wrinkle with gratitude as he looks at me. He places his hands over both of ours.

"Bethany . . . I have no words. I know you must have been

the Only Choice

through hell and this is selfish of me but I have only just got you in my life . . . if . . . if anything had happened I know I would've lost both of you. Ethan lost it when he got the call from Marco. I could feel him slipping—"

"Dad. .not now." Ethan tries to shrug it off.

"It's true Ethan . . . It's not like I haven't seen it happen before . . . Bethany you are part of us, a part of our family, so precious. And you two are my life and for a moment . . . a moment I don't ever want to live through again . . . I thought I had lost you. Just don't ever do that again . . . Ok?" His kind smile is filled with love and relief.

"Ok" I agree and give Ethan and extra squeeze which he acknowledges with a tentative smile.

We stay like that for a little while, it's not awkward and I think we all feel the need to draw comfort from each other. Tom is the first to break the quiet when he notices my eyelids droop. He bends down to kiss my cheek.

"Bethany. ." He bites his lip and forces a tight smile. "I'm so happy you are. . . ." He clears his throat and I smile, this heavily emotional situation seems to have us all a little tongue tied.

"I know . . . me too." I offer to help him out and he returns my smile and kisses me once more before stepping back to allow Ethan to do the same. Ethan holds my hand but has trouble holding my gaze. This is really hard but I think it's just going to take time and what he needs to understand is that because of him and Daniel, that is exactly what I have now, time.

Chapter Twenty-Three

A FEW DAYS pass and I feel much stronger. I can eat by myself and Marco has brought in some of my favourite pasta dishes from the restaurant, delicate and tasty and a welcome change from the bland dishes of the past five weeks. Daniel has been officially discharged but is constantly at my side, something I didn't want as I gave my statement to the police. I could see his knuckles whiten with anger and half way through it was evident he wasn't coping quite as well as I was with the retelling. It was hard but it was over and that's what I focused on but when the police finally finished and Daniel was quiet for so long I started to worry.

"Have I done something wrong?" The silence is broken and he looks startled at the interruption and shocked at my question.

"Why the fuck would you think that?" His tone is stern and he walks to my side gently picking up my hand which is now free of wires.

"You know we are both going to have to watch our language." I meant it as a joke but I draw in a stuttered breath when I think of how I was reprimanded by Angel for swearing.

"Hey . . . forget that Ok, this isn't about her." His eyes hold mine and I know he knows what I'm thinking. He has just heard

the Only Choice

the crazy fucked up story in tortuous detail. "I'm sorry, I just didn't know that every time I questioned her, she came and beat the shit out of you. That she did it because she was mad at me. I fucking hate myself for what she did to you."

I laugh because I think we have been through enough to ever need to start self-flagellation, we are neither of us blameless in this. "Oh believe me I hated you too but lucky for me . . . no mirrors." I wink and he throws his head back and laughs pulling me into a tight hug that doesn't make me scream. "All that changes today though. I am taking my first bath and I am walking myself there." I say with a good deal of pride, he cocks his brow like he is impressed. "Just as soon as Sofia comes with my stuff."

"I can help you, you don't need Sofia." He almost growls like I have insulted his manhood.

"Daniel, I'm filthy." I moan and then snicker at his obvious salacious grin.

"Oh baby, don't tempt me." He leans in and plants tender kisses along my collar bone and up to just below my ear. "But I'm helping you, end of." He sucks on the soft flesh and I feel the familiar draw of heat in my core, it feels normal, it feels welcome, it feels delicious and I moan my appreciation. Sofia barges in cooling the instant heat that has return with vengeance between us and drops her Louis Vuitton Tote bag on the end of my bed. There is a fight over who is helping and I have to credit Sofia and her fiery self for standing up to Daniel in all his intimidating glory but I negotiate a compromise. Sofia is helping me in the bathroom and after some girlie time Daniel will help me with the bath.

My walk to the bathroom feels like my own personal marathon and I have Daniel on one side, a nurse on the other and Sofia hovering front and back. I am glad Sofia is here, really its best friend above and beyond but there is no shame in wanting to retain a little mystery in my relationship with Daniel. Even if I am not doing anything remotely mysterious in the bathroom. I stand and Sofia unties my gown. I have a clear plastic film covering my wound which is badly bruised and dark with dried blood and healing tissue. The scar looks nasty, my tummy is swollen and looks misshaped against my obvious weight loss elsewhere but I can't help but cry out when I see myself in the full length mirror behind the door. It is only for a second before it flies open and Daniel is standing in its place. I feel my legs buckle and Daniel's arms are around me, supporting my weight before I fall and I am crying, crying like a big girl.

"Hey hey what's the matter? Are you hurt? Did you hurt yourself?" His words are trying to sooth but they are edged with panic and he looks to Sofia for help. I continue to sob and shake my head, my ugly head. The image was only fleeting, my face looks drawn, dark eyes and yellowing bruises on my cheeks and chin. The shock was enough without the result of my losing battle with Angel's knife. My hair, clumps of short cropped hair sticking up like its allergic to my scalp, tufty long straggles she missed and uneven bob length pieces showcase my ordeal to perfection. I am hideous and no one said a damn word.

I manage to sob into his chest as he has me pressed tight, one arm around my waist one hand cupping the back of my head. "I look . . . I loo. ." I sob the words, more sound than speech. "My hair, my face, my . . . my body." My sobs muffle into his shirt.

"I know baby, and I want to believe me but the doctor said we should wait." His gravelly words are whispered in my ear.

My head snaps up to see his mean joke reflected in his face but there is no humour. He is deadly serious. "What?" I gasp.

"What? You are naked, what do you think I mean?" He looks intently in my eyes, his expression both confused and curious.

"Daniel, look at me, I'm hideous!" I shout, he is obviously blind maybe he is deaf too.

He scoops his arm under my knee and lifts me easily. He lowers me into the bath of no bubbles Sofia had run and kneels beside me. "Bethany, you are the most beautiful woman I have ever seen and it's only because you look a little fragile that I'm not fucking you right now." He turns to wink at Sofia, "no offence

the Only Choice

Sofia but I really wouldn't care if you watched or not but I'm trying to be a gentleman about it. Which is pretty fucking hard, because you are in fact naked and you don't have a hideous bone in that delectable body." He scoops up some water and starts to wash my not at all delectable but entirely battered body, he places one strong arm around my neck and I let my head flop back. The tears stop when I realise they were pretty stupid tears under the circumstance, my image in one hit was just a little shocking especially compared to Daniel with barely a hair out of place. I am alive, Daniel is alive, our baby is alive, the bruises will fade, scars will heal and my hair will grow back.

The next day a hair dresser arrives and works her magic transforming my hair of many lengths. Leaving it the shortest I have had it since I was maybe eleven years old and still a Tomboy. But to be fair she didn't have a great deal of choice and the dark chestnut pixie cut is soft around my face and Sofia assures me it is cute as a button. Daniel isn't around this morning and Sofia has brought the prettiest silk slip of a nightie with matching gown and when I look in the mirror this time I smile. I certainly look well enough to be discharged and I am kind of excited that Daniel is going to take me for a spin around the hospital gardens later, fresh air and sunlight. Sofia insists on a little tinted moisturiser to cover the last of the bruises and hands me a cashmere wrap in case it is chilly outside. She looks distracted but she is very dressed up so she probably needs to stop playing nurse and go wherever she is supposed to be. She gives me a quick kiss on my cheek and dashes away, strategically deflecting my questions. I may only have half a spleen but the bullet didn't affect my brain and I just know she is up to something.

I can see Tom walk toward me pushing an empty wheelchair and carrying a tight bouquet of white avalanche roses. He parks the chair and comes to sit beside me. He takes my hand and holds it firmly but I can feel him shaking. "Bethany, Daniel asked me to come get you but I need to say a few things first before I hand you over." He clears his throat with a deep cough and straightens his back.

"Hand me over?" He holds my gaze and I get a sudden surge in my tummy and those butterflies high and low start somersaults inside.

"Yes, hand you over." He smiles a knowing smile filled with love and concern. "I know I haven't been a part of your life for very long and there are people much better qualified than I to do this, but I do love you. We all love you so much and want what's best, want you to be happy. I have been here the whole time but felt like a fraud because these people, Sofia, Marco, Tony and Viv, all of them, they are your real family and it gives me immeasurable comfort knowing you have such amazing people around you. I want you to know that you have me and Ethan too now. But all of that is nothing compared to what that young man feels for you, he never left your side for a moment. I know he loves you like you deserve to be loved, and I'm relieved he does because I couldn't give you away otherwise. I know it's traditional and I am honoured I get to do this but I do also feel since I haven't held the title long I have asked someone who *is* more than qualified to accompany us, if that's Ok with you?"

I think my jaw must be on the floor because he is definitely talking like I am all clued in to what is about to happen. Marco steps into the room in his navy Armani suit with a white rose button hole and silver grey tie to match the ribbon wrapped around my flowers. I feel the first burst of tears on my cheek. Oh shit I am not nearly stable enough for this intensely emotional event.

"Hey Bets you know I love a two-fa, so let's do this." He holds the jackets collar of his suit, the same one he wore to Sofia's wedding, which seems like a lifetime ago. He ruffles my cropped hair and plants a kiss on my cheek wiping the tear as he does. "It's inevitable" He says in his best Matrix Agent Smith accent. He helps me stand and then sit back down in the chair that I wish I didn't need and he starts to push as Tom walks beside me. Its then I notice the collection of nurses with gushing grins and clasped hands, great, so everyone knew but me.

the Only Choice

The short lift ride and walk along a blank corridor has us stopped outside a set of double oak doors. Marco walks in front of me and squats down on his haunches. "You ready for this Boo?"

I bark out a light laugh that might sound a little hysterical, "Not even remotely," he laughs but stands as the doors open. My heart is in my dry throat at the vision of Daniel stepping through the door. God he looks breath taking, dark suit, darker eyes and emanating intensity that makes my whole body shudder.

"Would you give us a moment please?" His eyes are fixed on me as he addresses Marco and Tom, the soft footsteps indicate their departure. "Hey." His lips curl into a grin that wouldn't look out of place on the devil himself, it causes me to laugh my 'hey' back at him.

"This is all arse backwards you know that right?" I continue with my nervous laugh. He has crouched in front of me like Marco, so is eye level with me.

"Oh! How so?" He bites his lip and I love that his intensity isn't stopping his playfulness.

"Well we are supposed to get engaged, hen-do, wedding, honeymoon, then baby." I tilt my head happy with the normal list of traditional sequence of events involving getting hitched.

"Well, the baby is a done deal *baby* and an engagement didn't work out so well for us in the past, besides it is just a period of time, this . . ." he takes my hands all playfulness gone, "this, is forever."

"I like the sound of that." I breathe out as he covers my lips with his but I continue to speak, "I still get a hen do though, you promised." I can feel his smile against my mouth.

"And I am a man of my word." He kisses me again but doesn't stand and I can almost hear his heartbeat as loud as I feel mine.

"We can do this again, have the big day thing with all that shit but there is just no way I am going one more day without you as my wife." His voice is gruff and urgent.

"I take it everyone I love is right behind those doors?" I tip my chin and he nods not needing to look where I'm pointing, in fact he doesn't seem to want to take his eyes off me, which is perfect. His gaze pierces me, fixes me and holds me.

"I need to make sure; I wanted to make sure this was your choice. I know I'm not great at letting you do that and even today it might look that way but I want this to be your choice as much as I know it is mine." I can see he is holding his breath and it surprises me that he could have the slightest doubt and he sighs with pure relief when I whisper.

"It's the only choice."

The End.

Epilogue

"**FUCKING LAS VEGAS!**" Sofia squeals and with her arms tight around my waist jumps up and down like a giddy child and with enough force to lift me clear off the floor. In fact, she is worse than a child because she should know better. I try in vain to shush her excitement as I look over her shoulder at a heavy browed scowling Daniel and a none too happy Paul. My attempt at a placatory smile falls on sterner features than I have the capacity to melt but after five years of dealing with my stubborn streak Daniel knows better than to argue this little trip, besides he promised and he is many things and one of which I love the most, is that he is a man of his word. That doesn't mean he isn't going to make me pay; my tongue quickly darts to lick my suddenly dry lips and my whole body responds with an involuntary full-on shudder, he notices, of course he notices. He feels me every bit as much as I feel him but the way my body responds is as potent and reactive as the day we met, only now I get to call him mine and he gets to call me Mrs Stone or Mummy when the kids are near.

He walks slowly down the front steps of our family home, out of the city, surrounded by acres of farmland, woods, lakes and wildlife but not so far as to feel isolated. He continues to focus his intense stare at me but flashes a scowl at Sofia, my partner in crime. I don't think Sofia has ever been intimidated by him and she completely disarms the faux tension with a fit of laughter. I can't help but snicker too, especially when he scoops me up and cups the cheeks of my arse, gripping and squeezing, pulling me hard against him as I automatically wrap my legs around his waist. "While you are away I want you to think of all the ways you will be punished when you return." He growls in my ear and I flush bright red that he hasn't had the decency to speak in a hushed tone. His soft lips languidly move from embarrassing me to biting and sucking on the soft flesh on my neck. God, I love it when he does that, its like a mainline of molten heat to my core, utterly delicious and utterly distracting and I know that's his plan.

"Punished? Why am I being punished?" I tilt my head just out of reach of his soft seductive mouth.

"Mmm, well you are abandoning us. I think that warrants at least a whole week of punishment don't you?" He hitches me up so I am just high enough to feel the heat and tip of his erection and I can't help wriggle a little lower and swallow back a throaty moan. His breath is warm against my neck as he whispers. "Oh baby, we could just start your punishment right now if you want." I stop wriggling and pull back, I learnt early on, not to under estimate Daniel's capacity to administer punishment, whenever, where ever and I have my best friend and her husband all gathered on our drive ready for our departure. I know we are going to Vegas but I have no intention of getting the 'show' started here. I try to wriggle free again and he throws his head back and laughs but holds me just as tight.

"No no we'll miss the plane." I am still trying to escape his steely grip but I think he likes to feel me wriggle because he is un-phased by my efforts and continues a deep throaty laugh that I feel vibrate through my body. He moans and takes a deep draw of the scent in my hair like he is committing it to memory and the thought warms my soul and makes me laugh in equal measure. We are only going away for five nights. My body still aches from his need to consume every inch of me last night, making it very clear that this first separation, since we married and I left the hospital is only barely tolerated. Every touch, every kiss full of passion, desire and need; and his relentless pursuit of my pleasure left me exhausted, begging and sated but not before I admitted to myself if not to him that this trip was a stupid idea.

"Since it is my plane, what makes you think I'll let it take off anyway." He lets me slide down his body, holding me still, for a moment too long in company, over his straining jean clad erection.

"Man of your word, Hmm?" I raise my brow but I know he is just trying to delay the inevitable.

"Fucking Vegas!" He moans but playfully slaps my bottom as I turn to hug Paul goodbye. Our bags are in the car and Peter is waiting to drive us to the airport. I hear the noise from the garden start to get a little louder and with a quick look of shared panic between Sofia and I, she grabs my hand as I hesitate and turn toward the house. She drags me into the back of the car. I wind the window down and lean out to take one more kiss.

"You'll be Ok?" I suddenly hate that I am going away and he doesn't help when he grumbles that he doesn't really have a choice but Sofia presses her head beside mine and grins at him.

"Suck it up Stone, it's not like you are left holding the babies on your own. Mum is here with Marco, you've got Paul to show him the ropes and you've got a fucking housekeeper!" She turns her head and presses a kiss on my cheek and now we both look like Cheshire cats with our fixed wide grins. "and I haven't even said 'what happens in Va—'

"Don't even fucking think about finishing that sentence Sofia, if you don't expect me to drag my wife back out of that damn car!" Daniel growls his interruption and Sofia may not notice but I see the fire in his eyes and his jaw start to tense. This is hard for him, I know and not because he doesn't trust me. He has proven over and over that trust is no longer an issue but he still blames himself for not protecting me from Angel. Saving me was only a minor sop because for him, she should never have gotten to me in the first place but to me, saving me was the only thing that mattered. I nudge Sofia hard in the ribs but she chooses not to tease him anymore. A wise decision because if you can hear the reverberating anger of the hornets' nest within, it is best to put the fucking stick down. Peter takes the timely decision to slowly pull away and I blow him a kiss and wave like a crazy fan at a concert. I sit back and try to process the swirling riot of emotions driving away from my family evokes.

I am grateful my wish for Groundhog Day never came true. I am grateful I didn't have to repeat my wedding day on a promised grander scale because mostly I am grateful that my wedding day and every day since has been more treasured than the one before. When Daniel left me to take his place at the front of the tiny chapel in the hospital I couldn't have been more amazed at how perfect, *our perfect,* was. Marco opened the doors and because there was no way I was being wheeled up the isle Marco and Tom escorted me the short distance to Daniel. The sight took my breath away and only made my decision conclusively inevitable. The sight and scent of a thousand avalanche roses couldn't mask the love and excitement from everyone there who had played a part in Daniel and I reaching this day. Ethan stood smiling to the side of Daniel, the room was filled with everyone I loved and cherished as my own family. Sofia, Paul, Marco, Tony and Viv, Joe and everyone from the restaurant; Jack Wilson and his wife, Lili, Gaby, Saskia and Sam, Jason and even Colin, Daniel's PA. I know even if I couldn't see them at the time because my eyes were glassing up, I knew everyone I loved was there. I remember trembling as Daniel held my hands in his and before the Priest could begin he swept me into his arms and softly consumed my lips with his, before he grinned and whispered that he wasn't sorry that he couldn't wait.

My vows were to the letter a repeat of the priest, as I was unaware this was my wedding day I had nothing prepared but judging by the grin of Daniels face he was more than happy with my declaration especially as the outdated 'promise to obey' had snuck back in. Daniel had had a little more time to prepare and he stole my heart again with his vow:

Bethany, you are my light, you are my fire,

I don't deserve you, I know

But somehow you chose to give me your kindness, your love, your soul and

Just so you know, you have mine, all that I have and all that I am, only means a damn because your are mine, I breathed my first breath when you walked into my life,

And I promise to spend every moment of the rest of my life trying to justify that you made the right choice,

You may obey me but you also own me, slay me and hold my heart,

So have mercy because you are my life, my world, my only choice.

I love you Bethany, with all my heart. Always.

How could I possibly want a re-do when he got everything so right.

The honeymoon we spent travelling the Mediterranean on his yacht. Never too far from the mainland because he was a nervous wreck about my pregnancy, because I was apparently the first woman to have a baby. He spent this time handing much of his workload over to Jason because he wanted to be more Dad than businessman and that was perfect because I still wanted to finish my studies but didn't like the idea of handing our baby over to strangers, however well qualified. But when Lucas Jack Anthony was born it never looked like that would be an option. Daniel barely let him out of his sight for a moment and with Auntie Sofia and Uncle Marco and the grandparents all champing at the bit to babysit, calling on strangers was entirely unnecessary. It turned out Jack was Daniel's fathers name and Tom's middle name and when I put a stop to 'Daniel' being the second of our sons middle names, Jack Daniel is funny for about five minutes, then we settled on Anthony in honour of my other dad.

There is only fourteen months between Lucas and Leia Rose, we call her 'L.' Her middle name is after my mum and her first because it means *choice* even if her arrival was anything but. Not such great planning but perfect all the same, *our perfect* but it did mean it took me the full five years to finish my degree. It was a promise I made long ago not only to myself but for myself and it may not be necessary for my life now, but it is mine, it was my choice and no one can take that away from me. I work part time in the Stone R & D department but with two under five year olds that is mostly for my sanity and as crazy as Sofia might think I am she will understand exactly what I mean in about four months' time.

"I'm sooo freaking excited!" Sofia squeal's in my ear and I flinch and cup my hand against my ear a little too late to protect my hearing.

"You know we're not really going to Vegas right?" I turn to face her utterly shocked expression making me laugh out but bite my lip as her face turns to a scowl. "Oh come on Sofs you're nearly six months pregnant and you want an eleven hour flight for a five night stay, you're nuts! Besides I promised Paul, he was really worried about the distance and—"

"Fuck!" Sofia interrupts dramatically, throws herself back hard against the seat and I flash a quick glance at Peter who raises as brow in the rear view mirror. He has been witness to one or two tantrums in the back of this car but not from a fully grown woman. "It's not fair. It's not like he's all swelled up like a balloon. I should be allowed a little fun, a little R and R, a little *me* time." She huffs and it's my turn to raise a brow because from what I have seen, her pregnancy has been all about the R and R and quite a bit about the 'me time.' "Don't look like that, I know I'm being a brat but I figure I have only got a few more months I can get away with it so I'm making the most." She pouts and crosses her arms for effect.

"Do you want to know where we are going or do you want to

sulk?" I can see she's not really pissed but she's a little like an infant in the 'surprising' stakes. It seems that surprises are great as long as you know about them otherwise they are just a bit disappointing. A surprise Disney trip for Jack and Leia last year was disguised as a normal visit to see Nanna Viv and Grampa Tony but the aftermath of the revelation was tears and desolation at not actually visiting Nanna and Gramps not joy and uncontainable excitement at visiting the six foot mouse and friends; lesson learnt never to be repeated. She mumbles something about 'go on then' and I take her hand and give it a gentle squeeze. "All right then, we are heading to that spa just outside of Milan, you know the one you wanted to go to for your hen weekend. So lots of R and R and lots of you time, I promise." She tilts her head against my shoulder and sighs.

"It sounds wonderful but why did you say Vegas?" Her tone indicates her complete turn around and it makes me smile she can be placated so easily.

"Oh just keeping my husband on his toes" I quip and gain another raised brow from Peter in the rear view mirror and a snort from Sofia.

"Oh yes because that always works out so well. Trying to get one over on that man is like trying to get one over on Santa; he just knows and he doesn't tend to react very well to surprises either as I recall. Do you remember the time we tried to do a surprise dinner with cake for his birthday and because he couldn't get hold of you he practically had the restaurant on lock down and surrounded by armed guards and all because you were up to you elbows in cake mix and couldn't answer the damn phone; Geeesh!" We giggle at this but to be fair this was only six months after the Angel thing and one month before Jack was born. He has relaxed a little since then, well I think he's relaxed a little since then. We arrive at the airport and Peter takes our bags to the plane.

"The captain said Daniel has already called to check the flight details and once you have taken off he will have to submit the correct flight plan and Daniel will know you are not going to Vegas. He also said he hoped he doesn't lose his job because he quite likes working for Daniel and I kind of think the same." He pulls me in for a hug.

"He'd have to get rid of me first Peter." I give him a wink

"Well, in that case I'm safe then aren't I?" He chuckles and waves us off as we climb the narrow steps to the small but utterly luxurious plane.

I don't think we even make it to the channel before my phone starts to vibrate. I slide the screen open to accept the call and take a sip of my champagne as Sofia scowls and sips her sparkling elderflower water.

"Mind telling me where you are going Mrs Stone?" His stern gravelly tone sends delicious shivers all over my skin.

"Vegas?" My reply is more a tentative question and I bite my lips together to prevent a snicker.

"Oh you want to play?" The air conditioning in the plane is going to need to kick up a gear from his tone alone and I struggle to swallow the instant lump in my throat.

"I have company," I whisper and Sofia does her best to pretend she is reading a magazine but her lips are curling to the side and I know her quick glance has just added to the flame of my cheeks.

"And that makes a difference because?" His question is rhetorical and I feel a shift of heat from my face to between my legs because I know it doesn't make a scrap of difference where I am or with whom. I smile when I hear him groan at the same time a small moan escapes my mouth. I shift in my seat and decide I need to change the course of this conversation or I am going to be spending the rest of the flight in the bedroom 'playing' and I think that might be the height of bad manners.

"Ok so not Vegas, we're going to the spa in Italy. The one we were supposed to go to for Sofia's hen weekend before it changed to Ibiza." I add because it was a long time ago, I'm sure he doesn't remember.

the Only Choice

"The one near Milan?" He asks, his tone brusque and I shouldn't be surprised he's like a computer for holding information.

"Yep." I hesitate when the call goes quiet. "I thought you'd be pleased. You know, no wild parties, dodgy tattoos, drugs or hookers." I add as a joke but he remains silent. The seconds tick by and I can just see his hand raking through his untamed dark locks. He's worried and it's not because of the drugs, hookers or inappropriate tattoo opportunities because none of that is real. He is worried because he doesn't like uncertainty when it comes to me, when it comes to my safety. The fact that I know I am safe is irrelevant, this is his job and I have taken that away from him. I draw in a deep breath, "I'm sorry."

"Oh I will make sure of it." His tone laced with sensual intent; a direct shift from cool and stern. "Enjoy your rest Bethany, you are going to need it and Bethany?" He pauses and I hold my breath before I realise I need to reply.

"Yes." I exhale.

"No more surprises.'" His words are more a command than a statement.

"No." I reply softly. I know he is holding on for more so I quickly stand and walk through the door leading to the bedroom. "Sir." I add as I close the door behind me.

The next five days are heaven, I mean pure undiluted heaven. Every day we have peen pampered and preened, massaged and manipulated, in a good way. We have been served food of the Gods, decadence fit for a deity, did I mention it was heaven, good, because after five days I'm actually in hell. I miss my husband and I miss my children and I know I sound ungrateful but I am more than happy to be ungrateful as long as today I am going home, to them. My bag is packed and I am waiting in the foyer while Sofia has one more treatment because the car isn't due for another hour. Daniel has been in meetings all day and I can't wait to speak to him, I have Skype called every day, sometimes with the children sometimes alone which makes me all the more eager to actually get home and have some *real* face time. Sofia finally appears and seems a little sad to be leaving where as I am pushing the doorman aside and carrying my own bag to the damn taxi. It's my turn to be giddy with excitement.

I don't pay much attention to the drive until we exit the motorway and start to climb the narrow winding road up through the mountains. Sofia asks where we are going because even if I could ask I wouldn't be able to interpret the reply; my Italian is very basic and very slowly spoken. I relax when we are told it's a change of route because of some road works but when we pull off the main road and start to work our way down a dirt track I quickly grab my phone because now I know this isn't right. Daniel answers on the second lengthen dial tone. It takes only a moment to know he is abroad and only a second more to know that is why we are parked outside the most amazing Italian mountain villa.

I gasp and scramble to open the door as he appears on the wide stone steps that lead up to the arched porch with ornately curved terracotta tiles on the sloping roof. The wooden slated window shutters are all open and I can hear a riot of noise coming from the rear of the villa. I run flat out, Sofia forgotten, into his waiting arms and relish the strength and feel of his body as he wraps around me and holds me tight. Secure before his hand creeps into the hair from the back of my neck and up, he grips and winds his fingers in a firm hold pulling me back with a growl. His dark eyes are fierce with lust and I wouldn't care who was watching at this moment because I know my lust for him is matched with the desire in his eyes and the heat from his iron hard length pressed against my light cotton skirt. I gasp again as he tightens his grip and his mouth covers mine, we both moan. God, that was a fucking stupid idea to go away but this is fucking amazing now that we are back together. He lifts me easily with one arm and I wrap my legs around his narrow waist. He turns

the Only Choice

and walks with purpose through the villa.

"I should say hi, don't you think?" I nod to the splashing noise from the pool, not sure who is out there but I have a pretty good idea.

"Not a fucking chance, they won't let you go and I'm not waiting another minute. Still struggling with the sharing thing and they are *my* children too. Fuck I need to be inside you right now and I don't think Nanna's going to approve if I bend you over the sun lounger." He hasn't broken his stride and I don't mind, there is plenty of time for catch up and by the sounds of it they are having too much fun to even notice I'm there.

"It's gonna need to be quick then, as soon as Sofia shows herself they'll know I'm here and hunt me down." I giggle as he takes the stairs two at a time.

"Not a problem." He draws in a deep breath as the door of our bedroom slams shut and in the next breath he has me pushed flat against the weathered oak with him flush against me. I feel the tight tug of my panties and the sharp sting as they disintegrate in his fingers. He smoothes the skin on my hip before he grabs the flesh and squeezes, his hands then travel at a rapid speed all over my skin sending a trails of fire in their wake. His lips cover mine, his tongue dives and swirls and tastes, his kisses along my jaw and up my neck are feather light, his kisses on my neck are fierce and proprietary and I moan as he sucks and draws my blood to the surface. I cry at the point of pain as he marks me, the moment he surges hard into me and with a guttural groan of his own. I throw my head back with a thud against the door and writhe in ecstasy against his relentless driving thrusts, deeper, harder, every grind, every step closer sending me higher as I gasp for the air to breathe. My body starts to tremble when he stills and holds my chin delicately, his eyes boring into mine.

"Wait baby, come with me." He pants, my mind is fuzzy and my body isn't listening to me, it just wants to take what he's giving. "Baby, I want you to come with me and I want you to look at me. I need to see you fall apart." I know I whimper at his words and he smiles when I manage a slight nod. Honestly, it is a big fucking ask given our separation and the fact that I am so desperate to let go I feel a little insane right now but he just asked so damn nicely, I have to try.

He pulls back and slides back in, slow and deep, deeper than he had been, if that was possible but it is and he hits such sweet spots inside a tiny cry escapes and he lets his head drop to my shoulder with a moan. He picks up his pace and I can't stop the build inside, he lifts his head to gaze once more into my eyes, his passion, lust and love sears my soul. He can feel me and I can feel him and just like him I loved to watch him fall apart too. I cling to his broad shoulders and he pounds hard once, twice and swallows my cry as I fall. I fall and he catches me and I catch him right back; holding him tight as he regains his even breathing and gently lowers me to the floor. His head resting on my forehead, my legs feel like jelly and he scoops me into his arms before I collapse.

"Well I did say you'd have trouble walking but I'm really looking forward to the bit where you aren't able to sit down." He kisses my hair and sits me on the edge of the bed. He walks over to the chest of draws and it's the first time I have time to take in what a beautiful room we are in. The white plastered walls are edged with thick stone and the depth of the window ledges indicate just how thick the walls are. The exposed wooden beams are pale and the floor boards are natural too and highly polished. There is a small writing desk and a full length mirror and what looks like an ensuite from the tiling on the floor. The room is light and the décor is modern and in keeping with the region, stylish and elegant. The four poster bed has white with black striped linen, the black lacquered posts don't reach the ceiling or connect in anyway but I know they will be put to use. Daniel grins as he kneels in front of me and threads my feet through some new panties.

"I like what you're thinking Mrs Stone." He runs his hands up my thighs lifting my skirt as he pulls my underwear into place,

the Only Choice

I lift to help his progress. "But there are little people waiting. . . ." He pauses as he traces his finger along the edge of my newly restored panties. "Actually on second thoughts, they can wait a little longer . . ." He starts to kiss on the inside of my thigh and I fold over onto him in a fit of giggles, his longer than normal stubble tickling the sensitive skin but before I can argue or acquiesce, he sighs as the simultaneous sound of what seems to be a heard of wildebeest charge up the stairs and fly into the room. Lucas splats himself against Daniels back as he is still crouched on the floor and L bumps into the bed beside me and I quickly lift her into my lap as she squeals and wraps her tiny arms around my neck. They are both wet from the pool and too excited to actually make any sense so I just cuddle and tickle and laugh with them. Daniel throws Lucas onto his shoulders and points at me and mouths that he's not done with me and I can feel my cheeks flush and mouth back 'good.' I carry L and Daniel follows with Lucas back down the stairs to the pool to find the others.

We carry them back up the stairs several exhausting hours later, not exhausting for us but certainly their Uncle Marco and Uncle Paul were put through their paces. We set them down on the low beds and cover their tiny bodies with a light sheet as the heat from the day persists into the night. Having fallen asleep in our arms during dinner they both remain undisturbed by the change in location and I take a moment to marvel at the little carbon copies of Daniel before me. Only the slight difference in sizes marks that they aren't twins with their dark tousled hair and crystal blue eyes. The lazy afternoon bled into the perfect evening. The terrace was laid out with one long table and benches either side, at one end was an alcove of large cushions and hammocks for lazing around after the meal. The food, was simple, rustic and plentiful and the company couldn't be better, Marco, his Mum and Dad, Sofia and Paul, Ethan, the cousins Pip and Fia, Pip has been working as an intern under Jason at Daniels London office, since graduating last year. Daniel gave out an open invitation and anyone who was available jumped on the plane. I never take for granted the privileged position I am in but I am in awe that Daniel understands how important this family thing is, given his own limited experience, his love of privacy and his dislike of sharing. But he does understand and when he does something like this, I just manage to love him a little bit more.

We must have taken longer to put the kids to bed than we thought or the day had taken its toll because the terrace is bereft of bodies and the table clear of dinner debris. Daniel takes my hand and we walk to the edge of the pool, sit and dangle our legs in, the cool water swirling and swishing around our legs as we drag them back and forth. The night is alive with the sounds from the surrounding mountain and the evening scents of lavender and citrus fill the air, the villa is softly lit and the whole evening feels magical. I let my head fall back and gaze at the sky bursting with too many stars to comprehend but the moment is instantly gone when I hear him slip into the water and feel the tug on my hand to follow. He is submerged and pulls me in without resistance despite being fully clothed and I reach for him and we wrap around each other before returning to the surface for air. He starts to peel my sundress that is slick to my skin down my shoulders and off my waist and I unbutton his shirt, the water is just shallow enough to reach the bottom on my tip toes but he is easily standing firm. He unties the straps of my bikini, top and bottom and the materials glide over the surface of the water and out of reach. He grins as I take a furtive glance around, the only sound is nature, wild and cacophonous and a little bit breathless. There is not another soul around, just our souls entwined and helpless for each other. I tug at the cord in his shorts and my fingers slide to push the material free from his body, freeing him, hot and hard against my water cooled skin. I am surprised I can't see steam rising from the pool or hear the sizzles as his skin touches mine.

"You are too naked." He grumbles and I pull back to see he actually seems serious and I look around again to check why now he would think this when he was the one that has made me naked but there is still no one but us around.

the Only Choice

"I thought you liked me naked?" I let my legs float around his waist and squeeze to pull him into me; he groans a deep throaty sound that vibrates through the water.

"Mmm not any more, I want you to put something on." He is trying to sound stern but I can see in his eyes the wrinkle and crease as he fights one of his breath taking smiles that is just waiting in the wings, but why?

"Something on or in?" I tilt my hips and use the weightlessness to roll my core softly against his rock hard erection that is bobbing just against my folds and I snicker as he takes a sharp breath.

"Fuck, you're making this very hard." His voice is gruff and he coughs the last part which just makes me giggle more.

"So it would seem and your point is?" I am now hovering just above him and I can feel the tip of his cock bob at my entrance but I need him to take this further because I have no purchase.

"My point." He starts to swish his way to the edge of the pool, where I know I will find my purchase. "My point is I want to do this in a *not* arse backwards way and you are distracting me." His lips cover mine as I am about to ask what he is talking about. I love that our perfect is arse backwards, so what is it he wants to do now that isn't and that involves me putting more clothes on. My questions dissolve as his tongue delves deeper, demanding and devouring and all I can think is I really want his other point right now. But he stops and gently cups my cheek, his eyes intense, serious and his jaw is clenched like he is suddenly nervous.

"Our normal was arse backwards; the baby, the wedding, the other baby, this hen trip and I love that about us . . . So this should be an engagement ring but I hate the idea of a limited period of time with you, even if that time is now irrelevant, so this . . ." He takes my left hand that was resting on his shoulder and slides something on my finger. I can't see it because my brief glance down only saw his fingers over mine and I can't seem to take my eyes away from his. "*This,* is the only period of time with you that I do like the idea of." I feel his hand slip away and I get my first look at the stunning diamond eternity ring that is now nestled next to my wedding ring.

"Eternity," my thumb strokes the underside of the ring to feel more diamonds and I look back into his eyes which, tonight sparkle brighter than any precious stone and whisper my understatement of a lifetime, "I like that idea."

The End (Again)

Acknowledgements

Because I wrote these book back to back before I sent them to my editor, my thanks are pretty much to the same people. Having said that I am adding a few, and I hope I get everyone but if I don't i'll try and make it up in next time. (ooo I hope there is a next time!). As a complete unknown and a social media virgin I have been overwhelmed by the help and support from the Indy Author and Blogger community. So thank you to Francesca at Francesca Romance Reviews for my cover reveal and Blog tour, to FMR Book Grind for my blitz promotions: Kelly at Kellys Kindle Konfessions and Schmexy Girl, Book Bellas, Shh Moms Reading, SBC, Red Hot Reads, EscapeNBooks, J J Book Bangers and Philomena at 2 and Friends who Promote and all of the other lovely bloggers (I'm sorry if I;ve missed anyone feel free to kick my arse)... I'd like to thank Stylo Fantome and Georgie Ramsey for their collective wisdom. Also the Indie Writers Unite—there is not a question that goes un-answered and it helps to know there are many of us bobbing around, if not in the same sea certainly in a similar rickety floating device.

Kymme and Lynn, I know you got top billing previously but you deserve it for your tireless encouragement. That goes to for you too Katie for shamelessly pimping me to all your friends and pestering them for reviews—you're a star. To Joan for the inspirational photographs... you know the ones ;) and for pushing my work in your groups... Super happy you are on my team.<3.

To other authors who take the time to reply to even the silliest of query or message . . . you probably have no idea how disproportionately happy each bit of communication make me so thank you . . . Jodi Ellen Malpas, Kitty French, Christine D Reiss, Ker Dukey, Pepper Winters

My husband and children for tolerating my long absences from the family, in both body and mind.

My editor Philippa ,Angela for my beautiful cover designs and Stacey for making it all pretty for the publishing! And not lastly but certainly importantly (again) all the bloggers that have taken the time to reply to my review requests and have shown an interest in wanting more; THANK YOU :)

But mostly, I'd like to thank you, for choosing to buy my book and taking the time to read it—a huge, I mean really huge, thank you. You will never know how incredibly grateful and honoured I am that you have. I would like to ask one more favour, if you enjoyed my book please leave your review at your book retailer's website or Goodreads (or go cut and paste crazy and leave it at both :)

Reviews are the life blood for an unknown like me and I am really grateful when you do take the time to post. Also, I will always answer emails and messages, it may take a while but I promise I will get back to you.

<3 <3 <3

The People who make it all happen.
Dee Palmer—Author
Website—www.deepalmerwriter.com
Follow me here
https://facebook.com/deepalmerwriter
https://twitter.com/deepalmerwriter
Editor- Philippa Donovan —www.smartquilleditorial.co.uk
Formatter— Champagne Formats
www.ChampagneFormats.com
Cover Design Angela—www.angieocreations.com

Choices Playlist

Thinking Out Loud—Ed Sheeran
Take Me To Church—Hosier
Run—Snow Patrol
Chasing Cars— Snow Patrol
Make This Go On Forever—Snow Patrol
Changing —Linkin Park
Best of You —Foo Fighters
Halo—Florence and the Machine
The Only One —James Blunt
My Immortal —Evanescence
Focus—Emma's Imagination
Big Big World—Emilia
How Long Will I Love You —Ellie Goulding
Figure 8—Ellie Goulding
Tessilate —Ellie Goulding
I Know You Care —Ellie Goulding
(Had a bit of an Ellie Goulding thing going on)
Wheels —Lone Justice
Heavy Cross —The Gossip
Stay With Me—Sam Smith
Orbiting —The Weepies

About the Author

I have been asked recently what I hoped would happen from publishing my first book. Honestly, I hadn't thought that far ahead. I enjoyed taking a bit of me time . . . still do. I never expected anything from my writing . . . my reward was that I had been allowed some this time to write this story . . . I mean how self indulgent is that when you run your own business with the family and you still have a family that depend on you? Precious time to do what I really enjoyed was what I wanted . . . Oh and perhaps that a few others would enjoy what I had written, because lets face it . . . who doesn't like a little external validation once in a while. It's been three months since I pressed the publish button on Never A Choice and I have been blown away by the response, reviews and personal messages I have received. So in case I missed it previously I would like to thank everyone that took time to message me, write a review or simply buy my books . . . You totally rock!!

Stalk me On Facebook, Twitter and Instagram

Sign up to my Newsletter and I promise I won't spam you but you will be the first to get any free stories and news about promotions and New Releases :)

Go—http://eepurl.com/biZ6g1

or find the form on the Contact page at www.deepalmerwriter.com

Printed in Great Britain
by Amazon.co.uk, Ltd.,
Marston Gate.